Deeper

Deeper

a novel

ROBIN YORK

Bantam Books Trade Paperbacks

New York

A Bantam Books Trade Paperback Original

Published in the United States by Bantam Books,
an imprint of Random House, a division of Random House LLC,
a Penguin Random House Company, New York.

BANTAM BOOKS and the HOUSE colophon are registered trademarks of Random House LLC.

This book contains an excerpt from the forthcoming book *Harder* by Robin York. This excerpt has been set for this edition only and may not reflect the final content of the forthcoming edition.

LIBRARY OF CONGRESS CATALOGING-IN-PUBLICATION DATA
York, Robin.
Deeper : a novel / Robin York.
pages cm
ISBN 978-0-8041-7701-6 (pbk.) — ISBN 978-0-8041-7702-3 (eBook)
1. Women college students—Fiction. 2. Cyberbullying—Fiction. I. Title.
PS3625.O7545D44 2014
813'.6—dc23   2013037832

Printed in the United States of America on acid-free paper

www.bantamdell.com

9 8 7 6 5 4 3 2 1

Book design by Mary A. Wirth

Deeper

Sometimes I hate the girl I was back then. It's like how, when you see a horror movie, you can't help but feel contempt for the virgin who goes for a walk in the woods after midnight. How can she be so stupid? Doesn't she know she's about to get gruesomely hacked to death?

She *should* know. That's why it's so hard to watch. Because you want her to know. You want her to defend herself, and you look down on her for not knowing, even though obviously it's the guy who hacks her up who's at fault.

The thing is, the movie makes him seem like a force of nature—unstoppable—so the virgin comes off as a total dumbass for not checking the forecast to see if it calls for serial murder before she skips off into the night.

These days, if someone sent me a text that said nothing but *OMG*, I wouldn't wonder if whatever I was about to find out was going to be bad. I'd only wonder how bad and how long it was going to take me to crawl out of whatever pit I was about to fall in. But in August of my sophomore year at Putnam College, I didn't worry. I thought maybe Bridget, my best friend and roommate, had gotten distracted before she could finish her train of thought.

I towel-dried my hair and stood up to lob the damp towel into my laundry basket in the closet. Missed. By the time I'd picked it up and put it where it belonged, another message had popped up on my phone, this time with a link.

You need to see this, it said.

And then, immediately after, *I'm so sorry.*

I clicked the link.

I think part of me knew even then. Because the thing about being a good girl is, you spend your whole life developing a finely honed radar for detecting anything that could potentially cause people to love you less.

Girls like me—or, I guess, girls like the one I was last August—we eat approval. We live for it. So when we do something dumb—or, say, when we do something really monumentally idiotic—we know.

The screen filled up with a picture of me, topless, with Nate's dick in my mouth.

I looked, and I took a deep breath. I closed my eyes.

I could actually *feel* it—the solid ground of my life, cracking open.

It sounds too drama llama when I put it like that, I know, but I can't think of another way to describe it. One minute, I was on firm footing—a nineteen-year-old overachieving politics geek, on track to go to law school and take the world by storm—and the next, my feet had lost purchase on the floor. I sagged against the desk. I couldn't get enough air.

The shock of it didn't take any time at all to sink in. It sank in immediately, traveling some kind of shortcut path from my eyes to the area of my brain that had made a quiet, private list of the consequences of those photos the second Nate took them.

Everyone will see you, mock you, hate you.

You won't get into law school.

You'll never get a Rhodes.

You'll never be a judge or get elected to office.

This changes everything.

Seeing those pictures—I was devastated. Immediately. Because I'd known.

That night when I'd gone down on Nate and he'd lifted his iPhone in the air and aimed it at my head, my good-girl radar was working fine. *Bad idea,* the radar told me. *Such a bad idea.* But I overrode it, because Nate was in a mood, and I thought if I went along, it would bring him out of it.

You trust him, I told myself. *Nate would never.*

But he did. He must have. The website identified me as Caroline Piasecki from Putnam, Iowa, and Nate was the only one who had those pictures. Either he put them there, or he gave them to someone who did.

There were two shots of my face smiling. One duckface from my car that I'd sent him just to be an ass. One of me in my favorite animal-print bra and panties, which I'd taken in the mirror in my high school bedroom, sucking in my stomach and pushing out my chest because I'd wanted to look sexy. I'd wanted so much to be sexy for him.

And the other, even dirtier pictures. The ones I almost couldn't look at.

Three of them.

At the bottom, my face again, with a cartoon bubble that said, *I'm Caroline Piasecki! I'm a frigid bitch who needs to get FUCKED!!!*

I couldn't cry.

I couldn't breathe.

I couldn't really believe it.

The page had four hundred sixty-two comments.

Four. Hundred. Sixty. Two.

If someone had asked me ten minutes earlier how I felt about Nate, I would have told them, "Oh, there are no hard feelings." Three years together, and we'd just grown apart. I guess it was college that did it. By the end of our freshman year, I'd started to feel like maybe Nate and I didn't have all that much in common. In high school, I'd been dateless until he asked me out—a late bloomer, my dad said. Nate was cute, popular, smart. Flattering to be noticed by a boy like that. But at Putnam, I had started to think maybe there was something missing between him and me. Better chemistry. A deeper connection.

I'd broken up with him before we came back to school. We shared a pizza and drank soda, and I tried to explain my reasoning without hurting his feelings. I thought I had pulled it off pretty well. By the end of dinner, he'd been smiling and agreeable again.

I would have said he was a nice guy. That we were still friends.

So even though I wasn't exactly surprised, I was, too. I'd followed the rules, worked hard to get good grades, dated a nice boy, and made him wait a long time for sex. This wasn't supposed to happen. I hadn't expected my prom date, my first boyfriend, my *first,* to use the Internet to call me a cum-loving slut who loves jizz in her face or to list the name of my college and my high school right there beneath the blow-job picture.

Because who expects that?

I sank down into the desk chair and thumbed through the first few screens of comments. Then the next few. Screen after screen.

She has nice tits.

I'd hit that.

fap fap fap fap thx Carolina, you hoor!

What an ugly slut. I want more vag!

Every word I read—every filthy thing some basement-dwelling Internet creep said about me—I thought, *This is my fault.*

My fault, my fault, my fault.

I never should have let Nate take the pictures. I knew it. I knew it when he took them, I knew it after, I knew it when we broke up and I had this fleeting, urgent impulse to beg him to let me delete every single photo of me off his phone. An impulse I shrugged off because I didn't want to offend him.

I didn't want to be *rude.*

I sat there for a long time, scrolling and reading, wiping tears from my eyes with the back of my free hand. I was panting more than breathing, panicking more than thinking, too disoriented to have anything like a coherent plan.

I think I was mourning the end of something without even knowing it had ended. My youth, maybe. The sunny, perfect part of my life.

It wasn't until Bridget messaged me again—*R u ok?*—that I really understood. I thought about how she would come back to the room and she would have seen. She would know, and I would have to face her.

I thought about how it wouldn't be just Bridget. It would be everybody.

That's when it hit me that I would never be okay again.

Caroline

Two and a half weeks after the photos appear online, I have everything under control. Right up until I walk out of Latin and into West Leavitt's elbow.

I'm striding with my head down, my mind on the upcoming student-senate election. I thought I would run this year to represent my dorm, but now I don't see how I can. The girl who *is* running is . . . Well, I'm trying not to be uncharitable. She's not my top choice.

I'm my top choice.

My feet are moving out the door and steering me to the right, away from most of the other students. I used to go to the left, but Nate has Macroeconomics in the classroom next to mine, and I don't want to run into him. I've started going right instead and then detouring around the outside of the building to head toward the dining hall for lunch.

Today, though, my path isn't empty—the hallway is crowded, heaving and alive. But since I've got my head down,

I don't notice until I crash into some random person's back. The bag I'm carrying gets knocked out of my arms and onto the floor. I go to pick it up, saying sorry, noticing just how many legs are in this hall, starting to wonder what's going on. I'm still trying to figure it out when I stand back up and get nailed in the nose.

I'm not aware, in the moment, that it's a body part that strikes me, or who it belongs to. I only know that there's a lot of flailing movement happening right in front of me and that the bridge of my nose has connected with something that's in motion and deeply unforgiving.

It hurts.

Oh, holy mother of God, it hurts.

Cupping my nose protectively, I crumple, ducking my head and folding my body over the pain. My eyes fill with tears. Warm liquid slips over my lip. My tongue pokes out to lick it before I understand that—*ugh, blood*—I'm bleeding. Then it's coating my mouth, warm all over my chin, and I don't even care because my nose won't stop exploding.

I've never been hit in the face before.

It is distressingly AWFUL.

I know there's something I should be doing other than bleeding on my own fingers, which I've pushed firmly up beneath my nose as though they have the power to do . . . anything at all. Which they don't. Blinking, confused, I look around for what I've collided with and why it hates me. Considering the state of my nose, I'm expecting a brick wall, or perhaps a monster with cinder blocks for hands.

Instead, I see big male bodies shoving and grunting. There's space all around them, but I've breached it, which is probably why I got nailed in the face, and which also puts me in a perfect position to see the punch coming.

I don't see it land. The man who gets hit is standing with

his back to me, directly between me and the fist. But the taut smack of skin against bone sours my stomach.

The guy goes down, right in front of me. The other guy straddles his waist, chest heaving, leaning over so I only see the top of his head. He looks like he's ready to take another swing, and I *really* don't want him to, because this is all so primitive and brutal that I'm not sure I can stand it.

Then there's this terrible noise—this high-pitched, reedy gasping noise—and the guy on top looks right at me.

Oh, God. I made the noise. That was me, that wheezy scream, and now I can't breathe at all, because the guy on top is West, and the face he punched so hard belongs to Nate.

West's eyes go wide. "Jesus, Caroline, did I hit you?"

He stands, stepping close, reaching out. It's as if he completely forgets he's beating the shit out of Nate, and he just comes after me. The look in his eyes, the outstretched hand—it's so much like the first time West reached for me, more than a year ago, that I have a moment of déjà vu. My knees buckle, which annoys me. My body is the enemy right now—my incompetent knees, that noise my throat decided to make, my leaking nose, the pounding pain in my face.

Not to mention my heart, which is trying to escape my chest by flinging itself violently against my ribs.

West's hand lands on my waist, steady and firm, and it's stupid. My body is stupid. Because his hand feels kind of awesome.

Obviously I'm concussed. West is the one who hit me, probably, and he's definitely the one who hit Nate, who—

Fuck.

Nate is sprawled out on the floor, bleeding from the mouth.

Worse, I can't really bring myself to focus on Nate, because West's other hand landed on my shoulder briefly, and now he's lifting my chin. The blood makes his fingers slippery. I'm bleeding on him. And I like it.

This happens with West. He's only touched me once before, but it isn't the kind of thing a girl forgets.

God, there are so many, many reasons this is not good, though. Most of them aren't even health-related. For starters, I'm not into guys who punch people. I'm not into guys at the moment, period. And if I were, I wouldn't be into West, because West is trouble, and I'm allergic.

"You're bleeding," he says.

"You hit me."

"Let me see."

He tugs at my wrist, and I let him drag my hand away from my nose, because basically I will let West Leavitt do anything. It's possible that he's some kind of magical creature. I mean, he's not. I know he's not. He's a twenty-year-old sophomore at Putnam College, majoring in biology. He shelves books at the library, waits tables on weekends at the Gilded Pear—which is the only fancy restaurant in Putnam—and works the overnight shift at the bakery in town. All that on top of at least a couple of shady, unofficial sources of income, plus classes, makes him busier than just about anyone I know.

He's tall—around six feet, maybe a little taller—with messy brown hair, light blue-green eyes, and a great tan.

He's a guy who goes to my college. That's all.

But that is not all.

His face is . . . You know how they say human beings are more attracted to symmetrical faces? Well, West's face is slightly off in every conceivable way. One of his eyebrows tilts up a bit, and the other one is bisected by a thin white scar. His eyes are a color that isn't actually a color, with these tiny little flecks that sometimes look shiny, and I don't understand how that's possible. His mouth is wider than it ought to be, which makes him look like a smart-ass every time he smiles or almost smiles or thinks, vaguely, about smiling. His nose must have been broken once—or maybe more than once—because it's not quite where it's supposed to be. It's shifted a titch to the left. And honestly? I think his ears are too small.

When he looks right at me, I can barely make words.

That's why I'm standing here, bleeding, letting him inspect my nose.

"Is it still there?" I ask. Only unfortunately it sounds more like *Ib id till dere?*

"Yeah. I think I must have elbowed you. It's not broken, though."

"How do you know?"

"It'd be bleeding more."

He traces the bridge with one finger.

It doesn't hurt anymore.

A groan from the floor draws West's attention away from my face, at which point my nose resumes throbbing and I remind myself who's groaning and why.

Nate's lip is split. The whole front of his shirt is crimson and wet. His teeth are pink when he spits.

Pink teeth. That wakes me up a little.

That's Nate, I think. *West hit Nate. He's bleeding.* You're *bleeding.*

My brain keeps offering up these declarations, one after another, as though I might eventually locate a story to string them all together. But whatever part of me is in charge of analyzing and processing data, it's off-line.

Blood drips from my chin. I follow its path and see that it's landed on the scuffed toe of West's black boot.

"I need a paper towel," I say.

West's friend Krishna grabs him by the arm. "You have to get out of here."

Krishna is tall, with dark skin and black hair and a frighteningly beautiful face. He's also usually so laid-back that he's right next door to comatose, so his urgency is a whiff of ammonia under my nose.

The students at the fringes of the crowd have all turned to look down the hall, where something is happening. Someone is coming.

West Leavitt punched Nate in the face.

I'm bleeding.

He's still touching me, and I can't think.

"Take care of her." West is speaking to Krishna, but he's looking right at me when he says it, his expression apologetic.

Krishna gives him a small shove. "Fine, dude, just *go*."

West turns, glances at me one more time, and jogs down the hall. Krishna picks up my bag off the floor—I hadn't even realized I'd dropped it again—and puts an arm around my shoulders. "Come on, we'll find you that paper towel."

"Do you think Nate's okay?"

"I think Nate's a dick," Krishna says. "But he's still breathing. Can you walk any faster?"

I do my best. We end up in a women's bathroom on the second floor, Krishna standing by the door and propping it open with his body as I press a coarse brown paper towel to my nose and examine myself in the mirror.

I look like something out of a slasher flick. There's blood all over my face, clumping up the ends of my long brown hair. My hand is covered in gore, and the formerly white edge of my shirt sleeve where it sticks out under my sweater has gone crimson and wet.

Got what you deserved, didn't you? Slut.

My stomach heaves up, a sudden lurch that makes me close my eyes and suck in a deep breath.

I look at Krishna, but of course he isn't the one who said it.

It was *them*. The men.

They follow me around. Their voices. Their vile opinions, now an endless stream of negative color commentary on my life.

I'd still fuck her, they say when I turn on the tap. *Fuck that bitch until she walks funny. I don't care about her face.*

I stick my fingers under the stream of cold water and wait for it to warm.

"You all right?" Krishna asks.

He looks uncomfortable. We're friendly, but we're not really *friends*. He's closer with Bridget, my roommate, than he is with me. All four of us were on the same hall last year, Bridget and I rooming across from West and Krishna.

I like Krishna, but he's not the kind of guy I'd ever choose to lean on. He's kind of a manwhore, actually, and a slacker. I don't imagine that standing here watching me bleed is high on his list of things he wanted to do today.

Experimentally, I take the paper towel away. The bleeding seems to have stopped. "I'm fine. You don't have to stay."

"I wouldn't mind, except I have someone I need to meet. But if you want—"

"It's okay."

I'd rather be alone. My hands are shaking, and my knees still feel a little untrustworthy.

"I'll tell West no harm, no foul, okay?"

"Huh?"

"I'll say you're not hurt."

But I am hurt. Inside me, under my rib cage, hiding somewhere deep beneath my lungs, there's raw, sliced-open flesh that won't close up. It hurts all the time. My tender nose and the dull throb in my head have nothing on that pain.

"Tell him whatever you want."

He still looks awkward, but he says, "Later." When I say it back, he goes.

The door closes with a quiet thud.

I lean against the paper-towel dispenser, listening to the water run, and take deep breaths.

In. Out.

In. Out.

By the eighth breath, I've managed to banish most of the fear and tune out the pain. I've had a few weeks to practice. I'm getting good at not feeling things.

The key is to keep busy. To set goals and tick them off the list, one after another. I can't stand here all day breathing. I have to get to lunch, because I've got a buttload of studying to do before my group-project meeting at three. I need to look at my email—I heard my phone vibrating during Latin, and I know I'm going to find a fresh crop of links in my daily Google alert. I have some time set aside to deal with them before the meeting.

This is what my life is like now. Always something to do.

Before, I was a diligent student. I printed out my color-blocked class schedule, with designated study sessions neatly labeled and shaded to match. I three-hole-punched all my syllabi and made special binders, one for each class, with custom dividers.

Now I pour all my diligence into designing spreadsheets to track my progress in wiping out my sex pictures from the Internet. I note the URL for each image, the site host, the date and time posted. I've mastered reverse image searching and developed mad skills at tracking down site owners' contact information and bombarding them with legal-sounding messages until they remove every last photo of me from their servers.

The only way to succeed at this horrible game I don't even want to be playing is to spend a lot of time online seeing things I wish I didn't have to. I know more about file-sharing porn sites now than the average frat boy does. I have seen eleven lifetimes' worth of veiny, erect penises. Whenever I lie down and close my eyes, my brain treats me to a clip show of the Day in Porn, and I hear the men accusing me from their dark, seedy corners of the Internet.

You're nothing but a cockgobbling whore.

I'll hold you down and fuck those tits. See how hot you feel then.

I know what they think of me, because they won't shut up about it. Some nights I can't sleep, so I sneak out of the dorm room I share with Bridget and drive in circles around Putnam.

I hear those men because I don't have a choice.

I drive because I don't know what else to do.

But I don't have to fall apart. I thought I did at first, when I saw the pictures. That life as I knew it was over, and I just had to deal.

I was wrong. I have choices. Not falling apart is my choice. Every morning, whether I've slept or not, whether I've made it through the day without crying or given in and sobbed in the shower, where no one can hear me—the sun comes up, and I make my choice.

Today won't be the day this breaks me.

I throw away the disgusting wad of bloody towel and rinse my face off, drying it on a fresh towel. My sweater is a lost cause. I pull it over my head and toss it in the trash can. It was cheap anyway, and starting to pill.

I stick the cuff of my shirt under the tap, trying to remember if you're supposed to use cold water or warm to get blood out. I never get it right. I should look it up on my phone. I should—

—*figure out why West just punched Nate.*

Yeah. That, too.

Unless I already know why. I hope not, though. God, I hope not.

I have to treat this whole deal as one more thing to cope with. That's all it is. A problem to be solved. I can solve any problem if I work hard enough.

The men can laugh at me, fill my head with their poison. They can look at me naked, jerk off to me, post comments with photos of their dicks covered in semen, their fists wrapped around, the screens of their computers in the background with my body on them.

I can't help it, Caroline, they can tell me. *It's your fault for being so fucking hot!*

They've done all of that already. They've made it so I can't walk around campus in shorts without feeling slutty and stupid and completely at fault.

But I won't let them beat me.

I pull my arms far enough into my sleeves that I can wring out the wet, then shove my hands back through the holes. I'll have to change my shirt later. For now, this is the best I can do. Lip balm. Hairbrush.

One step after another, hour after hour, day after day, until it gets better.

If I keep going, eventually it has to get better.

I cross campus with my arms wrapped around my torso, scanning the blue sky, the cheerful red flowers, the students heading off in all directions, alone and in groups, purposeful as ants.

Before, I was so excited to be back at Putnam again. I love the campus, with its redbrick buildings and the arched open-air walkway that connects the dorms marching alongside an expanse of green lawn. I love my classes and the challenge of being at a college where I'm not the smartest. Unlike kids in high school, no one here gives me a hard time for caring too much about my classes or nerding out about Rachel Maddow. Pretty much everybody at this school is at least a little bit of a nerd.

But in the past few weeks, Putnam's been spoiled for me. Maybe forever.

The thing is, Nate didn't just post the pictures. He used the website where they went up to forward an anonymous link to a bunch of our friends. It got emailed around, and when I forced Bridget to tell me if anyone had sent it to her, she admitted that she'd gotten it in her college email *seven times*. Seven. There are only fourteen hundred students at Putnam—three hundred fifty in our class. I can't imagine how many times the message circulated among the ones who *aren't* my best friend.

The original post Nate put up is gone, but the photos keep popping up on different sites, and some of the posts still name my college, my hometown, me.

When I walk around Putnam now, I look at every guy I pass, and I think, *What about you? Did you see me naked? Did you save my picture onto your phone? Do you whip it out and wank to it?*

Do you hate me, too?

It makes it difficult to get excited about dancing with them at parties or cheering them on at a football game.

My phone vibrates in my back pocket. Bridget is texting to ask if I'm heading to lunch.

I type, Yes. You?

Yep! Gardiner?

I'm 5 min out.

Cool. Did u hear abt West?

I'm not sure how to answer that, so I type, Sort of.

She replies with *Swoon*.

Bridget likes to pretend West and I have a silent, simmering affair going on.

I like to pretend he and I are complete strangers.

The truth is somewhere in the middle.

When I met West, it was move-in day for first-year students, and it was hot. *Iowa* hot, which means in the mid-nineties with 98 percent humidity. The best thing to do under those conditions is to lie on a couch in someone's cold basement and watch TV while eating Cadbury eggs. Or, if you *must* be outside, to seek shade and ice cream. Not necessarily in that order.

Instead, I was carrying all my earthly possessions from my dad's car up four flights of stairs to the room I would share with Bridget. I have a lot of possessions, it turns out. I'd gotten a little dizzy on the last trip up, and my dad had insisted I plant my butt on the step by the dorm entrance and sit this one out.

So at that particular moment he was on his way up to the room, Bridget hadn't arrived yet, and Nate was off moving into his own room on the east side of campus. I was alone— sweaty and grimy and red-faced and *hot*. It's possible that I was mentally griping a bit about my tired hamstrings and the lack of trained helper monkeys to do the moving work for me when the ugliest car I have ever seen rolled up.

The car was the color of sewage, dented and rusty, with a

passenger-side door that had been duct-taped on. As I watched, it cut across an open parking space and slow-motion-bounced right up over the curb onto the manicured college lawn, rolling to a stop in front of my sneaker-clad feet.

I glanced around for the RA, good-girl radar pinging like mad. There were tire tracks in the grass! The car was farting out oily-looking clouds of noxious exhaust! This could not possibly be allowed!

No RA in sight.

The driver's-side door opened, and a guy got out.

I forgot my own name.

Now, probably that was because I stood up too quickly. It was *hot,* and I'd only had a Pop-Tart for breakfast, too excited to eat the eggs and bacon my dad tried to push on me. I definitely didn't get woozy because of how this guy looked.

I mean, yes, I'll admit, the way he looked might have contributed. The lizard part of my brain greedily took in all the details of his height and build and that mouth and his face oh my *God,* and then the rational part of me filed them carefully away in the appropriate mental binder.

That would be the binder neatly labeled If You Weren't with Nate.

But it wasn't the way the guy looked that got me. It was the way he moved.

I want to say that he *swaggered* out of the car, except that makes it sound like he was trying too hard, and he just obviously *wasn't.* He was naturally that graceful and loose-hipped and, God, I don't even know. You'll have to take my word for it.

He glanced all around. His gaze settled on me. "You the welcome wagon?"

"Sure," I said.

He stepped closer and stuck out his hand. "I'm West Leavitt."

"Caroline Piasecki."

"Nice to meet you."

His hand was warm and dry. It made me conscious of my clammy, gritty grip and of the sweat under my arms. My deodorant had failed hours ago, and I could smell myself. *Awesome.*

"Did you drive here?" I asked.

The corner of his mouth quirked up, but he sounded very serious when he said, "Yes."

"From where?"

"Oregon."

"Wow."

That made his mouth hitch up a little more, almost into a smile.

"How far is that?"

"About two thousand miles."

I looked at his car. I looked *in* his car.

Okay, so the truth is, I stepped closer to his car, *away* from him, and leaned over and peered inside. The backseat was crammed with camping gear and an aquarium full of light-bulbs and tangled electrical wire, plus a giant clear trash bag that was moist with condensation and contained what appeared to be dirt. There was also a huge box full of cans of Dinty Moore beef stew and a few randomly flung shirts.

The car looked like a hobo lived in it. I was fascinated.

I was also kind of afraid to keep looking at him. I could see from his reflection in the car window that he was stretching his arms behind his back, which had the effect of tightening his T-shirt and putting things on display that I was probably better off not looking at.

"You drove by yourself?" I asked.

"Sure."

He lifted his arms up into the air to stretch his shoulders. His shirt rode up, and I glanced away from his reflection, embarrassed. "With the windows down?"

I was just making words with my mouth at that point. All sense had abandoned me.

"Yeeeeeah," he said slowly. When I snuck a look at him, his eyes were full of mischief. "Sometimes I even got crazy and stuck an arm out."

I felt my throat flush hot. Returning to being unforgivably nosy about his car seemed the wisest course of action.

I noticed a sleeping bag on the front seat and wondered if he'd been using it right there where it lay. Did he just pull over on the side of the road, lower the passenger seat, and sleep? Did he eat cold stew out of cans? Because that was definitely a can opener in the cup holder.

And that was definitely a slightly crushed, open box of condoms on the passenger-bay floor.

"Don't you worry about botulism?"

Now, in my defense, I actually did have a reason for the question. I saw the cans, noticed that a number of them were dented and dinged up, and then remembered this high school bio class where we learned about anaerobic bacteria and how they grow in airless places. Sometimes cans get dented and there's a teensy tiny hole that you can't even see, but bacteria get in and they go crazy replicating themselves. When you open the can, the food just looks normal, so you eat it, but then you die.

It all made sense in my head. It wasn't until I straightened and turned around—which made me dizzy again, I guess because I'd been bent over too far, peering into his car like some kind of peep-show freak—that I realized it hadn't made any sense to *him*. His eyebrows were all knit together.

"From the cans. With the dents," I said.

No change in the eyebrows.

"Anaerobic bacteria? Gruesome, painful death?"

He shook his head slowly back and forth, and then he did the worst thing.

He grinned.

It was like a nuclear attack.

"You're a weird one, aren't you?" he asked.

I'm not the guy with condoms and beef stew in my car.

I didn't say it, though. I was too busy smiling like a complete idiot.

West's grin has that effect on me. He doesn't deploy it often, but when he does, I go brain-dead.

Also, the world had gotten kind of fuzzy and sideways at the edges. My hip hit something hard, which upon further investigation turned out to be his car door, and then I was sinking down, resting my forehead against the hot front tire and saying, "It's because they don't have helper monkeys."

I don't even know what I meant. I was all addled and sleepy suddenly, and he was really close, reaching for me. I felt his breath on my neck, heard him mumble something about *get inside* and *you*.

I liked the sound of that.

A heavy weight on my shoulders turned out to be his arm coming around me, easing me down onto my back. For one slow, perfect beat of my heart, he was poised on his elbows above me, his hips pressing into mine. He smelled good. Warm and rich, like something amazing to eat that would melt on my tongue.

Then he shifted away, and we were lying side by side on the ground. I wondered vaguely if my desire for him to climb back on top of me made me a bad girlfriend. Did it count as cheating? Because I liked his hands on me. I liked the smell of him.

I closed my eyes and breathed in West Leavitt and green grass and warm earth.

I'm pretty sure I was still smiling when I lost consciousness.

Bridget hails me from beside the glass-paned doors that mark the entry to the dining hall.

She's beaming the whole time I cross the lobby, right up until I get close enough for her to see my face.

"What happened to your *nose*?"

"It collided with an elbow."

"You're going to have to explain that."

"Yeah, I know. But give me a second."

We go through the doors, grab trays, and wait for the handful of students in front of us to make their way down the line before I dive in. "You know the fight? West and Nate? I kind of got caught in the cross fire."

"Nate *hit* you? Oh my gosh! That's terrible. Did you call security? Because that's serious, Caroline. I'm not even kidding, you can't let this keep going on like it is, or—"

I touch her arm to stop the stream of words. Bridget talks like a faucet. She's either on or she's off. You have to interrupt the flow if you want to get a word in edgewise. "It wasn't Nate. West elbowed me, I think. Neither of us was too sure, actually."

Her eyes get huge. "You talked to him?"

I know what she's imagining—West and me huddled somewhere private and intimate, and him holding a warm compress to my forehead. That's how I met her, in fact. I had passed out next to West's car, and I woke up on my dorm bed with a cold paper towel on my head and Bridget leaning over me, all forehead wrinkles and concerned blue eyes, like some kind of adorable red-haired, freckle-faced angel.

"Not really," I say. "That's a good color on you."

It's the truth: Bridget looks good in blue. But mostly I tell her because she's a jock—a long-distance runner on the track team—and I make a habit of complimenting her whenever she wears normal clothes, just to encourage the practice.

We're making our way down the hot-food line now. "Do you have chicken without the fried stuff on?" she asks the student worker.

"No, just what you see."

"Okay, thanks." She's in training, so she's super careful about what she eats.

I take a plate of chicken-patty parmesan and two chocolate mint brownies. I have bigger things to worry about at the moment than calories.

"Don't even think I didn't notice you changing the subject," Bridget says when we've made our way from the line to the salad bar, where she loads up on hard-boiled eggs and greens. "I need to know what he said. Like, was he still mad from fighting, or was he nice? Did you guys go somewhere quiet, or were you in a crowd? How upset was he that he hit you? Because Krishna says—"

"He didn't say anything," I clarify. "He had to leave so he didn't get caught and end up expelled or whatever."

"But you said you talked to him."

"No, I didn't."

She rolls her eyes. "You *implied* it, lawyer girl."

"We exchanged a few sentences. He wanted to make sure I was okay."

We're on to drinks now. Bridget goes for the milk. I get myself a Coke with ice. "Did he say anything about why he did it?" she asks.

"No."

"Did you ask? Did you hear them arguing? Give me something here. Only you could act like West and Nate hitting each other and you getting whacked in the face is no biggie. Hey, where's your sweater?"

"I had to throw it out. Blood all over it. And, no, I didn't hear them or ask."

"That sucks. I liked that sweater." We swipe our cards at the checkout to put the food on our meal plans, and she starts walking toward the closest free table. Looking back at me over her shoulder, she smiles. "Want to know what *I* heard?"

"What?" I set my tray down on the table a little too hard.

Her smile falters. "You're upset."

"No."

I'm not. I'm just . . . confused. Something's going on, and these days when something's going on, it's rarely good. And if the something involves West and Nate, I'm very much afraid I don't want to hear it.

We sit down. I brace myself. "Just tell me, okay?"

"I heard they were fighting about you."

Crappity crap crap crap.

"Who told you that?"

"Somebody in their class. They've got Macro together."

"Nate and West?"

"Yeah, and Sierra, you know her? She said that after class Nate made some random joke, and West got on his case, and it turned into an argument about you."

"What did they say?"

There's a rock in my stomach, dense and hot. I sip my Coke, closing my eyes against the doomed feeling slipping over my shoulders.

"I'm not sure." Bridget's tone is cautious. "Sierra didn't catch all of it, only your name."

I push at my chicken with my fork, but I can't even bring myself to cut it. When I put it in my mouth, it will taste like ashes. The burned-up remains of the life I used to have.

People talk about me. Not to my face, but behind my back? All the time. I'd made Bridget promise to tell me whatever she heard, because I need to know. It's the only way I can be sure they're forgetting, like I want them to.

I'm nothing special—just a normal-looking college girl. I should be able to fade into the background if I keep my head down. In a year, I'm hoping that barely anyone will remember this. *Caroline who?*

It's not what I had planned, exactly. I'd thought I might shoot for student-body president my junior year, senior year at the latest. But I can table that ambition if I have to. I'd rather be anonymous than notorious.

"Sierra said it was kind of romantic," Bridget offers. "He was defending your honor."

It's such a preposterous idea—that I have honor. That West would defend it.

I barely know him. I've only talked to him one time.

West and I are not friends.

And for the past few weeks, the only people who have cared about my honor are Bridget and me. None of my old friends can look me in the eye. Nate and I came as a unit, and when they had to pick sides, I guess his side looked like more fun.

"I would never do something like that," Nate had said, straight-faced, when I confronted him in front of a bunch of those friends in this very dining hall. "How could you think I would?"

And then, after I sputtered and he denied for another few minutes, he'd said, "I guess a lot of those girls just want attention so bad, they'll do anything to get it."

I look out the window at the lawn, unable to chew up and swallow the idea of West Leavitt defending my honor. Unable to process it at all.

Last year, when I regained consciousness after fainting by West's car, the first thing I heard was an angry male voice in the hall. My dad was shouting, which was nothing new. He's a judge, so he spends most of his professional time being calm and rational, but outside of work he's the single parent of three young daughters, and he has a tendency to get shouty when he feels threatened. Which is *a lot*.

You just have to know how to handle him. My oldest sister, Janelle, sucks up. Alison usually cries. I present him with reasoned arguments, appealing to the logical brain until the ranty brain calms down.

Dad must have been all the way down the hall by the stairs, because I couldn't make out what he was saying. Occasionally a lower, calmer voice broke into his tirade.

West's voice.

I didn't sort all this out until later. At the time, my head felt overlarge and tender, and I asked the girl leaning over me, "Who are you?"

"I'm Bridget," she said. "Are you okay? You fainted. This cute guy carried you up the stairs, and I don't know what he said to your dad, but your dad is *ticked,* and is he always that scary? Because, if so, I'm glad you're here—it's going to be a lot more pleasant for you—and also . . ."

She kept going until the door flew open and my dad came back into the room, red-faced and sweaty under the arms of his golf polo. He sat beside me on the bed, so obviously agitated that fume lines might as well have been rising off his head.

"How are you feeling?"

"Okay." This was a lie.

"I'm going to get you moved to one of the girls' dorms."

I sat up abruptly. "What? Why?"

"That boy out there—he's not a good influence. You shouldn't be living near a kid like that."

"Like what? What did he do?"

Well. That was the wrong question. For the next several minutes, I learned how entirely alarming it is for a father to leave his youngest daughter for just a few minutes and then rediscover her laid out on the ground underneath an unknown male. Especially when your daughter turns out to be unconscious, the kid has "an attitude," and you don't "like the look of him."

All of this was compounded, according to my dad, by the "drug paraphernalia" in the backseat of the punk's car. By which I think he meant the aquarium and lights and the bag of dirt, not the Dinty Moore. Although who knows? I was entirely out of my league. I heard the words *drug paraphernalia,* and I imagined short lengths of thick rubber, bags of heroin, syringes.

My dad was still lecturing when Nate showed up and made everything worse. Dad had invested three years in trying to guarantee that Nate and I were never alone near a horizontal surface, and now here Nate was, sauntering into my bedroom without knocking.

Dad turned a deeper shade of red.

Quickly, I introduced Bridget to Nate and Nate to Bridget and Bridget to my father. I smiled a lot, making an effort to seem healthier than I felt, because this was the first stage of what would turn out to be an arduous campaign to ensure that when he left—three days later instead of one, because the campaign was freaking *long* and hard fought—I'd still be in this dorm, in this room, with Bridget.

I won, but West was the necessary sacrifice. My dad wouldn't leave until I'd agreed I would have nothing to do with "that boy."

It was laughable, really, to think I might have. It turned out Dad was right about the drug thing.

West and Krishna's door was always closed, the curtains pulled shut. They had a steady stream of guests, played loud music, and annoyed me with their late hours and the whiff of sandalwood and sticky-acrid smoke from their room that infested our entire floor.

West set up that aquarium and those lights someplace secret—no one seemed to know where—and grew a bumper crop of weed. This was according to Krishna, who hung out in our doorway a lot, chatting with Bridget and me.

Krishna I can talk to. But West . . . no. The way he walks—that swagger that isn't a swagger—it's like he knows his way around, even if he's somewhere he's never been before. His confidence makes him seem older than me, and Bridget is always telling me stuff about him that cements the impression. Apparently he loaned money to this guy in Bridget's psych class so the guy could buy a plane ticket to see his girlfriend. West charged him interest. It makes me wonder whether he breaks kneecaps if someone doesn't pay him back.

He's just more than I could handle, even if I were allowed to talk to him.

I confined my relationship with West to staring from afar—and I wouldn't have done even that, except I can't help it. When he's around, I have to look at him.

He knows it, too. He smirks at me sometimes. One time, when he was coming down the hall in a towel? *God*. I think I was red for an *hour* afterward.

I never found out what he said to my dad. I have a feeling that, whatever it was, he wasn't defending my honor. It's hard for me to see why he would start now.

Maybe I should be grateful, but I can't. I don't need guys like West Leavitt defending me. He's infamous. Between the drug dealing and that face, that smile . . . pretty much everyone on campus knows who he is.

He'll draw attention to me. My primary purpose in life at the moment is to disappear.

When I mentally come back to the table, Bridget is peeling a hard-boiled egg and watching me. She's gotten used to my long silences. She's fiercely loyal, endlessly supportive. The best person I could possibly have on my side.

"If people want to know what I think about what West did?" I began.

"Yeah?"

"Tell them it was all a misunderstanding. It had nothing to do with me."

Her forehead wrinkles. "But I figured it was good. Somebody else on our side, right?"

"I don't want to be on a side, Bridge," I say gently. "I want people to get amnesia on this whole issue. Fighting tends to be a thing people remember."

She bites her lip.

"I don't need people linking me up with him, okay? I need to keep a low profile."

"If that's what you want me to say, that's what I'll say," she assures me. "That'll be the end of it."

I try on a smile and push my chicken across the tray, then pull my mint brownie closer and sink my fork through the thick layer of frosting. Dark fudgy black over a green so bright it's almost neon.

That'll be the end of it.

I wish I could believe her, but I can't make assumptions like that anymore. I've learned that when evil crawls out of a snake pit, you have to track it down and squash it. Then you have to assume it had babies and go looking for them.

I have a past to erase if I'm going to claim the future I've always wanted—a future that requires me to get into a good law school so I can clerk with a great judge and start making the connections my dad says I need if I want to be a judge myself someday. Which I do. I want to go even further. State office. Washington, D.C.

Dad always says the first step to getting what you want is to *know* what you want and what it takes to get it. There's no shame in aiming high. For my sixth-grade History Day project, I wrote a book of presidential limericks, one for each president. By ninth grade, I was volunteering to canvass door to door, and I got on the mailing lists for the Putnam College Democrats *and* the Putnam Republicans before I even received my acceptance letter.

I know what I want, and I know what it takes to get it. It takes a lot of hard work and sacrifice—but it also takes a clean record. No arrests, no scandals, no sex pictures on the Internet.

I don't need anyone going around beating people up on my behalf. I can't chance it happening again.

I need to talk to West.

I find him on the fourth floor of the library.

It's all journals up here, the shelves shoved together in the middle and study desks lining the outside walls, plus a Xerox machine where I spent way too much time copying literary criticism of T. S. Eliot last year.

West is standing by a cart full of books with his back to me, shelving a fat red volume of something. It takes me a minute to realize he's him. I'd already looked all over the first three floors, and I was starting to panic that he might not be here. I've noticed that I often see him with his cart on Thursday afternoons, but that doesn't mean much.

He's got earbuds in, and I don't think he's seen me, so I take a second to think about what I want to say to him. I feel kind of sweaty and unkempt, even though I took time after lunch to change my shirt and slick on lip gloss.

I've never done this before.

I've never initiated a conversation with West.

It feels more intimidating than it should, not only because of who he is—the *forbiddenness* of him—but also because this is the fourth floor. It's an unwritten rule of Putnam that the fourth floor of the library is a space of sacred silence.

West grabs another book. He has to reach above his head to shelve it, which means his shirt lifts and I see he's got a thick brown leather belt holding his jeans up. It doesn't match. His boots are black, and so is his T-shirt. It's got this big jagged orange seam sewn across the back, as though a shark came along and bit a giant rip in it and then he handed it over to a seven-year-old to fix.

I can't imagine how such a T-shirt even happens. Or why anyone would wear it.

West's clothes are sometimes like that. Just . . . random.

I kind of like it.

When he lowers down to his heels and bends over the cart, his shirt rides up, exposing some of his lower back.

I clear my throat, but his music must be too loud, because he doesn't turn toward me. I step closer. He's got his head down, his hand reaching for a book on the lower shelf.

Crap. Now I'm so close that I'm bound to startle him when he finally figures out I'm here.

There's nothing I can do to prevent it. I reach out, meaning to touch him just long enough to get his attention, but I end up pressing my palm flat against his lower spine instead.

It's an accident. I'm almost sure it's an accident.

Eighty percent sure.

He doesn't jump. He just goes completely, utterly still. So still that I can hear the music playing over his earbuds. It's loud, with angry vocals and an insistent, pounding beat that matches the sudden pulse between my legs.

Oh, I think.

Maybe it's not an accident, after all.

West's back is indecently hot beneath my palm. I stare at my fingers, ordering them to move for several long seconds before they actually obey. When I pull my hand away, it feels magnetized. Like there's this drag, this force, tugging it back toward West.

I'm pretty sure the force is called *lust.*

West straightens and turns around, and I know even before he does it that I've miscalculated, and now I'm totally at his mercy, which means I'm doomed. I'm not sure he *has* mercy. He sure didn't seem like he did when he was hitting Nate hard enough to make me physically ill.

He pulls out his earbuds, and I try to think something other than the word *doomed. Doomed, doomed, doomed.*

I try to remember what I was going to say to him—I had a whole speech planned—but I can't. I can't.

I stare at his belt instead. I think about grabbing it and

yanking him closer. As if this is a thing I could do. A thing I have ever done, with anyone, much less West Leavitt.

Dooooooomed.

"Hey," he says.

Which isn't fair, because it means I have to look up.

I do, eventually.

Our eyes meet. His pupils are huge, and there's something so intense about the way he's looking at me, it's kind of scary. Only *scary* is the wrong word. I've felt a lot of *scary* in the past few weeks, and this is different.

This is scary like pausing at the top of the steepest hill on a roller coaster, bracing yourself for the drop.

"Hey," I say back.

"What's up?"

"Can I talk to you?"

He considers this request. "No."

It's not what I was expecting him to say. All I can come up with is "Oh."

Then it's silent again except for his music, and there's this . . . this *atmosphere*. I think it must be him. I think he's *making* the atmosphere with his skin and his eyes, which look almost silver right now, and maybe he's also making it with all the muscles in his forearms, which are clenching and unclenching his hands in this way that's just—

It's just something. Intense, I guess. *Menacing,* but without the menace.

I have never stood this close to him before. I've never been alone with him since the day he parked his car right next to my feet and made me pass out.

I've never felt this excited, awkward, and senselessly worried in my whole entire life.

Until he takes a step toward me. That's worse.

Better, too.

Better-worse. It's totally a thing.

I back up.

He's supposed to stop stepping toward me when I back up, but he doesn't. He keeps coming. He moves right into my zone of personal space, and I get pinned up against the stacks, my butt pressing against a low shelf, West's hands braced on either side of my head.

"I'm working," he says. As though I'm a book, and he's shelving me.

I try to say, *I'll come back later,* but instead I make this sort of clicking, gargling noise that makes me sound like a bullfrog. I can feel my throat flushing—always a dead give-away that I'm embarrassed. I clear it and manage to say, "That's fine. I can . . . come back. Or I'll c-call you."

I don't have his phone number. Or any intention of calling him.

I don't know why I'm imagining I can feel the heat off his skin, because that's impossible. He isn't that close, surely. I cast my eyes up, trying to visually measure the number of inches between our faces.

It's not very many inches at all.

West doesn't touch me, but he is *much* closer than he needs to be, and the way he's looking down at me, his chest rising and falling rapidly, color high in his cheeks—I can't help but think about his fist connecting with Nate's mouth. The way Nate fell to the floor, heavy and limp.

He did that for you, I think.

I came here to ask him, but I already know.

He did it for me, and this is how he looked afterward. Dilated everywhere, his skin warm and his breathing rapid and shallow.

This is how he would look in bed.

I close my eyes, because I need to get my bearings. I had

imagined a businesslike talk with West. *Please don't do that again,* I would say. *Okay, if that's the way you feel about it,* he'd reply. *Yes, that's the way I feel,* I would tell him. Then maybe I'd give him a lecture about the importance of settling conflict without violence, followed by a brisk handshake.

I didn't imagine the ruddy skin of his neck right by the collar of his shirt. The stubble on his jaw where it curves into his ear. I didn't anticipate his smell, like spearmint and library books, detergent and warm skin.

God, he smells *fantastic,* but he's also kind of scary, and I have no idea what the rules are right now. No idea at all.

I need rules to get through this. I'm a rules kind of girl.

"West," I whisper.

It's supposed to sound calm and businesslike, but instead it sounds like I'm begging him for something, and I guess he takes that as a cue. He drops his head toward my shoulder. His lips . . . I can't be sure, but I think his lips are *really* close to my skin. I feel his breath near my ear, and my nipples harden.

"West, what the hell?"

"Why'd you come here, huh?" he murmurs.

And then—this is the worst-best part, by far—he turns his head and kisses my jaw, openmouthed.

It's like satin. Like lightning.

I don't know what it's like.

I *do* know that it's not what's supposed to be happening at all.

Except that the atmosphere West is creating makes me feel like this *is* what's supposed to be happening. Exactly this. The West menace is, like, sex in aerosol form. He's making it with his body, and then he's putting it all over me.

My body is into it, too. My body is *on board.*

My body is such a traitor.

"Why'd you have to come?" His voice is low and husky. Languid. His voice is a hook, catching on me. Reeling me in.

The music from his earbuds is a faraway drumbeat, and West doesn't move his hands. I do, though. Mine have slid up to his neck, tangling in his hair, pulling his head down.

Okay, no, they haven't. But they want to. They are positively itching to go rogue, and maybe he can see that in my eyes, because he makes this sound that's not even a sound. It's just an explosion of breath that does incendiary things to my panties.

"Tell me," he insists.

Tell him what? I have no idea what he's talking about. The only thing I know is if he doesn't kiss me soon, I'm going to die. He's so *hot*, and it's not just that his skin is warm, although it is. It's that I can feel all the energy from the fight coursing through him. He's still jacked up and high on adrenaline and chemicals. He's not himself. I'm not sure how I know this, but I do. West isn't West, and I'm not Caroline. Not with him so close. Braced over me, heating me up, breathing against my neck, he feels like a guy who's barely keeping it together. A guy who would beat the living shit out of the wrong someone if the wrong someone happened by, but who'd rather spend the rest of the afternoon and half the night fucking the *right* someone raw.

The right someone could be you.

I can't believe I just thought that.

"Tell me," he says again.

"Tell you what?"

"Why you're here."

I look away, to the side and up, because I want him to kiss me and I shouldn't. I don't know him. I'm not sure I like him. He *scares* me. His knuckles are split where they grip the metal shelving—gripping it so hard, they've turned white.

West is holding himself back from what he wants to do to me, and I wonder, what happens if he lets go?

Do I let him turn me around, bend me over this shelf, sink inside me?

I try to be disgusted by the idea, but, God, I can feel a ghost of what it would be like. It would be *electric*. Hot and slick, full and fast, the most erotic thing that's ever happened to me. I know it. I *know*.

But then it would be over, and I think I know what that would be like, too. West silent and stiff-jawed. A closed door.

I've never even had a *conversation* with him.

I push at his chest, trying to break the spell. "West. We have to talk."

"We're talking."

But I don't have his attention. His attention's lower, as it should be, because when did his knee get between my thighs? And am I really . . . ? Oh. I am. I'm kind of almost riding him.

"Get off," I say.

I'm whispering, nervous again about being overheard and despised by studying students—though I haven't actually seen any—or, worse, being seen here, doing this. They would talk about me. They would never *stop* talking about me riding West's thigh in the library barely an hour after he punched Nate in the mouth.

This is the worst possible thing I could be doing right now.

"West, get *off*."

He lifts his head. His dark hair is falling in his face, and his eyes look like chips of sky.

He eases back. "What is it?"

"I have to talk to you."

"I'm not in a talking mood right now, Caro."

My head is clearing. Nobody's getting bent over anything.

This is all just hormones. Adrenaline. It's got to be. West is biologically driven to want to rut with something after his testosterone-fueled display of masculinity, and I'm . . . I guess I'm biologically driven to be rutted on.

But I'm strong. I can rise above my biology.

I think.

"Too bad," I say, "because that's why I was looking for you. So we could converse like civilized beings."

West just levels that stare at me.

"Not rutting beasts," I add.

"I'm a beast," he says slowly. "And we're *rutting*?"

He doesn't like the word *rutting*. He spits it out like he's disgusted with it.

"What would you call it?"

"I don't know what to call it. Maybe you should tell me what you're chasing me around for."

"I'm not *chasing* you. I just—"

A pissed-off male voice says, "*Shh.*"

Fourth floor. Shit.

When I open my mouth again, my thoughts have scattered like marbles, and I can hardly even look at West. He's crossed his arms. His split knuckles are wrapped around his biceps. It looks hard.

Everything about West is hard.

Talk, Caroline, my brain urges. *Words. Sentences. Go.*

"I wanted to, um . . . About earlier. See, I heard from Bridget that—"

"*Shhhhh.*"

The same irritated voice again. I lose my words, flustered and ready to bail on this whole thing.

West says, very calmly, "There's three other floors, buddy. Pick one or shut the fuck up."

"This is the quiet floor," the invisible guy complains.

"Show me where it says that."

"Everybody knows."

West shakes his head. "I'm not everybody."

There's silence for a moment, then the resonant sound of a chair being pushed back. A backpack zipper. Footsteps announce the approach—a student glares at West with angry eyes—but he keeps going, and I hear the stairwell door opening.

A beat later, just before the door slams shut, the words *stupid slut* drift through it.

The ugliness of those words cuts into my hurt place, deep.

He's not the first person to call me a slut, but he's the first one to say it so I can hear him. And honestly? It doesn't help that he says it right after I let West push me against the stacks and stick his knee between my thighs.

It doesn't help that my panties are wet. I *feel* like a slut. I feel like I'm rattling apart, unable to stick to a direct line for more than five minutes.

Stupid cunt would spread for anyone, the men inside my head say.

I'd like to see him fuck her. I'd pay good money to watch that.

I look up at West. I feel despised and powerless, and it's so frustrating that he's seeing me this way—that he's watching so intently and really *seeing* what I try not to let anyone see, ever.

That I am right on the verge of falling apart. All the time.

His eyes soften, gentle with pity, and that makes it a hundred times worse.

Stupid, pitiful slut.

"It's fine," I say. "I've heard it before."

"It's not fine."

I wave my hand in the air, pointlessly, because I have no response. It isn't fine. But it's my life now.

"Caroline, it's not *fine*." West puts his hands on my shoulders.

I shrug him off and step sideways to get out from under him. "I know, okay? You don't have to *yell* at me. I know. He's going to tell everyone, and then the whole campus is going to be whispering about how we were practically screwing on the fourth floor of Hamilton. I get it. I'm sorry, all right?"

I think his eyes could burn holes through me, they're so fierce. The little flecks seem to flash. The grooves beside his mouth carve themselves deeper. "What are you sorry for?"

What am I *not* sorry for? I regret everything I've ever done with a guy. My first kiss, which took place after an eighth-grade dance, with a boy named Cody. My first French kiss, which was with Nate. Letting Nate take off my bra, put his fingers inside me. Sleeping with Nate and thinking we were making love. Buying lingerie for him, going down on him, letting him take the pictures when I thought it would bring us closer.

West, too. I regret what just happened with West.

"Everything," I whisper.

It's the wrong thing to say. His hands push into his hair, clenching. "Christ. I can't even—what's the *matter* with you, huh?"

"Nothing you can fix."

"So *why are you here*?"

I take a deep breath. I can do this. "I need to know it's not going to happen again. That you're not going to go around punching people because of me."

He frowns, a deep slash between his eyebrows. "Who said it was because of you?"

The question catches me off guard. "I heard—I heard you guys were arguing about me. Sierra told Bridget."

"I don't know a Sierra."

"I guess she knows you."

His face goes even darker. "It's not her business. Or yours. It's between Nate and me."

"I think we're way past the point where you can play the none-of-your-business card."

That makes him even more agitated. He wheels away, stalking to the end of the row. Then he comes back and grabs the cart with both hands. He looks like he wants to shove it at me. "He pissed me off. That's all you need to know."

"Yeah, but—"

Head lowered, he kicks the toe of his boot against the cart. Not hard, but hard enough to make way too much noise.

"You have to tell me what happened," I say, as calmly as I can manage. "Then I'll leave you alone."

His head comes up. "You think that's what I want? For you to leave me alone?"

I don't know what he wants, so I keep my lips pressed shut.

"He pissed me off because he's a smug, arrogant prick," West says. "And I was fucking sick of hearing him talk, all right?"

"So it had nothing to do with me."

He rakes his hand through his hair again. Turns away.

"West?"

"I wouldn't say that."

I wait.

It occurs to me that I'm good at waiting, and maybe that's one thing I have on West. He's more worldly, more confident, but he's volatile and I'm not. I'll stand here until he's done throwing his tantrum, and then he'll have to tell me.

I wait some more.

He turns back around. "I didn't do it *for* you, okay? I just couldn't take it anymore. He deserved to get beat down, and nobody else was doing it. But if you have some kind of hero fantasy, you can forget it."

"What's that supposed to mean?"

"You know. If you're getting your rocks off thinking I hit your ex because I've got a thing for you."

"Are you serious?"

"Why wouldn't I be serious?"

For a few seconds, I can't speak. He's just yanked me so rapidly from ashamed and awkward to righteously pissed off, my brain is having trouble keeping up. "That's so . . . conceited," I finally manage. "I mean, so, *so* conceited. After what you just—why would you even say something like that?"

He steps closer. He's vibrating with emotion, and I can't sort him out. I don't know what he's thinking, how he feels. I only know he feels it a *lot*. "Why did you touch me?" he asks.

"I was trying to get your attention."

"People tap when they're trying to get someone's attention. That wasn't a tap."

"It was . . ."

I've got nothing. I groped him, and we both know it. The only thing I can do now is lie. "It was an accident."

I hate when he does this. Looms over me this way with those eyes and that face. *Looks* at me. It is my new least-favorite thing: being looked at by West. Like he's trying to sex me to death.

"Honey," he says finally, "that was one hell of a long accident."

"Don't call me honey."

"I think you like it."

"I think your ears are too small."

I nearly groan after I say it. Stupid blurting mouth.

But I had to say something, because *honey* is degrading to women, totally inappropriate, utterly unexpected. And I do kind of like it.

West exhales a laugh through his nose, smiling. "You have a gap between your front teeth."

"It's useful. I can spit through it."

"I'd like to see that."

"Well, you won't get to."

"Won't I?"

"No. We're not going to be friends. We're not going to be anything. That's what I wanted to tell you."

He doesn't like that. His mouth doesn't, and his eyes don't. "It's not what it seemed like you wanted to tell me a minute ago."

"I don't care what it seemed like." If he keeps leaning closer, I'm going to pinch him.

He leans closer. I pinch him.

Okay, I try. But my hand gets near his arm, and lust sucks me in, and then I'm just kind of groping his sleeve.

His biceps is as hard as it looks. I take my hand away before it can declare its allegiance to the enemy.

"Looked to me like you wanted me to kiss you," West says.

I cross my arms and examine the books on the shelf behind his shoulder, a neat row of thick blue spines that say *PMLA*.

"It doesn't matter," I tell him. "I can't afford it. If people think we're together, or that what happened between you and Nate was about me, they'll keep talking about it, and this whole mess will go on and on. That's not what I want. I want it to go away."

"You want it to go away."

The doubt in his voice fires up my anger again. I hate that some people think I published those pictures myself, just for the attention. I hate that *he* might think it.

"Yes." The word comes out a little louder than I intend, so I say it again. "Yes."

"Rich Diehms called you a slut three minutes ago, and you didn't say anything to him. You said it's fine."

"What do you want me to do, chase him down and punch him in the mouth?"

"Maybe," he says. "Yell at him, at least."

"What would that accomplish?"

"Does everything you do have to be about accomplishing something?"

Here, at least, is a question I can answer easily. "Yes."

"So what are you trying to accomplish now?"

"I'm trying to get my pictures off the Internet, and I'm trying to keep a low profile so people will forget it ever happened."

He laughs at me.

My hand comes up so fast, I don't even realize I'm about to smack him until he catches my wrist.

"Honey—"

"*Don't* call me honey." I'm struggling against his grip, so angry that he caught me and won't let go. Caught me *easily*. I've never tried to slap someone before. I'm breathless and too emotional, balanced on the brink of tears. "Let me go."

"You gonna hit me?"

"Maybe."

".Then no."

I wrench my wrist, then try pounding at his chest. He captures my other wrist.

"It's a lost cause," he says. "Trying to get at me. Just as hopeless as the idea you can erase something from the Internet or make people forget what you look like naked. Completely hopeless."

Once his words sink in, I stop struggling, and he lets me go. I spear him with the iciest glare I can muster. "Thanks for the pep talk, but you are the *last* person on this campus I would ask for advice."

Something in his eyes shuts down. "Oh? Why's that?"

Because you're a drug dealer.

Because you're the kind of person who punches people when they piss you off.

Because you're trouble.

I can't tell him any of that. I can't make myself sound like an angel. I suck dick on the Internet.

"Because I was with Nate. And you're . . ."

When I trail off, he lifts one scarred eyebrow. "I'm?"

"Not Nate."

This time, his laugh is bitter. "No," he says. "I'm not Nate."

I want to apologize, but I'm not sure how, or even what to say.

West doesn't wait around for me to figure it out. He takes his cart, checks the spine of the next book in line, and begins rolling down the aisle away from me.

"I'm sorry," I call to his back. "I didn't mean it like that."

"Don't worry about it, princess," he says without turning around. "I won't say a word to anyone."

"Okay." I wrap my arms around my stomach. "Thank you."

He doesn't answer me. I guess we're finished, and I'm relieved. Sort of.

I'm also shaky and weak. It seems possible I might puke.

West pauses, right in the middle of turning from our row to the next one. He leans over the cart, balancing his forearms on the books, staring down at them for a long, awkward minute that feels like a year.

He lifts his head and looks right at me. "This wasn't a good day for us to have this talk."

"No," I agree. "Probably not."

He blows out a breath. "I shouldn't have hit him. It was a dumb-ass thing to do, and I'm still pretty wired from it. Sorry I . . ." He waves his hand at me. "Sorry for all that."

I don't know what to say, so I nod.

"Is your nose okay?"

"It's fine."

"It hurt?"

"A little. But it's not a big deal."

He flexes and releases his swollen hand a few times, staring down at it. It's his left.

"What about your hand?" I ask.

"It'll heal."

The floor falls silent. I wonder if anyone is up here. If there's a girl around the corner, sitting in silence, listening to this whole thing.

Maybe she's like me. Scared and stuck, frozen in place.

"You know," West says, "you didn't do anything wrong."

"Yeah. That's what Bridget tells me."

But she only says it because it's what she's supposed to say. I know what she really thinks. It's the same as what I think— what everyone thinks.

I *did* do something wrong. I trusted the wrong person. I

made a stupid mistake. I made it possible for Nate to take advantage of me, and it's my responsibility to own up to it.

West shakes his head, as though he can hear all these thoughts, but he doesn't buy it. "You took some sexy pictures with your guy. Lots of girls do it. If some girl gave me pictures like that, I'd never fucking stick them on the Internet, no matter how pissed at her I was."

"You saw them?"

"Everybody saw them."

I close my eyes against a stinging pressure in my sinuses and behind my eyes.

Crying isn't on my schedule.

"He says he didn't do it," I whisper.

"That's because he's a douchebag. Douchebags lie."

"Can we not talk about this?"

His head drops, his gaze falling back to the books. "All I wanted to say was, I don't think you can make it go away. Not the way you're doing it."

I have no reply. It hurts too much to hear him articulate it—my worst fear—and for the second time today I feel as if *he's* the one who hurt me, even though both times I did it to myself.

I've just run into his elbow all over again.

"Caroline."

The way he says my name forces me to look up.

"You know what?" he asks.

"What?"

He starts wheeling his cart away. Turning his head toward me, he smiles the tiniest bit and says, "Except for that gap between your teeth, you looked fucking hot."

He turns the corner. The wheels squeak as he moves into the next aisle.

He's a pig.

I won't think about what it means that I'm not disgusted with him.

Or that I'm standing here, arms wrapped around my torso, smiling at my feet.

It's too screwed up, so I just won't think about it.

I won't wonder if he's right and I'm wrong—if everything I've done to try to rescue my future is pointless and really I should be doing something different. Fighting for myself, somehow.

Right now I can't handle it. I can only breathe in deep and try to remember what's next on my schedule. Where I have to be. What I have to do to get through the rest of this day.

This is my fight. The only thing I know how to do to get my life back the way it was. Bury the pictures, rebuild my reputation.

This is my fight, and I'm not giving up.

Two weeks later, a nightmare wakes me.

It happens a lot.

I roll out of bed and slide my feet over the cool floor until I've found my flip-flops in the dark. Grab my keys from the dresser. Cup them against my palm so they won't jangle.

When I pull a sweatshirt over my head, holding my breath because I want to be quiet, Bridget's comforter heaves on the top bunk. Her head pokes out from beneath the covers.

"Where are you going?"

"Just out. I'll be back in a few hours."

I feel guilty for waking her up, but I can't really help it. It's hard to be an insomniac when you have a roommate.

"Be careful."

"I will."

She rolls over, and even though she's awake, I ease the door shut slowly until it latches and locks with a quiet *snick*.

I'm always careful.

I walk to my car with my keys gripped in my fist, looking left to right across the parking lot, listening for anything, anyone. I'm parked under the security light. From ten feet away I unlock my doors with the remote, and my heart beats so fast, so fast. The gasping sound of relief when I shut the door behind me is too loud in the clean, safe interior of my Taurus.

I turn on the stereo and crank up the volume and drive.

I have a series of loops that I do. First I go in a circle around the college, which is four blocks long and three blocks wide. Then I do widening circles around the surrounding college-owned buildings, the downtown, the fast-food strip and box stores, the Little League diamond and Frost-E-Freeze shack. I pass fields of cornstalks starting to break ranks and turn brown. My high beams spotlight the blank landscape of my home state.

One of these loops used to be my evening run, but I had to stop. After my naked body and my location became public information, being alone outdoors lost its charm.

I make only right turns, because I hate turning left, and my dad isn't here to tell me I need to get over that.

I don't know how to talk to my dad anymore. When I call him, I can't figure out what words I would have said before, when I never had to think about it. I knew just how to make him laugh and love me. Now when we talk, it's like I'm acting, only I don't know my lines, and I suck at improv.

I can't remember how to be the Caroline Piasecki who graduated from Ankeny High with her smile white and perfect, wearing her graduation cap and gown, walking onstage to give the valedictorian speech with her two sisters and her father in the front row of the bleachers, beaming with pride.

I haven't told him about the pictures. I can't.

I'm a mouth with a boy's dick in it, a body to look at, legs to spread.

I spin the wheel, turning my car to the right. To the right. Always to the right.

I haven't seen West for thirteen days, but I think about him. I walk myself through that afternoon at the library, trying to follow all the twists and turns of our conversation. Why did he push me back against the shelves? What was he thinking when he told that guy to leave? What was he trying to accomplish?

I think about him asking me if everything I do is about accomplishing something.

I pick over my relationship with Nate, trying to answer all the unanswerable questions.

Was he always bad and I just didn't notice? Did he *turn* bad?

How could I have trusted him?

I think about West saying, "You didn't do anything wrong."

I remember the way his thigh felt, pressing between mine.

One time last year, I was writing a paper at my desk, and I heard shouting and laughter in the hallway, periodic smacking thumps that made me flinch. Nate was lying on my bed, reading his Intro to Econ textbook. Bridget went out to see what was going on and didn't come back. Then I heard her laughing and West's raised voice.

"What are they *doing* out there?"

I tried to sound like I didn't care. Like I was slightly annoyed and I didn't feel this tug in my chest. This pressure to find out, join in, become part of it.

Nate shrugged. "Go see."

I can still remember exactly how I felt when I stood up and headed out there. Balanced on a knife's edge between good and bad, unsure which way I might tip—but aware, deep in my bones, in my tight lungs and tense shoulders, that *something was about to happen.*

In the hall that night, I found Bridget and Krishna, bowling with rubber chickens.

Yeah. It took me a minute to get it sorted out, too.

I don't know where Krishna came by the chickens—probably he stole them from somewhere—but whoever had owned them before couldn't possibly have enjoyed them as much. Krishna and the chickens were famous last year. The chickens showed up all over—occupying toilets, hanging from the rafters in the dining hall, perched on top of the big phallic metal sculpture in the middle of the campus, or dangling from the party keg.

But this time Krishna was standing at one end of the hall, twenty feet from a neat arrangement of pins, and winding his chicken through several tight arm revolutions. As I watched, he let go, an underhand throw that whipped the chicken through the air with surprising speed. It hit the pins, and they exploded, scattering all over the hall. Bridget shrieked, then bent over, laughing.

It was totally juvenile—the game, Bridget's girlish reaction, Krishna's red eyes and his stoned grin. I had a paper due in the morning and a lot of polishing still to do. I had Latin homework to get through, and if I had to go to the library because of these guys, I'd—

Suddenly the door right across from mine opened. West came out with a chicken in each hand and a two-liter bottle of soda under one arm. "Okay, so here's what I'm thinking about chicken rockets," he said, before he caught sight of me and stopped.

We looked at each other. Probably not for ten entire minutes, but that's how it felt. Like an indecently long time spent staring at his face, when I almost never allowed myself more than a glance. A day of watching his mouth twitch. His nostrils flare. His too-pale blue-green eyes lit up with mischief.

I got all tangled up in those eyes of his, mentally tripped and fell, and then couldn't untangle myself.

West arched an eyebrow. "Want to play?"

He didn't mean anything by it. I'm almost sure.

Or, I mean, he *did,* but all he meant was, if I said yes, I'd get a chicken of my own and a free pass to indulge in this silliness, blow off my homework, act like a different girl.

He didn't mean did I want him. Did I want to learn how to cut loose. Did I wish I could be different.

But, even so, my heart beat like a bass drum in a halftime show, and I couldn't quite catch my breath to answer, *No, thanks.*

This isn't for me.

You're not for me.

The denial was too thick in my throat. If I tried to say it out loud, I would choke on *no,* because I wanted to say *yes.*

In the end, I didn't say anything. Nate came up behind me and wrapped his arm around my waist, resting his chin on my shoulder. "What's with all the noise?"

A door shut behind West's eyes. His face closed off, and the tipping point where I was standing flattened out beneath my feet into the familiar, unexceptional terrain of my hallway, my state, my whole boring life.

"Just blowing off some steam," West said.

"Could you keep it down, maybe?" Nate asked. "We're trying to study."

"Sure thing."

Nate pulled me inside, closed the door, kissed my neck. His hands roamed under my shirt, over my bra, and then I stopped him because Bridget was in the hallway and I had a paper to write.

And also because I felt deflated, as though some rich possibility had been taken from me. Something more than a juvenile game of hallway bowling.

The alchemy of a boy who could turn two-liter soda bottles into chicken rockets.

I wonder, sometimes, whether the pull I felt toward West is the reason why I broke up with Nate. Whether it gathered power until it got so strong, it cast a shadow over all my other feelings, and I didn't even realize it.

When I think about Nate, about West, it's hard for me to tell what's my fault and what isn't.

When I sleep, there's no peace in it. I dream of being chased, attacked, hurt. In my dreams, I'm a victim, and the dreams start to feel more real than the daytime does.

Semitrucks idle behind the Walmart and the grocery store. The guy at the gas station has gotten to know who I am, and he asks how things are going when I pay for gas and orange juice. He's in his forties, with a salt-and-pepper beard and a gut. He seems like a nice man, but how nice can he be, really, working the night shift at the Kum and Go?

Even the name of the gas station is too gross. Before, I thought it was funny. Now it gives me flashbacks, and I've started driving twenty miles to the next town to buy gas there, because I can no longer talk to the Kum and Go guy without wondering if he's seen me with my clothes off.

I drive by knots of drunk students walking back to the

college from the bar or the pub, gripping one another's elbows, laughing and shoving. One time I saw a girl fall down. She was alone with a guy, and I thought he was going to rape her, but he helped her up. I pulled the car over and took deep breaths, close to hyperventilating. Because, seriously, what on earth is wrong with me that I thought that?

I never would have before. Never.

I don't want to be like this for the rest of my life. If I had an UNDO button, I'd hit it so hard. But if there's some way to go back to how I was before, I haven't found it.

Most nights, I end up at the bakery.

I tell myself I won't, but I do.

I'm under strict personal orders to stop driving here, stop parking out front, stop looking through the window for a glimpse of West.

Yet here I am.

Light spills from the kitchen in the back of the shop, through the plate glass and over the sidewalk. I set the emergency brake but leave the engine idling. With the car stopped, my music sounds too loud, so I lean forward to turn it down.

I imagine it's warm in the kitchen and it smells good. The mental taste of it is sweet, an antidote to all the hours I spend on my laptop, sifting through the worst that humanity has to offer.

West's figure crosses the doorway. By the time I'm standing up, one hand holding the door open and the other tucking my keys into my hoodie, he's already disappeared. A gust of cold wind blows across my exposed feet and over the back of my neck. I hunch down, pushing my fists deeper into the kangaroo pocket of my hooded sweatshirt.

The men in my head want to know what I'm staring at and why I'm such a dumb cunt.

I don't know. I don't know why.

I'm about to get back in the car when the wind shoves at me again, a cold, hard push right in my face, and I squint my eyes and raise a hand to shield my eyes.

I'm annoyed.

I'm angry.

I'm *pissed*.

I'm standing in front of a bakery at four in the morning, furious, staring at an empty window.

I squeeze my keys so hard, they bite marks into my palm. West walks by the open kitchen door again.

Go in there and tell him you're sorry. Tell him you like him. Tell him something.

But I don't. I can't. West isn't what I need. He's only what I want.

I want him because he punches when he's mad.

I want him because he drove a wheezing car two thousand miles by himself, eating stew out of cans as if that's something you can just *do*.

Because he looks at a soda bottle and sees a chicken rocket.

Because I feel like, if I was with him, he might fix me. He might save me.

He might ask me, *Want to play?* and this time I might say yes.

But I know that's not what would happen. He wouldn't save me. He'd ruin me.

I'm already ruined enough.

I turn around, get back in the car, and drive away.

It took me ten years to learn how to hate my dad.

He blew through town just often enough to fuck with Mom's head until she lost her job, gave him all her money, turned her heart over to him one more time, and then watched him drive away.

That year—that summer when I turned ten—Mom cried for a week. I visited the neighbors in our trailer park, telling them what had happened in a way that made it all sound funny, hoping they'd give me something to eat.

In the busted-ass, nothing place in Oregon where I'm from, there used to be jobs in lumber, but now there's nothing but part-time work, hourly pay, wages you can't raise a family on.

Where I'm from, women work, and men are only good for two things: fighting and fucking.

I got good at fighting early. When I was twelve, my cousin's friend Kaylee took me into the unlocked supply closet beside the laundry and showed me how to fuck.

I got good at that, too, with some practice.

Maybe it should have been enough for me. Seemed like it was enough for everybody else.

But there's something in me that's like a weed, always pushing up through cracks, looking for light. Looking for a deeper grip in inadequate soil.

I'm curious. I want to know how things work, fix them if they're broken, make them better. It's just the way I am, as far back as I can remember. When three out of the five dryers are sitting broken in the trailer-park laundry, I've got to know why. If I can't get a good answer, I'll take those fuckers apart and try to figure it out.

When there's something I can do, I need to do it.

I think that's what makes a real man. Not whose ass you can kick or how good you can fuck, but what you *do*. How hard you work for the people who depend on you. What you can give them.

That time my dad came around when I was ten—the time I stood up to him and he beat me hard enough that I finally learned how to hate him—he got Mom pregnant before he left.

My sister, Frankie, came into the world with two strikes already against her. Mom hadn't planned on another kid and wasn't real thrilled. Frankie showed up early, way too puny. She slept a ton.

Because I'm curious—because I can't help myself—I read this pamphlet that had come home from the hospital in a bag of free formula. It said babies were supposed to wake up every three or four hours to eat, but Frankie wasn't doing that. Not even close.

"What a good baby," everybody said.

Nobody wanted to hear she was starving.

I didn't want to love Frankie. I just wanted to fix her. But the thing about babies is, you mix up formula for them in the middle of the night—unwrap their blankets, change their diapers, run your fingernail across the bottom of their tiny bare feet until they're awake enough to eat—and the next thing you know they've got their little fingers wrapped around your soul, and they don't ever let go.

I had to do things for Frankie. Whatever needed to be done. I just had to.

So I learned what hours DHS is open. What paperwork you have to take to the office, who to call if you swipe your Oregon Trail card at the grocery store and it turns out there's no money on it because your mom missed the appointment and didn't tell you. I learned where to go to get secondhand onesies. Who gives out free formula on what days. How to turn in cans for quarters to pay for laundry, where to find work when people say there isn't any.

I learned. I've got a knack for it.

By the time I turned fourteen, I was making more money than my mom was, and I guess I started to think I was the man of the house. The rock the surf broke over. Invincible.

Then my dad showed up.

If I was the rock, he was the tide. Nothing I could do to keep him from dragging my mom back out to sea. All I could manage was to keep Frankie sheltered, give her somewhere to hide and huddle so he couldn't drag her under, too.

After that, I started thinking about what else I could do.

Just working and keeping shit together the way I was already—it wasn't ever going to be good enough. I had to give Frankie a life somewhere else, somewhere better, or she was going to end up like all the other girls, screwing twelve-year-old boys in supply closets, getting screwed over again and again by some worthless bastard she's decided she's in love with.

I couldn't stand the thought of it.

When I was old enough to drive, I got a job at this ritzy golf course twenty-five miles away. I got that job on purpose, because I knew if there was anywhere I could meet the right people, study them, figure out how to *become* one of them, it was there.

I worked my way up to caddying, which is how I met Dr. Tomlinson. I caddied for him once when his usual guy was sick, and then he requested me and I got to be his usual guy.

This golf course I'm talking about—when I say it's ritzy, I mean it's so ritzy that people fly there from all over the world just to play golf, and once they pick their caddy they keep the same caddy for as long as they want. It's swank.

So, anyway, Dr. T is rich—an anesthesiologist—and his wife comes from money. I've been in their house, high up on a bluff with a view over the golf course. It's huge, clean, everything immaculate, nothing broken or out of place.

That house looked like everything I wanted for Frankie. A fortress that would protect her from my dad, from pain, from making stupid, fucked-up decisions and wasting her life.

I saw that house, and I wanted it. I wanted what he had.

I guess Dr. T saw something in me, too. The weediness in me. My willingness to work, to grow toward any kind of light I can find. He said I reminded him of himself back when he was a dirt-poor farm kid in Iowa, desperate to do something with his life.

I make him feel big, is what he means. Show him who he was and how far he's gotten.

Dr. T made me his project. He taught me how to talk so I don't sound ignorant. He told me when I was acting like trash, how to fit in among people like him. He and his wife don't have kids, and he kind of adopted me.

His wife—she didn't want a kid. She took me out in the

woods and told me to lift up her skirt. Took me in the pool. Took me into her bedroom when Dr. T wasn't around.

She wasn't the only woman to use me, or even the first. She wanted into my pants. I wanted her money. A fair exchange, I figured.

Dr. T told me they would send me to the college where he'd gone, the *best* college, according to him. If I could get the grades and get in, they would ship me off to Putnam, Iowa, with full tuition. Room and board would be up to me.

The Tomlinsons would do that for me. They liked me that much.

I worked my ass off to get in to Putnam. I did things I'm proud of, and I did things Dr. T would kill me for if he found out. I did them so I could get here, and I'm here so I can get a good degree and meet the right people to give me a leg up in life.

I did them for Frankie and my mom.

I'm not ashamed. The world isn't some flawless place where everything works. It's a fucking mess, and if I have to cut corners or break the law to get where I need to be, fine. If I have to trade sex for money, for opportunity, I'm still better off using my dick than wasting my life, losing my heart.

Love is what fucks people up. Love is the undertow.

My mom taught me that.

At Putnam, I wasn't the same person I am back home. I was a student, a worker, an actor mouthing lines. I was an impostor, but a good one. I knew exactly how I was supposed to behave, what I could get away with saying and doing, when I needed to shut the fuck up and keep my head down, no matter how much I didn't want to.

I knew the rules. I knew where they bent, and I was good at bending them, because for a guy like me, bending them was the only way.

But bending is bending and breaking is breaking. Except for that one fuckup with Caroline, I didn't break the rules. I broke the *law* but not the *rules*.

I guess when I fuck up, I tend to go epic.

"Get your fingers out of there."

Krishna is bent over the mixing bowl, poking at the nine-grain-bread dough. I take the towel out of my waistband and snap him across the back of the neck.

"Ow!"

"I said get your fingers out."

He straightens and wipes his hand on his jeans. Flour released from the towel drifts in a cloud around him. "I just want to see if it feels like an ass."

"That is some perverted shit."

"You're the one who told me."

"No way did I say that. Wash your hands if you're going to touch it. That's all I ask."

"I did before I came over here."

"You did not."

"I did too. I always wash my hands after."

After, in this case, means, *after I roll out of her bed.* Half the time Krishna crashes my night shift, he's wasted. The other half the time, he's just gotten laid.

Tonight, I'm pretty sure it's both.

"Maybe you should wash your hands before, quit spreading scabies all over campus."

"Scabies? Dude, that's sick. My body is a fucking *temple.*"

"And I'm sure your women appreciate it, but I don't know where those fingers have been, so you're going to wash them again before you touch that dough or I'll smack the shit out of you."

He lifts both hands in surrender. "All right, Captain, all right. What crawled up your ass tonight?"

"Nothing."

Krishna scrubs his hands. I clean the bowl of the mixer with a scraper and soapy water, then dry it and polish it until it shines.

I like working alone. There's no one around to make a big fucking deal of what mood I'm in.

There's no one to make me notice I've been in a bad mood for weeks, because every time I see Nate Hetherington, I want to punch him again.

I must not have hit him hard enough last time. He's still smiling that smarmy fucking smile.

Krishna puts both hands in my nine-grain dough and starts massaging it with his eyes closed, his expression all blissed out. He acts like such a dipshit, you'd never know he was some kind of math prodigy.

"I'm not going to let you fuck it, if that's what you're thinking."

"Shh," he says. "I'm comparing."

"To who?"

"That girl I was with tonight. Penelope."

"With the dark hair?" I ask. "Kind of big?"

"Yeah."

"Jesus."

"Why, you like her? You know if you'd told me, I wouldn't—"

"Nah, it's fine. She's my lab partner."

"She's got an ass on her," he says.

"I don't want to hear about it."

It's not that I care about Penelope one way or the other. I just don't want to go to lab and have to think about Krishna bending her over a railing or whatever.

He'd tell me all the details if I didn't forbid him to. Krishna will tell anybody any goddamn thing. Back home, a guy who bragged as much as he does would get his ass beat on a regular basis. When I met him last year, I thought I'd probably kill him inside of a week, and there goes my big chance.

He has a way of making you like him, though. Fuck me if I could tell you what it is.

He smacks the dough lightly. "This doesn't compare. It's all lumpy."

"It's the nine-grain. It's supposed to be lumpy."

When he thinks I'm not looking, he pinches off some dough and puts it in his mouth. Then he licks his finger.

"That's it. If you touch one more thing, you're leaving."

"You'd get lonely without me here to keep you company."

"Yeah, I'll cry all over the baguettes and tell Bob to charge the suckers extra for artisanal salt."

Bob owns the bakery. He hired me as extra labor for the Thanksgiving rush last November, but I made myself so indispensable that he kept me on, eventually giving me a few overnights a week. He's close to retirement, and he doesn't really give a fuck anymore as long as the place opens and closes and there's something to sell. He's been letting me experiment with the bread, make new kinds to see if the customers go for it. It's a kick.

Plus, the bakery is a great place to move weed. There was already a tradition of Bob selling warm muffins and cookies to college students in the wee hours—stoners with the munchies, students pushing the edge of an all-nighter. I keep up the tradition, but the ones who text or call me first and slip a wad of cash into my hand get more than a muffin in their paper bakery bag.

Krishna's running the finger he licked around the lip of the giant mixing bowl. I go for the towel again, but he sees it

coming and grabs it out of my hand. I let him. I'm not fighting over a hand towel.

"I've got work to do, you know."

"What have you got to do? Watch dough rise. This is the
most boring job in the world."

Since he got here, I've been washing dishes in water hot
enough to scald his never-worked-a-day-in-his-life skin.

I don't know why I keep him around. He skips class,
doesn't have a job, drinks too much, sticks his dick in anything that moves. I shouldn't like him.

He just kind of attached himself to me.

I'd planned to live by myself this year. I found a basement
apartment for cheap and got permission from the college to
live off campus, which saves a fortune on room and board.

Krishna saw the lease on my desk and begged me to take
him with me.

He ended up finding a bigger place, above a shop, and
promised to pay the rent if I'd lease it and let him take a
room. I agreed, because he's good for it. Krishna's parents
are loaded.

He dusts off the countertop with the towel, hops up on it,
and draws a grid in the flour on the cool metal surface. "Will
it cheer you up if I tell you your girl's sitting out front in her
car again?"

I look up, which is just stupid. First off, I can't see her
from back here. I can only see her if I walk to the other side
of the room and look out the front window—and then she
can see me, which I don't want her to.

Second, she's not my girl.

Third—

"Ha!" Krishna says. "You're so easy."

Yeah. That's the third thing. He picked up on my Caroline
fixation real quick last year, and he taunts me with it.

Ever since I hit Nate last month, she's been parking at the bakery a couple of nights a week. She doesn't come in. She just sits out there when she's supposed to be sleeping.

I saw her at the library today, bent over her notebook, writing something. The sun was streaming in over her table, making her hair and her skin glow gold. She looked fragile. Tired.

I can't stand her being out there. I want her to go away.

I want to not have to think about her.

Of course, maybe she's not even there. Krishna could be yanking my chain. He's hoping I'll ask, and I don't want to give him the satisfaction.

"You know anybody Vietnamese?" he says.

"What? No."

"I need to find somebody Vietnamese to teach me how they play tic-tac-toe. I'm working on this combinatorics thing—"

"Is she out there or not?"

He grins. His teeth are blinding. The grin is at least 50 percent of the reason he gets so much tail. "Yeah, she's out there."

"Did you talk to her?"

"You told me to leave her alone."

"Good."

I put the yeast away in the fridge and look at the list of stuff I need to get finished before my shift's over.

I glance at the clock.

Krishna's still talking about tic-tac-toe.

My phone buzzes in my pocket. I pull it out, see my mom's number, but the text sounds like Frankie.

What r u doing?

I text back. Working. Why are you awake?

Cant sleep, she writes. Sing 2 me

It's after ten back home. She should have been asleep hours ago. She's only nine.

Why not Mom?

Shes out.

That's what I was afraid of.

What song do you want?

Star one

So I type out the first verse of "Dream a Little Dream of Me," line by line. She sends me a smiley face.

Go to sleep, Frank.

Im trying

Be good.

Always

Love you.

Night west

Night peanut.

When I put my phone back in my pocket, it feels heavier.

I don't like Frankie texting me after ten o'clock.

I don't like that my mom's not home or that she emailed me asking for five hundred dollars this morning but didn't say what it was for. I tried to call Bo, Mom's boyfriend, who they live with, but he didn't pick up and he hasn't called back.

A couple thousand miles away from them, I can only know what they tell me, and Mom only tells me what she thinks I'll want to hear. I'm supposed to have faith they'll all be fine without me.

When you've had my life, faith is in short supply.

And God damn it, I don't like knowing Caroline is out there in the dark, alone, awake when she needs some rest.

I'm sick of fucking *worrying* about her all the time.

That's the worst thing about Caroline—the endless nagging *worry* of her. It was bad enough last year, when I met her and fell for her and swore to myself I'd never touch her again, all in the same day.

It was bad enough when I started dreaming about her, waking up with my cock hard and jerking off in the sheets, thinking about her mouth on me, her legs wrapped around my waist, what her face might look like when she comes.

Bad enough, but fine. Whatever. I can ignore that kind of shit forever. I could jerk off a million times thinking about Caroline and still not need to talk to her.

The problem with Caroline isn't that I want her. The problem is that I want to *help* her, want to *learn* her, want to *fix* her, and I can't do that. I can't get caught up with her, or she'll distract me and I'll wreck everything.

I've got too much at stake to let myself get stuck on some impossible girl.

I'm not going out there.

I look at the clock again.

Krishna sticks his head in the big industrial fridge. "You have any cookie dough in here?"

"No. It's time for you to take off. I've got to start baking soon."

He cocks his head and gives me an assessing look. He has a streak of wet gunk on one cheek and a drift of flour in his hair.

"You're trying to make me leave because you're gonna go talk to her, aren't you?"

Fuck it, I am.

I am, because I can't *not* do it anymore. I've been *not* going out to talk to her for weeks.

"I'll bring you some breakfast later," I tell him. "What do you want, a lemon poppy-seed muffin?"

"Bring me one of those ones with chocolate chips."

"You can have all the fucking chocolate chips. Just get out of here." I push him toward the back door, into the alley.

"Far be it from me to get between you and your lady friend."

"You know it's because you say things like 'lady friend' that I'm making you go, right?"

"Nah, it's because you've got serious privacy issues. You could be a serial killer, and nobody would know. Or, like, a secret stripper."

"As if I have time for another job."

"That's true. You'd have to stop sleeping. But it might be worth it to have chicks shoving cash in your jock."

"They do that, anyway, whenever I go out dancing."

"Oh, yeah?" Krishna's face lights up. "You got moves?"

I don't dance. If I need to get drunk, I do it at the bar in town that doesn't card.

If I need to get laid, I find somebody who doesn't go to the college, take her home, make her happy, and clear out. Townie women don't expect anything from me.

"No," I say. "I don't need moves. I've got tight pants and an elephant dick."

Krishna laughs.

"You're not driving, are you?"

"I walked. I can knock on her window if you want. Send her your way."

"Thanks, but no." I turn him in the other direction, pointing him toward the apartment. It's only two blocks, and I've never heard of anybody getting mugged in Putnam.

"Don't forget my muffin," he calls as he turns the corner.

After Krishna's gone, the kitchen is so silent it seems to echo. This is my favorite part of the night, what comes next—the part when I dump out the proofed dough, weigh it into loaves, shape it, fill the pans, and fire up the ovens. It's an act of creation, and I'm the god of the bread.

I look at the clock and measure out the minutes. Ten.

Ten, at a minimum, before I go look out the window. Maybe she'll be gone, and I won't have to do this. I can rule over this tiny world, messing with temperatures and proofing times, how much flour and how much liquid, how many minutes in the oven. It's like pulling levers. Up or down. More or less. Simple.

I wish Caroline would let me do it—let me be the god of the bread and leave me alone. But she's out there, messing up my kingdom, and I'm afraid of how much I want to go talk to her.

I think of Frankie on the phone. Of the money I sent my mom this afternoon.

I promise myself I won't go to the door for fifteen minutes.

Fuck it, twenty. I won't go for twenty.

I can't give in to this, because the worst thing about Caroline is that I've never promised her anything, but she's here, anyway. It's as if she knows.

She doesn't know. She can't.

She can't know that when I make a promise, I keep it.

Or that I'm afraid if I start promising her things, I won't ever be able to quit.

"You want to come inside?"

That's all it takes. When she says, "Yeah, sure," I turn and go back in, and she closes her car up and follows me.

I put my iPod on shuffle and start it playing. I like having music for this part of the night—put it on any earlier, and the mixers are too loud to hear it. While I wash my hands,

Caroline wanders around, doing a slow circuit of the room. Unlike Krishna, she doesn't touch anything.

I tie my apron on over my jeans and go back to what I was doing.

"Bob makes the sweets," I tell her. "I just stick them in the oven at the end of my shift. Not sure if you want to wait that long."

As though she's here for a cookie, and not because . . . fuck if I know. I clocked her ex, she showed up at the library, I mauled her, and she told me she doesn't want to have anything to do with me. Then she started stalking me at work.

What am I supposed to think?

She shrugs.

I fling a chunk of bread off the scale onto the floured surface of the table. "So how's it going?"

Caroline leans a hip against the table's edge, all the way down at the far end. "Fine."

Fine.

Everybody says they're fine. It's bullshit.

It's not as though every conversation I have back home is deep and meaningful, but I never wasted so much time being polite as I do in Iowa.

Caroline's wearing sweatpants and flip-flops and a hoodie you could fit seven of her in. Her toenail polish is chipped, and her hair's in one of those lazy half ponytails, like she started to put it up but her arms got tired and she had to abandon the job before she finished.

There are chicks who dress the way Caroline is dressed all the time, but she's not one of them. On the first day of history class, she wore jeans and a bright-blue sweater even though it was still ninety degrees outside. She lined her pen and her highlighter up perpendicular to her binder, the textbook and the syllabus all out in front of her.

There's something about her that's totally pulled together, even when she's just wearing jeans and a shirt. Not the way she looks, I mean. Something *inside* her. Like she's got it all figured out, knows what she wants, knows she deserves to get it.

I can still see how her face looked when she was sticking her nose inside my car, checking out all my stuff, asking me, "Don't you worry about botulism?"

Tonight—lately—she's all wrong. She isn't fine. Not anymore.

And I can't let it be.

"How come everybody lies when you ask them that?"

"What, how they are?"

"Yeah. You say, *Hey, how's it going?* and everybody says, *Oh, fine.* Their hair could be on fire, and they'd still say, *Fine, fine.* Nobody ever says, *You look like shit,* or *I don't have enough money to make rent,* or *I just picked up a prescription for a really bad case of hemorrhoids.*"

"People don't like talking about hemorrhoids. It makes them uncomfortable."

"But who decided it was the end of the fucking world to be uncomfortable? That's what I want to know."

She shrugs again. "I think it's supposed to be like lubrication for society."

"Lubrication?"

"Grease."

I frown at her and toss a loaf down the counter. It's filling up. I have to throw them down to her end. This one lands with a little *pouf* of flour that gets her black sweats messy, but she doesn't brush the flour off.

I know what lubrication is. I just don't get why we need it. We didn't need it at the library, when I was so fucked in the head from hitting Nate that I forgot I was supposed to even try to be polite.

It felt good punching that jackass.

It felt fucking great backing her up against the stacks, smelling her, getting my nose full of Caroline and my leg right up between hers, getting the taste of her on my tongue.

"It's something my dad says," she tells me. "Being polite is a form of social lubrication."

"I thought that was booze."

"What was?"

"I thought booze was for social lubrication."

She smiles a little. "That, too."

"I'm not sure you and me need lubricating."

That earns me Caroline's I'm-so-offended look. Those big ol' brown eyes narrowed to slits.

I'd like to see her make that face at me when I have my tongue between her legs.

And that is not even a little bit what I'm supposed to be thinking about.

It's impossible, though, to *stop* thinking about friction and lubrication, tongues and fingers and mouths, when she goes all red like that. When I know I'm getting her good and rattled. She pinked up that way once when I walked back to my room from the shower in a towel. Stared and stared at me with her neck flushing and her eyes huge.

I had a hard-on for a week.

"Why'd you come tonight?"

"You asked me to."

"Before that. Why do you keep driving here, parking out front? What do you want?" I throw the last piece of dough down the table, and it skids across the floured surface, stopping right in front of her.

"I don't want anything."

"I don't believe you."

She stares at me, nostrils flared, chin up. Starting to get pissed that I'm pressing.

Good. Let her be pissed. When she's pissed, she talks.

"How's it going, Caroline?"

This time, I lean into the words the way I might lean into the bread dough, pressing down hard with the heel of my hand. I want a real answer, because it's the middle of the night and we can lie to each other in the daytime, on campus, in the library.

We do it already. Every time I pass her in the hallway and don't grab her and push her up against a wall, kiss her stupid—*every time* it's a lie.

I'm sick of it. I took this job expecting to be left alone, working when nobody was awake, not having to be polite or to say words I don't mean, to act like I'm somebody I'm not. I need the job to give me that because I don't get it otherwise, and it fucks it up when Krishna shows up and we have to pussyfoot around the fact that he drinks too much and hates himself. It fucks it up to have Caroline sitting outside in her car, not coming in. And now that she's in, it's fucking it up that she's telling me she's fine.

"It's going," she says.

"Yeah? Enjoying the fall weather? Classes treating you well?"

She pinches the bridge of her nose instead, high up, and closes her eyes. "You were right. Is that what you want me to say?"

"I want you to say whatever the truth is."

"Why?"

"Because I don't think you ever tell anybody the truth. You're awake at two in the morning. You look like shit.

You're exhausted. When I invite you in here, when I ask you how it's going, you think I'm going to fucking buy it that you're *fine*? You think that's what I want you to say?"

"That's what everybody says."

"Yeah. It is. And if you're going to get out of bed and come here and talk to me, the bare minimum you can do is assume I'm not everybody. When I ask you, I actually want to know how you are."

"What if I don't feel like telling you?"

"Then say that. *How's it going, Caroline? None of your fucking business, West.* See how that works? It's easy."

For a minute she's quiet, and I have a chance to appreciate what an asshole I am. I've got no right to be this way with her. I don't know why I always *want* to be—to push at her, peel her apart, find out what's underneath—but I do.

That's the thing about Caroline. I want to strip her naked, and *then I want to keep going.* I want to learn what makes her tick. Not even want—I *need* to.

I need something from her, and that's what I have to guard against. The most dangerous thing about her. Because if I need her, she'll hurt me, distract me, maybe even break me into pieces and grind them under her heel. I've seen it happen with my mom.

And it's not like I'm so dumb that I think love does that to everyone. Bo, Mom's boyfriend, he loves her, but he doesn't love her *that* way—like a typhoon, a fucking tsunami knocking his feet out from under him. I know there's love in the world that's take-it-or-leave-it, easygoing, slow and steady.

But that's not what I feel around Caroline.

She could knock me on my ass so hard.

It's not what I'm in Iowa for.

She exhales, a long whoosh of air. "Okay," she says. "Okay." And then, after another pause, "Ask me again."

"How's it going?"

"Terrible." She looks at the floor. "Every day," she whispers. "Every single day is the worst day of my life."

I flour the table in front of me, preparing to shape the loaves.

Bread practically makes itself, if you do it right. You just have to quit fighting it.

Caroline watches my hands. The way my fingers shape and pinch, set the bread on a tray to rise—I have a way of making not fighting it look like fighting it. I guess I've been digging my heels in so long, it's hard to remember there's another way to do things.

I don't think I was ever like Caroline, though. Never privileged like her, confident of my place in the world, thinking the future was some gilded egg I could pluck out of the nest and take home. I've always known the world isn't fine, that it's broken, that it fails you when you least expect it to.

When you know that, it's easier to take the blows. Automatic to fight back.

"I can't make it go away," she says softly. "Not by myself. Not without . . ."

"Not without what?"

Her nose wrinkles. "Telling my dad."

"What can he do that you can't?"

"Lots of things, potentially. But mainly there's this company you can hire to scrub your name online. Push the bad results down in the search engines. But it's expensive."

"Ah."

"Yeah."

"That sucks."

"It does."

"So what else is new?"

She blinks at me, obviously not expecting the change of subject. "Not much," she says.

"Huh." I push some dough in her direction. "You want to try this?"

"No, thanks."

"C'mon, I'll show you how."

"Thank you, but no. I think my talents lie elsewhere."

She sounds so much like the old Caroline that I almost smile. "No problem."

She starts to wander around the room again.

"Have you thought about anything at all besides naked pictures since they first popped up . . . when, early last month?"

"August twenty-fourth." She tilts her head, considering. "Yes."

"What else have you been thinking about?"

Caroline peers into the clean mixer. When she puts her finger inside the bowl and traces the curve of it—the curve I polished until it was shiny enough to attract her attention—I don't tell her to stop, even though I'll have to clean it again after she goes.

She can touch whatever she wants.

"My constitutional law class. Latin homework. My sister's wedding coming up. Whether my dad is eating okay now that I'm not at home to nag him. How to cover up the circles under my eyes. Rape. Evil. Whether law school admissions committees routinely Google applicants or just in special circumstances."

She glances at me. "If I should get the space between my teeth fixed. The usual."

"Sure you don't want to pile on a few more things? Global warming, maybe? Declining newspaper circulations?"

She almost smiles. "What do *you* think about?"

I guess I'm supposed to make a list, too, but fuck that.

I've got three years of undergrad before I can start med school, followed by four years to become a doctor, another four or five to become an anesthesiologist, and then years of hard work to build a practice. I've got three jobs, Frankie to think about, Mom to take care of.

Maybe what I can have of Caroline is this little slice of space and light in the darkest hours of the night. I can give her permission to not be fine. Let her talk about what's bugging her. Distract her from her problems.

If she wants to come here, I'll do all that, but I won't make her problems into mine, and I'm not going to bare my fucking soul to her.

"My ears, mostly," I say. "You really think they're too small?"

I touch them with my flour-covered hands, trying to look self-conscious. It works—she smiles.

That gap between her teeth kills me. I need to measure it with my tongue.

"Are you sure they're full-grown?" she asks. "Because my dentist told me that it might be a few years before my wisdom teeth finish coming in. Maybe it's the same with your ears."

"You're saying I might hit a growth spurt. Grow some manlier ears."

"It's possible."

"You know what they say, though. Small ears, big equipment."

"That is *so* not what they say."

"No? Maybe it's only in Oregon they say that."

She laughs, a husky sound. I don't like how it slips over me. I don't like how I can just about feel myself filing it away in the stroke book for later—Caroline laughing as I unhook her bra. Still smiling when I take off those shapeless sweat-pants and see what she's got on underneath. What she looks like naked.

You already know what she looks like naked.

Everybody does.

I shake off the whole train of thought. Doesn't matter, and it's not happening between her and me, anyway.

"Here's my point, though," I say. "There's all this other shit you could be worrying about, and you're wasting too much worry on something you can't fix."

"Like what? Worrying over the size of your ears isn't going to fill much of my time. I'll still have, like, twenty-three and a half hours a day to worry in."

"What are you saying, you only care about my ears half an hour's worth?"

"Maybe not even that. I have to be honest with you."

"Please. Be honest."

"Okay. The thing is, if I never have to see another guy's ears so long as I live? I'll be a happy girl."

"Now you're starting to sound bitter."

"Maybe I *am* bitter. Maybe I've just seen waaaay too many close-ups of ears lately."

"Red, swollen ears?"

She leans in, like she's telling me a big secret. "Veiny, hor-rible, giant, disgusting, *dripping* ears."

That cracks me up.

"What *is* it with you guys taking pictures of your ears?" She's all indignant now. "It's like you're so proud of them."

"If you could make stuff shoot out of your ears, you'd be proud, too."

She's biting her lip, looking away toward the mixer like it's going to rescue her from the fact that we just had a conversation about dicks, and she wants to laugh but she won't let herself. "I think we need a new topic."

"Something more polite?"

"Yes." Then she glances up at me from under her eyelashes, and, for one hot second, she's wicked. "Something a little less *lubricated*."

I have to look away from her. Take a breath.

I point at a lump of dough. "Wash your hands, and I'll let you knead that."

"Will you, now?"

"I will. I'm going to teach you to make the best sourdough loaf in Putnam County."

"Is anybody else in Putnam County making sourdough loaves?"

"Not that I'm aware of."

She makes a face at the bread, but she's pulling her sweatshirt over her head. "All right. I'm game."

The shirt she's got on underneath—it's got to be her pajama shirt. She's not wearing a bra.

I get four more loaves ready while she's washing her hands at the sink. It takes two before I've managed to push the surprise away.

I do another one with my eyes closed, willing the soft bounce of her breasts from my head.

When she comes back from the sink, her face is serious. "Listen. I'm . . . I'm just going to say this. I meant what I told you at the library."

"Which thing you told me?"

She's picking at her thumb with her fingernail. "I can't be your friend. Or—or anything else."

I get it.

Doesn't mean it doesn't hurt, a little, to hear it again, but I really do get it.

For all that I had my reasons for not talking to her last year, she's got her own reasons, too. There was Nate. There was her dad, who hated my guts even before I set about deliberately lighting his fuse. But underneath all that, there was this other thing.

Caroline's not the kind of girl who gets mixed up with a guy who's dealing. She's the type who plays it safe, does what she's supposed to, follows all the rules.

Maybe if I were who I'm pretending to be when I'm at Putnam, me and Caroline would be possible, but I'm not. We don't make sense together.

It's fine.

"Tell you what," I say. "Tonight I'm going to show you how to make a decent loaf and bake it. If you come back tomorrow, I'll teach you something else. We don't need to be friends. We can just do this . . . you know, this nighttime thing. If you want to."

"Can we?"

"When Bob's not here, it's my bakery. I can do whatever I want as long as I get the bread made."

"And you won't . . ."

When she looks right at me, my hands twitch.

You won't, West.

You fucking won't.

"We'll make bread and be not-friends. You don't have to come within ten feet of my ears. I don't want that from you, anyway."

What's one more lie on top of all the others?

She pokes experimentally at the dough in front of her. "All right. Show me how you do this thing, then."

I show her, and then I show her the rest of it. She stays until her loaf comes out of the oven. By then she's yawning.

I send her home to bed with warm bread tucked under her

arm. I make her text me when she's back at the dorm, safe behind a locked door.

The next night, she comes back.

She keeps coming back, and I keep letting her.

That's how I get to be not-friends with Caroline Piasecki.

When I think of the bakery, I think of all of it together.

The crunch of fall leaves piled up on the threshold of the back door where they'd blown down the alley and stuck.

The gleam of the mixing bowls and countertops underneath the banked fluorescents when West finished cleaning and locked up.

The smell of baking bread, the crumbling clay of live yeast between my fingers, West's voice behind my ear as he leaned over my shoulder and watched me drop it into the bowl, saying, "Just like that. Exactly."

The way he moved his arm in short, sure strokes when he sliced open the tops of the loaves right before he pushed the rack of trays into the oven.

Winter came late. October turned into November, and I spent a long, crisp autumn of flour-strewn countertops and rising dough, sticky fingers and loud music and West working with his ball cap turned backward, an apron tied around his waist, and that smart-ass grin on his face.

West is the bakery. I can't imagine the point of it without him in it, and I can't imagine him—the best version of him, the one he rarely lets people see—without that kitchen as the backdrop for his movements.

West bending down to measure out a scoop of grain.

West nudging the oven door closed with his shoulder, setting the timer.

West kneading with both hands, flour dusted all the way up to his elbows, moving to the easy rhythm of some cheesy club music Krish had picked out.

There, in the bakery, while the rest of the world was sleeping, time buckled and we found something outside it. We became us in that kitchen. Long before he kissed me, I passed a whole lifetime with West, bathed in yellow light, baptized in lukewarm tap water, consecrated at sunrise when we broke a loaf open and looked. Dug our hands into it. Tasted what we'd made.

It wasn't perfect, what we made. One night I forgot the salt. Another time, the water I put in was too hot, and I killed the yeast. There were nights when West forgot to tell me some vital thing and nights when he decided not to remind me, just to see if I'd remember.

He held himself back, and I wasn't always brave enough. I didn't trust myself.

We failed as often as we succeeded, West and me.

But I think about what would have happened if he hadn't come out to get me.

I think I might have stayed in my car forever. I might have made only right turns.

I might never have learned how to stop being afraid, and those men would have kept chasing me around, always.

I can't be anything but glad that's not the way things went. Instead, West came out, and I went in.

After that, I rarely wanted to be anywhere else.

"You're buzzing again."

I'm in my nook, a little area on the bakery floor between the sink and the long table against the wall where West lines up his mixing bowls. I like it here because I can only usually see a slice of him at a time.

I watch his boots, his pant legs from the knees down, his apron.

During this part of the night, when he's mixing, he's always moving. Rocking from one foot to the other if he's feeding and stirring the sourdough starter. Pacing from the sink to the mixer to the refrigerator to the storage room, back to the mixer, back to the sink, over to the counter to pick up a tool he's forgotten.

The way he moves is almost more than I can take. His lazy grace. His competence.

His arms come into view as he lifts one bowl off the stand and puts the next one on. He bends over, and I see his hat and his neck, his face in profile, his jeans tight over his bent leg, the shape of his calf.

I can handle him in pieces. They're all nice pieces, but they don't make me break out in a nervous sweat, like I did last night when it was time to head home and he walked me to the back door, propped his hand up on the jamb, and said something that made him smile down at me and lean in. I don't know what it was. I couldn't hear him, because the way he had his arm braced made his shirtsleeve ride up to reveal his whole biceps, a defined curve of taut muscle engaged against the doorframe. I fell into a biceps wormhole, and then I made the grave error of looking at his mouth, the shape of his lips and his cheekbones, his chin and his eyes. I forgot to listen to him.

I forgot to breathe or exist outside of West's face.

Yeah. That's a thing that can happen, apparently, and when it happens, it's really bad. He had to snap his fingers in front of my nose to wake me up. It made me startle, and I stepped backward and nearly fell down. West just smiled kind of indulgently.

"Text me when you get home," he said, and I said something that sounded like *gnugh*.

I guess he's used to me being hopeless around him. We both just pretend I'm not. It sort of works.

West and I are like that. We sort of work.

I've been coming to the bakery two or three nights a week—almost every shift he's on, I'm here. Insomnia has made her bitch, but it doesn't matter so much when I can hang out with West and study in my little nook. I nap after class. I'm turning into a creature of the night. It's all right, though. I guess I'd rather be Bella Swan hanging out at the Cullen place than, you know, school Bella—all pissy and defensive, clomping around Forks High, convinced everyone hates her.

The men in my head are quiet when I'm at the bakery. I think if they called me names, West would glower at them and tell them to shut the fuck up. If they were real, I mean. Which they're not.

West's phone is still buzzing, vibrating itself partway off the edge of the tabletop. I poke out a finger and push it back to safety. "Dough boy," I say, loud, because it's hard to hear with the mixer going. "Your phone."

"What?"

"Your phone."

I point, and he finally understands. He walks over and picks it up off the metal countertop right beside me.

I made the mistake of grabbing it once, thinking I would hand it to him. The look on his face—he has this way of shutting down his whole expression so it looks like there's no feeling in him at all.

He's hilariously funny when he wants to be, wickedly smart, open and teasing—and then suddenly I step over some invisible line and he's a robot. Or too intense, complaining about how something is bullshit, like he did that first night I came here.

He takes his phone into the front of the store, where I won't be able to hear him talking.

I go back to my Latin, though it's hard to concentrate, knowing, as I do, that in ten or fifteen minutes someone will show up at the alley door. West will meet him there, positioning his body so I can't see who he's talking to, mumbling in this low voice that makes him sound like just another dude, a slacker. His shoulders will slouch. His hands will dip in and out of his pockets, propelled along by his soothing, nonthreatening voice.

I try not to see. It's better if I stick to the slices. That's the only way we can be friends—or not-friends, I guess.

And I need to be not-friends with West. He's the only person in my whole life who doesn't treat me like nothing happened but who also doesn't treat me like *everything* happened. He says, "How's it going?" when I walk in the door, and I tell him the truth, but afterward that's that. We're done talking about it.

Tucked in my nook at the bakery, for a few hours two or three nights a week, I feel like myself.

When he comes back, he hops up on the nearest table opposite me and says, "What's that, Latin?"

"Yeah. I've got a quiz tomorrow."

"Need help with your verbs?"

"No, I'm good."

"Are you staying long enough for me to teach you all the finer points of muffin glazing?"

"Probably not. I've got to write a response paper for Con Law, and I didn't bring my laptop."

"You should've. I like it when you write here."

I do, too. He's quiet when I need him to be quiet, and when I want a break he'll teach me some bread thing. If I read him my draft out loud, he'll suggest some change that sounds small but always ends up making the paper more concise, the argument stronger.

West is smart. Crazy smart. I had no idea—the one time I had a class with him, he didn't talk.

It's possible he's actually smarter than I am.

"Next week, then," he says. "Tuesday you will learn the secrets of the glaze."

I smile. I think he likes teaching me stuff nearly as much as he liked learning it in the first place. He's almost insatiably curious. No matter what homework I'm doing, he'll end up asking me fifty questions about it.

"Sounds good. Are you on at the restaurant this week-end?"

"Yeah. What about you, you got plans?"

I want to hang out with you. Come over Sunday, and we'll watch bad TV.

Let's go to the bar.

Let's go out to dinner in Iowa City.

Sometimes I invent a life in which my being more than not-friends with West is a possibility. A life where we get to hang out somewhere other than a kitchen at midnight.

Then I mentally pinch myself, because, no, I want *less* scandal, not more.

"Bridget is trying to get me to go to that party tomorrow night."

"Where's that?"

"A bunch of the soccer players."

"Oh, at Bourbon House?"

"Yeah, are you going?"

"I'll be at work."

"After you get off?"

He smiles. "Nah. You should go, though."

When Bridget suggested it, the idea filled me with panic. A crush of bodies, all those faces I would have to study for signs of judgment, pity, disgust. I can't have fun when I'm so busy monitoring my behavior, choosing the right clothes, plastering a just-so smile on my face and watching, watching, while the men in my head tell me I look like a whore and I should pick somebody already. Take him upstairs and let him suck my tits, because that's all a slut like me is good for.

Bridget thinks I need to get out more, pick my life back up where I left it. Otherwise, Nate wins.

I see her point. But I can't make myself want to.

I look at the corrugated soles of West's boots, swinging a few feet from my face. At the way his knuckles look, folded around the edge of the table. The seam at his elbows.

If West were going to the party, I would want to.

"I might."

"Do you some good," he says. "Get shit-faced, dance a little. Maybe you'd even meet somebody worth keeping you busy nights so you're not hanging around here harassing me all the time."

He grins when he says it. *Just kidding, Caro,* that grin

says. *We both know you're too fucked in the head to be hooking up with anybody.*

Before I've even caught my breath, he's hopped down and moved toward the sink, where he fills a bucket with soapy water so he can wipe down his countertops.

I look at my Latin book, which really is verbs, and I blink away the sting in my eyes.

Video, videre, vidi, visus. To see.

Cognosco, cognoscere, cognovi, cognotus. To understand.

Maneo, manere, mansi, mansurus. To remain.

I see what he's doing. Every now and then, West throws some half-teasing comment out to remind me I'm not his girlfriend. He smiles as he tells me something that means, *You're not important to me. We're not friends.*

He pulls me closer with one hand and smashes an imaginary fist into my face with the other.

I know why he does it. He doesn't want me to get close.

I don't know why.

But I see. I understand.

I remain.

We're a mess, West and me.

He cleans the tables off, his movements abrupt and jerky. Agitated. When he switches to dishes, he's slamming the pans around instead of stacking them. He's so caught up with the noise he's making that when a figure appears at the back door, West doesn't notice.

I do, though. I look up and see Josh there. He used to be my friend, before. Now I see him around with Nate. I think he's going out with Sierra. He's standing with his wallet in his hand, looking awkward.

"Hey, Caroline," he says.

"Hey."

West turns toward me, follows my eyes to the doorway. He

frowns deeply and stalks toward the door. Josh lifts the wallet, and West kind of shoves it down and aside as he moves out into the alley, forcing Josh to step back. "Put your fucking money away," I hear him say as the door swings closed. "Jesus Christ."

Then the kitchen is empty—just me and the white noise of the mixer, the water running in the sink.

When he comes back in, he's alone, his hand pushing something down deep in his pocket. "You didn't see that," he says.

Which is dumb.

I guess he thinks he's protecting me. If I can't see him dealing, I'm not an accessory. I'm the oblivious girl in the corner, unable to put two and two together and get four.

"Yes, I did."

He levels this look at me. *Don't push it.*

I haven't seen that look since the library. It makes me dump my book on the floor and stand up, and when I'm standing I can feel it more—how my chest is still aching from the hurt of what he said a few minutes ago. How my heart pounds, because he hurt me on purpose, and I'm angry about it.

I'm *angry*.

He turns his back on me and starts to wash a bowl.

"What kind of profit do you make, anyway?" I ask. "On a sale like that, is it even worth it? Because I looked it up—it's a felony to sell. You'd do jail time if you got arrested. There's a mandatory minimum five-year sentence."

He keeps cleaning the bowl, but his shoulders are tight. The tension in the room is thick as smoke, and I don't know why I'm baiting him when I'm close to choking on it.

He's right to try to protect me. My dad would have kittens if he found out I was here, with West dealing out the back door, selling weed with the muffins. He would ask me if I'd lost my mind, and what would I say to him? *It's only weed? I don't think West even smokes it?*

Excuses. My dad hates excuses.

The truth is that I don't make any excuses for it. I turn myself into an accessory every time I come here and sit on the floor by West, and I don't care. I really don't. I used to. Last year I was scandalized by the pot.

Now I'm too busy being fascinated by West.

And then there's the money. I think about the money. I wonder how much he has. I know his tuition is paid, because he told me, and that he caddies at a golf course in the summer, because I asked why he had such stark tan lines.

I imagine he's paying his own rent, paying for his food, but as far as I can tell he doesn't have any hobbies or vices. I can't figure out why he works so many jobs and deals pot, too, if he doesn't need all that money just to get by. And he must not, right? He must have more than he needs if he's buying weed in large quantities and making loans.

"Drop it," West says.

I can't drop it. Not tonight. Not when the pain in my chest has turned to this burning, angry insistence. I'm too pissed at him, and at myself. "I'll have to ask Josh," I muse. "Or Krish. I bet he would tell me. I bet when people show up at your apartment, you don't turn your back on Krish and make him sit alone while you deal outside on the fire escape."

I've never been to his apartment. I only know about the fire escape because I drove by.

I'm possibly a little bit stalking him.

West drops the bowl in the sink and rounds on me. "What are you in a snit about? You want me to deal in front of you?"

Do I?

For a moment I'm not sure. I look down at the floor, at the spill of flour by the row of mixing bowls.

I remember the first night I came in here and the first thing that's happened every night since.

How's it going, Caroline?

"It's bullshit," I say.

His eyes narrow.

"It's bullshit for you to pretend not to be dealing drugs out the back door, like you're going to protect me from knowing the truth about you. It's not fair that I'm supposed to come in here and bare my soul to you, and you don't even want me to touch your stupid cell phone."

West crosses his arms. His jaw has gone hard.

"You're a drug dealer." It's the first time I've ever said it out loud. The first time I've ever even mentally put it in those words. "So what? You have some dried-up plants in a plastic bag in your pocket, and you give them to people for money. Whoop-de-do."

He stares at me. Not for just a moment, which would be normal.

He stares at me for *ages*.

For the entire span of my life, he looks right in my eyes, and I suck in shallow breaths through my mouth, my chest full of pressure, my ears ringing as the mixer grinds and grinds and grinds around.

Then the corner of his mouth tips up a fraction. "Whoop-de-do?"

"Shut up." I'm not in the mood to be teased.

"You could've at least thrown a *fuck* in there. Whoop-de-*fucking*-do."

"I don't need your advice on how to swear."

"You sure? I'm a fuck of a lot better at it than you."

I turn away and pick up my bag and my Latin book off the floor. I don't want to be here anymore. I don't want to be around him if he's going to hurt me, bullshit me, and tease me. That's not what I come here for, and I hate how the pressure from the way he stared at me has built up in my face, prickling behind the bridge of my nose, sticking in my throat.

"Caro," he says.

"Leave me alone."

"Caro, I made forty bucks. Okay? That's what you want me to say?"

I stop packing my bag and just stand there, looking at it.

He made forty bucks.

"How much did you charge?"

"Sixty-five."

"For how much?"

"An eighth of an ounce."

I turn around. "Is that a lot?"

"A lot of money, or a lot of weed?"

"Um, either."

He smiles for real now and shakes his head. "It's a little more than anybody else is charging, but the weed is better. It's the smallest amount I'll bother to sell. Why are we talking about this?"

And that's when I lose my nerve. I shrug. I look past his left ear.

I don't want to ask him.

Before this year, I never gave money a lot of thought. My dad is pretty well off. I grew up in a nice house in a safe neighborhood in Ankeny, outside Des Moines, and even though Putnam isn't cheap, I didn't have to worry about tuition. I always knew my dad would pay it, whatever it was.

But that was before the pictures, and it was before I figured out that, no matter what I do, I can't make them go away. Not by myself.

I need fifteen hundred dollars—maybe more—to hire the company that will push my name down in the search rankings and scrub my reputation online. The guy I talked to when I called said that cases like mine can be more involved, which means a higher fee.

I don't have a job. I had one in high school, but Dad says I'm better off concentrating on my schoolwork now. I have a hundred thousand dollars in a savings account—my share of the life-insurance settlement when my mom died from cancer when I was a baby—but until I'm twenty-one, I can't touch it.

With no income and no credit history, I can't get fifteen hundred dollars on a credit card without my dad cosigning on the application. I tried.

"Caroline?" West asks.

"What?"

He steps closer. "What's this really about?"

And I blurt out the stupidest thing. "You don't have to protect me."

Because I'm sick of it. Of being protected. Of *needing* to be.

"I'm not."

His eyes, though. When I meet his eyes, they're blazing with the truth.

He is. He *wants* to.

"You know what the worst thing is?" I ask. "It's knowing I was *always* stupid and sheltered and just . . . just *useless*. Everyone telling me I'm smart, like that's so great and important. Going to a good college—*oh, Caroline, how fantastic*. But one bad thing happens to me, and I can't even . . ."

I trail off, because I think I'm going to cry, and I'm too angry to give in to it.

West takes another step closer, and then he's rubbing my arm. The flat of his palm lands against the back of my neck, over my hair, and he's tipping me forward until my forehead rests against his chest.

"You're not useless."

"No, seriously, I can't—I need you to hear this, okay? Because the thing is—"

"Caroline, shut up."

The way he says it, though—it's definitely the nicest anyone's ever shut me up. And his rubbing hand comes around my back and presses me into him, and that's nice, too. I can feel him breathing. I can smell his skin, feel my hair catching on the stubble underneath his chin.

It's better here. I like it.

I like it too much. So much that I spend the longest possible span of time I can get away with savoring the heat of him, the weight of his hand on the back of my neck, the way his boot looks stuck between my flats. But then I have to ask. I have to.

"West?"

He makes a noise like *hunh*.

"Do you have a lot of money?"

I lift my forehead to ask him, which puts me in startlingly close range of his face. I'm close enough to see the frown begin at the downturned tips of his eyebrows and spread across his forehead.

Close enough to see his eyes go baffled. Then angry. Then blank.

His hand drops away from my neck. "Why are you asking me that?"

It's too late not to say, but the butterflies in my stomach have turned to lead ingots, and I know this is all wrong. I know it is. But I don't know why or how to get out of it. "I, uh . . . I need a loan."

He steps back. "What for?"

"Remember when I told you about that company that can clean up my reputation online?"

"You said it was expensive, so you'd have to tell your dad."

"Yeah."

I wait a beat.

"You didn't tell your dad."

"I can't, West. I thought about it, but I . . . What if he sees?"

It could happen any time. My dad could be sitting at his desk and type my name into a search engine, just because. Or somebody he works with could point him in that direction. A friend. One of my sisters. *Anybody*.

I close my eyes, because the humiliation of it, the shame of asking West to help me fix this thing—I can't.

I can't look at him at all.

"How much do you need?"

"Fifteen hundred dollars. I heard you . . . I heard sometimes you do that."

He sighs. "You have any income?"

"I get an allowance."

I open my eyes, but I can't lift them above my shoes. My black flats are dusted with flour. It's worked its way down into the buckle, and I doubt I would be able to clean it out, even if I wanted to.

"How long would it take you to pay me back?"

"I could pay you a hundred fifty a month." *If I never buy anything or eat outside the dining hall.*

West kicks my toe with his boot. Waits for me to look up. His eyes are still dead.

"I'm charging you interest."

"I would expect you to."

"I'll have it on Tuesday."

And then there's nothing left to say. He's gone, empty, and I'm too full—like there aren't any edges to me. It's just pain and disappointment, all the way through.

"Thanks," I say. "I'm . . . I'm going to head out. I have to write that paper."

He just grunts at me and weighs out dough. A thousand miles away.

I don't see West on Friday, because he's working at the restaurant, and we're not friends.

I don't go to the soccer party. Bridget just about breaks something trying to sell me on the idea, but I can't. I tell her I have to study, and then I hide in the library and replay my conversation with West over and over again. I should never have asked him for the money. I don't know who I should have asked, but not him. The look on his face . . . I can't stop thinking about it.

I don't see West on Saturday, because he's working at the restaurant, and we're not friends.

The next week is more of the same thing. On Tuesday he gives me the money, and he teaches me how to make lemon glaze for the muffins. Everything's like normal, but there's this thin coating of awkwardness ladled over our conversations, and when I'm not around him, it hardens and turns opaque.

I convert West's cash into a money order and send it off to the Internet-reputation people, but I wish I hadn't. I wish I'd never opened my mouth.

The next weekend I eat dinner with Bridget, and we walk

to the Dairy Queen in town afterward, leaves crunching under our feet. I eat a hot-fudge brownie sundae so big that I have to lie down on the red lacquered bench afterward and unbutton the top of my jeans. Upside down, I look out the front window and down the street. I can just make out the chalkboard easel outside the Gilded Pear.

Nate took me to dinner there last year before the spring formal. West was our waiter. Every time he came to the table, it was more awkward than the last. By the time he brought the check, his conversation with Nate was so thickly laced with irony that I felt like they were performing a scene in a play.

The kind of play with sword fighting.

I didn't break up with Nate because of West. Honestly.

But I probably broke up with Nate because of the possibility of someone *like* West.

"Did you finish your paper last night?" Bridget asks, and because I'm distracted by the memory of West in his waiter uniform—black slacks and a white dress shirt—I say, "Mmm-hmm."

"And your reading for Con Law?"

"Yeah."

He had his sleeves rolled up. His deep tan against crisp white cotton.

"So you have no excuse not to go to the Alliance party with me."

"What? No."

I sit up. Bridget is smiling her worst, most evil smile. "Yes."

"I really don't want to."

"You really have no choice. You don't need to study, it's time for you to get back out there, *and* this is the easiest, best party, because at least half the people there will be gay. Possibly two-thirds, if you count the bis and the people who are 'experimenting.'" She does the air quotes with her fingers. "Plus, we had so much fun last year. *Please.*"

Two hours later, I've got a beer in one hand and Bridget tugging at the elbow of my other arm, pulling me toward the dance floor.

The Queer Alliance party is in the Minnehan Center, which is the campus building designated for large-scale fun. It's got the movie theater and this room, which is a huge, high-ceilinged hall with a stage, a disco ball, and a little cubby on one wall where the party's hosts push an endless parade of Solo cups across the counter to the crowd of students.

You can't get in to parties at the Minnehan Center without a student ID, but once you're in, there's no such thing as underage. The student worker who hands out wristbands performs a cursory ID check that miraculously results in everyone at the party being legal.

The beer is always free. The music is always loud.

The Alliance party has a sound track that brings out the inner ABBA in everybody—and also a lot of exhibitionist streaks. As far as I can tell, I'm the only person in the room in jeans and a T-shirt. Bridget's got on a gold sequined tube top and tight black pants that flare out over platform shoes. She's a disco queen.

She picks a spot at the edge of the dance floor just as "It's Raining Men" comes on. Arms raised, jumping up and down, she hoots along with a hundred other people. "Dance with me!" she shouts.

I shake my head.

Then I drink the beer, downing it quickly so I can get away from her disappointment and grab another.

By the time we've cycled through half the sound track to

Priscilla, Queen of the Desert and all the good Gaga, the dance floor is roiling, and I'm relaxed enough to join in, bumping hips and slapping hands with Bridget. I smile to see Krishna come up behind her. He grinds on her, and she rolls her eyes, but she likes it. He pulls us into the group he's dancing with—some people I don't know, although I'm pretty sure one of the girls is named Quinn.

I recognize her because she hung out in Krishna and West's room last year. She's blond and big—a good four or five inches taller than me, with broad hips and a generous chest and a smile that seems to include a lot more teeth than it ought to. She keeps grabbing my hand to spin me, and I get sweaty and a little dizzy. Krishna fetches us another round of beers, and we drink them quick, licking the foam off our lips. He pulls out his phone. The screen lights up his face in the dark room, making him look mischievous and almost enchanted. He glances at me, grins, and types something.

"What are you doing?"

"Texting West." He lifts the phone, and before I can stop him, he takes my picture.

I grab his arm, blinded by the flash and by my panic. "Don't send that." The sudden brightness sent me reeling back to my memory of that night with Nate. The surprise of the flash. His hand on my head, dick in my mouth, choking me so I had to concentrate to keep from gagging. "Krish, *don't.*"

But he's not listening. He's grinning, jabbing at the screen, and I'm trying to wrest the phone out of his hand when I hear a little whoosh that means it's sent.

"Damn it!" I punch him in the shoulder, frustrated and upset, frustrated with myself for *being* upset. It's just a picture. It doesn't matter.

Except that I'm crying.

"What'd I do?"

Quinn reaches out for me, but I'm already gone. I rush toward the door, pushing through bodies, the music and the lights pounding too loud. I had more to drink than I should have. I let my guard down, feeling safe, feeling *okay*, but there's nothing okay about me.

Frozen on the screen of Krishna's phone with my hair falling all around my face, my T-shirt scooped too low, askew, sweat shining on all that exposed skin—I look like a mistake waiting to happen.

Then I see Nate, and I remember I'm a mistake that's already happened.

He's between me and the door. By the time I realize it, he's looking at me, and there's nowhere to escape to. I can't dance now. I have to get out. So I keep going, chin up, hoping my mascara isn't streaky and pretending the men in my head aren't shouting at full volume.

Let's see that dirty pussy, baby. I want to eat it out. I'm going to nail the living fuck out of you.

"Caroline!" Nate props his hand in the doorway so I can't get past. He smiles his drunk smile. "Didn't think I'd see you here."

I think of West, leaning in the doorway at the bakery as he walked me out. Telling me to text him when I was home safe.

I look at Nate, blocking my exit. His eyes crawling down my shirt.

Was he always this way?

He's got a beer in his other hand, and his sandy-brown hair is a little long, curling around his ears. He wears a polo that brings out the blue of his eyes over these horrible navy pants with tiny green whales on them that he loves to put on for parties. He insists he wears them ironically, but I always used to tell him it's not possible to wear pants with irony. You put on whale pants, you're wearing whale pants.

Douche, West says in my head.

"Why shouldn't I be here?"

"You haven't been around much."

"I've been busy." I try to look like West when he's gone blank. Like I could give a fuck about Nate.

"Josh said he saw you with that sketchy guy from across the hall last year. The dealer."

"So?"

"So I'm worried about you, Caroline. First those pictures, and now you're hanging out with *him.* . . . What's going on with you?"

I'm speechless. I mean, literally, I can't make words. There are so many, they jam up at the back of my tongue, and I don't know which ones I'd say even if I could shake them loose.

The nerve of him. The *nerve.*

He hitches his arm up higher and takes a sip of his beer, as though we're going to be here awhile, shooting the breeze. "We're still friends," he says. "We'll always be friends, you know that. I just don't want to see you getting hurt."

That's the thing that unlocks my throat. *We're still friends.*

He betrayed me. He *broke my life,* then pretended I was the one who did it. He lied, because he's a douchebag, and douchebags lie. And now he's standing here, *blocking my exit,* telling me we're still friends.

"You know what, Nate? Fuck you."

I duck underneath his arm, half expecting him to hip-check me and pin me in place. Half certain that he really hates me enough, wants to hurt me enough, that he'd do that.

He doesn't, though. I get past him, run down the hall to the bathroom, lock myself in a stall, and climb up on the lid of one of the toilets, feet on the seat so I can drop my head down between my knees.

I keep it there until I can breathe.

I keep it there until I figure out that the low humming sound I hear isn't inside my head. It's my phone. In my pocket.

When I pull it out, there's a message from West. Are you ok?

I'm not okay. Not at all. But seeing West's name on my phone—seeing that he's asking, when he's never texted me before except to type out one- or two-word replies to my home-safe messages—it helps.

I'm fine, I type.

Well, actually I type, im gun3. But somehow the miracle of autocorrect sorts it out.

Where are you?

Minnehan party.

I know. K sent me your pic. Where at M'han?

Bathroom.

There's a pause. Then, K's a fucking idiot.

I overreacted.

It's ok. Everybody has an off night.

Why is it that when other people tell you things you already know, it's soothing?

Why is it that when West tells me I'm okay, I believe him? Not that he can make me okay, but just to have that touch-stone.

I want to tell him about Nate, but I want to forget it happened even more.

Are you still at work?

No. Just got off. A pause. That sounded dirty.

I smile at the phone.

You should go back in there. K said you're helping him pull chicks. Another pause. But they're all dykes.

Homophobe!

Not me. Quinn will tell you—all those girls call themselves that.

They call themselves women, I type, but that's not what I meant to say.

Womyn, I try a second time, but it autocorrects to Women.

I give it a third shot. W-o-m-y-n. Fucking autocrochet.

There's a pause, and then West writes, Autocrochet? I'm dying.

I blink at the screen. Oh. Yeah, it seems I typed that. Glad I can amuse you.

I take a deep breath. It takes my fingers three tries to make the words Come dance?

A longer pause.

Need to sleep.

I'm sure it's true. He only sleeps about four hours a night during the week. He told me he uses the weekends to catch up.

OK. Sleep tight.

Another pause, and I'm starting to think we're done, that I should leave the bathroom, go home, and go to bed, when another bubble pops up. Caroline?

Yeah?

Tuesday is cookie day.

Tuesday, back at the bakery. I don't want to wait that long to see him, but that's the way it is. Right. See you then.

By the way.

Nothing for several seconds.

You look fucking hot.

No tooth gap in sight.

Those words—what they do to me. My heart is so light, I

think it might be made of air. It might float up and escape through the gap between my front teeth.

I take a screenshot and put the phone away.

Still smiling, I climb down and wash my hands, listening to the thumping bass beat from down the hall. My toes move back and forth on the floor, one foot's tiny acknowledgment of the rhythm.

My eyes are like that, too. Sparkling with their own tiny acknowledgment.

It's the second time he's told me that.

When I come out of the bathroom, Bridget is making her way toward me with Quinn.

Or, more specifically, Bridget is weaving down the hall, and Quinn is watching her like a hawk, moving in to steady her every time it looks like Bridget might hit the deck.

The sad thing is, Bridget only had two beers. She has no alcohol tolerance whatsoever.

"Caroline!" she shouts.

"Bridget!" I shout back.

"I saw Nate."

"So did I."

"And I kicked Krish in the nuts for taking your picture. I mean, not really, but metaphorically I did."

"She chewed him out like you wouldn't believe," Quinn says.

"Did Nate make you cry?"

"No. I'm okay."

"Do you want to go home? Or we could get you some more ice cream."

I consider it. But I recognize the song that's on, and I don't want to go back to the room and hide. "No, I want to dance."

"Really?" Bridget peers at me, blinking blearily.

"Kind of. I mean, mostly I want to kick Nate in the nuts. Or smash his perfect nose in."

"Your boy already did that," Bridget says. I widen my eyes at her in the universal signal for *oh my God, shut up, you idiot*. I am hoping against all hope that Quinn didn't hear or won't understand.

"Your boy?" Quinn asks.

She's got one eyebrow up. That eyebrow knows *everything*.

"Bridget is a little drunk," I say apologetically. "And we have this kind of running joke about West—"

"Which is . . . ?"

I try to think of a diplomatic way of putting it, but Bridget beats me to the punch with: "That she wants to climb into his pants."

Yes. Those words actually come out of her mouth.

"I am going to *kill* you," I whisper.

I can't look at Quinn. I might possibly never look at Quinn again.

She clears her throat. Taps her foot.

God. I have no choice. I look.

She's *still* got that eyebrow up. There is no tiring her eyebrow. It is an endurance athlete.

"*Do* you?"

I don't know how to answer the question. I mean, yes. Yes, of course I want to climb into his pants.

And no. No, no, no, I don't want her to know it, or for West to, or for anyone alive to, basically, up to and including Bridget.

I say something that comes out a lot like *Hnnn?*

She grins. "I'll be sure to tell him that."

"I will hurt you if you do."

"Man, you are all over the threats. First that guy Nate— oh, shit, is he the one who published your naked pictures?"

She says it straight out, without any sense of shame or the least hint that it's a thing we're not supposed to talk about.

It shocks me so much, I just say, "Yeah."

"No wonder you're so full of rage. You know what you should do? You should play rugby. Are you fast?"

"Um, no?"

Bridget says, "She is *so* fast."

Quinn is smiling. "You can tackle people to the ground. It's awesome."

"That *sounds* awesome." Bridget again.

"We practice on Sundays at eleven. You want to come, too? We could use a new hooker."

"Thanks, but I have to save my athletic awesomeness for track."

"Oh, right. I'll settle for the blow-job queen here, then." Quinn says this completely without malice. She rubs her hands together. "Now, are we dancing or are we going to stand out here jerking off for the rest of the night? Because you know if we don't get back in there inside of two minutes, Krishna's going to have his tongue down some poor girl's throat."

Bridget wrinkles her nose. "He *is*. And I want him to dance with. He's so pretty. Like a Christmas decoration."

"He would make the world's most beautiful gay boy," Quinn agrees. "Let's go reclaim him."

I'm not really done with the rugby conversation, but Quinn sticks out her elbows, so we link arms and kind of half-run, half-skip down the hallway like drunken Musketeers. We wave our wristbands at the security guy, who is so, so bored with his job and utterly unfazed by us.

By the time we get back on the dance floor, I've got another beer in my hand, and I'm laughing, thinking of Quinn and Bridget and Krishna.

Thinking of my phone in my back pocket and that screen-shot I took.

I don't have one thought to spare for Nate.

"I brought you a present."

West looks up from the floor scale, where he's dumping big scoops of flour into the largest mixing bowl. "Yeah?"

I shake the white plastic bag I'm holding. "Corn nuts, Mounds bar, two Monsters."

"You know the way to my heart."

"I know the way to keep you from turning into a little bitch on Wednesday nights."

West smiles and takes the bag. He cracks an energy drink right away, closing his eyes as he takes a swig from the can.

He looks tired. Wednesdays are his worst, because he's got lab in the afternoon. Most days he naps after class, but on Wednesdays he has to get through all his classes on four hours of sleep, then go to lab, work his library shift, and head straight to the bakery again.

"What are you mixing, the French?"

"Yeah. You want to start the dill?"

"Sure."

I check the clipboard hanging by the sink to see how many loaves Bob needs. West comes right up behind me, flattens one hand against the cabinet where the clipboard is hanging, and rests his cold drink against my neck.

"Aaagh! Don't!"

He exhales a laugh and moves it away, but he doesn't stop caging me in.

If I shifted over a few inches. If I pressed into him. His whole body, solid against mine.

"You have a good day?" he murmurs.

Gah. What is he doing to me? I don't even think West needs to check the clipboard. It's all in his head already.

He's wearing this red plaid flannel shirt, unbuttoned. The sleeves are turned up, cuffs loose, and they flap when he uses his hands. I think about running my palm up his forearm. Feeling the soft fuzz of hair, the satiny skin underneath.

I think about turning around to face him.

But I just breathe in. Breathe out. Keep my voice normal when I answer, "Yeah, not bad. I ran into Quinn at lunch, and me and Bridget ended up sitting with her and Krish."

"Second time this week you had company at lunch."

I get up the nerve to turn around and smile as though I don't want anything from him, expect anything from him, *need* anything from him. "I know. I'm practically a social butterfly, right?"

West is sort of almost smiling. I feel like I'm an experiment he's running. *What will she do if I do this?* "You get any sleep before you came here?"

"A few hours. And I took a loooooong nap after class, too. See, look." I turn my cheek to show him the imprint from the throw pillow. "I was trying to read for English, but I fell asleep on the couch and permanently branded corduroy into my face."

He steps even closer to see the faint lines that remain all these hours later. He lays his fingers lightly along my jaw, using them to tip my face up toward him.

This is how he'd kiss me. Just like this, with a drink in one hand and a casual half smile, competent fingers putting my lips where he wanted them.

I inhale. *Don't get too excited, Caroline. He's just looking because you told him to.*

"Nice," he says. "I'm jealous."

"Of my nap?"

"Of your pillow."

I stand there with heat crawling up my cheeks, breathing through my open mouth, trying to convince myself he didn't mean it.

Yeast, idiot. Dill and onion flakes and poppy seeds. Focus on the work.

I can't, though, because it's impossible to look away from his eyes. They're gray-blue today, storm clouds and tiny sparkling flashes of lightning.

What do you want from me? Take it. Whatever it is. Please.

He swigs the rest of his Monster drink, and I watch the column of his throat. He's all stubbly, like he always is on Wednesday nights. No time to shave. With his head tipped back, his eyes closed, I notice how blue and bruised the skin beneath them looks. I notice how the brim of his black ball cap presses into the back of his neck, how his dark hair's longer than it was last month, curling behind his ears and up into the fabric of his hat. He looks weary and . . . I don't know. Precious. I wish I could give him something other than snack food I picked up at the Kum and Go on my way here.

I wish I could give him rest. Ease.

I wish he'd stop torturing me like this, where I'm so tuned in to him I feel like I might explode, and he's so mellow I can't even tell if he's doing it on purpose.

His forearm tenses when he takes the drink away from his mouth, then contracts when he crushes the can. My attention catches on what looks like a black leather cuff on his wrist.

"What's that?"

He looks where I'm looking. "Bracelet."

"I know, doofus. Is it new?"

"Yeah."

Abruptly, he turns, tosses the can across the room into the recycling bin, and goes back to measuring out ingredients.

I don't even think. I just walk to where he is and grab his hand while he's got the honey container tipped upside down over the bowl. "Careful!"

I don't think he's warning me about the honey.

"I want to see."

It's the kind of bracelet you can buy at a booth at the county fair—a stiff strip of leather, with an embossed pattern of a few red and blue roses, and his name pressed into it and painted white. The black dye has turned his wrist slightly blue.

"Fancy."

He tugs against my grip, and I look up into his eyes. I want him to tell me where he got it, because someone must have given it to him. It's new. He's wearing it to work, even though it's kind of cheap and tacky, so it must *mean* something to him. But I can't just come right out and say all that, and I feel like I shouldn't have to.

"My sister sent it." He pulls his wrist away.

Even though there isn't really room between us, he squats down, forcing me to take a step back so he's got enough space to pull the bowl off the scale and carry it over to the mixer. I can't even lift those bowls when they're full, but West makes it look easy. He turns the mixer on. The dough hook starts its banging, rattling song.

He has a sister.

"How old is she?"

"She's nine. Ten in the spring."

"What's her name?"

"Frankie."

"Frankie like Frank?"

"Frankie like Francine."

"Oh."

When he looks up from the machine, his eyes are full of warning. "You got any other questions?"

I shouldn't. I know better. The more I ask him right now, the faster he'll shut down.

"Why didn't you ever say?"

"You didn't ask."

"If I'd asked, would you have told me?"

West shrugs, but he's scowling. "Sure. Why not?"

"I don't believe you."

He shakes his head, but he doesn't say anything more. I watch as he goes over to the shelf, flips the top bread recipe to the bottom of the pile, and starts working on whatever is next on his list. His lips move in a whisper, words he's making only for himself. He could be repeating the ingredients on the list, except it's just like the clipboard—I know for a fact he already has those recipes memorized.

I go back to the dill bread, furious and hot, my heart aching.

He has a sister called Frankie. He's wearing her love for him on his wrist, and I'm glad for him. I'm glad there's someone else in the world who cares about him enough to press the letters of his name into leather, word into flesh, an act of memory.

I do it sometimes, in the dark. Lie in my bed, staring at the crosshatched pattern of springs supporting Bridget's mattress above my head and drawing the letters of West's name on my body.

W-E-S-T across my stomach, around the side. I use my fingernail, only my fingernail, and bring up goose bumps.

W-E-S-T along my sternum. Over my collarbone and down the swell of my breast, tripping and catching on my nipple.

His name feels like a secret, and now he's wearing it on his wrist. I want to know all about this girl who put it there. What she looks like. If she's got freckles, fair hair or dark, like his. If she's scrappy or ethereal, funny or serious, scrape-kneed or ladylike.

I know that she loves him, so I want to know everything else.

But West doesn't want to share her with me.

I shouldn't keep trying to scale these walls he puts up. I'm a terrible climber.

I don't like arguing, and he doesn't owe me a thing.

"Get down on your hands and knees," Quinn says, pointing. "And put your arm over Gwen's back."

The grass is cold. Dampness soaks through the knees of my sweatpants more or less immediately, but I have a feeling it's not the worst thing that's going to happen to me in the next few minutes. I'm tacking myself on to what Quinn calls the "scrum"—a word that sounds enough like *scrotum* to make me uncomfortable.

But not as uncomfortable as I feel slinging my arm around a stranger's back.

We are a tightly formed cluster of three rows of women, hands clutching shirts, shoulders into shoulders, hips into hips. Quinn says that in a minute our eight people are going to shove against their eight people, and then the ball will get rolled down the middle and . . . something. She briefed me on a lot of these rules on the way over, but when she said I'd be tackling people, she failed to mention the largeness of the people I'm meant to tackle.

Behind me, another player puts her head down and jams her shoulders into the two second-row players I'm flanking. She grasps a fistful of my T-shirt with one hand.

"All set?" Quinn asks.

"Um, no?"

She gives me a sunny smile. "You'll figure it out." She starts jogging backward to the sidelines, where she grabs a ball. "All right, let's do this thing!"

Seconds later she's rolling it between the two halves of the scrum, and my whole side of the formation is lurching forward. I have to scramble to hold on to Gwen as the grass tries to slip out from beneath my shoes. There's grunting and shoving, another rapid forward lurch, and someone shouts, "Ball's out." The whole thing kind of collapses and dissolves at the same time, and I just stand there, dazed, as everyone else on the field runs away.

"It's your ball, Caroline!" Quinn shouts. "Follow it!"

I spend the next half hour feeling like a very dumb kid sister, trailing after the older girls and shouting, *Hey, wait up!*

Since I have two older sisters, this is, at least, a role I'm familiar with.

Whenever I get the ball, I get rid of it as fast as possible. I am, it turns out, deeply terrified of the idea of getting tackled. Tackling also scares me. One time the opposing team's ball carrier runs right at me, and I tell myself I'm going to take her down, but then when the moment comes, I just grab ineffectually at her shirt. Because I suck.

Still, it's kind of fun. Right up until the parking lot beside the playing field begins to fill with cars and a van that says Carson College on the side.

Carson is a school about twenty-five miles from Putnam.

The van is full of college women in black rugby jerseys and matching shorts.

It occurs to me that perhaps Quinn made me wear a blue shirt for a reason.

And that Quinn is, in fact, a lying liar who lies, and she's manipulated me into a rugby *game,* not a practice.

The Carson girls who pile out of the van are so much bigger than our girls. Sooooo much bigger.

Also, they have a coach—a real, honest-to-goodness, grown-up faculty-member *coach.* Putnam Women's Rugby doesn't even have proper shirts. It's just a club whose membership seems to consist mostly of Quinn's friends, many of whom were complaining a few minutes ago of being hungover.

Whereas the members of the Carson team look like they ate rare beefsteak for breakfast. The coach has a male assistant, who appears to be our age but has a whistle and a clipboard and therefore looks far more official.

I am in way over my head. I start trying to think of a good reason to beg off.

I have to study.

Lame.

I sprained an ankle.

When?

I need to do . . . things. Elsewhere.

Right.

I lace my fingers behind my head and look at the sky, searching for inspiration.

But I find something else there instead.

I find that it's a perfect November day in Iowa.

The sky is so blue, it *hurts.*

The wind feels good on my face. The Carson players are chattering with our players, Quinn's talking to their coach, and everyone seems so happy.

I have nowhere else I'm supposed to be today, and I realize suddenly that there's nowhere else I *want* to be.

I like this.

I try to remember the last time I did something completely new and scary—something I *liked*—and I think of West at the bakery, his backward black hat and his white apron.

I'd like to send him a text that says, I'm playing rugby with Quinn, but instead I turn around and jog toward her so I can ask her to give me a better idea of what on earth it is I'm supposed to be doing.

Shit is about to get real.

Half an hour later, Quinn is muddy and smiling, and she yells, "Isn't this great?" from across the field. We are getting our asses kicked by the Carson team. I have no idea what I'm doing at least 80 percent of the time.

"It's awesome!" I yell back.

Because it is. It *is* awesome. I'm high on how awesome it is—how good it feels to run, how solid the ball is when I catch it, how firm beneath my arm.

It is awesome, and then I get hit by a truck.

Okay, fine, the truck is a person. But she *feels* like a truck, and she knocks all the air out of my lungs. I lie on my back, blinking at the sky, trying to breathe with these air bags that completely refuse to work. I bend my knees and lift my hips up for reasons that are unclear to me. Probably I look like I'm trying to mate with the sky, but it doesn't matter, because down at the other end of the field something exciting happens, and no one's paying attention to my death.

A dark shape blocks my view of the sky. A male voice says, "You got the wind knocked out of you."

I'm not dying. This is excellent news.

I'm so grateful, I could kiss him.

I still can't breathe, though.

"Turn over on your side," he tells me, and his hands urge my hip toward him. I turn, because he has a soothing voice, and I like his whistle. I stare at his hairy calves and his black socks and his shoes that look like they might actually be specifically for rugby, with cleats on them and everything.

I experiment with breathing again. Nothing happens. My eyes are starting to feel like they might pop.

"Don't panic. Your diaphragm is having a spasm, but it'll relax soon. Just take it easy. Close your eyes."

I do as I'm told. After a few seconds, the constriction in my chest eases and I'm able to inhale.

"Good."

I breathe. I open my eyes. The grass is blurry. I blink at it, but it doesn't come into focus.

"I can't see."

He hunkers down and squints at my face. "Do you wear contacts?"

Oh. "Yes."

I blink again, and now I recognize this. This is what the world looks like with one contact in.

The guy is kind of blurry, too, but in a nice way. He has really short brown hair in tight curls and a dimple in his chin.

"You think one got knocked out?"

"I do. Was that woman made of bricks?"

He smiles. Dimples there, too. Dimples all over the place. "She probably outweighs you by a hundred pounds. That was pretty hard-core. You want a hand getting up?"

I take his hand, thinking, *I got hit so hard I lost a contact.*

"I'm Scott," he says.

I'm so distracted, I barely hear him. I'm too busy thinking, *Oh my God, I got tackled and I'm not dead. I'm totally hard-core.*

"Caroline," I say, but I guess I must have mumbled, because he spends the next five minutes calling me Carrie while he fetches me some water from the Carson Athletic Department cooler and insists I use his folding chair.

I watch the game and try to figure out more of the rules. I ask Scott to explain the tricky bits. He does, and when he dimples at me, I go ahead and smile back at him.

What can it hurt? He doesn't know my name.

The whistle goes off a few minutes later. Quinn looks at me with that eyebrow up. I nod my head and jog back onto the field.

Afterward, I learn that all rugby games end at a bar. This is, it seems, nonnegotiable. The Carson team's coach shakes Quinn's hand and drives away, and the rest of us form one huge mass of muddy, bruised womanhood—plus Scott— and walk along the railroad tracks that bisect Putnam's campus. We pass the science center and the phallic sculpture that reminds me of Krishna's rubber chicken. One of the Carson girls tries to climb it.

By the time we burst through the door of the bar, most of the players are singing a song so filthy it makes me blush. Scott is beside me, somehow, at this exact most inopportune moment. "Not going to sing?" he asks.

"I don't know the words."

He smiles. "You really are new at this, aren't you?"

"I never touched a rugby ball before today."

My vision's a little blurry with just one contact in, but I can still see all his dimples deepen. There are two in his left cheek, one in his right, plus the one in his chin. Quadruple dimples. When he steps up to the bar with one of the women on his team to order the first pitchers in an endless stream of beer, I close one eye so I can appreciate how broad his shoulders are, the chiseled shape of his calf muscles.

The Putnam players start shoving tables together in the main part of the bar. It's only two o'clock, so we rugby women have the place to ourselves. I grab a seat and am gratified, a few minutes later, when Scott sits by me and not by any of the Carson College players.

When he throws an arm over the back of my chair, I'm threaded through with excitement and wariness in a combination I'm not sure what to do with.

He's flirting with you. He likes you.

He looks nice, but how nice is anybody, really? What does he look at when he jerks off?

Maybe he's seen my pictures, and that's why he's being so friendly. He thinks I'm an easy mark. He's imagining my mouth on him. Calling me a slut inside his head.

"So, Carrie." He's half smiling, his body loose, everything about him relaxed and easy. "What brings you to the game of rugby today?"

I remind myself that just because my pictures are online doesn't mean every man alive has seen them. I'd never even heard of these gross porn picture sites before August, and while I know guys look at a *lot* more porn than girls do, I don't think that means they're all scouring the Internet for crotch shots in every second of their free time.

It's possible that Scott is just a guy who thinks my name is Carrie and wants to get to know me better.

More than possible. Likely.

So I take a deep breath. I smell yeasty beer and dirt and perspiration. I look around the table and think, *I'm safe here. These women have got my back. And if they trust Scott—if they* like *him, which they obviously do—then it's okay for me to trust him, too. At least a little bit.*

"Quinn strong-armed me into it."

"Really?" His eyes kind of flick over me, but not in a perverted way. Just in the normal way that a guy looks at a girl when he's about to say, "You don't strike me as someone who's easily strong-armed."

"Well, I was kind of drunk at the time."

"Ah. I know how that goes."

One of the Carson girls is standing on a chair, pint glass in the air. Everyone is shouting and happy, and I can't concentrate on more than snatches of conversation.

"Blow jobs." "Six tries." "The best rucker in the universe." "World Cup."

Quinn grinning her widest grin, wiggling her fingers, saying, "Some of us don't *need* a cock to get off."

Gwen pours and pushes a glass in my direction. "Drink!"

When she turns away, I tell Scott, "Just so you know, I'm not drinking this whole thing. I have a quiz tomorrow."

"That's fine. I'm not drinking, either." I look at his glass and see that he's got water instead of beer. I hadn't noticed. "I'm the designated driver."

"Is this, like, your job?" I ask.

"No, I get paid to assist the coach during the games, but now I'm just here because a bunch of these girls are my friends, and I don't want them to get themselves killed on the way home."

"That's good."

He smiles. "It's not like it's a hardship. You want me to get you some water?"

"No, thanks. I'm good."

He lifts his own glass and clinks it into mine. "To your first game of rugby. Cheers."

"Cheers."

"Wait, whose first game?" one of the Carson players asks.

Scott points at me. "Carrie's. She never played before today."

"Ladies, we've got a virgin in the house!"

Before I know what's even going on, I'm standing on top of a table, and forty women are singing to me.

Oh, rugby women are the biggest and the best
And we never give it up
And we never give it a rest
And we build a better ruck
And we give a better fuck
And no matter who we play, we can never get enough
Out in the field! Down in the scrum! Rugby women will
make you come!

My throat is so hot, but I'm smiling.

It is impossible not to smile. I feel strong and fast, bruised and shaken, surrounded by affectionate solidarity.

I feel normal again, like I used to, before everything went off the rails.

In Massachusetts, there's an office building where it's someone's job to erase Caroline Piasecki's vulva from the Internet. If it works, in a year, that girl won't exist anymore. She'll be dead, and part of me will be dead along with her.

Maybe in the meantime what I'm supposed to do is grow into someone new. Find something green in me, feed it, watch it shoot up toward the sun. Turn into a girl who plays rugby and dances at parties and flirts with boys who are sunny and open and who don't deal drugs or avoid discussing even the smallest details of their personal lives.

Rugby is awesome.

I'm so flipping hard-core, I can't even stand it.

———

The first time I see the inside of West's apartment, he's not home.

I feel weird about it, but it's not as though I snuck in. Me and Bridget ran into Krishna at the student center, and he invited us over with him and Quinn to watch bad TV and drink "even worse" alcohol. None of us could resist the allure of the mysterious "even worse."

So here we are, sprawled out on a big leather sectional couch, sharing a bottle of butterscotch schnapps that Krishna produced from the depths of the coat closet, and watching reruns of *What Not to Wear*, which Krish has stored up on his DVR in numbers that kind of frighten me.

West is working at the library, but he should be done soon. I text him, Are you off yet?

Yeah, he replies. I'm walking home. You?

I'm in ur apartment, poking all ur things.

This isn't true, but it gets his attention. DID YOU BREAK IN?

Yes. I keep a set of lock picks in my cheek.

Houdini used to do that. I find the idea repulsive, but I also sort of love it.

Very tricky. Are you really there?

Yes, K invited me. I like what you've done with the decor.

This is a joke, of course. It's obvious what happened here: Krishna bought all the stuff he thought was important—the couch, the TV, the alcohol, a king-size bed I can see through the open door to his bedroom—and then he and West purchased everything else in the place for two bucks at a rummage sale. Probably they got their dishes in big paper bags marked *25 cents,* because I'm drinking butterscotch schnapps out of a Flintstones jelly glass. I've propped up my sock-clad feet on a coffee table made of plywood and cinder blocks.

I put a lot of creative effort into it, West says.

I can see that.

If you find my collection of Pound Puppies, DON'T MOVE ANY.

Are they in the bedroom?

You could go in & find out. Look up.

Why?

I keep my stuffies in a hammock.

Smiling, I glance at the closed door to his room.

I could go in. I could sit on West's bed. Touch the bed-spread, whatever color it is. See what he's put on his walls, what books are on his shelves, how much laundry there is in the basket.

I want to.

Are you in my room, Caro?

The question makes my throat hot—as hot as if he'd asked me what I'm wearing. As hot as if we're cybering, which we're not. Not even close. So why is it that when I take a sip from my jelly glass, the schnapps goes down wrong and I start to cough uncontrollably?

"What are you doing over there?" Quinn asks.

"Texting West," Bridget says. "You can tell because she's biting her lip and kind of hunching over the phone, like pos-sibly Skittles are going to come out of it, or a rainbow, and—"

"I know *that*," Quinn interrupts. "I just want to know what he said to make her choke."

"Nothing," I croak.

"Ooh, what?" Bridget asks.

"You two need to fuck and get it over with," Krishna says.

"Shut *up*." I am a genius with the witty retorts.

The door opens, and West walks in. Seeing me on the

couch, he smiles. "Thought I was going to find you in my bed."

I burst into flame.

Not really, but I might as well. It would be a better way to dispel heat than sitting here, glowing red.

"Not with those ears," I say.

West snorts and drops his bag by the door. "Hey, Quinnie. Bridget. What's Krish got you drinking?"

"Butterscotch schnapps," Quinn says.

"Gross."

"It is some broke-ass shit," she agrees.

"I was just saying to Caroline about how the two of you need to fuck," Krishna says.

"Again? You're way too obsessed with who I'm fucking."

"I'm not obsessed. I'm concerned. You're a twenty-year-old guy with too many jobs and a permanent James Dean loner frown. If you don't start using it to get laid, you'll probably die of repression. And here's Caroline—"

"Could you guys maybe stop talking about me like I'm not in the room?"

"And stop saying 'fucking,'" Bridget suggests. "It's degrading. And I think—"

"See, that's your whole problem," Krishna tells her. "You think fucking is degrading."

"Like I'm the one with the problem. This from the campus manwhore who—"

"You are the one with the problem! You never have any fun."

"I'm here, aren't I? This is fun, right?"

Quinn groans. "Only for you two."

West comes up behind me and puts his hands on my shoulders. I tip my head back to look at him upside down, worried how he's taking this, but his mouth is soft, his eyes amused. "Caro and I aren't like that."

I smile at him, because his denial sounds like a confirmation, and because his hands on my shoulders are smoothing back and forth. His thumbs find a spot to rest and press on the back of my neck, which makes my breasts feel full and heavy and the pit of my stomach go molten.

I'm ridiculously pleased with Krishna's implication that West is in the middle of what sounds like a long dry spell. Although, considering the source, Krishna could just mean West hasn't had sex in a week.

I don't like thinking about West having sex. At all.

"So what are you two like?" Krishna asks.

"They're friends," Bridget says.

"No, we're not," West says.

Bridget looks confused.

I understand. It's kind of confusing. "Can we not talk about this?"

But Krishna is invested now. "No, I need to figure this out. Every time I go to the bakery the past few weeks, there you are. Seems like West's always texting you all of a sudden. He just came through the door smiling at you like the sun rises and sets on your ass, and now he's got his hands all over you."

Quinn chimes in, "He's *always* got his hands all over you."

"That's not true."

But, actually, is it? His hands on my shoulders are familiar. At the bakery, he often touches me like this. Casually— tapping my kneecap on the way past, dropping a hand on top of my head when I'm about to leave, rubbing my shoulders in an idle moment when we're both chatting with Krishna.

He's a physical person. It doesn't mean anything to him. I'm the one whose heart stops, every time.

"It's nobody's business but ours," West says.

Any normal person would be dissuaded by how forbidding West looks right now, but Krishna isn't normal. "If you're not going to fuck, we should start thinking about hooking Caroline up. It's about time she got back in the game, don't you think?"

Bridget punches him in the arm. "It's not a *game*."

Krishna pitches his voice in a spot-on imitation of Bridget. "It's not a *game*, it's not *fun*, she's not a piece of *ass*." Then, in his normal voice, "Swear to God, woman, it's like you're allergic to everything in the world that might accidentally make you feel good."

"Don't be a dick."

"Don't be a prude."

She sticks her tongue out at him, and Quinn mutters something that sounds like "Talk about two people who need to fuck."

"What?" Bridget screeches. "What are you implying?! Because if you're trying to say—"

"Never mind."

I expect Krishna to be all over that comment, but he surprises me by getting up off the couch and disappearing into the kitchen. He comes back with a beer, even though he already has a drink. He pops the top and takes a long swallow. He doesn't look at Bridget at all, and we just watch him, fascinated.

Or, I have to confine myself to glances, actually, because West has dug his thumbs deeper into my neck muscles, forcing my head forward. My hair hangs down in my face. His thumbs are branding irons, blunt and hot, searing parallel lines into my skin from my hairline to the low-dipping collar of my shirt. Again. Again. His fingers wrap around my shoulders, gripping like he owns me, and I'm melting.

I'm liquid.

I'm his.

"Let's not get distracted from the point," Krishna says. "The point is, Caroline needs a rebound lay."

"Oh, do I?"

I sound drugged.

I am drugged.

Bridget protests for me. "She does not."

"Seriously, Krish, you're being a jackass," Quinn says.

"We've got to find her a hookup. After Thanksgiving, I'm going to make it my personal goal in life to get Caroline some action."

"Caroline can get her own action," Bridget says. "I mean, if she even wanted to, which—"

"Which I don't."

"Because you're traumatized," Quinn says.

"I'm not *traumatized*."

I'm flustered and hot. I'm hoping, rather desperately, that the prickling in my nipples doesn't mean the headlights are on and everyone in the room can see what West is doing to me, right in front of them.

"It's all right," Quinn says. "Nobody's judging you. This is your safe zone."

"Caroline doesn't need a safe zone," Bridget says. "She's doing great. Tell them about—"

She sees my face and stops, but it's too late.

"What?" Krishna asks.

"Nothing."

"Doesn't sound like nothing."

"It's nothing. Really." I reach forward for my drink, breaking contact with West because things are about to turn ugly. I can feel it. The air has gotten heavy. My arousal has fled like a rabbit startled back into its hole.

I knock back a big gulp of butterscotch schnapps and start to choke *again,* which is a tactical error, because while I'm debilitated, Krishna goes after Bridget.

"Tell me what you were going to say," he demands. I tip sideways on the couch, coughing so hard that I have to pull my knees up. West rubs my back.

"Breathe," he says in a low murmur.

Even that's sexy. I'm choking to death, racked with guilt over what Bridget almost revealed, and I still have a corner of my brain devoted to fainting at the hotness of West. I'm a hopeless case.

Bridget crosses her arms, squared off against Krishna. "I'm not telling."

"Tell me."

"No."

"Tell me tell me tell me tell me tell me tell me tell me tell me—"

"Oh, all *right.* I was just going to say about this guy she met."

"There's a guy?" Quinn asks.

I'm barely capable of inhaling. When I say, "There's no guy," I drool a little on the leather, and I have to wipe it off with the palm of my hand.

I can't look at West.

"It's too late to deny it," Krishna says. "Bridget already spilled. Who's the guy?"

I don't see any way out of telling them. I sit up. "You re-member Scott?" I ask Quinn.

"Rugby Scott?"

"Yeah."

"He asked you out?"

"No! No. It's nothing. It's just . . . I just mentioned to Bridget that I might try to find out his last name. From you. In case."

"So you can call him?"

"Maybe?"

"He was into you," she says. "You should definitely call him."

"You think?"

"Sure. Why not?"

"Who's rugby Scott?" Krishna asks.

"He goes to Carson," Quinn says. "You wouldn't know him. And he's really nice. And *hot*. Well done, Caroline."

"I haven't done anything yet."

She chucks me on the shoulder. "Sure, but you should. Get back out there, you know?"

I duck my head. Sidelong, I glance at West.

He's gone blank.

Krishna is looking at him, too, and I can't make out whether he pushed West into that blank face on purpose or if he's oblivious. That's the thing with Krishna—I can never figure out if he's an asshole or if he's *pretending* to be an asshole.

Either way.

He drops to the couch beside Bridget, chugs the rest of his beer, and says, "Maybe we should find something else to watch."

West opens his bedroom door. "I've got to study."

He closes it, and then there's just the sound of the TV and Bridget shifting uncomfortably on her end of the couch.

"I didn't *do* anything," I say. "I don't even know his last name."

But I'm not sure who I'm talking to.

No one replies.

"So when are you heading home?" West asks.

"Tomorrow."

It's the Tuesday before Thanksgiving—or Wednesday, I guess, since it's three in the morning. Campus has been a ghost town since lunchtime, and West has been at the bakery all day. He had to come in early. He'll stay late. He has an insane amount of baking to do to help Bob get the holiday orders filled.

It doesn't matter, he told me. He's got the whole rest of break to sleep.

"Early?" he asks.

"Yeah."

"Can you go vent the oven for me?"

I walk over to the oven—which is more like a metal closet with glass in the door—and push the button to vent the steam so the loaves will start to dry out during the last few minutes of baking.

"Thanks."

I hop up on the counter and study the room. Since October, it's become almost as familiar to me as my dorm room, and I've stopped noticing how crowded it is. How the vented steam smells of moist dough, raw and wet. How West's hands are always busy, the floor is always dirty, and I'm always safe, even if I'm not always comfortable.

Officially we're on break, and I should be at home.

Home has become an increasingly difficult concept. I still talk to my dad once a week, but I've come to dread our conversations. I've been a daddy's girl my whole life, and now I don't know what to say to him. He asks me how Con Law is going, if the class is as tough as I feared. He reminds me that I should look into summer internships at the career center, because I ought to have some experience before I start applying to law schools in a few years.

He tells me he loves me and reminds me to be safe.

I hang up the phone with a piercing pain in my stomach. I feel like a liar, but I haven't told him a single lie.

For the first time since I got to Putnam, I don't want to go home for break. Dad gets into the whole turkey thing, and I'm in charge of stuffing. My sister Janelle and her fiancé do cranberry sauce and rolls. Alison, my other sister, is in Lesotho with the Peace Corps, but if she were home she would do pumpkin pie.

I guess I should take over pie duty.

I'm supposed to get fitted for a bridesmaid's dress for Janelle's wedding, which is coming up in the summer. She emails me details about the venues they're looking at, the colors she likes, the save-the-date cards they're having made on Etsy. I know I'm supposed to be excited, so I act that way, but I can't drum up any enthusiasm.

"You ever call that guy?" West asks.

It's been two days since he shut himself up in his room. This is the first time either of us has mentioned that conversation.

"Scott," I say.

"I didn't forget."

"No. I didn't call him yet."

His phone buzzes. West checks it and taps out a message to someone. He's been glued to it all night, distracted. He hasn't told me who he's talking to. It could be his sister, his mother, some girlfriend back home he's never mentioned.

He doesn't tell me anything.

Tonight he has nothing to teach me. All these weeks of glazing and proofing, I feel as though we've never talked about what it is I'm actually supposed to be learning.

I never asked him to be my teacher. It's not what I want from him.

But on the other hand, I've found proof of West's lessons scattered all over my life. Proof that what Nate did to me isn't the only thing about me worth talking about. Proof that just as I could have walked into the bakery any night, I can also walk into a party or out onto a rugby field.

I'm still here. I'm basically okay. I don't require coddling, and I'm not going to buy into any more bullshit.

I am overproofed, utterly sick of pretense. Because the other thing I've figured out since October is that West tells me *nothing,* and if there is nothing I can teach him, we'll never be more than we are in this room.

He's staying here over the break. It costs too much and takes too long to fly to Oregon for the paltry few days off we get, and, anyway, Bob needs his help.

West told me all that.

What he didn't tell me is that he wants to go home—but I know he does, even though I'm not sure where home is, what town he's from, what's there for him. I don't know because he doesn't *say.* He doesn't tell me why his attention is so riveted on his phone, why he's distracted all the time lately, what he's worrying about.

I know he's worrying. I know something about him isn't right. But I also know he's never going to look up from the bread and say to me, *Caro, can I tell you something?*

An awkward sort of finality has settled between us to-night, and I think it must be because of that conversation at the apartment.

Maybe I'm wrong, though. Maybe it happened when he

handed me the envelope full of money. The money changed something.

If West shared his own weed with friends, he'd be a guy who was fun to party with. Since he sells it to them, he's a felon. That's because of the money.

I'm supposed to be rich. He's supposed to be poor. He gave me fifteen hundred dollars, and now something is different between us, but he won't tell me what, and I won't ask.

I'm not brave enough to push him, but I wish he would tell me. I wish he would *need* me. Because I'm not sure how much longer I can stand to be the only one in this kitchen who will admit to being vulnerable. And I'm not sure, either, how much longer I'm going to need this—these late-night drives to the bakery, these hours with West working and the mixers going.

There is so much more we could be saying to each other, and aren't.

Tonight the mixer's rattling song sounds like a dirge, and I feel nothing but grief. I woke up from a nightmare to come here—a dream where I was out on the rugby field in a night-gown, wading through a thick fog, and I couldn't find something I needed, couldn't hear anyone calling for me. I felt irrevocably lost.

This night—this moment—this is the end of something, and we've failed at it.

"I'm going to miss you," I tell him.

He's got his back to me. Without responding or even ac-knowledging that I spoke, he turns up the mixer to high. It bangs around so loudly, I can't hear the music. I cover my ears and listen to the beating of my heart with my eyes closed. When I open them, it's because his hand is on my thigh, and he's standing right in front of me, filling my whole field of vision.

His eyes are silvery-blue, cast into shadow by his indrawn eyebrows, startling and intense.

Krishna and Quinn are right—West is always touching me. I always feel it.

His hand on my thigh makes me throb. Between my legs. My heart. My throat.

Everywhere.

Stupid girl.

When he moves his hand, I clutch at it. I overlap our fingers, mine on top of his, and press down, hard.

West looks at our hands, and he sighs. "What am I supposed to do about you? I think you'd better tell me, Caro, because I don't have a fucking clue."

I gaze at the knob of his wristbone. At the dark hair on his forearms, the divot of his throat, the patch beneath his lip where he missed a few hairs when he shaved.

His mouth. His eyes. His mouth.

Always his mouth, wide and smart-alecky, generous and withholding.

I wait for West's mouth to make words I'm never going to hear.

I'll miss you.

I care about you.

I don't want you going out with that guy, because I want you with me. I want us to be more than this.

I want to say, *Tell me everything, West. Please.*

But in the morning I'm going to drive home and see my father. Whatever it is West might have to say, tonight isn't the right night for him to say it, and I'm not the right person for him to say it to.

It's not just him. It's me. I'm not brave enough.

My fingertips skate over the shapes of his face. The arch

of his eyebrow and the scar that bisects it. The curve of his ear. The lush fullness of his mouth.

I want to breathe in when he exhales, rest against his body, wrap my legs around his waist, and take him inside me.

I don't know how to get rid of this.

I don't know how to give him up.

The oven timer beeps. West steps away from me and turns it off. Opens the door. Takes out the bread.

The whole rest of the night, he keeps his distance.

In the morning, I get in my car and put sixty miles between us, but it's not far enough.

I don't know how far I'd have to go for it to be far enough.

THANKSGIVING BREAK

West

Don't get involved, I told myself in the beginning. *She's not your problem.*

But I was already involved, even then. By Thanksgiving, I was so involved with Caroline, I almost couldn't stand to see her.

Everything I told her was a lie.

We weren't going to be friends, I'd promised. But what else do you call it when you text somebody a million times a day and look forward to seeing them even though you just fucking *saw* them?

What do you call it when you know when somebody has class and what material their next test is about, and they know when you're going to be working and how many hours it is since you slept, so they bring you all your favorite junk food to help keep you going?

Caroline and I were friends.

I was lying about it.

I told her I wasn't going to touch her, but I touched her every chance I got. Brushed my arm against hers. Leaned into her with my knee. When she turned her back, I checked out her ass and thought about how it would feel in my hands. When she leaned over the table, kneading, I looked down her shirt.

I'd find reasons to get inside her personal space. I'd watch her skin get pink and patchy, and I'd love it.

I wasn't any kind of saint. Even though I couldn't have her, I did my best to make her want me. I made sure she was thinking about me, and I didn't stop when I found out she wanted to ask out some guy she'd met playing rugby.

I ramped it up.

I treated her like she belonged to me, even though I wouldn't have her and I wouldn't let her have me, either.

I told Caroline to admit how she was feeling—how she was *really* feeling—but when she'd ask me, "What's on your mind?" I wouldn't say, *I'm worried about my mom because she said her back went out and I think she must be missing shifts at the prison. If she gets fired, she's going to get whiny, and Bo's never been around her when she's like that. He might dump her for being a useless drag—which she is, I swear, my mother whines like nobody else alive—and if that happens, I'll have to go back home.*

What would be the point?

I was two different people, and only one of them was real. The real West Leavitt lived in a trailer in Silt, Oregon. He talked to me all day long. *Check on your mom. Make sure she gets groceries so Frankie's got something decent to eat. Pick up another shift at the library, because you never know. You just never know.*

Whereas the guy I was in Iowa—he was the clothes I put on

to get where I needed to go. He was me, pretending to be the kind of person Caroline has been every minute of her life.

Whoever you are when you're born, you can't just shake that off. We like to pretend we can. That's the American dream, right? No limits. But the truth is, you might get rich, but you can't buy the way rich people *are*. You can't just put the right clothes on and belong. You're still going to think like a poor kid, dream like one, want like one. You'll still flinch every time another student asks you, *So what does your dad do?* or *Where are you going for break?*

It's hard work, teaching yourself not to flinch. Learning to be someone you're not.

That's what I was doing at Putnam. I was working. I wasn't there for laughs, or to party, or to find the girl I wanted to spend the rest of my life with. I was there to make the rest of my life *happen*, and it was a full-time project.

People like Caroline don't have to worry about the groceries or the rent. They can assume all that shit's taken care of, and then they just have to figure out what they want and go for it.

Where I'm from, assuming you're going to get into med school is like assuming you can walk on water. It's a fairy tale, and people who believe in fairy tales are idiots.

I didn't get to Putnam assuming anything. I got there on the charity of a rich alum whose wife I fucked.

I knew what I was doing. I would have done it again.

I hated it, but I would have done it.

I hated lying to Caroline, but I lied to her. If I'd told her the truth, it would've broken her heart.

I couldn't have her. That was the truth.

I could only have this one thing, if I worked hard enough. Nothing else.

———

Caroline texts me on Saturday. What are you doing?

I've been sleeping.

I woke up at dawn and walked around campus in a fog—a literal fog, I mean, the air full of thick white mist—and felt like some lost ghost haunting the place. I stayed out there too long, not dressed right for the wet invasiveness of the weather.

When I came back to the apartment, I was shuddering, and it was so fucking quiet that I got this creepy feeling, like maybe I didn't exist at all. I got out my phone and scrolled through yesterday's texts from Caroline and Frankie and my mom.

It's Thanksgiving break, I told myself. *Not the apocalypse.*

But I still felt strange. I sat on my bed, staring out at the fog, and polished off the last few inches in Krishna's bottle of butterscotch schnapps.

I stared at the ceiling until I fell asleep.

When Caroline's text wakes me up, the phone says it's four o'clock, but it takes me a few seconds to figure out that means afternoon. I slept all day. My fingers are stiff, my mouth tastes like garbage, and my dick is half hard for no reason.

Nothing. You?

The phone rings. It's her. "Hey."

"Hey."

"You sound sleepy. Did I wake you up?"

"Yeah."

"Sorry. I can go. You go back to sleep. I know this is, like, your one big chance to be lazy."

"It's all right. How's your break going?" We've only exchanged a few texts since she left on Wednesday. I haven't known what to say to her. She's pissed at me. I'm pissed at myself. I think we'd be better off not seeing each other at all, but if we're going to stop, it's going to have to be her who stops it.

"Okay, I guess. I mean, Thanksgiving was okay. Now everybody's gone, and it kind of sucks."

"Where'd they go?"

"Janelle and her fiancé already went home. My dad went over to some friends of our family's in Marshalltown."

"He left you home by yourself?"

"He wanted me to go with him, but I didn't feel like it."

"When's he coming back?"

"Late, I guess. It's for dinner, but this friend is a judge, too, and they usually drink after dinner and sit around telling judge stories for hours."

"Huh. So what are you up to?"

"Nothing." She makes this soft sound, kind of laughing at herself. "I'm bored. Three days off school, and I officially have no idea what to do with myself. Plus, I'm lying on my bed in my room, which hasn't changed since high school, so I kind of feel like I'm in this weird time warp, like I never went to college at all, and nothing that happened at Putnam was real."

I reach down to adjust myself. I'm picturing her on her bed, and it's not helping the hard-on situation. In real life she's probably got her sweats on and her hair in one of those floppy-mess ponytails, but in my head she's wearing that pajama top from the first night at the bakery, white panties, and nothing else. Lacy panties—the kind that go down over her hips like shorts, her pussy a pink shadow underneath.

"But then you wouldn't be talking to me," I say. "Since you know me from Putnam."

"Yeah. It still kind of feels like that, though."

"Like what?"

There's a hitch in my breathing. I've got my hand on my cock, stroking.

Fuck. I shouldn't. She's interested in another guy, and I'm an asshole.

But I don't stop. I haven't heard her voice in a few days. I've been alone so much, I'm not sure I *can* stop. My hand is dry and hot, pulling so hard it's almost cruel.

"Not real," she says. "Like my worlds are colliding, only not, like, colliding. More like mingling or something?"

"Are you sober?"

She laughs. "I am. That just makes it weirder. Are you?"

"Yeah, why?"

The reason I'm picturing those white panties so vividly is she wore them in one of the pictures online.

I know her pussy is pink beneath those panties, shaved, because I've seen it.

I don't deserve to be her friend.

I have to stop.

"Your voice is all scratchy," she says. "You don't sound like you."

I'm not who you think I am.

I'm an asshole with my hand on my cock, picturing you, because I want you.

I want you all the goddamn time, and it's making everything impossible.

"Who do I sound like?"

She's quiet for a second, and then she laughs again, shy now. "I don't know."

I want her to say something dirty. I want this to be phone sex, for Caroline to tell me she's blowing me, I'm fucking her, she never wants me to stop.

I'm loathsome.

It only makes my hand jerk faster.

"Tell me what your room looks like," I say.

Tell me what you're wearing. Tell me what you want me to do to you.

So she describes it—purple walls painted when she was eleven, a desk that she got in trouble for carving her name into, a daybed, whatever the fuck that is—and I turn my face away from the phone so she can't hear my breath, broken.

"West?"

"Yeah?" I sound strange. I've lost track of everything but the sound of her voice and the slick flesh moving under my palm.

"Will you come, West?"

The sound of my name, the way her voice wraps around it. The breathy intimacy of her request. She wants me with her, and I do come. All over my hand.

"Sure." I'm so wrecked, I have to clear my throat and try again. "Sure, yeah, I'll come."

It's only when I'm getting in the car, asking her for directions, that I understand what a terrible idea this is.

By then it's too late to back out.

"Boost me," she says, and she giggles. Actually giggles, like a kid. "C'mon, West! Give me a boost!"

She's got her hands on the roof, one foot denting the gutter—though it's already pretty trashed at that spot, she must always go up this way—and her ass wiggling in my face. I'm pushed up against the railing of this tiny balcony off Caroline's bedroom on the second story of her giant house, the cold of the metal seeping through my coat, wondering how I got myself into this insane situation.

She slips, shrieks, and knocks against me, hard. Without

thinking, I get an arm around her waist, the fingers of my other hand wrapped tight around the rail. I wonder how this balcony is attached to the house. A few bolts? What's the weight limit? What's this fucking thing *for,* anyway? It's not as if she's going to string the laundry out her window to dry.

"You're crazy," I tell her, but she just laughs.

"I've done this a zillion times. Give me a boost, and I'll help you up."

"It's November."

"There's no snow or ice. The stars are good up here. Come *on.*"

I figure either I help her up on the roof or I spend the next hour of my life trying to talk her out of it. Plus, if we keep trying to do this her way, we're going to end up dead.

She's already got her foot up again, her ass pressing into my groin. My hands grip her hips automatically, guiding that sweet, soft pressure right where I want it.

I've forgotten all about helping her up, but Caroline finds purchase with her other foot, and then she's gone, up, up, and away.

I've just helped a stoned girl onto the roof of her suburban mansion. After getting her stoned.

I'm going to hell for this.

Her hand is in front of my face now, white and small. "I'll help you up."

"I can do it. Move over."

Her hand disappears. I climb up. She's flopped onto her back, looking at the sky. The black coat she's wearing kind of disappears into the dark shingles, and the moonlight catches the row of silver buttons like a landing strip that leads to her smile and the sparkles in her knit cap.

"Lie down," she tells me.

I just stand there and look at her for a minute, because she's perfect. Her hair is loose. Her guard is down. She told me she was worried the pot would make her paranoid, but she wanted to try it anyway. Instead, it's made her soft and receptive, blown her pupils up so her eyes look huge and dark, full of wonder.

I feel like I've performed some kind of miracle.

"Wow," she says. "You look *so weird* from here."

That makes me smile. I kneel on the roof next to her, enthralled by her teeth. I only took a few hits off the pipe I brought, but it's been awhile since I smoked. I could look at her face for an hour. I want to touch her hair, feel how soft it is. Run my fingers through it, over her throat, down that line of buttons and up under her shirt, pushing it out of the way to expose her skin to the moonlight. I want to make her cold so I can warm her up with my body, my mouth, my hands, my tongue.

I want to make her belong to me.

"What is it?"

"Promise me you're not going to fall off the roof and get killed."

"I'm not. I told you, I've done this a million times."

"Why'd you need a boost, then?"

"I never come up *alone*. Janelle usually boosts me."

"You allowed?"

"Sure! Oh, wait, you mean by my dad? No. Well, sort of. He knows we do it, and we've never gotten in trouble or anything, but it's definitely frowned upon. We never come up when he's home."

She told me when I got here that he's not going to be back for hours. That he'll probably end up staying over with the Marshalltown friends. Too much booze to drive. But she made me park around the side just in case.

If she were a girl back home, there wouldn't be any mistaking the invitation. *My dad's gone. Come over. Bring weed.*

If she were a girl back home, I'd have a string of condoms in my pocket and a shit-eating grin on my face.

But she's Caroline, and I'm not sure she has any idea what she does to me. Not like I've been subtle, but I said I wouldn't come after her, and she said she doesn't want me to. She's thinking about some other guy. Scott.

So I don't know. If she has an agenda, I don't have a clue what it is.

"Lie *down*," she says. "You're blocking my stars."

I lie down, elbows behind my head, and look up.

"It's cloudy."

"Shh."

"There's no stars."

"*Shhhhhhh,*" she says again, with a lot of drama. "Shut up and enjoy the firmament."

I smile up at the sky. Stoned out of her gourd, Caroline's even bossier than normal. And she still says shit like *firmament.*

We look at the cloudy dark mess in the sky for a while. The night's actually not half bad. The clouds are thick, but they're moving in fast masses, and sometimes the moon escapes and brings some stars with it. Better than the usual Iowa sky, so often gray-white and thick with moisture. Fucking oppressive. The sky seems taller back home somehow.

It's crisp out, but not as cold as it ought to be for the end of November. I'm wearing a heavy zip-up sweatshirt over a flannel shirt and a T-shirt, and I'm comfortable enough, except for the strip of skin along my lower back where my shirts have all pulled up because I've got my arms above my head. I feel the roof through my jeans, numbing my ass.

It doesn't matter. Being high makes everything crisp and

sharp, but it also makes it so I just don't care about shit like whether I'm warm. The buzz turns down the radio station in my head, constantly tuned to Oregon, and tunes in to Caroline.

She's lying on her side, staring at me.

I feel her breath on my face. The warmth off her body.

I know exactly how far I'd have to move to kiss her, and it's not far enough.

"I can see every single hair on your face," she tells me.

"I shaved."

"No, I mean, like, your pores. I can see all the places where the hairs come out. It's weird."

"It's not weird. It's my face."

"Your face is *weird,* though, West."

"Thanks."

She laughs, a wash of spearmint-scented breath over my ear. "Please. You don't need me to tell you how pretty you are."

"Guys aren't pretty."

"Have you seen your roommate? He's the prettiest girl on campus."

"You should tell him that sometime. He'd be so pissed."

"It's not like it's hurting him in the dating department."

"Krish doesn't date, Caro."

"You know what I mean." She leans closer.

"Why are you hovering over me like a vulture?"

"I like watching your jaw move when you talk. I can see, like, muscles and stuff. I never noticed before."

"Maybe 'cause we don't usually talk with your face three inches away."

"That's probably why," she says solemnly.

"Or because you're stoned."

"Another strong possibility."

I close my eyes. I feel like something important is slipping away from me and I'm supposed to want it back, but I don't. I don't want anything that means I'm supposed to keep apart from her.

"You are, though," she says.

"What am I?"

I want her to tell me what I am. I walked into this house of hers, this house with its big white columns marching along the front and its granite countertops, the deep white carpet in the living room that must be new because there's not a stain on it. I walked in and got lost.

I don't know who I am. She's the only thing here I recognize, and it makes it harder to remember why I'm not supposed to put my hands on her hips, pull her on top of me, kiss her cold lips, and push my fingers underneath her hat to feel the warmth of her hair, her head in my hands.

The only thing I know in this place is Caroline.

What am I?

When I open my eyes, she's right there, looking at me. Looking into me.

She strokes one light fingertip along the bridge of my nose, pausing at the tip. Then skips down to the groove above my mouth. Over my upper lip. She's drawing me with her finger, and it brings something up that I've shoved down inside me, buried in earth, covered over with a rock.

I don't know what to call it. Greed. Need.

She's touching me like I'm fragile, precious, and it's making me want to flip her over, pin her wrists down, climb on top of her and do things to her until she feels boneless, desperate. Until the only word she can make with that mouth is my name, over and over. I want to know every fragile hollow of her body, and I want my tongue on them, my name inscribed in some secret language only Caroline and I even know.

"You're beautiful," she says.

I'm dangerous.

I sit up, scooting over a few inches and trying not to be too obvious about it. My hands are shaking.

"You're high," I tell her.

"I know."

"How's the Internet treating you lately?" I ask because I want to remind her of the money. I want us to be a transaction, logical, bounded. I miss the bakery walls. When I'm on the clock and she's nothing more than a visitor, we both have a role to play. On this rooftop, there aren't any boundaries. I'll put them back up, if that's what it takes. "That company you hired doing what you want them to do?"

She's turned away from me slightly, not giving me her back but not showing her face, either. I think I must have hurt her feelings. She asked for it, though, touching me like that. "I'm supposed to get a report every month, but so far I haven't seen one. Maybe because of the holiday, they're delayed or something."

"Does it *seem* like it's working?"

"I don't know. I decided I was better off not Googling myself all the time, so I stopped."

"Makes sense."

She wraps her arms around her knees. "I've been thinking about changing my last name."

"Seriously?"

She doesn't answer me. She's looking out over the backyard.

"To what?"

"Fisk. That was my mom's name."

"Don't let him do that to you."

"I wasn't thinking of it like that. I just think—"

"Don't let him win. Not like this. It's not who you are. You're no coward."

She whips around, eyes flashing. "I didn't say I was going to do it. I was just thinking about it, and I have every right to think about it if I want to."

I lift my hands. "Fine. Think about it."

That just pisses her off more. "You have no idea what it's like. I walk around campus knowing people are talking about me behind my back. I look around my classes, and I can't tell who's seen me with my legs spread. Could *you* stand it, if it were you?"

"If everybody on campus had seen my dick? Sure. It's just my dick. It's not me."

"Maybe. But it's different for guys. Nobody would call you a slut if that happened. They'd just think you were, you know, kind of a tool. Or that you had too much to drink. Not that you were *worthless*."

"If people think that, they're idiots. Why should you care what a bunch of idiots think?"

"Because the world is full of idiots, West! And because it matters to people who aren't idiots. My dad's not an idiot, okay? He's smart. But if he finds out . . . if my sisters find out? Or what if I go to law school and I try to get a good clerkship, but I can't because my vagina's on the Internet? You know how much that would suck?"

"It would, okay, I get that. But changing your name— that's who you are. That's *you*."

"Women change their names when they get married."

"Apples and oranges."

"No. It's *always* arbitrary. It's a decision I can make if I want to. And I'm surprised you're being a jerk about this. I thought you were on my side."

"I am on your side, I just . . . He put those pictures up there so people would call you names. He was pissed at you, right? He wanted you to feel shitty. And I think if you change your name—that's what he *wants*. That's probably even more than he ever wanted. That's what all of them want, for you to be ashamed of yourself, but you didn't do anything to be ashamed about. You took off your clothes with a guy, sucked him off, let him fuck you—big fucking deal, Caroline. So they call you a slut, and they call you a frigid bitch, and it doesn't even make sense. I mean, pick one, right? None of it means anything about who you are. Those pictures aren't *you*."

"They *are*, though. I'm the pictures. The pictures are me. There isn't anything else anymore. I think about this guy I met, Scott? You know why I haven't called him? It's because I'm wondering, *How long will it take him to find the pictures?* And he doesn't know my name yet. When I met him, he actually thought I said 'Carrie,' so he thinks my name is Carrie, and it's like . . . What if it was? What if I were Carrie Fisk? Then I wouldn't have to worry, *How long until he knows? What will he think? What will he do?*"

"If he'd judge you for that, he's a dick and you're better off not knowing him."

"It's not . . . It's not even *him*, West, it's everybody. Everybody says, *Be careful what you do with pictures. The Internet is forever. Don't post drunk shots on Facebook*. I could be sixty years old, and they might still be online. They could be there for the rest of my life. So what if Scott doesn't care? What if we date for years and get engaged, and then his mom finds out? Or his dad, or his great-aunt, or whoever? What if he has some pervy cousin who jacks off to my pictures and tells Scott, you know?"

"What if you die in a freak accident next week? What if your firstborn gets leukemia? Jesus, Caroline, don't make this the center of your entire fucking life!"

I hear what I sound like in the silence afterward.

Pissed off. Accusing.

I feel like the lowest thing. Worse than a worm. Something rotten, disgusting. Something decayed in me.

I'm as bad as every guy she's worried about. I jerked off talking to her on the phone a few hours ago, and if that doesn't make me a pervert and an asshole, I'm not sure what would.

I just hate hearing her talk about this other guy. I hate that her hope is attached to a name that isn't mine, her future to a name that isn't hers.

Shame floods through me, a hot impulse that makes me angry she's not talking. Makes me fill the silence with more stupidity. "It's normal," I tell her. "It's tits and a cunt, legs, an ass—it's not the end of the fucking *world*, Caro. You think you're so fucking special, but there's a million other girls' cunts online, and most of those girls aren't moaning that their lives are over just because some random dude is getting off looking at them."

Quiet again. In the nice neighborhood where Caroline lives, everyone is sleeping tonight. That makes me feel vile, too. That she should live in this place that's *exactly* the kind of place where I want to put Frankie. Surrounded by safety.

That I am the thing here, tonight, that's making her unsafe.

I risk a glance at her face. She looks like I slapped her.

I did slap her.

The worst part is, there's no reason for me to be mad at her. I'm not—I'm just mad in general.

I'm mad the world sucks so much, that this should have happened to her, that she should feel so bad about it.

I'm mad that sex can't just be sex, it has to be everything else, too—money and power and misery and pleasure all mixed together. Because I want her, I'm mad at her, and it's fucking stupid.

The whole thing. Stupid.

I sigh and stand up. Pace out the rooftop. This giant house where Caroline spent her whole life, sheltered from anything half as bad as what her punk-ass ex-boyfriend did to her. He probably grew up in a house like this, too. Probably wrecked her whole world without a second thought.

I walk back toward Caroline.

"I'm sorry," I tell her. "That came out . . . I'm just sorry, all right?"

She shakes her head. She's got her arms wrapped around her legs, her head turned away. "You know, I never called it that?"

"It?"

"Cunt," she says, like the word tastes bad in her mouth. "Pussy. Slit. Tits. Cock. All those words—they never had anything to do with me before."

She angles her head toward me, and I see her eyes, full of tears. "I don't want them to have anything to do with me."

I sit down a few feet away. Not sure what to tell her.

"There are so many things I'm not sure I can ever get back," she says quietly. "I mean . . . I understand what you're saying. I get that life doesn't end because of a couple grainy pictures online. But it kind of does, too, you know? Because now everything I've seen people say about me is *in* me. I have

a cunt, I am a cunt, I'm dressed like a slut, I am a slut, I'm
frigid, I'm a bitch, I want cum on my face—all those dirty
things that never used to apply to me and now they do. They
just eat away at me. So if I feel something, if I want a guy, if
I get . . . if I get wet for a guy, if I want somebody to kiss
me—it's not the same anymore. It's always going to be full of
that stuff, either because I'm pushing all those words away or
because I'm trying to figure out how to make them mine.
And I hate that."

I wish I didn't know what she meant, but I do. I can't tease
a woman, work for a smile, get her off with my tongue inside
her, without thinking about what she wants from me. What
I'm going to get for it.

That's the thing about trading sex for favors. It makes
everything feel like a transaction.

"Do you want somebody to kiss you?" I ask. "Is this all
theoretical, or . . ."

Her arms wrap tighter around her legs. "It's not theoretical."

"Scott?"

"Sure, Scott. I mean, maybe. I just met him. But what if,
right? Why does it all have to be spoiled before it's even
started?"

"It's not spoiled."

"It *feels* spoiled."

"That sucks."

"It does."

She traces a circle on her kneecap with her fingertip. "I
only talked to him for a couple minutes. I liked him. He's
easy, you know? And Quinn got ahold of his number for me,
but I just haven't . . . I don't want to think of him like that. I
want all those words and body parts to have nothing to do
with any of it. Except they do."

"Yeah, that's pretty much inevitable if you're gonna date the guy."

She looks right at me for a second, then back at the roof. "I was starting to feel almost like I could do it, earlier today. Call him up and ask him out after break. I thought . . . But I have to say, you kind of ruined that whole idea, so thanks."

There's a smile in her voice, though. A small one, but it's there.

"I get that I was a prick, but I don't get what I ruined. You're gonna have to explain that."

"I don't think I can do it. Any of it. I'm going to become a nun."

"That would be a waste." Now I can see the smile, the apple of her cheek lifting, though she's still not looking at me.

"No, I can see now it's the only way."

"Sister Caroline," I say. "Martyr of Internet Porn."

She lifts her head. I can't look away from the brilliance of her teeth, her lips, because I have this sudden, awful, amazing idea, and I'm focusing all my attention on keeping it from coming out of my mouth.

I *could kiss you,* is what I'm trying not to say.

I *could make you forget all about those fucking pictures.*

I *could make you feel good, wipe out all that shame, show you what's supposed to be going through your mind when you're with a guy.*

I *could. Me.*

"You like him a lot," I say instead. Because she's already made her choice, and I'm not it. I wasn't even an option.

"He's fun."

"Fun is a little lukewarm."

"No, don't. Don't pick on him. He's great. Or he could be great. He seems like he could."

"Too bad he's so ugly."

"No, he's hot, too. Quinn said."

"Quinn's into girls."

"Quinn's bi."

"Seriously?"

"You didn't know that?"

I shake my head.

"Well, she is. And she thinks Scott is hot."

"So you ask him out, and then you dive right in and kiss him. See what happens."

I watch her when I say it, because whatever her reaction is, I'm going to memorize it. I'm going to use it to remind myself whenever I need reminding.

She's not mine. I can't have her. That's final.

"I will," she says. "That's a great idea."

But the face she makes—it's not going to work out as the reminder I wanted.

"You look like you're thinking about licking a slug."

"Don't tease me. I'm working on it."

I want to tease her, though. I feel suddenly, thoroughly stoned on this idea I've had. It's made it to my brain, I guess. It's worked through my system in one fast heady rush.

Nothing is real but her and me and this ocean of dark we're drifting in.

Nothing is real but the way I feel lighter when she smiles. When I'm teasing her, I feel like maybe I'm somebody after all, and not just a son and a brother, an employee, a quick fuck. I'm more than a student, an impostor, an arrow on its vector toward a goal. Like I matter to her.

Like I matter for *me* and not for what I can do for somebody else.

"If I said you should suck him off, maybe, *maybe,* I'd expect that face. But kissing? How can you be into a guy and make that face when you think about kissing him?"

"It's complicated. Shut up."

"I'll shut up when you answer the question."

"No. I'm not—why are we even talking about this?"

"Because you're stoned. You have no filter."

"I do too."

"We just talked about your cunt. The filters are definitely off-line."

She laughs and buries her face in her hands. "That was your fault."

"Everything is my fault."

I can't stop this. Can't stop myself. Not when she's making me feel this way.

Her shoulders are shaking. I'm not sure when she quits laughing and starts crying, or if she even does quit. It's maybe all the same thing. Laughing and crying together.

I just know that when she looks up, the tears make her eyes shine, and that's where the stars are.

That's how it looks to me. Like the stars are in Caroline, and the whole world is just me and her.

Because I'm stoned.

And because I'm in love with her.

"This, too, Caro," I say, leaning in. "This is completely my fault."

When our lips meet, she breathes in, and that's all that happens. Maybe for a second, maybe forever—it's hard to tell when you're stoned. Time gets unpredictable. Sex gets much bigger and much smaller, both, because you can feel *everything*. Every hair, every breath, every heartbeat, every firing inch of skin. It's distracting. I get distracted by how Caroline's mouth feels soft but dry, and it's like shaking hands, this kiss. Taking her measure. Saying hello. It's not sexy. It's . . . interesting.

"Weird," she says against my mouth.

"You're weird."

"Look who's talking."

I lick her bottom lip, and she sinks to her elbows.

I follow her down and do it again. "Still weird?"

"You're licking me," she murmurs.

"How's that working for you?"

She closes her eyes. "I think . . ."

I draw her lip into my mouth and bite it gently. It feels fleshy between my teeth, more substantial than it looks. I want to do this to every part of her. Lick it and taste it, bite it, test it. Consume her, piece by piece.

"Don't think. Thinking isn't your friend."

"You're not my friend, either."

"Funny." I get my hand in her hair, my thumb under her jawline, tilting her head where I want it so I can really kiss her.

I think, fleetingly, *Don't,* and then I do.

Our tongues meet. Our teeth bump gently, and she makes this sound with her breath that would be a laugh if she weren't so busy sinking her fingers into my hair and kissing me back.

If we were friends, it would be disgusting. Spit and tongues, teeth and lips.

But we're not friends.

It's fucking amazing.

I kiss her hard. I control her, use her mouth, direct her head.

I kiss her soft. Tongue that sexy gap between her teeth. Pull back, let her take over, show me what she likes, how she wants it.

She does want it. Maybe only tonight, maybe for all the wrong reasons, I don't know. I'm not thinking about it. I'm kissing Caroline, which is better than thinking.

We fall into this kind of haze, nothing touching but our mouths, hands stroking over hair, necks, shoulders. I'm hard, but it feels like a faraway piece of information, with no urgency to it. This isn't sex. It's kissing. The forever kind of kissing, where there's no urgency and no time. Kissing like waves lapping. Perfect kissing.

"Still weird?"

"So weird."

She's smiling when she pulls my head back down.

Caroline's smiling, and we're kissing, and everything is perfect until light cuts across her face and she says, "Oh, shit."

Headlights in the driveway.

"My dad."

Her Romeo and Juliet balcony turns out to be the perfect height for dropping into the backyard.

My car turns out to be in just the right spot for getting out of Dodge without being spotted.

But the drive between Ankeny and Putnam is way too short for me to sort out what the fuck it is I thought I was doing and way too long to endure the memory of Caroline's mouth against mine.

The apartment looks alien when I get back. Small and cold and ugly. Empty.

I go into my room and shut the door. I flop onto my back on the bed, feeling tired and used up.

My phone rings. I almost decide not to answer it, because I know it's got to be Caroline.

I can't talk to her. I have to get my head on straight first, figure out what that *was*. Figure out why, when I snuck down her driveway at a crawl with my headlights off, half of me was hoping I wouldn't get caught and the other half was disappointed, ashamed, fucking *furious* with her for making me feel like her dirty little secret.

When I glance at the screen, though, it's not her. It's my mom.

"Hey, what's up?" I ask.

Frankie's voice. "Dad's here."

My heart jolts. I sit up so fast that my vision narrows. I have to put my palm to my forehead to steady myself. "Where are you?"

"At home. At Bo's. He's—he won't go *away*, West. You have to make him go away."

She sounds like she's about to cry, her voice high and reedy, right on the verge of losing it.

Frankie never cries.

"Okay, take a deep breath, kiddo. You're inside, right?"

"Yeah."

"And he's outside."

"Uh-huh. And I locked the front door, but he's pounding and pounding on it. I'm afraid it'll break!"

Now that she says it, I can hear the pounding. I'm thousands of miles away, and the sound scares the fuck out of me. I still remember him outside the trailer, yelling at my mom in the middle of the night.

"Michelle! Let me in! Let me into my own goddamn house, you worthless slut!"

He was drunk, Mom told me. He was angry. He didn't mean it. But I shouldn't worry, because she would never, ever let him hurt me.

It wasn't even forty-eight hours later that she let him into her bedroom.

He hurt me plenty.

"West?" Frankie's voice is wobbly. "I'm scared, West."

My hands are shaking from adrenaline. I push myself until my back is in contact with the wall. I need something hard to brace against. "I know, sweetheart, but that's a solid door, and he's not going to get through it. Where's Mom and Bo?"

"They went out."

Drinking, I guess she means. It's only ten in Oregon. They won't be back for hours.

"Did you lock the back?"

"Nuh-uh."

"All right. Can you go do that now for me?"

"Yeah, but West—"

"Just lock the back door. One thing at a time, Franks."

The pounding grows faint. She's breathing heavy, fast. Scared to death. I try to focus on the sound of my own inhalations and exhalations.

When she was little and she had a bad dream, I'd take her into my bed and let her curl up beside me, matching our breathing until we both fell back asleep.

"I got it," she says.

"Top and bottom?"

"Yeah."

"Okay, now the windows."

"What about the windows?" Frankie asks.

"Check them, just to be sure."

One thing about Bo—he's a paranoid guy. Name a conspiracy theory and he's a believer. Plus, he grows weed in a clearing in the woods behind the house and works as a guard at a prison that regularly releases men who hate his guts back into the stream of society. Bo's house is a flimsy one-story POS ranch, but he's got solid locks on the doors and bars on all the windows.

I murmur reassurances.

"It'll be all right, baby.

"He's not going to hurt you.

"He won't get inside."

But I don't know. I'm not there. It's taking everything I've got not to grill her for details.

"I checked them," she says finally. "They're locked."

"Good girl. Now get as far from the door as you can so you don't have to hear it."

"He's crying, West."

"Just tune him out."

"I feel bad for him."

"Don't. He made his bed. Go sit in the tub, okay?"

"Why?"

"You won't be able to hear in there. It'll be like you're in a bubble."

"That's dumb."

"Hey, who called who for help here?"

I imagine her smiling, even though I'm not. I've got nothing to smile about.

I hear the shower curtain rings sliding over the rod. Then her breathing is louder.

"You in there now, Franks?"

"Yeah."

She'll have her arms wrapped around her knees, just like Caroline up on the roof. I see Frankie in her nightgown, her dark hair hanging over her arms, down her back. Her skinny legs, mosquito-bitten, covered in scratches and sores. Bare toes dirty.

Summer Frankie. But it's November, and when I talked to Mom on Thanksgiving she said there was snow on the ground. I haven't seen my sister in three months.

"Should I call the police?" she asks.

I think of Bo's crop, the plants up to his chin. I know it's not like that now. He's harvested for the season. Last time I talked to him he told me he was letting the Indica buds mature, but pretty soon he's going to be heading down to California to sell.

He doesn't usually keep any of it in the house. He knows the law. He taught me it's essential to know what you can go down for, if you're gonna go down. Never carry enough to get charged with felony possession.

Still. What if he's not following his own rules? I don't want to be responsible for calling the cops out to Bo's house and getting him in deep shit. If he loses his job, goes to jail, then Mom probably loses hers, too, and we're all screwed.

Frankie's just a little girl, defenseless, huddled in the tub.

"What happened?" I ask.

"I was watching TV. Mom said to go to bed by nine, but there was this movie on and I knew she wasn't going to be back, so I watched it, and then I heard him knocking. It was so *loud*, West."

"Did you open the door for him?"

"No. Mom said not to."

"Mom knows he's back?"

"We ran into him in town. He's living at the trailer."

"He's not. Franks—tell me you're joking."

"Yeah, he is! He says it's his, and we got no right to keep him out of it."

"That fucker. What happened to Hailey?"

"She moved in with her boyfriend."

I put my cousin Hailey in that trailer on purpose. I paid up the lot rent for the whole school year. I wanted Mom and Frankie to have a place to go if things went to shit with Bo, but I never thought of this. I never thought I'd be paying for that low-life son of a bitch to have a home base to terrorize my little sister from.

I shove my heels into the blanket, pressing against the springs. I've got my head down, elbows between my knees, and I wish I was with Frankie. I wish I was there for her.

I wish I was where I belong.

"What's he saying?"

"What do you mean—now?"

"No, I mean, what did he say when he got there? What's he want?"

"He says, 'Come out, baby girl. Your daddy wants to see you.' And he called Mom a bitch, but then he said he didn't mean it, that she broke his heart and that crap."

"Don't go out there, Frankie."

She huffs. "I know, West. I'm not *stupid*."

"Did he sound mad?"

"He sounds drunk."

"Why do you say that?"

"He's all, like, slobbery."

"Jesus."

She's silent a moment. "I don't hear him pounding anymore."

She's more herself now. I think she feels better in the shower with the doors all locked. Plus, she likes knowing something I don't know. Being the one who tells me things for a change.

"I'm going to see if his truck is still there."

"Be careful."

"I will."

I hear the shower curtain again, and then her breath is quieter, more even, as she moves through the house to the curtain. "He's gone."

"Good. But keep everything locked up."

"I will."

We're quiet. Just breathing.

"Stay with me awhile," she says.

"As long as you need me."

It's hours before she's asleep. We watch a movie together, talk about nothing—her petty friendship dramas, the new hair bands she got, a singer she loves who's going to be in a movie she wants to go see next time Mom is off work.

I hang up, finally, to the sound of Frankie breathing, heavy and slow.

She's safe. She's fine.

But I feel like I'm falling, and there's nothing solid for me to grab hold of.

Caroline

I wonder, sometimes, why I couldn't see what was happening.

I mean, it was obvious to absolutely everyone. It should have been obvious to me. That night on the roof, how it ended, how my lips felt soft and changed for hours afterward, how I kept touching them, how I couldn't think of anything else. Not for days.

That ridiculous deal we struck.

My impatience for Bridget to go to her Tuesday/Thursday morning class so I could sit on my bed and wait for his knock. Two taps, always two. And I would go to the door and pull it open, and there he'd be. Back again, when I'd been afraid that this was the day he wouldn't show.

Back again to lie on my bed and put his mouth all over me, his hands all over me, to breathe hot and short against my neck while I pretended that my heart wasn't dark and rich, full to bursting with the sound and smell and taste of him.

I don't know why I didn't understand. I guess I was afraid.
I never knew there could be so much ecstasy in fear.

He's been avoiding me for a week. *More* than a week. Ten days.

At first I didn't realize. I was too wrapped up in my brain fog of what-the-heck-happened, and then I went out to brunch with my dad, who wanted to talk about My Future. Only now the conversation was more awkward than ever, because part of me was happily nodding along, thinking, *Yes! I'm going to get a great internship this summer,* but I also had to contend with the chorus of Internet Asshats saying, *Not with your cunt online!*

And, meanwhile, the new, completely West-centric part of my brain was busy squeeing, *I got stoned and made out with West on the roof—O-M-effing-G.*

All of which means that I missed a lot of cues, said weird things, and got frowned at by my dad, who didn't understand why I'd turned into such a freak.

I drove back to school on Sunday afternoon and sent West a text when I arrived. He wrote back, Cool.

Cool.

Who even says *cool*?

I don't know, but I told myself maybe it was good that he didn't seem too enthused to see me. We probably needed some time apart, a few days to sort through what that . . . that *episode* on the roof meant. And since I'd just had a serious talk with my dad, I'll admit, I figured I could use a little space from West, to think about what I was doing.

I watched a lot of TV and bad movies with Bridget. I went to Quinn's room with Krishna and split two six-packs and laughed at *Harold & Kumar.*

I didn't think about what I was doing.

I didn't go to the bakery, either. I would have on Tuesday night, but West usually texts to ask if he's going to see me, and he didn't. So I didn't. I slept instead. Straight through the night, like a normal person.

I did it again Wednesday night.

Thursday I sent him four texts, but he didn't answer them.

Friday I sent him a fifth. WTF, West?

He wrote back three hours later. Sorry. Busy.

Saturday, Sunday—nothing. I went to rugby practice and accomplished my first really great tackle. I hung out with Quinn and Bridget after. I asked Quinn if she'd seen West since break, and she said, "Yeah, why?"

No reason.

By Monday, though, all the stuff I didn't want to think about was making its existence known. I was starting to feel shitty. The Asshat Chorus was getting loud.

You knew when you invited him over, the men said. *You knew when you had him bring the weed. You wanted him to fuck you on top of that roof.*

Did I? I can't remember. I can't decide. Everything seems so murky.

That night, I broke down and told Bridget what had happened, and she got so pissed at West.

"He can't treat you like that! It's not right!"

She convinced me to call him. I left an angry voice mail. I texted again, demanding he get in touch with me. Bridget grabbed my phone out of my hand and called him a "fucker," which I then apologized for, but he still didn't text me back.

I couldn't sleep after that. Bridget snored softly in her bunk above me, and I pulled out my phone and wrote: I feel terrible about what happened on the roof.

I feel dirty.

I feel ashamed.

Why aren't you talking to me?

In the morning, I wished I could take those texts back. Overdramatic much, Caroline?

But they were sent, and that was that.

It's Tuesday after class when he texts me back. The phone chimes when I'm lying on my stomach, staring at my fingernails and trying to work up some enthusiasm for lunch.

Nothing dirty about it, West writes.

A whole sentence fragment. How about that?

Then why are you avoiding me?

I'm not. I'm busy.

That never stopped you before.

Sorry.

I wait to see if he's going to give me a better explanation, but he doesn't, and I'm so sick of it. I'm sick of him.

I'm sick of myself, too. How am I letting this happen? After what Nate did, I didn't let the misery get me down. I took action. Now one kiss from West and I'm reduced to this text-groveling?

Fuck that.

Come over to my room and talk to me, I text. Right now.

I have class.

I look at the clock. Not for an hour.

Nothing for a moment. I scroll back through the blue and green bubbles of our conversation, trying to recognize myself in these demands. Trying to recognize the West who rubbed my neck in the apartment, who put his hand on my thigh and asked me what he was going to do about me. The West who said, "This is completely my fault," right before he kissed me senseless.

Ok, he texts.

And then I wait.

Well, all right, I change into jeans and put my hair down and then I wait.

I don't know why we have a cliché about watched pots and boiling water. Clearly there should be one about waiting for a boy you kissed while stoned on a roof to come by and explain himself.

A watched West never shows up.

But, you know, less lame.

Finally, after an eternity, he knocks twice. I open the door, and I don't know. I don't know. His pale eyes are West's eyes, and his face is West's face, and how did I not see him for ten whole days? How did I forget what he does to me?

I want to sink into him, weave our fingers together, kiss his closed eyelids, and welcome him back.

I don't do it. I'm not completely crazy. But the wanting is there, oppressive as a hand pushing me under.

Kind of beautiful, too.

I look away, desperate to get ahold of myself. He's wearing a coat that seems gray at first, but when you get close up you see it's made of black and white stripes close together in a kind of chevron pattern. I can't imagine where somebody would get a coat like that, except maybe my grandpa's closet. It should be strange or ugly, but it's like everything West wears—he makes it seem sexy. Like old-man coats are the thing this year.

"Nice coat."

He gives me that blank look. As though I'm the woman at the dining hall who swipes his ID. Some anonymous person he barely knows. "Thanks."

I step back. He's never been in my room before. It's a little surprising how small he makes it, just by walking into the middle of it.

"You want me to take that?"

He shrugs off his old-man coat and drops it on the couch. Then drops himself down next to it.

One of his eyebrows is a little lifted, which I guess is supposed to mean, *Well, Caroline?*

I sit on the bed. I pull my pillow onto my lap, pluck at the pillowcase, which has Smurfs on it. They're supposed to be ironic Smurfs, but maybe that's like ironic whale pants. An impossibility.

I remind myself why I made West come over here. Because I kissed Nate and he put my naked pictures online. Then I kissed West and he stopped talking to me. I'm tired of this shit.

"What's the matter with you?"

"Nothing."

"You're mad at me."

"I'm not." He's fixated on this spot on the floor, like all the world's secrets are written there, pinhead-small.

"You're disgusted with me."

"No."

"You wish you'd never kissed me."

He meets my eyes for a fraction of a second. Looks at the secret spot again. "Yeah." But then he looks back at my face. "No."

"Which is it?"

"Both."

"What am I supposed to do with that, West?"

He sighs. His hair falls forward, covering his eyes, and he clasps his hands between his knees, that bracelet at his wrist spelling out the letters of his name, a symbol of everything he won't share with me. "I told you from the beginning how it's going to be with us."

"You said you wouldn't touch me."

He nods but doesn't look up.

"You did touch me, though."

"I fucking *know* that, Caroline."

"Don't get snippy with me. You don't have any right. We were both up there. We were both kissing."

"Yeah, but I'm the one who had to jump off the balcony, aren't I?"

"That's why you're pissed at me?"

"I'm not *pissed* at you!"

Finally he's looking at me, but it's not any help. His indrawn eyebrows and scowling mouth mean he's mad about something. If it's not me, then what? "You sure seem like it."

He stands up. Paces back and forth a few times. Glances at the bunked beds, Bridget's empty desk, my cluttered one. He picks up the framed picture of me with my dad and my sisters at my high school graduation and sets it back down.

He points to the picture. "You know what I said to him?"

"Who, my dad?"

He crosses his arms. "I said, 'So that's your daughter?' This was after I'd carried you up the stairs and laid you out on the bed. I stood right over you, staring at your tits, and I said, 'I'm right across the hall. Coed dorms, man. This is going to be *sweet*.'"

He uses his drug-dealer voice, his stoner voice—utterly fake if you know West but convincingly awful if you don't. I can hear exactly how it must have sounded to my dad. Like his baby girl was moving in across the hall from a date rapist, or at the very least a lecherous creep.

It's a miracle Dad ever left Putnam.

"Why?"

"So you'd have a good reason to keep the fuck away from me."

"Yeah, I get that, but I don't understand. And don't try to

feed me any garbage about me being rich and you being poor or you being too noble or whatever."

He makes a face. Walks away toward the window, turning his back on me. "I'm not noble."

"Then what are you?"

No answer. The silence spins out, Bridget's Putnam College clock ticking out the seconds—one, two, three, four, five, with no answer—until suddenly West spins around and says, "I'm fucking selfish, all right? I've got plans for the future, and you're not in them. You're not ever going to be in them, Caro, so it just makes more sense for me to keep away from you so I can focus on what's important."

What's important. Which is not me.

I gaze at Smurfette on my lap, her golden puff of hair and her stupid fuck-me shoes and her dress, and I want to punch her. I want to punch myself, right where it hurts, right where West's words lanced into the old burning pain beneath my lungs, that vital spot he keeps hitting me in without even caring enough to mean to.

He's not trying to hurt me. He's just selfish.

"Don't look like that," he says.

"I will look however I want." I enunciate every word, slowly and carefully, because I don't want him to know that he's hurt me.

I turn the pillow over. I trace the outline of Brainy Smurf's hat. I always identified with Brainy.

"Caro—"

"Maybe you should go."

He picks up his coat. He walks over to the door. I wait for it to open, wait for him to walk out, wait for the part of my life that doesn't have West in it to begin.

But he stands there, and then he leans into the door and

kicks it viciously, three times. He kicks the door so hard that I jump.

The hair on my arms lifts.

The violence is a bell ringing inside me. An announcement that something is beginning, something's been unleashed.

He turns back toward me. "I don't want to go. Okay? That's my problem, Caroline. I never want to go."

"What do you *want*, then?"

I'm almost in tears. I'm almost shouting, because I don't know. I've never known.

He walks over, drops his coat on Bridget's bunk, braces both hands on the metal framework of the bed. His feet are wide, straddling mine, blocking out the ceiling light. I can't see his face, but when he says, "I want to kiss you again," I can hear the softness of his mouth. I can almost feel it.

West nudges my foot with his, boxes in my knee. "I could feed you a line about how I want that because I think you need somebody to show you you're not broken, how you're beautiful and sexy and if you're dirty it's only in the good way, the way *everybody* is dirty. I could tell you that, and it would be true, but what's really true is that I'm selfish and I want you. I don't know how to stop wanting you. I'm just really fucking tired of trying."

He shifts slightly, letting the light loose around his head. It brightens his ear, shows me his eyes. They are hard and glittering and full of something I've seen there a hundred times but never knew what to call it.

Need. Greed.

This is what West looks like when he's greedy.

His greed is for me.

I can't think. Breathing is all I can handle. Breathing and watching him.

"I wanted you from the minute I saw you," he says. "I want you right now, and you can barely stand me. *I* can barely stand me, so I don't know why you put up with my shit, but even right now, when I hate myself and you're pissed at me, I still want to push you down on the bed and take off your clothes and get inside you. Get deep inside you, and then, deeper, until I'm so deep I don't even know what's me anymore and what's you."

He squats down and crosses his arms over my thighs and leans way in. Our noses are a millimeter apart. I want to turn my head away, except I don't. His mouth moves so close to mine that it feels like kissing when he says, "That's what I want, Caroline. That's what I never told you. I see your face when I close my eyes. Over break, when you called? I jerked off to the sound of your voice *while you were on the phone.* I'm selfish and no good for you, I've got nothing to give you and no room for you in my life, and I want you anyway."

I'm still. So still, because I need to let his words sink in.

Not so I can figure them out. It's going to take me a long time to figure them out, and right now I don't care. I just need to feel what he said all the way through me, because his greed—his *need*—is all around me, touching my skin, and my heart wants to gather it in.

Deep and then deeper, just like he said.

So I do that while he waits. I pack his words around my heart, knowing I shouldn't, because they're not the right words. It's dangerous to want West so much that I'll take any crumb he gives me—any profane, broken piece of him—and turn it into a love letter.

It's desperate and damaged, stupid and wrong.

I don't care. I don't care.

"West?" I whisper.

"Yeah."

Our lips are touching, dry brushes of his mouth over mine when he speaks and then after—I guess after, which means this is a kiss, even though I haven't admitted I'm open to more kissing.

"You're a horrible friend."

"We're not friends."

His hands. His hands on my face again, cupping my jaw, framing my ear, fingers slipping into my hair.

"You would be the worst boyfriend in the entire history of boyfriends."

He drops, knees on the floor now, one arm at my hips pulling me closer so I'm practically falling off the edge of the bed, except he's there to catch me. His mouth is open. His tongue is hot. Licking me. Asking me to let him in. "Not gonna be your boyfriend."

"Then what. What."

It's not a question. I'm not capable of concentrating enough to ask him a question, because I'm falling into him, finding a way around his elbows and his roving hands to get him closer, tighter. My lips yield to his tongue. I'm pulsing and hot, slick and floating, lost and stupid, and it's better than anything.

He gets a knee between my legs, drags me up his thigh with both hands on my butt. He kisses me hard, hard enough that it hurts, but I don't care, because all I want is him closer. I don't care until he pulls my head back and nips at my neck and I look up at the ceiling, where the light is so bright it hurts my eyes. I close them, dizzy, and the brightness flashes like a strobe.

Like a camera.

This is nuts.

This is reckless.

"West," I say.

"Caroline," he mutters.

"Stop."

He stops.

When he lifts his head, his eyes are sex-drugged and sleepy. His lips are red, his skin flushed behind the stubble on his chin, and I feel the tingling raw spot on my neck where he scraped against me. I want him to do that everywhere on my body—leave marks behind, make me tingle and ache and then *fix* it—and I don't recognize this version of myself. I don't know who I am when I'm like this.

"I need . . ."

He braces his hands on my shoulders, setting me apart from him. But keeping me there, one arm's length away. "What do you need?"

"Rules. Boundaries. I need some idea . . . what this is."

He looks down toward the floor, but his gaze gets caught on my chest. I look down, too, and watch the sly grin spread over his face as he stares at my nipples poking through my shirt.

"Quit that."

"You're into me," he says.

"Shut up."

"You're *so* into me. I bet you're wet right now."

"I bet you're hard."

"It's like Thor's mighty hammer in my pants." He says it with a smirk.

"Didn't the hammer have a name?"

West says something that sounds like *Mole-near*.

"Spell it."

"*M-j-o-l-n-i-r.*"

"Jesus. Why do you know that?"

"A better question might be why we're talking about it."

"Because guys love talking about how big and hard their hammers are?"

"And what they want to do with them. Don't forget."

I ease out from under his hands and sit up on the bed again. "Yeah. That part."

West sits next to me, but he gives me some room to think.

So I think. About his hand on his hammer. "You really did that when we were on the phone?"

He smiles, but he looks kind of sheepish. Not an expression I see on West very often.

"I mean, really-really? You're not just saying that because you're trying to flatter me?"

"If I wanted to flatter you, I'd tell you that shirt looks pretty on you. Or that I like your eyes. Something that's, you know, actually *nice*."

I glance down at my knees and smile.

I think about what I want and what I need, what I can take and what I can't do without.

Maybe I'm traumatized. Maybe I'm being irrational. I don't know.

I want West, though. Any version of West I can have, any way I can have him.

And it isn't as though, if he were willing to give me everything, I could even take it. As my dad so recently reminded me, there's my future to think of. There's my reputation, which I can't really put to the test by dating the campus drug dealer.

I don't want to date West. I want him to show me what deeper feels like.

Deep and then deeper. All the way down.

"All right," I tell him. "Here's what we're going to do."

_____

Twice a week. Tuesdays and Thursdays, ten o'clock to ten-fifty, while Bridget's in class and West is in between and I've got nothing until lunch.

We're not going to date, and we're not going to tell.

Those are our rules.

I spend the time before West shows up on Thursday zoning out. Like, I keep thinking I have it together, but then my brain will wander off like a wayward child, and I'm helpless to prevent it. Bridget keeps asking me what happened with West, but I can't say. He and I made a deal. And, anyway, what would I tell her? That I decided to be West's friend with benefits? His fuck buddy? That we're going to do a Get Caroline Back in the Saddle training program twice a week?

I'm smart enough to know that to anyone else this would sound like an epically bad idea. Bridget would not approve. My father would have a stroke. The Internet Asshats, predictably, think I'm a sloppy cunt who needs a good dicking, or whatever.

I'm getting kind of bored with the Internet Asshats.

I know what good girls do, and this is not it.

But I put it on my calendar, anyway, fifty minutes twice a week that I round up to an hour and shade in orange because orange feels like his color. WEST, I type.

Bridget and I string Christmas lights around the windows of the dorm room, and I go out to Walmart and buy an extra string to wrap around the posts of the bed and along the edges. When Bridget isn't home, I turn off the overhead bulb and get under my blanket. The lights glow green and red, blue and yellow and orange.

I close my eyes, skim my fingers over my skin, thinking of West.

I have never been so excited.

He shows up right after his class. Knocks twice, then just opens the door and lets himself in. He's got that coat again, and a textbook and notebook under one arm. He won't quite meet my eyes.

"I was thinking," he says, with no warm-up.

Uh-oh.

"I don't want this to . . . hold you up. So I think we should agree, we're only doing this until—until you feel ready. For something normal."

"Like . . . what?"

"Scott. You need to promise me, when you're ready to go out with Scott, or some other guy like him—some guy who wants to take you to dinner and, like, meet your dad and all that—you'll tell me. And we'll quit."

With West in my room, I find it hard to remember what Scott looks like or why I would ever want anything more than I want this. But I recognize that he's trying to do the right thing. Some version of the right thing.

I kind of love that about him. He says he's not noble, but he's got his own code, and he needs the boundaries, the rules, just as much as I do.

We're going to do this, but first we'll box it in and wall it off and find a way to make it acceptable. To make it *fit*.

"Ooookay," I tell him.

That out of the way, he unlaces his boots and leaves them by the door. I've never seen him with his boots off before. His socks are just ordinary gray socks, and there is no reason they should make me hum with anticipation. No reason at all.

He drops his stuff on my desk, hangs his coat on my chair.

He pulls his phone out and sets it on the edge of my desk right by the bed, next to my pillow.

I'm going to have my head on that pillow. West is going to kiss me, and then he's going to look past me to the desk and see how many minutes we have left.

Fifty minutes seemed like a reasonable amount of time before. Not too long, not too short. Now it seems like an eternity. All I've done is kiss him, but no one kisses for fifty minutes.

This is insane.

I glance at West for reassurance, but he isn't helping. His eyes have found the same magic spot on my floor he stared at last time he was here.

Me, I think. *Look at me.*

He doesn't. So I walk to where he's trained his gaze, find the spot, and step on it.

I step on it because, insane or not, I prepared for this hour. Plugged in the Christmas lights. Put on my favorite dark jeans, a white shirt that's a little tighter than I'm comfortable with outside the room, a pretty bra. I brushed my hair out, left it down.

I didn't put shoes on, though. My feet are bare, toenails painted pink, and I want West to see my feet and think about the rest of me naked. I want him to own up to his desire again, although, seriously, how many times does he have to say it before I'll believe it? The way he grabbed me two days ago, dragged me up his thigh . . . I get hot flashes just thinking about it.

I get another one now, watching West's eyes travel up from the floor spot that I've obliterated, over my legs, lingering at my hips, my breasts, my lips. That look is back in his eyes, covetous.

He *wants* to touch me.

It's just that neither of us seems to know how.

You would think we were both virgins, rather than an Internet naked-picture sensation and . . . whatever West is. Not a virgin. I'm pretty sure.

Ninety percent sure.

He sits down on the mattress. "Come here."

I do.

I sit right next to him, thigh touching thigh, and I want to look at his face.

I do look. For fifty minutes, I'm allowed to look. I'm not sure what else I'm allowed to do, but looking is okay.

His face is beautiful. The Christmas lights cast a glow over his skin, blue across his cheekbone, red behind his ear. His eyes, slightly narrowed, seem to glow. The word I think of is *avid*. Like whatever I'm about to do, he's going to observe it, lean into it, take it and run with it.

I like being the thing he's avid for, because that same feeling is inside my skin. The strain of not touching him, a low hum that's always there, always something I'm pushing down, ignoring.

Only now I don't have to.

As soon as I think it, my fingertips drift up to touch his neck. I turn my hand over and feel the rasp of his stubble against the backs of my fingers, the bumpy texture that smooths out lower down, until I find a spot where his skin is like hot satin.

"Can I do this?"

What I'm really asking is, *How greedy can I be? How much will you give me?*

He smiles, a little huff of breath that isn't a laugh or a judgment, just a pleased noise. "Yeah."

He draws a line across my chest, above the swell of my breasts. "Above here."

I inhale and feel the line rise. The wake of his touch.

He strokes down my arm to my wrist. "And here." He rubs his thumb over my wristbone.

"There?"

"That's where I'll touch you."

"That's it?"

He looks hard and long at my body. Every part of me that was sleeping comes awake and puts out its arms and says, *Come in, come in, come in.*

He taps my knee. "From here down."

I hide my eyes against his shoulder, wanting to grumble. He's going to skip all the best parts. "Is there a weird, kinky reason for this that I'm not understanding?"

He puts his hand in my hair and lifts my face so I have to look at him. "It's just . . . what I want."

His eyes are cautious, saying this. As if telling me what he wants is the scariest thing he's done since he opened the door. It makes me certain that he hasn't always been able to draw lines, hasn't always set the terms.

It makes me wonder who he's been with before, and how.

"Do you want me to do the same thing?" I drag my finger across his chest. "Above here." Down his arm to his wrist, catching on his bracelet. "All along here." A lingering tap north of his knee. "From here down?"

"You could." His thigh shifts under my fingers, which have given up tapping in favor of fanning out over the muscle they've found. I want to stroke upward, filling the full width of my palm with soft denim and firm warmth until I reach the crease of his hip and have to decide where to go. Map him with my hands. "Or you could just go with the flow and trust me."

I try to think of something smart to say, or something funny. But those words—*trust me*—crumple up my confidence and toss it away.

I think, all in a rush, of the reasons I can't trust. Bad breath and body smells, stuck zippers, biting. The words on the birth-control chart that hangs on the inside door of the bathroom stalls that I've meant to look up but never gotten around to. Frottage. Rimming. I don't know what they mean, not exactly. I don't know how many girls West has had sex with, and it seems vitally necessary that I find out so I can compare myself to them unfavorably.

There are condoms in my desk drawer, but they could be the wrong size.

Trust me, he says, and I can't shut off my brain. Last time we kissed, I was stoned, so it was different. This time I have no defense, no way to hide from how close his eyes are, how much he sees.

It was like this with Nate. Over time I got better about it, but mental flailing was pretty much my constant make-out companion until I figured out that it worked better if I had a few drinks first. Then I tried to plan as many of our sexual encounters as possible for parties.

I'm not sure I've ever been kissed at ten in the morning, in the daylight.

I don't trust it. I don't trust *myself*.

"We should have some music," I blurt.

West sighs.

Then he shoves me.

I'm on my back with West above me, those eyes like smoke, that smart-ass mouth so sure of itself. "Trust me," he says again, and kisses me.

Then it's okay.

Way better than okay.

Kissing West is nothing like kissing Nate. His mouth is warm and sure of itself, and it says, *Shut up, Caro. Close your eyes. Stop thinking.*

Feel.

I do. I can't not. With West's mouth on mine, feeling is the only thing I'm capable of.

We kiss. Time passes, and we kiss.

I wish I had words, if only so I could press them into memory. This hot, wet slide of tongue against tongue, soft lips and angled mouths, fitting and refitting. This beautiful pulse, this damp haze, this foggy, hot, yearning ache.

There are more ways to kiss than anyone ever told me, and I want them all.

I get them. I get West, his mouth, his weight, his smell.

We kiss.

The lines we've drawn on our bodies aren't important. They're just pencil marks we need to put around this thing that's so big, it could get scary if we let it.

Kissing West is my hands in his hair, on his neck, spanning his shoulders. It's clutching his back when he plunges his tongue into my mouth, finding his waist, sneaking under his shirt to steal the heat and smoothness of his skin.

It's his body above me, his chest on me, a heavy crush I can't get enough of because he's always been so far away and now he's *here*. His palm cradling my head, his fingers curled around my shirt at the shoulder, fisted in a tight grip because they want to wander and he won't let them.

It's his pale eyes, a rim of bluish color around huge dark pupils, his eyelashes long and his eyelids sleepy.

It's the sighing weight of his forehead on mine when he has to breathe.

Lazy heat. Connection. Safety and quiet in a place where I've been alone and afraid and the voices in my head have been loud for weeks now. Months. He casts a spell on me, throws me into a gorgeous daze where I could kiss him forever and be perfectly content.

We have fifty minutes.

The thought is fingers snapping in my consciousness. Fifty minutes. How many are left? My lips feel full, bruised, tender and slick. I can't remember ever kissing this much. Surely I must have, with Nate, in the early months we were dating? But when I think that far back, I mostly remember arguments. We would kiss, and then he would want more and I'd stop him, and he would get distant, huffy, pained.

You don't know what it's like, Caroline.

West is carrying his weight on one elbow, his legs and hips off to the side. I don't know if he's hard. I haven't cared, haven't thought. I've been too busy kissing, and I don't know what it's like.

Cocktease, the Internet Asshats say, but this time they're right. I just forgot. I forgot about him.

I break the kiss so I can crane my head around and look at the time on the phone. Ten minutes left. We've been kissing for thirty-five, forty minutes. But ten minutes should be long enough, if we need to do something different. Finish West off.

The thought is spiky, uncomfortable.

I ask him, "Are you . . . ?"

"Mmm."

He's mouthing my neck. Paying zero attention to my attempt to question him.

I curl my fingers around the thick leather of his belt. Bring them to the buckle, heavy and threatening.

I pull the leather from the loop.

West's hand covers mine. "What are you doing?"

"If you're . . . you have class, so . . ."

West rolls away and sits up. He has to duck his head because of the bunked beds. "I have class?"

"I don't want you to . . ." I can't say. "Forget it."

He grabs my chin and turns my head and makes me look at him. He won't let me look away. It's freaking annoying, and I hate it.

"Trust me," he says. "I need this to be—need us to do this right. With you talking to me, telling me what you like, nobody trying to just guess or do stuff they don't necessarily want to. I *need* it."

I can't say no to that. To anything he needs. As much as I hate to, I have to tell him.

"I thought you were maybe uncomfortable. From so much . . . from kissing me, maybe that was making you . . . hard, and if we only had a few minutes left before class, I'd better . . . finish it."

He sits there, watching me with his eyebrows drawn in. I can't tell what he's thinking—if he's angry or frustrated, confused, or maybe wishing he were somewhere else. With some girl who isn't such a mixed-up freak.

Then he leans toward me, catches me by the waist, and pulls me into his lap.

He kisses my hair, right by my ear. "He really did a number on you, huh?"

I think about saying, *Who?* or *No,* but I'm trembling, and my mouth tastes like battery acid, so, yeah.

Yeah. I guess he did.

"I have to go in a minute," West says quietly. "I don't want to. But I have to."

"I know."

"I like kissing you, Caro." He puts his lips to my neck. His arm is wrapped around my back, his hand heavy at my hip. The weight of it—perfect. "You like kissing me?"

"Yes."

"Good."

His mouth moves down to my shoulder, to the sliver of

exposed skin at the neckline of my shirt. To the hollow behind my ear, where his breath makes me shiver. He finds my
mouth, and then our lips meet again, hot and wet and perfect, perfect.

"You like that?" His voice is a growl, a low thrum, explicit
as fingers between my legs.

"*Yes.*"

"That's it, then. You like it. I like it. Beginning, middle,
end. There's no finish. This is the whole thing, right now."

He's kissing me again, so I can't think about whether or
not what he said is true. I just wrap my arms around his
neck, rake through his hair, outline his ear with my fingertip,
and kiss him back. Under the Christmas lights, in our cave.
Kisses chasing kisses, hands and mouths.

Everything. Everything.

And then we run out of time. It takes me a second to figure out that the beeping I hear is his phone.

"You set an alarm?"

"Knew I'd never stop otherwise."

Reluctantly, he pushes me off his lap and reaches for the
phone, silencing it. Then he's standing, adjusting his belt,
lacing up his boots.

When he lifts his head, his eyes are sleepy and sexy, his lips
stained, color high in his cheeks. Looking at him does something crazy to me, a wet hot clench between my legs, heat
spreading outward, upward. I wish I'd gotten his shirt unbuttoned while I had the chance. Seen more of him. Pressed up
against his bare skin.

Next time.

God, I hope there's a next time.

"You coming to the bakery tonight?" he asks.

"Yeah."

"Cool. I'll be back Tuesday. If you want me back."

"Yeah. I do."

He retrieves his jacket from the couch and puts it on. When his hand is on the doorknob, he says, "For the record, Caro?"

"Yeah?"

"Hard as a fucking rock."

He slips out the door, and I'm still smiling at it like an idiot when Bridget comes back from class.

Tuesday.

Fifty minutes.

Outside, the sky is dark. It's snowing, blowing icy slush sideways, gray and miserable. I've put on Bing Crosby just to make West shake his head and pretend to lament my terrible taste in music.

His hair is cold and damp, his nose freezing when he presses it against mine, but his lips are warm. His smile is warmer. We have this dim room, this bed surrounded by color, our feet intertwined, his body pushing down on me.

We have slow, deep kisses that keep getting deeper.

I ruck up his shirt and follow the gully of his spine up. The muscles of his shoulders flex under my hands. I scoot down. My shirt hikes up. We kiss and kiss, and I find a way to wiggle until my bare stomach is touching his.

Do you feel this? Your skin and mine?

Because I feel it everywhere.

I want it. I want you.

I skate my palms up his sides. Over his shoulders, into the inner sleeves of his shirt until I run out of room over his hard biceps. His hips move into my thigh, belt buckle nipping at the top of my thigh, and I press my fingernails into his skin and scoot down another fraction, seeking better alignment.

Seeking pressure between my legs.

I want the knowledge of what I do to him, the heat of what we do to each other.

When I get there, he grunts and bites my lip. His eyes are slits, his nostrils flare as he breathes in deep, fast. "Caroline."

I lift into the ridge of heat in his jeans, loving that I can do this to him. Loving the pressure, the weight, the way his kiss gets darker and more desperate and we move together, synchronized.

It's not sex. It's better than sex.

It's West.

Thursday. I wore this shirt—this joke of a shirt. It's supposed to fall off at the shoulder. It's supposed to be layered over another shirt, but I didn't tell him that, and as soon as we lie down to start kissing, it comes off my shoulder and exposes my bra strap and a little bit of my bra.

Red lace.

Come on, West. Be tempted.

Everything is faster this time. His first kiss is hungry, and I'm glad because I've missed him, I've missed this, I've thought of nothing else for two days. His hands have a desperation in them, sliding up and down, into my hair, back to my arms. Starving.

It's not enough anymore. These limits he drew on my body, the pencil marks faint. I want more. We both want more.

I don't have to be sneaky in order to get him between my legs. I tug at his belt, and he's over me, as hard and hot as I remember him but better. So much better. The way he rears up suddenly to look at me. His eyes in this light, keeping no secrets. My stomach is showing, one bra cup half out, and his hands tremble on my wrists as he pulls them overhead and crosses them on the pillow.

I've never felt so desirable. It's a drug in my veins, a giddy ecstasy that makes me grin at him with well-kissed lips. Makes me powerful.

Do something, I order him with my eyes and the small, restless movements of my hips. *Do something, or I will.*

He sinks down, hair falling in his face, and kisses me again. He thrusts—really thrusts—and my head tilts back. My whole spine arches up, moving into him. I'm wet, and I want his fingers. I want his whole hand inside my jeans, fumbling into my panties. His mouth on my breasts. I want us to round all the bases, one after another, in the next half an hour.

"Please," I say.

West breathes against my ear. Licks my earlobe. Bites me. "That is not a shirt."

I grin at the bunked bed above me. "Please."

He sits up again. "Take it off."

Gladly. Gladly I do, and then his hands are just . . . everywhere.

Everywhere. More than once.

My bra hooks in the front. I show him, helpfully, and then the bra is gone and he's kissing me again, his shark-bit T-shirt so annoying, his warm palm on my breast. Long fingers. Gorgeous, capable, intelligent hands. He knows exactly what to do. *Exactly.*

"Take this off," I say, tugging at his hem, so he does, throws the shirt on the floor, comes back down on top of me, skin-to-skin, naked from the waist up—*oh my God, this is the best thing that has ever happened to anyone in the history of the universe.* I slide my hands all over his back. He kisses a trail from my mouth to my jaw, down my neck.

He licks my nipple, and I die. I just die.

We are hands and arms, colored light on smooth skin, heat and sweat in the sweltering dorm room. We are kissing mouths, thrusting hips, building tension between my legs.

"Here, this can't feel good," he says, and yanks open his belt, pulls it out of the loops, throws it on the floor. He is a cowboy, his belt a whip. It is the sexiest four seconds of action I have ever witnessed.

I miss the pinch of his buckle into my stomach, but not for long. Not for long, because he touches my breasts. He watches me. He figures out what I like, plucks at that tension with his fingers, presses against my clit just right until I'm openmouthed, gasping, embarrassingly wet. It sneaks up on me, unexpected, because I've come before with a guy but never from friction, never through my jeans. Never so easy. I don't recognize this effortless skip from good to great to unbearably amazing, but West must, because he figures out the angles and pushes himself into me in just the right spot, so hard, so perfect, until I'm coming apart against his hardness and his hands and his mouth, oh, God, his mouth.

When the alarm goes off, I'm still catching my breath, and he's smiling like I gave him a prize.

I think maybe he gave me one. Not the orgasm, either—although the orgasm was great.

The knowledge that it can be so *easy*.

He does it again before he leaves, with his thigh between my legs and his mouth on my breasts. He'll be late for class, I think, but I'm limp and my upper lip is sweating, and he licks right over it when he kisses me goodbye.

He pulls his boots back on and rakes his eyes over me, half naked, half dead from pleasure.

I've never felt so beautiful.

It's the shortest fifty minutes of my life.

The end of the semester arrives, and I'm not ready for it. Back in September, it seemed like an impossible goal—to get through the days, to keep my head up, to keep going. I'm not sure when it stopped being impossible, but I know that the difference has everything to do with West.

It's finals week, which means no class. No schedule, except for a few in-class exams I have to show up for.

No Tuesday and Thursday morning time with West.

Worse, I won't see him for an entire month. He's flying home to Oregon. Dad is taking Janelle and her fiancé and me to St. Maarten for Christmas, and then I'll be hanging around home, waiting for next semester to start. Last year, I spent most of Christmas break with Nate. Now it's like this yawning void up ahead—nothing to look forward to, and a lot to cringe away from.

Even though we don't have class, West has work, of course, so I see him at the bakery, the library, and his apartment. Bridget and I have been hanging out with Krishna and Quinn a lot, and with West, too, when he's around. The five of us are getting to be kind of a unit.

I hadn't realized how much I missed being part of a group of friends until I had one again. There's an unpredictability to it, a potential for fun—or at least for conversation, someone to talk to, something interesting to hear about. When it was just Bridget and me, I would see her in all the same places. We had fun, but I think I was sort of a fortress after August, and we were behind the walls.

Now when I walk across campus, I run into Quinn on the quad. She's trying to talk me into buying rugby shoes. She's planning a big party for right after break, and she wants me to help her with organizing. Quinn's been running the rugby club single-handed since the end of last year. I think she wants to recruit me to the dark side.

I walk out of Latin and see Krishna, and he and I head in the same direction, talking about nothing. TV. What his mom sent him in the mail. What he's up to for Christmas.

The pictures are still out there, but they're no longer everything I see when I look around. The first report I got from the service I hired is only a page long, miserly about details. I shrug it off, just happy to have it be someone else's responsibility.

West fills a lot of the space in my head where the pictures used to be. He crowds out my concentration when I'm trying to review my notes at the library. He pushes his cart past, earbuds in, eyebrows lifted in an understated hello.

I get one look at that smirk and I'm a goner, back in my bed, under the lights. Under him.

I can't concentrate for an hour.

During our usual Tuesday meeting time, I keep glancing at my bed, surprised by how much I miss him. The next night we hang out at the bakery, and I want to touch him, but Krishna's there, and I'm not allowed, anyway. Not at the bakery. Not in the library. Not where anyone could see.

I sit in my nook on the floor, flipping through my Latin flash cards, and when I look up he's staring at me from across the table.

He's got flour on the bridge of his nose. Dusted over his forearms.

He's got his jeans and boots on, and he's measuring ingredients, scraping bowls, emptying fifty-pound bags of flour into the wheeled bin. I can't stop thinking about this scene I saw in a movie once, where the man and the woman had sex with her sitting at the edge of a table and all their clothes still on, just shoved down out of the way.

It certainly wouldn't be sanitary, but I have a feeling I wouldn't care.

"What are you up to after this?" West asks.

It's toward the end of the shift. Krishna has left. He's done with his finals already, heading home to Chicago for the holiday.

"I'm going to grab a nap, and then I have my English paper to write still."

"That's your last thing, right?"

"Yeah. It's due Friday."

"You gonna be able to sleep?"

He means because Bridget's family will be here to pick her up first thing in the morning. Part of her family—her dad and his new wife, plus some stepkids. The room will be a zoo.

"I hope so."

"You could crash on our couch," he says. "Write it over at our place."

"Yeah?"

"Sure. Why not?"

West does the dishes, and I get drowsy. I fall asleep with my head against the leg of the sink, waking once when someone shows up to buy an eighth off West and again later when he drops a pan with a loud clatter.

On the walk to his apartment, I feel drunk. I fall asleep on the couch while he's taking a shower, barely coming awake when he settles a blanket on me, kisses my temple, and says, "Sleep tight."

I wake up shivering.

The blanket is a puddle on the floor, the apartment cold. Outside, the snow is blowing, nasty. I think of Krishna in his car and hope he's okay. But it feels like late morning—he's probably already home by now.

I reach for the blanket, wrap it around my shoulders, stand up.

I find myself on the threshold of West's bedroom, still drowsy, looking in at him.

He's a lump beneath a kids' comforter, dark blue with rocket ships and planets on it. I asked once if he got it at a yard sale, and he gave me an odd look. "Brought it from home," he said, as though that's what we all did. Picked up the comforters off our childhood beds and carried them with us to college.

Everyone else I know works so hard to separate childhood from college, to prove we're grown up and those years are far in the past. Not West.

It's not because he's still a child. I wonder if it's because he never was.

I can't imagine West's childhood. I can't imagine anything about his life away from here.

There's nothing much in the room. No decorations. No Christmas lights. No sign that he's loved or that he loves anything.

It's not inviting, but it's Thursday morning. Nine o'clock, according to the display on his alarm clock. I'm barefoot, wrapped in a blue fleece blanket from the couch, and I feel invited.

He invited me.

I walk to his bed and take off my jeans.

I flip back the covers. I climb in behind him.

I put my arm over him, nestling it up beside his arm. Tuck my knees behind his. He's not wearing pants; his leg hair is ticklish on my thighs, and I wonder briefly if I should be doing this. If he'll be angry with me for taking a liberty.

But West is the one who made it so we'd be alone, and here we are, on the verge of not being able to see each other for a month.

Mostly I do it because right next to West is where I want to be.

With my head on his pillow, I can feel him breathing, slow and steady. He's warm and heavy, safe and so dangerously essential.

I close my eyes. He smells like bread and soap.

I drift.

When I wake up, we've flipped positions. He's spooned behind me, and the energy is different.

He's awake.

All over.

"Caroline." His voice is low and husky, with an edge to it I've never heard.

"Mmm?"

"You're in my bed."

"Yeah. You looked cozy."

"It's ten o'clock. Thursday."

I roll to my back. He rolls right on top of me, lifting my arm above my head. Our eyes meet, and then our lips.

The kiss is sleepy, lazy, but insistent. *You're in my bed*.

This is how I get kissed if I'm in his bed.

My shirt is just a T-shirt. My bra is boring and white. I could probably use a shower. I have morning breath.

He kisses me like I'm delicious.

He peels off the layers of my clothing as though he's going to find some fabulous treasure underneath, then strokes his hands over my naked body as if to say, *This. This is it. You.*

His shirt comes off. He's gorgeous—tan and flawless,

muscular and lean. I lick his biceps. Bite his shoulder. He tastes clean and alive, like everything I want.

In minutes we're down to his boxer briefs and my panties, and I'm writhing. Actually writhing. It isn't a thing I knew I was capable of doing, but with West it isn't even a choice. I have to. Our tongues are at war, my hands on his ass, tugging him closer, closer, always closer.

I'm so wet. Wet through my underwear, I'm sure of it, and the tip of his erection is probing, pushing my panties a few centimeters inside me with the weight of his body and his slow, rolling thrusts. Two thin layers of fabric between us, moist, slippery, insubstantial. Our hips come together in time with our mouths, our tongues, our straining need.

I need him. I need him. I can't think about anything else. My hands find the waistband of his briefs and slip inside to find the clench of his muscles under my palms.

"Jesus," he says, with his face against my neck. "Don't."

I take my hands away, discouraged. West looks at me. Kisses the wrinkle between my eyebrows, the tip of my nose, my chin, my mouth. "Come on, I didn't mean it like that. You're killing me, that's all."

"I want to be killing you."

I want you inside me. Deep. Deeper.
Please.

The words are at the back of my tongue, piled up, and I can't make myself say them. I can't ask.

"I want to make you come," he says.

That would also be excellent.

He strokes his hand up my leg, and I make this sound that's like a squeak. I guess he likes it, because he kisses me hard. His palm starts over again, sliding from my neck to the cap of my shoulder. It slips over my collarbone to cup my breast and drag slowly over my nipple and then down, down to my waist, to my navel, to the space between our bellies. "I need to touch you."

"Please."

He shifts to the side, leaves his thigh slung over mine, his elbow by my arm, his breath at my ear as he caresses my breasts with the back of his hand. Brushes back and forth over my nipples. Traces circles, random patterns, until I'm ready to hurt him because the anticipation is killing me, and I say, "West, please, *please*," and he relents. He flattens his hand and slides it slowly—agonizingly slowly—down my stomach. Over my navel. Right to the margin of my panties, which are ridiculous red-and-white-striped cotton with holly berries on them and this cartoon Santa, the least sexy panties I own.

I didn't know I'd be here, that this would happen. I had no idea what this morning would bring. This cautious lifting up of the elastic. This wicked, knowing, dirty sneak underneath.

I never could have imagined the feeling of West's hand cupping me. His fingers parting me, tracing the secret shapes of my body, the sound of his voice saying, "Fucking hell, Caro," like a prayer and a compliment.

He presses his finger inside me. Then another. When he tries three, I whimper, and he finds my clit with his thumb. I arch off the bed, deliciously shocked.

There is a sense in which I've done this before, all of it, but it feels brand-new and astonishingly different. It feels so good that it hurts, it aches, and I hate it, but not nearly as much as I love it.

"You like that," he says.

I mewl. Like a cat. And his grin is so smug, I reach up to give him a playful smack, but he changes the angle of his fingers inside me and I end up yanking him closer by the hair, kissing him so hard that our teeth knock together and I bite my tongue. I don't care. Not with West's thumb circling my clit, over and over, just a little too hard, which turns out to be how I like it.

Not with his fingers moving in and out of my body, a steady rhythm that fractures me into a thousand desperate, craving pieces.

"That's my girl," he says, when I have to turn my face away because I can't concentrate on kissing, can't breathe, can't do anything but buck against his hand, senseless as an animal. "Just like that."

When I come, it's terrible. This low gathering tension winds and winds until I think I'll die, and then I *do* die, I do, and it feels so amazing that it *hurts*. West stays with me right through it, watches me, eases me down, and now I can feel the rush of it, the part that's all pleasure in one big push, a wave, a wake, a wave, until it's grabbed me everywhere, pulled me in and let me go.

I float.

"Oh my God," I whisper, when I can speak again. My voice is faint. Sweat has gathered at my elbows, in my armpits, on my temples. The wetness between my legs has spread down my thighs, and I'm conscious of the smell of sex.

Nate called it "that fish smell" once. He joked about it.

Fuck you, Nate, I think faintly, but there's no rancor in it. I honestly don't care.

I feel so good.

It wasn't like this with Nate. I came, but it was a goal that had to be reached. An obstacle to be laboriously climbed toward so that we could move on to the next thing, and then the next. It was never this . . . this *bliss,* this shared thing West and I make between us, a natural outcome of our being together rather than the product of our dogged efforts.

"Hey, where'd you go?"

West is propped on one elbow beside me, his hand flat on my stomach, resting. Poor hand, it must be exhausted. I give it a pat, then link our fingers together. He smiles and lets his elbow slide, settling onto the mattress. I'm too tired to do anything but look at him. His face, his chest, his stomach, his briefs, dark gray with their intriguing bulge and an even more intriguing wet spot.

I've never touched him there. I've been afraid to, always afraid that there are rules and I don't know them. Like if I wait long enough, someone will give me a book called *How To Touch West's Penis,* and I can study it until I'm confident. An expert.

Enough of that. In this bed, this cocoon, I'm allowed to reach out for him. To enjoy the sharpness of his inhale, his lowering eyelids, his lip caught between his teeth.

I'm allowed to trip my fingers down his happy trail, shimmy closer so we're belly to belly, my breasts pressing into his chest, my hand flat, slipping inside his underwear and investigating what I find.

Hard. Hot. Big—oh my gosh.

"You are like a *furnace*," I say, and he laughs.

I think it's supposed to be a laugh. He sounds like he hurts. I want to make it better.

I tighten my hand and stroke experimentally, watching his face to see if it's okay. If *I'm* okay, doing this. It's not my first go-round on this rodeo, but I don't want to be inept. I want to give him what he gave me.

When I stroke again, his mouth opens, his head falling back.

Okay, then. That seems to work, so I do it until he makes this noise that I guess, officially, is a grunt, but it's so sexy I could die. I find the wet spot at the head of his penis, slide

my palm over it, slick it downward. West's hand is there suddenly, rudely shoving past mine, gripping himself tight.

"I'm—do you want me to—"

"You're perfect," he says. "Fucking perfect. Keep doing
that."

So I do the same thing a few more times, stroking and
spreading, making him slippery. He starts to push up into my
hand, hard and then harder, flags of color rising in his cheeks.
I love that. I watch him, eager for more signs that he likes it,
likes this. I kiss him, wanting to push him off a cliff like he
did to me, but he can't kiss. He's turned crap at it, I guess
because he can't concentrate.

That makes me smile.

My hand speeds up. His face is hard and fierce and gorgeous.

"Caroline." He covers his eyes with his forearm, and the
hand that's in his shorts covers mine, guiding me into a
rhythm, a grip that's tighter and more cruel than anything
I'd have dared on my own. "Just like that, honey. Don't stop.
I'm gonna come, don't stop."

I can't decide what to watch, so I watch everything. Our
hands working together. The head of his penis peeking out
between them, his hips lifting off the bed, the helplessness in
his face when he comes, wetting our hands, my hip, his stomach. I listen to him groan, feel his body lift up underneath
me, dirty and sexy and glorious.

When it's over, his arm drops down and clamps me tight
to his side. His grip on my hand releases, his fingers slack.
Face slack. I pull the blanket up over us.

I listen to the wind outside, the snow hitting the window
in a thousand tiny taps.

I think about how many pictures I've seen on the Internet.
Shiny cocks, pinkish-purple heads, spurting semen.

I think of what we just did, West and me. How it would look in a picture.

A picture like that—it could never be more than a shadow of what we did. What we are together. It would only be parts, but the parts aren't the thing that matters.

It's all of it. All of West and me. The way it *feels*.

West is right. Pictures lie. I don't understand why I didn't get it before—that it's not *me* on the Internet. It's just some stupid pictures. Some lie Nate is fixated on telling the world.

They're about him, those pictures. They're not about me.

"You okay?" West asks.

I've never seen his face so relaxed. I kiss the corner of his mouth, and it tips up into a lopsided smile.

"I'm good."

His smile grows. "You're not. You're bad. Bad as the rest of us, Caroline Piasecki."

I kiss his chin. That smart-ass smile. "I know. It's more fun than I thought it would be."

His laugh is as soft as his face. "I better clean this mess up."

He drops his legs over the side of the bed, walks toward the bathroom, scooping up a pair of jeans along the way and throwing me a towel to clean myself up. I hear water running. "You want something to eat?" he calls. "I think I have chicken noodle soup. And I brought a loaf home."

I look at the clock, surprised to see how late it is. Our fifty minutes is up, but there are no alarms going off this time. No walls going up.

"Yeah, that sounds great."

I burrow down, pull the covers up to my chin, and give myself three minutes to indulge my stupid sappy heart, storing up memories for the lonely weeks ahead.

———

"I have something for you," I tell him.

He's sitting at the edge of the mattress, pulling on his socks. Preparing to go make me chicken noodle soup, which, I have to say, is the hotness. Even though all that's involved is a can and some water. Hot.

"I don't need anything."

There's tension in the way he shapes the words, and when he glances toward me, his eyes are cautious.

I don't let it bother me. Maybe West doesn't get a lot of presents. I sit up and press my breasts against his arm, kissing his neck. "Don't be a grinch. Hang on, I'll go get it."

I walk out into the living room in just my Christmas panties, rummaging through my bag with my ass in the air, putting on a little show because I know he can see me, and I feel so good. So happy.

When I come back, I hand him the book I bought him, wrapped in reindeer paper with a glittery gold bow. He puts it in his lap, reluctant, or maybe waiting for me to give him the card in my hand, so I do that.

He opens the card first, ripping it along the side in a way that causes it to flex inside the envelope and then release, slightly creased, into his palm. The money flutters out. Two hundred dollars in twenties, falling in an untidy pile on top of the book.

"What is this?"

Three words, but the way he says them—I shiver.

Something is wrong.

Something is wrong, and I feel suddenly scared, small. Ashamed to be standing here nearly naked when West is clothed and closed off. When he sounds so angry.

I start looking around the room for my bra. "You were supposed to open the present first," I tease. "Who starts with the card?"

"I do."

I've managed to locate my bra and I'm putting it on, fastening the hooks, when West's hand closes around my calf. "Caroline. What is this for?"

He asks the question very slowly and deliberately, leaning on every word. Fury etched into the lines of his face.

I can't imagine what he thinks I've done. Charity? Pity?

"The loan." And I tell myself not to say more, but I can't stop talking with his eyes so angry. I babble. "Sorry it's not more. That's all I could save in the past six weeks, with Christmas coming. I hope you aren't one of those people who think a book is a bad present, because I got books for everybody this year. I thought you might like it, though. It's about the science of bread, and there's a chapter in there— what?"

He's softened. The relief in his eyes—in his whole body— is palpable.

"Jeez. West, what did you think it was?"

He doesn't answer. I wait, and he unwraps the book, flips through the pages. I think if it were in Latin, or blank, he wouldn't notice. He's just pulling himself together, and I'm embarrassed to have to stand here and see it happen when he obviously wishes I were somewhere else.

"This is great," he says, after a long, awkward minute. "Thanks." A pause. "You don't have to pay me back."

"Of course I do."

He looks up at last. "I'd rather you didn't."

I'm not sure how to answer that. I'm so bewildered, but he sets the book down on the bed and puts his hands at my hips. He pulls me in between his legs and rests his face against my stomach.

"Really," he says. "Just don't."

His hands slide over my butt. I'm worried about what

happened, but West's hands are soothing. An effective distraction. As I'm sure he knows.

"I didn't get you anything," he murmurs.

"That's okay."

"Did I tell you how much I like these panties?"

"These? Why?"

"They're on you."

I exhale a laugh. I'm not sure what to do with my hands, so I rest them on top of his head. "I thought you were going to make me soup. That can be my Christmas present."

He hooks a finger in the elastic of my panties, drags them down, follows his finger with his nose. Inhales.

"I got a better idea."

I smack his shoulder. One of those smacks that turns into a caress. "West."

Something happened. I'd like to press him, but the truth is that I'm afraid to, and he's got his hands inside my underwear now. His palms are big and warm, his breath a tease that makes me think about his tongue and how I've never liked getting oral before but how, with West, everything's different.

With West, I have a feeling, I'm going to like it.

"Come back to bed," he orders.

So I do.

And oh my God. I like it.

Later on, the doorbell rings.

The gusts have died down outside, but the snow's still falling. I'm on West's couch, my laptop warming my thighs, my thoughts on Romantic poetry, Grecian vases, Mont Blanc. I'm gazing at the back of West's head where he's sitting on the floor by my hip, working out practice problems for his physics final. I'm trying to decide whether the sublime might actually be this moment. This glow in my body, my affection for his ears, the way my fingers want to rest on him when I'm thinking about the next paragraph I'm going to type.

The doorbell doesn't make any sense at all. I can't imagine why anyone would want to go outside in this weather or what possible reason a person who isn't West or me could have to be here.

He's standing up, though, almost immediately, sliding his phone out of his pocket, checking his texts or his email.

Oh, right, he's a dealer.

"You expecting someone?"

The bakery was busy last night, a lot of students wanting to ensure they had enough supplies to stay high through a month's worth of encounters with their parents or parties with their old friends from high school.

"No."

He goes to the door, opens it, and blocks my view of the fire escape. He's up on the second floor, the apartment above a store that sells gifts and women's clothes. The landing outside is small, and the couch has a better angle on the door than my nook at the bakery. I can see two figures beyond West.

I'm not sure why I get up. Because I don't want to feel apart from him today, I guess. Because I'm getting less willing to turn my eyes away from things that make me uncomfortable and simply pretend they're not happening.

This is going to sound strange, but it's a little bit because of West's penis, too. By which I mean: I was afraid to touch him there without clear guidelines. Afraid I wouldn't be any good at it, or I'd mess it up. But look how well it turned out when I did, right?

I'm afraid of this part of who he is, more afraid than I was of touching him. This West who breaks rules, who could get arrested or sent to jail—I don't even know why he does it. Just for the money? Because he wants to? Because he wants to prove he's not afraid?

Or maybe he does it because he likes it. He has an expertise that I don't share—words I don't know, mysteries of seeds and resin, weight and cost. He has that voice he uses when he's dealing. I think it's why I asked him to get me high when he came to my house. Because I want to know all the parts of him. Even the ones that scare me.

Anyway, I don't sort through all this consciously. I just duck under his arm, smiling, touching him, staking a claim on this evening and this part of his life, on him, on everything.

And then I stop short, the smile falling off my face.

It's Josh at the door, talking to West. And leaning against the rail behind him, wrapped in his winter coat, a hat, the scarf that I gave him last Christmas—it's Nate.

He looks as shocked to see me here as I am to see him. His eyebrows draw together, his mouth going tight and white around the edges—*pain*—and then just as quickly it's gone and he's trying and failing to look indifferent.

The conversation dies.

"Hey, guys," I say cheerfully. I'm not sure how else to play this. Someone has to smooth over this awkwardness, and I guess it's got to be me. "Getting something to tide you over the break?"

"They're not getting anything." West's tone is caustic. He looks at Josh. "What part of 'Text me first' and 'Don't come around where I live' was so hard for you to understand?"

Josh's chin comes up, defiant. "We just thought of it when we drove by. I figured you might be here, with finals going."

West shakes his head. "I told you how it works."

"Yeah, but—"

"*I* set the terms," he says curtly. "Not you."

"We'll buy a whole ounce," Nate says. He's lounging against the railing, faking relaxation. His expression is all holier-than-thou, and I recognize it as the face he made when he wanted me to do something for him that I didn't want to.

West has never looked at me like that.

"I had some of what you sold Marshall," Nate says. "It's good shit. He says it's one fifty for the half ounce."

"I'm not selling to you."

"I'll pay you four hundred." There's something smarmy in the way Nate says this—like he's trying to figure out West's price so he can pay it and then look down on him for being hard up enough to let himself be debased.

I'm kind of amazed. I mean, I saw him on the floor after West punched him. I can't believe he has the guts to be here, much less to be acting so superior.

"Maybe I'm not being clear." West is getting angry. "I wouldn't sell to you no matter what you paid me." He gestures at Josh. "I'm done with you, too. Get the fuck out of here."

Nate's jawline hardens. "You're an asshole."

"You're a cocksucker."

"Isn't that more Caroline's department?"

I have time to register what the words do to West—this weird ripple of tension through him as every part of his body goes hard and furious, all at once.

I have time to think, *Oh, crap.*

Then everything happens fast. West lunges forward and pushes me back into the apartment at the same time. I'm catching at his waist, trying to keep him from hitting anyone or getting hit, not on my account, not tonight. "Keep out of this," he says, and he's straight-arming me toward the door, but the fire escape is slippery and I lose my footing and bang my temple against something hard that makes me see stars, which I always thought was a figure of speech. Nate's against the railing, West is on him, Josh is shoving West, West's fist comes up—

I don't think it's West's fault, I really don't.

But when it's all over, West is the one who's standing on the fire escape in wet socks, absently rubbing his knuckles, and Nate is the one on his knees at the base of the stairs, cradling his ribs and spitting blood.

I think you need an ambulance.

I can walk.

Keep the fuck away from her.

She doesn't belong to you.

Doesn't belong to you, either, asshole.

Had your chance. Fucked it up.

Wish I'd had her longer. Miss that sweet ass. Or haven't you fucked her there yet?

Get him out of here. I won't be responsible.

Let's go. Nate. Let's go.

You'll be sorry.

I slide down the doorjamb, shake my head, blinking. It's cold.

I wish I hadn't come to the door.

West is there, his face right in front of mine, his intensity almost more than I can take. "Shit, Caro, are you all right?"

"I'm fine."

He pulls me to my feet, puts his arm around me, shuts the door on Nate and Josh. They're out there in the snow, Nate hobbling when he tries to walk, maybe hurt.

It's so ugly. All of it, this ugliness, because of me.

I hate it.

I think I'm supposed to like it. I think of all the movies I've seen where the guy takes a swing for his woman. The girl never gets hit in those movies. Nobody ever runs to the bathroom, hunched over, and throws up half-digested chicken soup in the toilet.

Clearly, I'm doing this wrong. I'm doing everything wrong.

I hear West come into the room, but I don't know what he wants from me. When I went to the door, before I even looked out on the fire escape, I put my arm around him and he shrank away from me.

It hurt when he did that. Everything that came after just made it hurt worse.

I think, inanely, of the present I gave him. The glittery bow. Two hundred dollars in an envelope.

What did he think I was paying him for?

The ugliness—it's not just in me. It's in him, too, and he doesn't want me to know about it, but that doesn't make it any less *there*.

I'm falling in love with a boy who sells drugs, who punches when he's angry, who knows my body better than I do.

I'm already in love with him. With West, who likes to set the rules, and who doesn't want me to hand him money in an envelope after I've taken his dick in my hand and made him come.

I don't know who he is, what his past looks like. I can't know, because he won't tell me. But his present is ugly enough to make me starkly, painfully aware of my own naïveté.

I'm shaking, clutching cold porcelain, crying.

West crouches down beside me. "Let me look at your head."

I let him. Even though I'm sick, sobbing more for him than for me. Even though I hate myself.

I curl up in West's lap on his bathroom floor and let

him look at my head, test me for a concussion, wrap his arms around me, and lean against the wall, holding me. Holding me.

Something is wrong with both of us, but I don't ever want him to let go.

West

My mom has a thing for *The Wizard of Oz*. When I was a kid, she found these blue-and-white-checked curtains at Fred Meyer and hung them up in the trailer, where they made everything look shabby. It was only a few months after Dad's most recent vanishing act, and she was still wearing the cheap sparkly red shoes he'd given her. You know the kind of shoes with a wide toe strap and a stacked heel like a wedge of cheese?

She loved them. Wore them everywhere, even though she was constantly turning her ankles. One night she put them on to go out drinking with Dad, and she came back three days later wearing new clothes, with a tattoo of Toto on her ankle and a shot glass that said Reno. She gave it to me as a souvenir.

After Dad left and Mom lost her job because he took the car and she couldn't find a reliable ride to town, she had this running joke where she'd click the heels of those shoes together and say, "There's no place like home, there's no place like home."

Then she'd look around the trailer and frown like she was disappointed.

"Still a dump," she'd say.

But she would lean into me if I was nearby, her shoulder against mine, our hair touching. "At least we've got each other, Westie."

All her jokes were like that—the humor at our expense, the silver lining in the fact that we were a team. A family.

There's no place like home.

But you can't go home again—I learned that from being at Putnam. Home changes while you're away, and you change, too, without noticing. You get in your car, watch the shapes of your mom and your kid sister get smaller in the rearview, and you think it'll all still be there the next time, as though you went out for groceries or worked two eighteens at the golf course, back to back, then pulled right into your spot in Bo's driveway like you'd never left.

It doesn't work that way. You come home on a plane. You land in Portland, hitchhike to Coos Bay, walk to the school to surprise your sister when she gets out for the day—and then when the group of kids with her in it goes by, you don't even recognize her.

You've never seen her clothes before. Her ears are pierced. Her face is different.

And the worst part is, she doesn't recognize you, either. She walks right past. You have to catch her sleeve, say her name.

I've never felt more like two different people than I did that Christmas.

One of me lived in Oregon, with Frankie, Mom, and Bo. Uprooted, worried, frustrated, cautious—but there, where I belonged.

The rest of me was with Caroline.

I fall asleep after my last final and wake up to sharp knocking at the apartment door.

Caroline's already left, on an airplane by now to the Caribbean with her family, so I know it's bad news.

I've been expecting bad news ever since I knocked Nate down the stairs two nights ago.

There's no way he's not going to retaliate. I humiliated him. Twice.

She's mine. That's what I was thinking when I did it. I don't care what happens to me—I'm not going to let anybody talk that kind of shit about Caroline in front of her, to my face, on my doorstep.

The worst part is, I knew she'd fuck with my priorities, mess with my head. I *knew* she would, and now that she has, I like it.

It's perfect. I want her to move into my apartment, sleep in my bed, shower with my soap, wear my old shirts around. I want to eat her out before breakfast every morning, rub off on her ass, bury my face between her tits, and come on her hip.

I'm two inches from being so whipped I've turned into one of those guys who does whatever his woman tells him to do and grins all the time, like he's high on the smell of pussy.

I'm a fucking goner for that girl. She *owns* me.

Which is why, when the knock comes at the door, I'm almost glad for it. I can't stand myself. Can't stand that she hit her head, bruising her temple. Can't stand remembering the wretched, ugly sound she made throwing up in my bathroom.

After she was asleep, I texted Bo, telling him there was a good chance I'd end up behind bars before I made it home for Christmas.

Don't let nobody in your place without a warrant, he wrote.

By the time I've got my boots on, the knocking has turned to pounding, but I take the time to pick up the book Caroline gave me off my pillow, dog-ear the page, and tuck it into my duffel bag.

It's a good book, and I don't want it trashed.

There are two of them at the door, a beefy guy with curly blond hair in a Putnam PD uniform and a skinnier, shorter black guy wearing a red Putnam College Security polo. "Are you West Leavitt?" the blond one asks.

"Yes."

"I'm Officer Jason Morrow with the Putnam Police, and this is Kevin Yates from campus security. We received an anonymous tip that you've been engaging in the illegal sale of marijuana. We need to come in and have a look around."

I can tell by the way he says this that it usually works. They knock on college kids' doors—twice a year, three times, whenever there's a serious complaint. They act civil and ask nice, and these other kids roll right over.

I've got nothing in the apartment for them to find, because, despite what Nate seems to think, I'm not fucking stupid. The amount of weed I'm holding—that's a serious misdemeanor for possession all by itself, a class D felony if they can prove I'm selling it. Which they can, of course, because nobody could smoke that much and function as a normal human being. I keep it in a locker at the rec center, and I go by there two or three times a week, run around the track, lift weights, shower, pocket a few eighths, a few quarters, whatever I know I'm going to be able to sell.

I haven't grown a plant on campus since the beginning of last year, when I did it more as a stunt than anything. I wanted people to talk. *He's the guy who's growing the good bud. He's the one who can hook you up.* Once that first crop was harvested, I shut the whole thing down. Too risky.

I know what I got myself into. I know my rights.

"No," I say to the cop at the door.

No, he can't come in.

No, I can't get out.

I'm trapped in this mess I made, and I have a month away from here—from *her*—to figure out how I'm going to escape.

My mom throws her arm around my neck from behind me, leaning close to plant a kiss that glances off my ear and lands mostly on my baseball hat.

"Ugh. Mom. You smell like steamed meat."

She's just home from a shift at the prison. I've never seen the cafeteria where she works, but if the way she smells when she comes off work is any indication, I'm not missing much.

I don't really mind the kiss, though. The cafeteria smell is in her clothes, but I can smell her skin, too, some flowery soap or lotion. Bo's bathroom counter is cluttered with Mom's beauty supplies.

I've been away so long that the strongest impressions when I walked in a couple days ago were all smells. Stale cigarette smoke, the plug-in air freshener, the waft of air that came off the couch when I sat down—dog hair and aging foam cushions layered over with Febreze.

The first time Mom hugged me, her scent made my throat catch, a physical reaction that wasn't quite tears and wasn't quite allergies, either. The boy in me saying *Mom* at the same time my hands itched to push her away, put a little distance between us.

"I just can't get over how good it is to have you back."

"Quit hanging on him," Bo says from across the table. "He's too old for that crap."

Mom takes off my cap and musses up my flattened-down hair. "He's my baby. You get something to eat yet, Westie? I can make you chipped beef if you want."

She's been plying me with my favorites. "Nah, I ate in town. Me and Frankie picked up Arby's after I took her to Bandon."

Bo looks up. "What'd you go to Bandon for?"

He was gone when we left, gone when we got home. I guess he didn't know. "I took Franks to the clinic for her physical."

His eyes narrow, and he turns to my mom. "You let him take her for that shot?"

My mom blinks a few times, too rapidly, and I realize she's stuck me in the middle of something. She said Frankie needed a physical in order to be allowed to do some kind of after-school indoor-soccer thing come January. When we got to the clinic, the nurse told me Franks was overdue for a hepatitis booster and that she needed to get it or she wouldn't be able to stay in school next year.

I figured it was a fluke. The state health plan covered it, so I told the nurse to go ahead, scrawling my signature across the form she handed me.

But now I remember, too late, that Bo doesn't believe in vaccines. He's got a book about it, a ready lecture about the fallacy of herd immunity and the toxicity of the stuff they put in those shots as preservatives. He'll go on about blood aluminum levels for an hour if you get him going.

"Did Frankie get a shot?" Mom asks.

When Mom had walked in the door, Frankie showed her the Band-Aid, first thing.

I glare at her, and she gives me this weak smile. Her eyes are pleading with me. *Come on, West. Take my side.*

I don't want there to be sides. Not between Mom and Bo.

"I went by what the nurse said."

Bo picks up his Camels from off the table and peers in the open mouth of the pack. Frowns, slides out the last cigarette. He's got a long fuse. If he and my mom are going to fight about this, it won't be now.

But he's not going to forget it happened.

"I'm going to grab a Coke," Mom says. "West, you want anything?"

"I'll take a beer."

"Get me another pack from the freezer, would you?" Bo asks.

Mom heads toward the fridge. "Didn't you just open those this morning?" .

"So what if I did?"

"So you're supposed to be cutting back. For Frankie."

Frankie's out in the living room, not visible from the kitchen, but Bo's house is small, and she can hear. She calls, "You're supposed to be *quitting*, Bo."

"Maybe next week."

Mom snags a beer for me. She doesn't ask Bo if he wants one, and when she twists off the lid and says, "You want a glass, West?" he makes a disgusted noise and pushes up from the table.

"Where are you going?"

"Out to the greenhouse."

He opens the freezer and takes a pack of cigarettes from the carton.

"You got some dinner?"

"Yeah, I'm good."

The corners of her mouth turn down as she watches him push out the back door. It makes her look old. My mom's only thirty-seven, but in her shapeless prison uniform she's middle-aged, the lines in her face deep-set, the disappointment at the edges of her mouth never quite disappearing.

She hates that uniform. In a little while she'll take a shower and do her hair, put on tight jeans and a nice shirt, chasing a youth that's getting away from her.

She was always more like a friend with a driver's license than a parent. A friend whose bad habits and flaws are obvious to everyone who knows her, but the kind of friend you forgive because she's got a good heart, and she can't seem to stop herself from getting it crushed.

I wish this were the first time since I got home that Bo's gone out to the greenhouse in a huff, but it's not. Something's not right between them.

There's a lot of things that don't feel right. Things I didn't expect. I want to glue down the flap of loose Formica at the corner of the kitchen counter, yellowed tape fluttering at its edges announcing three or four half-assed attempts to fix it, but it's Bo's kitchen, and when I search through the junk drawer for glue and find an envelope full of cash—one of Bo's many stashes—I feel like a thief.

I want to tell Frankie not to read this book she's got, this paperback that I remember girls reading when I was in high school, so I know it's got incest and blow jobs and other shit that's too old for her. But she's Mom's daughter, not mine.

Nothing here feels like it's mine.

I tell myself it's because I've never lived in this house. Back before I went to Putnam, when Mom decided to move in here with Bo, I stayed behind in the trailer. I've slept on Bo's couch before, but I've never called Bo's house my home.

The trailer is mine, and my dad is living in it.

"What's up with you and Bo?"

She waves her hand in dismissal. Picks up a Zippo that's lying on the table, flips it over a few times, tapping it lightly on the tabletop. "He's fine. Probably not sleeping enough. He hates when he has to work nights. Makes him grouchy."

"He's back on days next week, though, right?"

"Right." She drops into the chair Bo vacated, slides off the clogs she wears to work, and tosses them into the pile of shoes by the back door. Her socks have tiny little Totos on them, and she wiggles her toes at me. I gave her the socks for Christmas.

"Nice," I say.

"I love them."

She leans forward and picks up the lighter again, flicks it until she makes a flame. A sly brightness in her eyes tells me she's got an agenda for this conversation. "So this is the first time I've really got you all to myself. Tell me everything about school."

"Not much to tell."

"Ask him about his girrrrlfriend," Frankie trills from the living room.

My mom's eyes brighten. "I *knew* you had a girl. No wonder you never call me back."

"I always call you back."

She rolls her eyes and flicks the lighter again. "Yeah, when you're not *working*." She infuses the word with doubt, as though I'm working for the purpose of avoiding her.

Half the money I make, I end up sending her. I probably

paid for the magazines on the coffee table, just like I paid for her socks.

"Let me see a picture," she says.

"I don't have a girlfriend."

"He does!" Frankie's at the threshold of the kitchen now, her smile delighted. "She sent him a *bikini picture*."

God damn it.

"She sent *you* a bikini picture," I say, because this is the honest truth. I walked into the living room to find Frankie on my phone, texting Caroline, who'd just shared a vacation snapshot of her with her arm slung around a chunkier girl, her sister Janelle. Both of them in bikini tops with wet hair, smiling.

I need to stop texting her. Stop looking at that picture.

I need to draw better lines in my life, because *this* is what I'm supposed to be worrying about. The problems in this kitchen. How Frankie's getting C's in school and doesn't seem to know the meaning of the word *privacy*. How her boobs are growing and she's wearing a bra and shirts that advertise that fact for the world to see. My head should be on whatever's going on between Mom and Bo and whether Wyatt Leavitt has anything to do with it.

On how, when I asked Mom if she'd seen him, she said no, but she wouldn't meet my eyes, and then she went all falsely cheerful like she gets when she's lying to me.

I'm not supposed to be worrying whether Caroline's having any fun in the Caribbean, thinking about when I'm going to be able to steal twenty minutes to call her, if there's some way to get her alone behind a locked door when the house is empty so I can talk dirty to her, unzip my jeans, take myself in my hand.

"Let me see," Mom says.

"No."

But Frankie's coming up behind me, her fingers dipping into my back pocket for my phone, and I'm not fast enough to stop her. I grab her, tickle her, reach for the phone while I pinch her ribs just hard enough to make her squirm away, saying, "Ow!" even as she's laughing.

"Catch, Mom!"

She tosses the phone, and I get a glimpse of the screen with my text app open before the case hits the floor and skates across it. Then I'm down on my knees, scrambling with my mom, Frankie at the periphery, and it's the weirdest thing, because they're both laughing, but when Mom puts her hand out and pushes me away, she pushes hard. When she gets the phone and vaults to her feet—runs across the kitchen, saying, "Keep him off me, Frankie!"—it doesn't feel like a game.

It's not funny.

I dodge around Frankie effortlessly, grab my mom's wrist, wrench the phone out of her hand. My chest is heaving. I'm hot, out of control, full of misdirected rage, thwarted fury.

"Christ, West, lighten up," Mom says. But her eyes are glittering, offended and prideful, and when I look at Frankie she flinches.

I want to storm out of the house. Take a long walk out to the highway and along the road in the gathering dark. I want to fume, but I've got nothing to be pissed off about except my own failure to make the lines in my life black enough, dark enough to keep this kind of shit from happening.

I take a deep breath and let it out.

This is my family. My place.

These are my people, and this is where I belong.

If it doesn't feel that way, I'm doing it wrong. Closing myself off. And I can't do that, because if I lose this, who am I?

I thumb through a couple of screens on the phone and

hand it back to my mom, whose expression softens at the peace offering. "The one on the right, or . . . ?"

"The pretty one," I hear myself say. "Her name's Caroline."

What r you doing?

She texts back right away. Nothing.

What kind of nothing?

Laying on couch watching a movie.

What movie?

Breakfast Club. I've seen 400 Molly Ringwald movies today.

Why?

They were my mom's. I watch them sometimes.

A pause. My dad's at work. I'm bored. Break sucks.

Yeah.

Another pause. I'm calling you.

I'm on the couch, alone in the house. New Year's has come and gone, and Franks is back in school. Bo's on days again. He and Mom are both working, and the house is quiet for the first time since I got here.

I'm hard before the phone even rings.

"Hey," she says.

"Hey."

Then silence, and she laughs this breathy sort of laugh. "This is weird."

"Which part?"

I can imagine her biting her lip. Looking away from me.

I can imagine her throat turning red and blotchy. The way her breasts are rising with each quick intake of breath.

"You know the part of the movie where Judd Nelson is in the closet, and Molly Ringwald locks herself in there with him?" she asks.

"Which one's Judd Nelson?"

"The guy with the long hair and the flannel shirt."

"The bad boy."

"Yeah. And Molly Ringwald's the one—"

"I know who she is."

Caroline laughs. Kind of nervous. "That part's on right now."

"And?"

"And that's the best part. Molly's got her pink silk shirt on and her hair all perfect, because she's such a good girl, only now they're in the closet together . . ."

I start to laugh, realizing where this is going. "I thought you'd be into that other guy."

"Who? Anthony Michael Hall?"

"The wrestler one."

"Emilio Estevez? Ew."

"He looks like Nate, but with short hair."

Silence for a few beats. "God. He does. You're right."

She sounds so horrified, I start to laugh.

"But I always liked Judd best," she says. "Even when he spits in the air and swallows it."

"Got kind of a bad-boy thing, don't you?"

"*No.*"

I can hear the smile in her voice, though. "It's all right. Maybe I'm into poor little rich girls."

"Maybe you are."

"What are you wearing, rich girl?"

She exhales a laugh again. There's this shift I can almost feel, a click on the line, digital signals rearranging themselves from one stream to another. *What are you wearing?* The phone-sex starter pistol firing, and I'm on the block, ready for it. Jeans unzipped. Hand outside my briefs, because I can't go inside until I know she's playing along. Not this time.

"I've got my pink silk shirt on." I can hear the shift in her voice, too. Saying yes.

I slip my hand inside my shorts.

"And that long, tight brown skirt," she adds. "Brown boots."

"You have boots?"

"Sure. Every girl in America has boots."

A tight grip. A slow stroke. "You'll have to wear them for me sometime."

"Why?"

"I like boots."

The strain. There's nothing like it—so bad and so good. It's in every muscle in my body.

"Oh." The sound is a sigh.

"Hey, rich girl?"

"Mmm-hmm?"

"Turn the volume off on the TV."

I wait, working up a rhythm. The background noise fades to nothing. I can hear her breathing.

"What do you think they get up to in that closet?" I ask her. "You know, when the camera cuts away?"

There's a pause. "I never really thought about it."

"You wanna think about it now?"

"Maybe."

"Where's your hands?"

"Mmm. I'm not sure I'm saying."

"Put one of them someplace interesting."

She sniffs, a kind of laugh, and I wait a few seconds to make sure she's doing it. Then I say, quiet and low, "I think they started off kissing."

"Yeah."

"And the kissing got hot, and he pushed her back down onto the bench."

"I'm not sure there's a bench."

"There's a bench. It's long and flat, with no back on it, so he can lay her down and kneel next to her and push her skirt up past her knees."

"It's kind of long and tight, though. I don't think he could push it up."

"He's good with skirts. He doesn't have to take it off. He just pushes it up and leaves it up, so she feels the air on her thighs and starts to worry they're gonna get caught. It's exciting, thinking that. Maybe someone will walk in on them, the good girl with her legs spread, the bad boy kneeling there on the floor, kissing her. Touching her."

"Where's he touching her?"

"Everywhere except where she really wants it the most."

She inhales deep and her breath catches. I've heard her do that before. Seen her do that. The sound draws up a surge of heat from my balls, and I slick it over the head, draw it down. Slow and tight.

"What are you doing, Caro?"

"What do you want me to be doing?"

"I want you on your back with your skirt up and your legs spread."

That gets me a muffled *mmph*.

"You're there already, aren't you?"

"Maybe."

"That's my girl."

"What are *you* doing?"

"Honey, you know what I'm doing."

"Like last time?" she asks. "Thanksgiving?"

"Yeah."

She's just breathing.

"He's got her shirt pushed up now," I tell her. "His mouth on her stomach. Moving down."

"She's nervous."

"How come?"

"She's never done this before. It's exciting."

"He likes the way she smells. How smooth her legs are, how pale she is. Like a secret. She's wearing yellow panties under there, just plain ones. Are they wet, Caroline?"

She kind of squeaks, and my grip tightens. God, I love that squeak.

"Tell me."

"Yes."

"Yeah, I thought so. Wet through her panties, and he's going to go ahead and straddle that bench and get his nose right down there, pushing into the wet spot."

"That's crude."

"He's crude. That's why she likes him."

"That's not the only reason."

"It's one, though. She thinks he's exciting. She loves knowing he thinks about her when she's not around. That she makes him hard. Makes him come in his bed, in his shower, but he's never touched her."

"God. That's hot."

I smile.

"Why's he like her?" she asks.

I have to think about it—not the easiest thing to do with your hand on your dick, but I manage. "He likes that she doesn't know all the things he knows. That she hasn't seen the worst of life."

"She's seen more than he thinks."

"Maybe, but she's still got this air around her, like the bad things can never really touch her."

"She'd hate that," Caroline says. "If he told her that was why—she'd be disappointed."

"But that's not the only reason. It's not even the main one."

"What's the main one?"

I try to focus on the movie. Not Caroline on her couch, spread open, touching herself. "That she's there in the closet. She's brave, once she's made up her mind what she wants. Fierce."

"He likes her when she's fierce?"

"Yeah. Yeah."

Who are we talking about? I'm not sure. I'm starting to feel kind of stoned, dumb, like I might be saying more than I mean to, but I don't really care.

"West?"

"Yeah."

"What's he do next?"

"He puts his tongue on her, right through her panties. Gets his hands underneath the elastic, holds her there on the bench and licks and licks her until her panties are soaked through and she's just about dead from it."

"Does he like that?"

"He fucking loves it. Making her feel good, making her give up control, shut her head off and just feel—it's a trip. And he likes those panties, too. Those yellow panties. But he needs more, so instead of taking them off, he just eases them over a few inches. Enough to get his tongue in her slit, where she's soft and swollen and so wet. He can't get enough of her. He just buries his face in her, gets himself wet all over his chin and his mouth."

"West."

"She tastes incredible."

"God, West, I can't—"

I can't, either. I'm thinking about her pussy, the way she

felt under my fingers, under my tongue. Her thighs pressing against my head, her hands in my hair, on my dick—it's too much. "I want you," I say. "Fuck, I want you."

"You've got me."

"Right here, on this couch, *here*. I want you here, Caro. I want to taste you. Get my fingers inside you, tongue your clit. I want you naked."

She's panting.

"Use your hand," I tell her. "Pretend it's me. Come for me. I want to hear."

"West."

"Yeah."

"You, too."

"I'm close."

And then it's just breath. Noise. It's just moaning, grunting.

It's knowing what she's doing, picturing her doing it, her tits, her pussy, her eyes closed and her mouth open and the way her face looks when I make her come.

It's my hand working hard and fast, her fingers flying, this thread of connection between us, nothing real about it, nothing true, nothing right, but here it is, anyway. Nothing I can do about it. Nothing I want to do but this, but Caroline. Nothing.

She sucks in a breath, says, "Now," and I go with her with a grunt and a hot splash on my hand and a little bit on the couch, which, fuck, I'm going to have to clean that up, but I can't even care. She's trying hard not to make noise, and even so I can hear her, I can hear the not-noise she's making, and it's fucking glorious.

I come apart, a little bit. Lean back, close my eyes, listen to her. I go loose, unhinged, and break into pieces.

But I feel, afterward, like maybe some part of me got put back together.

———

It's late. I walk out to the greenhouse, dodging dog shit in the backyard and wishing I'd turned on the back porch light.

I step in something too soft. "Fuck."

I try scraping off my boot in the grass, but it's no use. The smell is in my nose now, my lip curling. I have to find a stick, try picking brown crap out of the treads, but that doesn't work, either, and I end up turning on the garden hose, covering the cold copper fitting with my thumb, blasting the sole of my boot and sending flecks of shit shooting all over the place.

By the time I've got the boot cleaned off, my pants are sticking to my shins. I'm cold and pissed, disgusted with everything.

I'm going back to school in a week, and my whole life has turned into a minefield of crap.

When I get to the greenhouse and open the door, I don't see Bo right away. I take a breath, trying to find a calm spot to do this from. It's not his fault I stepped in dog shit. Not his fault I've been waiting to talk to him for days and there's never a right time.

He's working. Mom's around. Frankie needs help with her homework.

Bo has been pushing away from the kitchen table and disappearing for hours at a time, and I've always thought of the greenhouse as his domain, where he goes to be alone, not to be pestered by his girlfriend's kid, who's sleeping on his couch, eating his food, getting in the way.

But I have to talk to him, because I'm leaving soon. Nobody else will tell me.

There's music playing in the back. I follow it, follow the light, and find Bo just leaning there, blowing cigarette smoke out a broken pane of glass into the night.

I recognize the song. Metallica. He's into all those old metal bands, but Mom can't stand the stuff.

The greenhouse is a rusted-out dump, a lot of the glass broken. Bo loves it. He likes growing things—not just weed, which he only plants back in the woods, but vegetables, herbs, all kinds of shit. He talks about finding a freeze-drier, storing up food against the collapse of civilization, but he mostly ends up putting bushel baskets of tomatoes and corn and peppers out by the road with a sign that says: HELP YOURSELF.

Bo is short, barrel-chested, with a shaved head and grizzled chest hair you can usually see because he goes around shirtless or half unbuttoned. In his prison uniform—belt weighed down with his radio, his phone, a nightstick, his Beretta—he looks like a badass.

He *is* a badass. He's got the scars to prove it. I saw him get into a fight once at a bar. He destroyed the dude who picked the fight. Just destroyed him.

It's partly because of Bo that I'm at Putnam instead of the community college. Because I trust him to keep his job, take care of Mom, watch out for Frankie, and not morph into a pervert or an asshole when I stop paying attention.

He loves them. Both of them.

I've never been completely sure Mom loves him back. He had to ask her out a bunch of times before she said yes. Had to court her for a few months before she started sleeping over at his place. She likes being with him, likes his house, but I don't think she likes the idea of being Bo's old lady for the rest of her life.

I think she's addicted to the way my dad makes her feel. That exciting, edgy, fucked-up rush she can only get from him.

"I fell in love with him the second I met him," she told me

once. "I was fifteen, and he drove into town on that motor-cycle, and the world stopped spinning."

Bo can't compare with that. Nothing can.

I know, because I felt that way the first time I saw Caroline, and I still do. If there's some way to turn it off, I haven't found it yet.

Bo taps ash on a jagged glass edge, dropping it into the weeds on the other side of the window.

"What happened with the cops?" he asks.

He doesn't mean did they search the place or leave—I already told him that. He means what did I do to get their attention.

"This girl I'm seeing—she's got an ex who doesn't like me much."

"You give him a reason? Other than stealing his girl."

"I didn't steal her. They were already broken up."

But I did steal her, a little bit. Freshman year, when she was across the hall, I watched her. Tried to get her flustered. I did things to catch her eye, and Nate knew it. He hated me even then.

He has every right to hate me.

"I got into it with him. For talking shit about her."

Bo takes a deep drag, eyes narrowed, watching me. Waiting for the rest.

"Twice. Second time was a little worse than the first."

I think of Caroline throwing up in my bathroom. The roaring pain in my hand when I connected with his face. His rib cage.

I gesture at the pack of cigarettes in Bo's shirt pocket. "Can I have one of those?"

He lifts an eyebrow. I don't smoke, but that doesn't mean I don't know how. I need the rush right now—the way the nicotine will sharpen up the edges of everything, make me wary, make me smart.

I need to get smart.

He hands me a cigarette, and when I put it in my mouth and cup my hands around the tip, he gives me a light off his Zippo.

"What's he got over you?" Bo asks.

"I knocked him down a fire escape. Might've cracked his ribs. Assault, I guess. Especially if he went to the hospital afterward."

"Was there a witness?"

"His friend. And Caroline."

He nods.

"I've sold to the friend," I add.

"More than once?"

"Yeah."

"So he tipped off the cops."

"Probably. I mean, anybody could have, but probably. You think they'll be back?"

"Yeah."

I purse my lips and inhale, grateful for the rustling sound of the paper igniting. Grateful to have this tiny curling spark to look at, this tight fullness in my chest as I hold the smoke in my lungs.

It's good to have somebody to talk to.

"You think I should just stop selling? Lay low for a semester?"

"If you can get by without the money."

I hesitate. Take another drag. Grow some balls and admit, "I end up sending most of it to Mom."

He makes this sound—I'm not sure what it means. Kind of a laugh, except with pain in it. He's not surprised, though. There's resignation in that laugh.

He doesn't say anything for a long time. Smokes his cigarette down to the filter, drops it onto the dirt floor, grinds it out.

"She don't need it," he says.

"What's she doing with it, then?"

He shrugs.

"You don't have any idea?"

"Presents I don't need. Clothes and shit for her and Frankie. I think she gave money to one of your cousins to get rid of a baby, but she won't talk about it."

I let that sink in.

"She's going out to see your grandma once a week."

He doesn't mean Mom's mom, who used to live in California but is dead now. He means Dad's mom.

He means a decade-old rift between my mom and my dad's family has been quietly repaired, and she didn't tell me. That *my* money's paying for stuff Dad's people need—or stuff they want—because that's the way Mom is with money. If she's got it, she'll give it to anybody, for anything.

If I've got it, she figures that's the same as if it's hers.

"Has he been back here?"

I don't have to tell Bo I mean my dad. We both know what this conversation is about, and it's a relief to talk around the undercurrents beneath the words, dig up the buried wires without having to name them.

The longer I stay here, the more obvious it becomes that, underneath, things are deeply fucked up.

Five miles away, living in a piece-of-shit trailer in the kind of trailer park nobody lives in if they have a better option, there's a man with my eyes. My mouth. Fucking things up just by drawing breath.

"Once," Bo says. "I drove him off with a shotgun."

"What's he want?"

Bo gives me a pitying look, and I take another drag on the cigarette and stare at my feet.

Stupid question. He wants what he always wants. Whatever my mom's got. Her heart. Her cunt. Her money. Her pride.

He wants Frankie's loyalty.

He wants to win everybody over, bring them around to his side, get them feeling sorry for him, looking at the world through his eyes, thinking, *Man, he's had some tough breaks, but he's a good guy. I'm glad it's all working out for him this time. I'm glad he's pulled it together.*

He wants to make my mom fall in love with him, and then when she's so far gone she can't even remember what happened before, he wants to punch her in the gut.

The last time I saw my father, he kicked me like a dog. Spat on me. Left me there, my lip split, curled around the pain.

I don't know why my mom can't understand. That's what he wants.

"Has she seen him?"

Bo doesn't answer for so long, I think he's not going to. He moves down the bench, swipes at an untidy spill of potting soil, rubs the dried brown leaves of a plant between his thumb and forefinger. "While I was down in California selling the crop."

"She tell you?"

His expression darkens. "You think I'd fucking let her live here if she told me? I heard it off a guy I know. She says it's bullshit."

"You don't believe her."

"I haven't made my mind up yet. But you know what happens if I find out she's seeing him behind my back."

Fuck. Yes. I know what happens.

He'll toss her out on her ass, and she'll deserve it.

Frankie, too. Bo's not going to be raising a nine-year-old kid who doesn't belong to him. Not without my mom in his bed.

He turns toward me. Walks close, clamps his hand over my shoulder. "I wish it wasn't like this," he says.

I can't look at him. I look out at the stars and finish the cigarette.

It's the weight of the past, suspended over our heads by a frayed rope.

It's a woman holding a knife in her hand, one cut that could ruin everything for me. Ruin Frankie. Ruin Bo. Ruin *her*.

It's like this, and there's nothing I can do about it.

Frankie flings herself over the back of the couch, her forearm pressing against my windpipe. "Do you really have to go?"

I tilt my head back and grab her by the waist to flip her over onto my lap.

In the air, she feels so insubstantial, her bones hollow like a bird's. I tickle her until she's shrieking.

"Quit it, West! Swear to God, quit, stop, please! West!"

I let up, and she scrambles away from me, skinny legs in skinny jeans, thick socks, a shirt with short little zippers at the shoulders that isn't warm enough for winter or young enough for her.

Mom and Bo are both at work. This morning it's just Franks and me and a bus I've got to catch if I'm going to make my flight back to school.

I'm leaving, but I don't think I'll be away for long.

Since that night out in the greenhouse with Bo, I can hear the clock ticking. The hands are flying around the dial like in some movie, blurring, blending, until time is tissue-paper thin.

My mother's eyes never light on anything for long. Her hands are nervous, her replies evasive.

Weeks from now, months if I'm lucky, I'm going to get a call that makes me drop everything and fly home. And the truth is, I don't have to go to Putnam at all.

I never had to.

I told myself when I left for school that I was doing it for Frankie and Mom, but I could have taken better care of them if I'd stayed here. Enrolled at the community college. Kept an eye on Frankie, kept my dad out of that trailer.

I went to Putnam because I wanted to.

I wanted to know who I could be if I wasn't tethered to this place. What I could accomplish on my own.

Anything, Caroline would tell me. *You can do anything.*

She believes it, too.

Caroline could never understand how selfish a thought like that can be. How selfish I am for having left and for being about to leave again when I know how things are here.

Frankie's smiling at me, breathing hard, her collarbones peeking out of the neckline of her shirt, her bottom lip chapped, her teeth a little too big for her face.

She's got black crap all around her eyes, long earrings dangling almost to her shoulders.

She's nine years old.

She needs somebody who will set limits, send her to bed, tell her to get off the phone and wash her face.

She needs me to make her do her homework and to manage Mom, who can only pass as a decent parent if there's somebody around to make her work at it.

She needs me.

Resentment spikes in me, dark and poisonous.

I wish I knew some way to give her back. If I knew how to stop caring—to become as faithless as my father—then I could go to Putnam and stay there. Send Frankie a card on her birthday.

I could make myself over into Caroline's West, with wide horizons and endless options.

"I'll miss you," my sister says.

Fists clenched, I have to close my eyes.

I would leave you behind if I could.

I wish I could. I want to.

But I open my eyes, open my mouth, and tell her, "I'll miss you, too. I'll be home in a few months. Then I'll take you somewhere cool. Portland, maybe."

"Really? What about San Francisco? Keisha says they have sea lions there, and there's this store that's all kinds of chocolate. That's where we should go."

"Yeah, I guess we could go to San Francisco. Maybe go camping on the way. See the redwoods."

"Camping? No way. Camping sucks."

"When have you ever been camping?"

"I know about it! You sleep in a tent and don't shower, and spiders fall on your head. No thanks."

I've never been camping, either. But who's going to take her if not me?

"We could have a fire. Make s'mores. We'll find a place to stay with a shower."

"A fire would be good," she says. "As long as there's a shower. And you would have to kill all the spiders."

"I can handle that."

Whatever has to be handled—spiders, nightmares, home-work, fathers—I can handle it.

What choice have I got?

I stand. "Hug me goodbye."

She gets up and wraps her arms around me.

I kiss the top of her head. Her hair is soft. It smells like pink chemicals, and all the resentment in me is gone, washed away as if it had never been.

We walk down the driveway together. She chatters about San Francisco.

She watches me from the road. Waves whenever I turn around.

She belongs to me. I can't do anything about it.

It's five miles into town, but I get lucky and hitch a ride with one of Bo's neighbors.

I look out the passenger window at the landscape, white and wheat, beige and brown, the sky wide open and relentlessly blue.

It doesn't look like Iowa. It looks like me. Those colors the colors I'm made of, the dirt of this place in my bones, silted up around my heart.

I can't keep being two people. The clock's running down, my time almost up, and I won't let myself string Caroline along, let her think I'm some other guy, some Iowa version of myself, when I'm not. I don't get to be.

I'm Frankie's.

I can't be Frankie's and keep Caroline. I wish I could, but there's no point in wishing.

Every time I kissed Caroline, I pulled her deeper in. Deep and then deeper, until I couldn't come home again without bringing her along.

"Here's my girl," I told my mother. "The pretty one."

I sat on Bo's couch in the dark and told Caroline, "I want inside you. I want you here."

But I was pretending. There's no world that has Frankie and my mom and Caroline in it, all of them belonging to me.

I've made a mess of things. That's what it all boils down to. A heinous fucking mess.

Caroline is in me, and now I've got to cut her out.

Caroline

Winter break was endless. I slept in late and padded around the house in my slippers. The rest of the world was working, productive, but I had nothing to do.

I played six million games of Minesweeper, which—yeah, I don't even know. Obviously there are better games. I couldn't bring myself to commit to anything that involved more than one level or any sort of complex strategy.

It was draining, being home. Christmas in the Caribbean wore me out. Having to smile so much. Having to talk about my classes, my friends, my interests, and never mention West or the bakery, Nate or the pictures, any of it.

Keeping secrets is exhausting. When your whole life turns into a secret, what then?

I told my dad about rugby. He didn't like the idea of me playing a tackle sport.

"You should play golf," he said.

"Dad, I hate golf."

"What's wrong with golf?"

Golf made me think of West. How he caddies, so he must know when to hand somebody a nine iron or a sand wedge. How he must have opinions about drivers and wear some kind of a uniform—a crisp polo shirt, khaki shorts. He must look so different.

I pored over Google maps, searching for golf courses in Oregon, trying to guess which was his.

My grades came. Two A's, two A-minuses. Dad put them on the fridge.

He asked if I was going to see Nate, and when I reminded him we broke up, he said, "You were friends before you were going out. Maybe it's better not to burn that bridge."

Obviously, I didn't call Nate. I took a four-hour nap instead.

For New Year's, Dad took me out to dinner and made a big thing out of letting me drink a glass of champagne. The next morning he gave me his credit card to buy myself "something nice." Because I got good grades. Because he was so proud of me.

When I showed him the cashmere sweater I'd bought at the mall—the exact shade of West's eyes—he kissed my temple, rubbed my shoulder, left me alone to watch bad movies in the den.

At night, long after Dad was asleep, I lay in the glow of the TV and waited for West to call.

I dozed off sometimes. I was so tired.

But when the phone rang, I woke up. I laughed. I craved. I yearned.

I flushed hot, dug my teeth into the flesh of my thumb, whispered words I never thought I'd own.

"Want you." "Need you." "Inside me." "God, West."

He would tell me things he wanted me to say. Dirty things that somehow weren't dirty with him, they were just *true*.

They were *real*. He would tell me, and I would say them. Anything he wanted.

There were words I didn't say, though.

I miss you.

I love you.

I must have thought there would be time for that later. After break, when I saw him again, we'd be different. We'd be close—as close as we were on the phone. We'd be *real*.

I hadn't learned yet that when your whole life is a sham, real isn't something that happens to you.

When you surround yourself with lies, all the real things start to break.

I'm back in Putnam for all of an hour before I head over to West's apartment.

I can't help it. I need to see him.

I wanted to pick him up at the airport last night, but he'd left his car in Des Moines, and he was getting in late. So I tracked his flight and saw when he landed, a quick twenty-minute drive from me in Ankeny. I imagined him driving to Putnam alone in the dark.

This morning, I'd promised my dad I would hang around for lunch after my sister and I went to the bridal shop to pick up my dress. Janelle grilled me relentlessly about boys, wanting to know if I was over Nate yet. "You should start considering meeting a new guy," she said at least six times. "It's not good to focus just on school."

Dad said I shouldn't jump into anything.

The whole time, I was thinking about West an hour away. Almost close enough to touch.

I want to take the fire-escape steps two at a time, but I stop myself. They're icy. I knock on the door, short of breath, heart pounding. I've been imagining this moment for weeks. The entirety of break spent anticipating this reunion, this kiss. West pressing me up against the wall. Pushing his weight into me, his hips. Me running my hands over his arms and his back. Getting lost in him, as surely as I've been lost in my own head all month.

When he opens the door, though, nothing's the way I imagined it.

His face is blank. As blank as the sky, as gray and cold.

I wait for him to recognize that it's *me*—to warm—but he just says, "Hey," and then I realize he *has* recognized me. And this is my reception.

He doesn't step aside to let me in. He's dressed for work at the restaurant—black slacks, white button-up, shined black shoes. So handsome it's a little scary, with his eyes that way.

"Hey. You're back." I have this nagging urge to check the door, make sure I'm at the right apartment. In the right dimension.

"I'm back."

"Did you have a good flight?" *Gah. We were supposed to be kissing by now.*

He turns away and grabs his coat out of the closet. "It was fine. I've got to go in to work."

"On a Thursday?"

"I picked up a shift."

"Can I walk over there with you?"

He shrugs like it's nothing to him one way or the other.

I'm baffled. Just the other night he said he wanted to get inside me, build me up, fuck me hard until we were both bruised and shaking, and then he wanted to do it again, slow, sweaty, trembling, and watch me when I came.

He said that. Two nights ago. I didn't make it up.

When he brushes past, he smells like wool and peppermint, and he doesn't even look at my face.

I follow him down the steps.

He's put on a hat I've never seen before, black-and-dark-gray stripes, thick and thin. I look at the spot where it meets the back of his neck. My fingers itch to touch him there.

His mood keeps me from doing it. His mood is a real thing dividing the space between us, as solid as granite.

Go away, his mood says, and it reminds me of the other times he's been like this. Weeks ago now.

I'd almost forgotten. All the rules we've had between us—I guess they were suspended over the break. Our talk of touching, of wanting, the dirty thoughts we exchanged, made me forget.

I'm not sure what the rules are now, but I know that whatever they are, they're fully in effect.

"What's wrong?"

"Nothing."

"Really? You seem kind of distant."

He turns partway toward me, hands shoved deep in his pockets. For an instant, his whole face is a wince. "I guess I don't feel much like talking."

You felt like talking the other night.

You talked me into two orgasms before we got off the phone.

I heard you come.

What the hell is wrong *with you?*

I should pick one of these things and say it, probably. But I just spent a month at home not saying any of the things I really felt. West was the only person I opened up to, and even with him, I censored myself.

My throat is tight.

We come to an intersection. The pile of iced-over snow reaches my waist, but there's a cut shoveled into it, and we pass through. I crunch over frozen gray slush in the road. The restaurant is half a block up on the right.

It's getting dark out, even though it's only four o'clock. The world feels dim and threatening. A car goes by, and the crunching noise its tires make sounds like a threat.

It's cold. So cold.

"What are you doing later?"

"I'm on until late."

He doesn't say when he'll be home. He doesn't invite me over.

That empty thing he does with his face—it's a trick. An act he's figured out how to do. It drives me crazy, because I don't know how to hide myself like that, and I haven't done anything to deserve his retreat.

It makes me think of that day in the library when I tried to slap him.

The way he was that day—that's West. That was me, too. Both of us *there* that afternoon, angry, intense, impulsive, *real*. Whereas this—this is just West being an asshole.

"What's your class schedule this semester?"

Another shrug. "I'd have to check. I haven't memorized it."

There's a slight sneer in that sentence. *I haven't memorized it, like I'm sure you have.*

West has never sneered at me before.

He's teased me, challenged me, seduced me—but he's never mocked me.

Something is really deeply wrong here.

I screw up my courage and catch at the sleeve of his coat, pulling him to a halt right in the middle of the sidewalk.

"Did something happen to you? Last night, or on your way back here?"

It's a long shot, but he could have an excuse. An explanation. He *could*.

"I told you, nothing's the matter."

"Then why are you acting like this?"

"Like what?"

I push at his biceps with my fingertips, looking up at his empty face. "Like *this*."

He kind of rolls his eyes at me. Not all the way, but he glances up at the sky, like I'm hassling him. Some random, troublesome girl. "I think you have the wrong idea about us."

"What does that mean?"

"Showing up at my apartment. We're not gonna be like that."

We're not gonna be like that.

That's what he's getting at with this routine of his. That's his purpose. "You're pushing me away."

He still won't look at me, and I think at first it's more of the same thing—a way for him to pretend I'm getting predictably whiny now, female histrionics in full effect—except his eyes are glistening. His Adam's apple works, bobbing as he swallows.

His voice is full of gravel when he tells me, "It's just, I'm gonna be busy." He clears his throat and continues, "I've got eighteen credits this semester, plus an extra bakery shift, and I don't think—"

"Who do you think you *are*?"

"What?"

"Are you the same person who I talked to on the phone two nights ago? And the night before that, and the night before that, and twice a lot of days, when the house was empty with Frankie at school? Was that you, or was that some other guy who just *sounded* like you?"

"You know it was me."

"So what are you saying?"

He crosses his arms. Completely unable to look at me. "I'm saying I want to back off this thing."

"This thing."

"Us."

"You're breaking up with me?"

"We were never going out."

The words drop onto the ground between us, and I look at the place where they land, right in front of his feet. The frozen gray slush. West is standing braced—his legs wide, his arms crossed, the restaurant door ten feet behind him, glowing like a beacon.

He planned this. He was ready for it.

And he's still doing a really terrible job of pretending not to give a shit.

We were never going out.

We're not friends.

He told me less than forty-eight hours ago that he wanted to tongue my clit until my thighs were trembling. I don't know what's changed. Something. Nothing. He hasn't bothered to tell me.

Because, after all, when does he ever bother to tell me anything?

I should be angry, but I'm so surprised and so fucking *disappointed*. I thought I'd be in his bed right now. I thought we'd be smiling, naked, rolling on a condom so I could finally, *finally*, feel him inside me.

Instead, he's so far away, I can't even find him in his own face.

"Right," I say slowly, looking at those five pathetic words on the ground. "We were never going out."

He glances at the restaurant behind him. "I gotta go."

I should let him.

I should tell him to go fuck himself.

But I need something, some rope to catch hold of, some idea what happens next. So I ask, "Will I see you? At the bakery, or will you come to the rugby party Saturday, or . . . ?"

"I'm sure I'll see you around."

"Yeah. Great. That's just fucking great, West."

His eyebrows have drawn in, like maybe I'm getting to him a little bit.

It could be because tears are making hot tracks down my face, puddling beneath my jaw, cooling on my neck.

It could be that.

"You have a great shift," I tell him. "I'll see you *around*. It's a good thing we're not friends, or else maybe I'd miss you. Or something more than friends—it's a good thing we weren't going out, or I'd be gutted right now. But, you know, we're not. Going out. Obviously. It's so obvious, I'm not sure why I didn't get the memo on that. Maybe it was the phone sex, addling my stupid female brain. Or, hell, maybe it was all those hours we spent together at the bakery, hanging out, or that time when I slept in your bed and cried on your lap on the bathroom floor. I just got *confused* about what we are. I didn't get the memo."

"Caroline—"

I take a step back. I lose my footing, slip, and fall on my tailbone. The pain pushes up more tears. When West offers me his hand, I swat it away. "No. I'm fine. Enjoy your night."

I lumber up, and if his eyes have thawed at last—if his expression is full of as much misery as I'm feeling—damn it, I'm not going to let it matter.

I'm going to walk away from him before all of it can catch up to me.

I walk fast, and then I start to jog, because I'm afraid if I let myself feel everything that's in me right now, I'll have to accept that he's breaking my heart on purpose, and he won't fucking tell me why.

The rugby party is legendary.

It's actually three parties. Starting right after dinner, there's a pre-party in Rawlins lounge that's just for the team. At nine, the whole-campus party kicks off in the Minnehan Center, which is always packed with bodies, because the rugby team throws the first big party after winter break, plays the best music, and never runs out of beer.

In between the two parties—well, that's why it's legendary. The blow-job contest.

Last year I missed it. I guess I was studying. But this time there's no question I'm going. I helped Quinn with the planning, showed up to decorate Minnehan with paper cutouts of fierce rugby-playing women and this sort of oversize mural thing on the wall, which I think was supposed to be a life-size representation of a scrum but ended up looking like a giant lesbian orgy, all tongues and hands. Really we're just lucky nobody from the college is paying attention to the decorations, because wow.

Wow.

Quinn says she's going to save it and put it up in her dorm room after the party.

I made cheese-and-salsa dip and cookies, but nobody's hungry. They're thirsty. Quinn brought three gallons of fruit punch and three bottles of vodka. We mix the drinks right in the red plastic cups. Mine makes my stomach hurt—vodka always does—but I sip it, standing on the fringes, watching the others dance.

I don't want to drink too much. I'm afraid I'll do something stupid, like show up at West's door and yell at him.

Like tell him that even though I know he doesn't *do* parties, and he wants to *back off this thing,* I wish he were with me tonight.

So I could kick him.

And then probably kiss him.

I'd like to drink six drinks in a row, but that would be kind of dumb. So. Here I am, sipping my Solo cup of punch slowly and carefully like a good little girl, and when Quinn tries to get me to join her in an interpretive dance-off, I just smile and say, "No, thanks, I'll watch."

I'll watch Bridget and Krishna laughing together on the other side of the room, my friends who aren't officially supposed to be here, except they helped Quinn and me set up, and nobody cares, really.

I'll watch Quinn undulate, pretending to be a jellyfish, because that's her assigned interpretive-dance theme.

I'll watch the door, even though he's not coming, wasn't invited to this party, would've said no if I invited him.

I'll stand here and watch my life pass me by, because I'm a good daughter, a party planner, a brownnosing rule-following coward. And the way things are going, that's all I'll ever be.

We leave the lounge wrecked, put on jackets and hats, twine on scarves, stumble out into the overcast night. The temperature is in the high twenties, the snow thick and slushy. We slog toward the rugby field along the train tracks to a spot behind the Minnehan Center that Quinn and I diligently cleared off earlier. Forty feet of snow-free track gleaming in parallel lines.

Already, some people are milling around—mostly players' friends, girlfriends, boyfriends. As we take bottles out of backpacks and unwrap disposable shot glasses to line them up along the tracks, the crowd grows. I've got a cloth envelope full of money. I'm supposed to be the cashier, but when Quinn sinks to her knees beside the tracks and says, "Let's go, girls. Line 'em up!" I don't want to anymore.

I don't want to be on the outside, looking in.

I find Krishna's head in the crowd and beckon him over. "You're the cashier," I tell him, pressing the envelope into his hand.

"Only if you do me for free."

"Fine. You can be my first." I catch Quinn's eye. "I want in on this."

"Sweet! We've got another virrrrgin!"

The idea that I'm a blow-job virgin is patently hilarious, but no one is mocking me here.

She makes some room beside her, gets me a shot, sets it up on the tracks in front of me. "All right!" she shouts, and the crowd starts to gather in around us. "You all know how this works! Ten bucks gets you two blow jobs—one for you, one for the awesome, amazing, ass-kicking rugger across the tracks. You pay your girl, she lets you stick your tenner down her shirt, it's all very kinky. We all go on the same whistle. The drink goes on the tracks, and you have to drink it with your hands free in one try. If you choke or spit it all over your face like a *loser,* go to the back of the line. If your rugger chokes or gets it on herself, you can have your money back. If you both swallow like big kids, you can pay another ten and go again if you want. You all know Krishna?"

Eyes turn toward Krishna. Heads nod.

"Right. Everybody knows Krish. You need change, talk to Krish. I'm also appointing him the asshole referee. This is supposed to be *fun* to raise *money* for *rugby.* Yes, the shots are called blow jobs. Yes, it's ever so naughty. But if you step over the line from fun and games to junk-grabbing or name-calling or any other form of small-minded assholery, Krish is going to give you the boot, and a dozen pissed-off ruggers are going to back him up. This is a safe space. For ev-er-y-one. Got it?"

More nodding and some cheers. The crowd's happy, we're happy. We aren't the only ones who threw a pre-party. "All right! Let's do it! Where's my whistle girl?"

Somehow, Bridget has the whistle. The first row of takers pays their money and gets down on their knees.

"Hands behind your backs!" Bridget yells.

I tuck my fingers into my back pockets, just so I won't be tempted.

Krishna winks at me.

"Suck them down, girls!" Bridget cries, and blows the whistle.

I dip my head. It's awkward just getting my face down to the level of the tracks, and I have to open my jaw wide to fit my mouth around the shot glass. Wide enough to make it ache. As I sit up, something flashes in my peripheral vision, a camera or a flashlight or just light gleaming off the tracks.

I see myself from the outside. Head thrown back. Eyes closed. A parody of exploitation.

The shot slides down my throat—Baileys, Kahlúa, whipped cream. Burning and cold at once, foreign and alarming. I stifle my gag reflex. My eyes tear up. It's impossible not to remember hands in my hair, pulling too hard. Nate's dick shoved farther down my throat than I wanted it, and this same sensation right at the borderline of gagging.

It's not funny. It's not.

But when I swallow and lift my head, nobody's got their hands on me. I have Quinn on my right. Bridget with her whistle, smiling. Krishna across from me with whipped cream all over the front of his black jacket, wheezing with laughter. "That is fucking *gross,*" he says.

"You lose!" Quinn taunts. "Back of the line."

It's the strangest thing, because I'm not drunk, and I'm not traumatized, and I'm not crazy.

I'm not a dumb cunt.

I'm not a slut, I'm not frigid, I'm not a disappointment.

I'm just a girl who did a shot off the train tracks, high-fiving her friends, savoring the warmth spreading down her throat and into her stomach.

It's stupid. But I'm okay. I'm actually kind of happy.

The next couple of shots are guys I don't know. I get the second one down but choke on the third, and that guy waves off the money when I try to give it back. I let him buy another round even though he's not supposed to. He chokes and dribbles whitish-yellow fluid all over his chin, which is sufficiently disgusting that we both bust up laughing. "I'm Aaron," he says, offering me his hand.

I take it. It's sticky. "Caroline."

He smiles. "I know."

I decide what he means is exactly what he said. He knows my name. Nothing worse than that.

"Maybe I'll see you at the party later," he tells me when he gets up, damp patches on the knees of his jeans.

Maybe he will.

There's another guy. After him, the thighs that plunk down in front of me belong to Scott.

Rugby Scott.

"Hi," he says.

"Hi."

"Fancy seeing you here."

I laugh at that. Actually, I kind of snort. I've had . . . uh-oh. Some drinks. Five. Or six? They're not very big.

Quinn taught us to make them with a lot of whipped cream and not so much of the hard stuff, because a few years ago one of the ruggers had to go to the hospital with alcohol poisoning. We're supposed to get rotated out every so often, but I'm still fine. I'm better than fine.

"Did you think you wouldn't see me?"

"Um . . ." His eyes flick to mine. "Does that question have a right answer?"

"Pay up, people!" Bridget shouts. Scott extends his hand, a ten-dollar bill sticking out between his fingers.

"Where am I supposed to put this?"

I've got money sticking out of my pocket, and the twenty plastered to my neck is poking me in my ear. I look heavenward, feigning exasperation. "Anywhere you want, big boy."

That cracks us both up.

He puts it in my pocket.

I wonder if he's been drinking, too.

I wonder why he's here. If he came thinking he'd see me. If he was looking forward to it.

One of the players sets a shot in front of me and plunks another down in front of Scott.

Bridget blows the whistle. "DRINK!"

I open my jaw wide. Put my head down, suck up my shot, knock it back. My eyes don't sting anymore. My lips are sticky and sweet, my hands cold from being out of my pockets so long. Scott gets his shot down, too, and pulls another ten from his wallet.

"I'm supposed to do this again now?" he asks.

"You're allowed."

"Oh, it's a privilege."

I beam at him. "It's *definitely* a privilege. And it's for a good cause."

This time, he tucks the money in my coat. It's zipped up

to my scarf, so when he wraps his fingers around the collar, just for a second, he's touching a perfectly innocent bit of chest real estate about five inches north of my boobs. And even that through a couple of layers of clothing.

But our eyes meet, and I know what he did, and so does he. Whistle. "DRINK!"

This one goes down funny. I start to choke, and I have to grip the train track for a second, cold iron through brown leather, sucking air into my nose. In my peripheral vision, I notice a disturbance. Movement. A ripple of aggression.

"Not your turn, dude," I hear Krishna say.

"I get to go again." Scott.

"I don't care."

I know that voice.

I look up and see West, down on one knee across from me.

He must have shoved to the front of the line. Barged right in and removed Scott, which is totally not allowed. If anyone else had done it, Krishna would have had them kicked out, but West is West, and they're friends.

West is West, and he's got some kind of point he wants to make. God knows what it is.

His jaw is tight. There's a line between his eyebrows, a hardness to his mouth. I wonder how long he's been watching and what kind of right he thinks he has here, anyway.

The muscle in his jaw flexes, his teeth grinding together.

"You're here for a blow job?"

"No."

I cross my arms, pouting. "Well, blow jobs are what's on offer. Are you in or are you out?"

Someone slides a shot down the tracks to the space in front of him. Bridget shouts, "Pay up!"

West frowns, opens his wallet, takes out a bill.

He extends it to me.

"You're supposed to put it *on* me."

"I'm not doing that."

"Everybody's doing that."

He hesitates, and I think he won't. He seems troubled by all this, not sure if I'm being exploited, exploiting myself.

I'm not sure, either, but I want to tell him that sometimes you just have to trust the way it feels. You have to believe that happy things can make you happy and wrong things feel wrong.

I want to tell him that tonight he has to trust me to know what I want, instead of making up my mind for me.

He's not in charge of me. He never was.

We were never going out. We weren't friends. And I haven't spent every hour since I last saw him two nights ago feeling brokenhearted, furious, betrayed.

Behind him, Scott is waiting. Hopeful Scott. Nice, ordinary, *possible* Scott. A guy I could take home to meet my dad. He must have driven all the way from Carson tonight for me.

It's a shame Scott's not who I want.

I reach out, grab West's wrist, and drag his hand to my chest. "This is a good spot."

Our eyes meet. He stuffs the bill inside my coat, down into my cleavage, his long fingers tamping it like an explosive.

I haven't been this close to him since before break. Only in my dreams. Only in my bed in the dark, remembering the sound of his voice in my ear, the heat of his body, the slide of his tongue.

The whistle blows. "DRINK!"

I keep my eyes on West as I bend down to take the shot. He doesn't drink his. He just watches me.

He watches me swallow it.

He's watching me when I open my eyes.

Maybe it's because I'm drunk, but I don't think so. I think

it's because I'm tired of doing what everyone expects me to. I'm tired of waiting around to be claimed, telling myself it's what I want.

I'm tired of being afraid of what might happen.

It already happened.

So I reach across the tracks, leaning way over with my ass in the air, pick up his shot, and knock it back with my eyes closed.

Then I look right into his eyes. I lick my lips, slow and seductive.

And that's all it takes.

West reaches out, fists his hands in my coat, and yanks me into him. We meet at the mouth.

It's the most obscene kiss of my life. Deep and hard, gasping hot, sticky-sweet, messy.

It turns out that West doesn't even need words to make the point he came here to make.

Mine, his mouth says. *Mine, mine, mine*.

But I'm not. I'm my own. And I grab his hair, pull it, scratch his neck, punishing him for not getting that. For doing this, for never having done this before—I don't know. Punishing him for torturing me.

It goes on, and I'm vaguely aware of somebody whooping. Maybe lots of somebodys. I don't care. My hands clench and unclench at his hips. He's saying my name. Kissing down my neck to my throat. He's catching his breath, pressing his forehead against mine.

And then he's standing up, leaving me cold. Alone.

He shoots a glare at Scott and walks away.

It's only then that I understand how deeply, righteously, incandescently furious I am.

———

I'm stripped to my bra, dancing in a heaving mass of shirt-less, sweaty, smiling, grinding women.

I'm safe, and I'm drunk, and I'm tired of men writing their claims on my body.

Slut, Nate wrote, and I believed him.

Mine, West wrote, and I let him, I melted, I gave him my surrender and my tongue, but I'm *mad* now. I've had enough of his shit. *Enough.*

Quinn's at my hip, bumping my ass, lifting my hand and twirling me around. Two girls are hugging, kissing with tongue in front of me. Bridget's dancing with Krishna, a beer in her hand.

There's a reason the rugby party is popular beyond the blow jobs, and it has a lot to do with the pile of shirts on the stage by the DJ. We're down to our sports bras, lace bras, acres of exposed flesh, girls who are too fat and too thin and just right, and none of us cares. We're here to dance. We're here for one another.

There's a line dance. I don't know the steps. They're sim-ple, but I keep forgetting them, crashing into people, spin-ning out too far on the twirl and losing my balance, finding it again. When I fall, hands reach out to clasp mine and lift me up. Bodies press into me, a hugging sisterhood of thrust-ing hips and lifted arms, sunglasses and duckface, bathed in disco-ball light.

I'm not bad. I'm not good. I'm just alive. I'm just here, dancing.

I love everyone. Everyone loves me. We're heat and sweat, young and beautiful, sexy, together. Not one of these women would hurt me.

I drink and I'm drunk. I dance and I'm breathing, moving, living.

We're in the middle of the dance floor, the center of

everything, and sometimes I think I catch sight of him at the edge of the room.

Boots and crossed legs, leaning against the wall. Hooded eyes. Watching.

Sometimes I think I see pants with whales on them. A smirking smile that knows too much. A dimple that made me think I was safe when I never was, no matter how nice his parents are or how good his manners.

But I'm angry and I'm dancing and I don't care.

Fuck them.

Fuck them both.

"I don't want to see him."

"Shh!"

"What? I'm *whispering*."

I trip over something, and Quinn gets my elbow and helps me up. We're in West's apartment. I'm still drunk, but I'm sober enough to know this is a bad idea.

"You don't have to see him," Krishna says. "He's sleeping. Keep your trap shut, and you'll be fine."

Quinn turns on the TV, and a wall of sound blasts out and knocks me down. "Whoa," I say from the floor.

"Shit!" She starts giggling.

She and Krishna are fighting for the remote. I'm thinking about whether I should leave, but Bridget helps me up and shoves a cold bottle of water in my hand, so I drink that instead. I close my eyes, savoring every freezing, quenching, amazing swallow.

The sound drops off to a hush. The apartment smells like West's apartment, and it's full of memories I don't want right now—except, of course, that I always want them and I always want *him* and there's nothing I can do about it.

The water soothes my throat, at least. My feelings will have to wait for some other night.

I open my eyes because my balance is off, which is much more obvious now that we're not at the party. Bridget is right up in my face, tucking my hair behind my ear, and I have to stick a hand out and brace myself against a cabinet so her beer-smelling concern doesn't bowl me over again.

"Why did you bring me here?" My question is supposed to be a whisper, but it sounds like a whimper. "I don't want to see him."

"I know, sweetie. I *know*. We weren't sure what else to do with you. We have to sober you up, and you were too loud for the dorm."

She leads me to the couch, where Quinn and Krishna are already sitting. When I sit, too, Bridget pulls my head into her lap and detangles my hair with her fingers. The air feels cool against my neck. The movie is stupid, something with cars and guns. Just when my eyes are starting to get heavy, food arrives—three huge containers of nachos from the pizza place. I sink down to the floor, wedging myself between couch and cinder-block coffee table props. I stuff chips and salt and cheese into my mouth.

"This is sooooo good."

"Don't forget to chew," Krishna says. "You know that's all coming back up later."

"No way," Quinn says.

"Are you serious?"

Krishna and Quinn are still arguing amicably over what the odds are that I'm going to puke before morning when the front door flies open. West blinks at us in dull surprise for several long seconds before Krishna says, "Fuck."

"Nice greeting." He bends down to take off his snow-covered boots and disappears from view. I'm down by the floor, covered in chip crumbs and probably smeared all over with nacho cheese. He hasn't seen me. I don't care.

"Dude, I thought you were asleep in your room," Krishna says.

"Not asleep."

"Yeah, so I gather. You been at the bar?"

There's a dull thud. "Yeah." Then a few seconds' silence and a loud crash. "Shit."

"You're drunk."

"No kidding."

Krishna turns to look at Quinn, eyes wide. She makes this shooing motion with her hands that means, *Get him into his bedroom.* Krishna stands up, nachos in hand, and it's the wrong move, because West zeroes in on the container, says, "You guys got food?" and walks toward the couch.

Then he sees me and stops.

"Have to talk to you."

"I don't want to talk," I tell him.

"Yeah. I bet. Listen—" He cuts himself off. Looks at Bridget, Quinn, and Krishna. "You guys should probably fuck off for a while."

"It's three in the morning," Quinn says.

"In *winter*," Bridget points out.

Krishna crosses his arms. "We're responsible for her tonight."

"I'll be responsible," West tells him.

"You're drunk."

"So?"

"So you can't take off your shoes without falling over. I'm not giving you Caroline."

"Hello? I'm down here? Alive and well? Perfectly capable of making my own decisions?"

"I'm taking her," West says.

"I'm not leaving her," Krishna insists.

"Fine. Stay. But we're going in the bedroom."

"Maybe I don't want—"

And then I'm upside down, with West's shoulder a hard pressure in my gut, and I have to focus, because my eyes are prickling and hot and I'm afraid I'm going to puke on him.

He picked me up. Picked me up off the *floor* and threw me over his shoulder.

That *dick*.

When he sets me down, I bump into the wall. He closes the door and locks it.

He's so dead.

"You *Neanderthal*. You fucking—fucking—*Piltdown Man*. How dare you? How *dare* you?"

He's over by his desk, pulling his wallet out and setting it in the drawer. Taking off his jacket. Unzipping his hoodie. He opens a drawer and pulls out a string of condoms and puts one in his pocket.

"What's that for?"

"Don't worry about it."

"Don't *worry*? How about you stop acting like an entitled caveman who can just kiss me when he wants to, throw me over his shoulder and carry me into his room and get out a *condom*, like *that's* ever going to happen, who can just phone-sex me when he wants to get off and throw me away when he's all done? How about—"

"Caroline." He sits down on the bed. His voice is slow and soothing. "We got things to talk about. Could you maybe give it five minutes without the screeching?"

"I'm not screeching!"

But it comes out pretty screechy.

I turn around and face the wall, covering my face with my hands because it hurts too much to look at him.

I need to be angry, because if I stop being angry, all that's left is disappointment and wanting, and I can't afford either of them anymore. They cost too much. They've been taking too much out of me for too long.

His bedsprings squeak. Even *that* seems poignant, a sound I remember from being in his bed, his hands on me, his mouth. My eyes flood with tears, and I'm so disappointed with myself.

"Caroline."

His voice is right behind me now. I've heard it like that, my name low and intimate, right before he comes. It's more than I can bear—the way my heart lifts, my body responds, even as I'm trying to locate my anger and push back the tears. "Don't."

But he doesn't listen. He puts one hand against the wall and the other at the small of my back. He leans in, his mouth by my ear, the heat of his body behind me close enough to feel, close enough to make me yearn, close enough to draw me back in if I let it, if I break, if I'm weak.

"Please," he says.

There's a knock on the door. "You okay, Caroline?"

Quinn's voice. I can imagine her and Krishna and Bridget, lined up out there. Worried about me.

I think about the party tonight, the dancing, the feeling of being surrounded by people who love me.

I'm not weak. I'm a little drunk—getting more sober by the second—but I'm strong.

I draw in a deep breath and find that strength. Wrap it around me.

Then I take my hands away from my face and turn to face West. "I'm fine," I call, loud enough for them to hear me. "He can have ten minutes."

"You sure?" Krishna asks.

"Go watch your fucking movie," West says.

After a moment, the volume on the TV goes up.

Then we're just looking at each other, West and me. His face so perfectly not-perfect. That wide, smart-ass mouth that can make me feel electric, make me feel like I'm drowning, make me feel like I could live on him and him alone.

His mouth is a lie.

I take him apart, one piece at a time. Chin, cheekbones, nose, eyebrows. Those eyes. His pupils blown, light rims around them, dark circles beneath.

It's just a face. West's face.

His breath is just breath, reeking of alcohol.

He's a man, sitting here. Not a problem for me to solve. Not an obligation, not a need, not love. Maybe not even my friend.

I can almost make myself believe it.

"What do you want?" I ask.

His mouth opens. His eyes narrow. He puts his hand to the back of his neck, lowers his head, exhales.

"Yeah," I say, because it's easy to see right now. I'm not sure if it's the false wisdom of all those blow jobs and beers or if it's because I've been so angry, but I feel like all the pretense has been stripped away, all the cozy lies I've hidden behind burned off on the dance floor. I feel wise, and there are things I know that I haven't known before.

Like this—this truth: West doesn't know what he wants.

"That's your whole problem, isn't it?"

He made that speech in my room last month, told me, "I want you, and I don't know how to stop wanting you. I want to get deep inside you, and then deeper, until I'm so deep I don't even know what's me anymore and what's you." He said that, but he hasn't made up his mind about it. He's afraid. He's still drawing pencil lines around us.

I could tell him that it's already too late. It's been too late for a long time, maybe from the start.

Instead, I tell him, "I'm sick of waiting for you to figure it out."

His eyes come up. Those little flecks glittering with something, some protest. Some plea.

"I'm sick of you acting like I'm just going to be whatever you want me to be. Maybe I have been so far. I guess I've done whatever you said, followed your rules. But I'm finished. This isn't a game, and you're not in charge of it. And I think—"

"Caro—"

"No. I'm talking now. You can fucking wait. I have been *patient* with you, but my patience is *gone,* West. You don't get to barge into the line at the rugby thing and kiss me in front of everyone—in front of *everyone,* when you *dumped* me, when you've refused to admit we have something even to our friends for *months* now—and then walk away, like you've said your piece and that's that. You don't get to pick me up and throw me over your shoulder and drag me into your room like I don't have a say in it. And put a condom in your pocket because, what? What if you feel like fucking me later? Might as well be prepared? No. You don't get to do that. You want to be friends? We could have been friends. You want to be fuck buddies, you know, I was up for that! Probably I would've gotten too attached, gotten my heart broken, if we're being honest, but so what? I wouldn't be the first girl in the history of the world to let that happen to her. But you're the one who said to let you know when I'm ready to see other guys, and you're the one who dropped me after break like nothing we said or did on the phone mattered, so don't pretend you have any right at all to play the jealous boyfriend when *you're not my fucking boyfriend.*"

I'm poking him in the chest now, and it's possible that I'm crying, but we're not going to examine that too closely, because I need to do this. It feels like such a relief to get it out, to accuse him, to beat on him with these words I've been holding inside me for far too long.

"I'm sorry," he says.

"You *should* be sorry. You've been a jerk to me, and I just take it. I let you. But I'm not letting you anymore. You want to be with me, make up your fucking mind."

He catches my face in his palms. I can't even hear over the rush of blood in my ears, my pounding heart, my fury. I'm not sure what's wrong with me. I said my piece. I should go, but he's trapped me here between his hands, his eyes on me, and I don't want to be anywhere else.

Everything I said is true, and I still want to be right here.

"*You're* the coward." My voice is hoarse. Low. Shocked, because I'm only now figuring this out.

"I know."

"And a liar."

"I know."

"You're *playing* with me."

He shakes his head. "No. I'm not—I don't mean to. I just can't."

"You can't what?"

Another shake, and our noses bump and slide past each other. He's not kissing me. He's right up against me, rubbing his cheek into mine. Scratching his stubble over my chin. *I need you.* That's what he's trying to tell me. *I want you.*

I need him, too. Want him, too. But it's not fair of him to give me this and nothing else. It's not *enough*.

"I can't," he repeats.

"I don't even know what you're talking about." I don't

sound so harsh anymore. I sound gentle. I feel gentle, because, God, I care about him, even though it's wrong and
dumb. He's hurting, and I care. "I can't know, because you
don't tell me *anything*."

"I know. I'm sorry."

Now I push his hands off me and grab his head, the way
he did mine. I want him to see me. I want him to hear, to
understand. I sink my fingers into his hair, hold him there.
Make him listen. "You could tell me," I say. "There isn't anything you couldn't tell me. God, anything—you *know* I'm on
your side. And if you just told me . . ." I trail off, thinking
what that would be like.

I should keep silent, but there's too much alcohol in me,
too much openness not to say all of this.

I look in his eyes.

"If you just told me, then we could get into that bed and
crawl under the covers. We could take everything off, and we
could really be together. Deep and then deeper, just like you
said. You know how it would be, West. We both know."

"Incredible," he says.

I dip my thumb down, run it over the arch of his eyebrow.
"Yeah. Incredible."

I put my arms around him, gather him close, tuck my
head against his neck, because I think he needs this. I'm
pretty sure I'm the only person in Iowa who's ever hugged
him, and in Oregon, who knows? Maybe no one hugs him
but me.

I hold him tight, and he's shaking. Actually shaking.

I feel sorry for him. That's a new thing. I think this is the
first time since I met him that I didn't feel like West had all
the power, held all the cards. The first time I've ever believed
he's maybe even more screwed up than I am.

I kiss his jaw. I stroke his back one more time, because it's broad and warm and strong, and the truth is I can't help it. I never could.

But after all that, I let go. Take a step back. Meet his eyes and lift my chin.

"It's deeper or nothing," I tell him. "So make up your mind."

This time, I'm the one who walks away.

January ended. February came.

I quit selling weed and got rid of my stash. Without Caroline around, the bakery was dead. I worked hard, studied while the bread rose, listened to the buzzing fluorescents.

It was boring. Boring and miserable.

Three weeks passed when I didn't see Caroline, and, even so, she was woven through my life. My memories, my dreams, my thoughts. It turns out you can't cut someone out of your heart just by wanting to.

I didn't want to hurt her.

I didn't want to hand her the power to wreck me.

I didn't want to fuck her and walk away like it meant nothing, like *she* meant nothing.

I just wanted to be with her. All the time. Every way. Even though I was leaving, and even though I didn't deserve her.

"Deeper or nothing"—that's what she said before she walked out of my apartment and out of my life.

I was too scared to pick. Too scared to follow her outside, tell her what she wanted to know, go down on my knees and beg if I had to.

I was too caught up in all these questions I didn't have answers to.

What if you go after the love of your life and it ruins you?

What if you don't, and you figure out you're already ruined?

What if there's no right thing? Only you and the girl you love and your fear. A ticking clock, a mother you can't trust, a sister who needs you, a father determined to fuck up anything good you manage to get your hands on.

I'd shied away from deeper, but I never gave much thought to the alternative.

Nothing, or deeper.

My choice to make.

What kind of dipshit chooses nothing?

Smoke fills my lungs, and it's been so long, the rush is immediate.

The high is ugly. It amplifies my bad mood, so much that I can feel my lip curl, the corners of my mouth turning down. My nostrils flare.

I take another deep drag.

I'm on the sunporch at the back of the restaurant, grabbing a five-minute smoke in the middle of the Valentine's Day service rush. It's cold out here, the sounds of the kitchen muffled by insulation and wood siding.

Tips are good tonight. I should be content to work, but I'm crawling out of my fucking skin.

I haven't seen Caroline in twenty-two days.

In the window, against the darkness outside, my reflection stares back at me, pissed off and mean.

I look like my father.

I'm the age he was in my first memory of him. He bought me a bike with training wheels and Spider-Man on the seat. I thought he was fucking amazing. My father, I mean. Not Spidey, although Spidey was pretty great, too.

My dad and my mom were always kissing, hands everywhere. I wasn't allowed in Mom's bed at night when he came around. They made noises in there, so I had to squint my eyes closed and send my thoughts away. I would lie on the couch under an old green nylon sleeping bag, rubbing the satiny lining under my chin, thinking about how awesome it would be when they got married. How I'd have two parents.

Kids with two parents lived in a house with a yard. I knew this because I watched the kids at school who had what I wanted, and the main thing they had was dads *and* moms. Dads with jobs and wedding rings who showed up for school concerts with video cameras and waved.

Five feet away, on the other side of the paneling, the headboard knocked out its rhythm. My parents' voices blended together, low and urgent, full of pain.

I figured that before too long I'd get a dog to go with the kitten my dad had brought home out of the blue the week before.

Before too long, everything would be perfect.

It didn't last, though. It never lasted. He argued with my mom, and she didn't manage to calm him down. He kept harping on how much she'd spent on some shirt she bought. The fight escalated into a tirade about her nagging, her neediness, what a useless fucking *burden* we both were.

He got behind the wheel drunk, backed out into the road with a spray of gravel, and jerked the car forward so fast he ran over the kitten.

He stopped then. I threw myself to my knees beside the car. He got out, and both of us looked.

That poor fucking kitten. I couldn't stop staring at it. My mom was standing against the door, crying like she was the one he'd run into, while I watched the kitten try to breathe with its chest crushed.

I thought we were united. I thought he was looking at the kitten the way I was, trying to breathe for it, soaked in remorse and confusion and a desperate, unraveling kind of hope for its rescue.

I kept thinking that. Right up until he hauled off and kicked it.

It wasn't even dead, but he kicked it hard enough to send it sailing on a low arc, inches above the ground. It rolled through the gap in the neighbor's trellis, coming to a stop underneath, too far underneath the trailer for me to reach.

It would rot there. I didn't know that yet.

"Quit crying," he said. "It's just a fucking cat."

When he got in the low-slung car, pulled the door handle shut, and drove away, I didn't hate him. I blamed my mom for all of it—the argument, his anger, the kitten.

I didn't hate him, but I understood for the first time that he and I aren't the same.

He's the kind of man who would kick a kitten.

I'm not.

My mom doesn't seem to get that. This morning she sent me a text that said, Happy Valentine's Day to the love of my life!

I held the phone in a tight grip. It was either that or fling it across the room.

The love of her life.

When she's with my dad, she calls him that. Wyatt Leavitt, the love of her life. Her sweet man. Her wanderer.

"There's nothing like passion," she told me last time she took him back. "You wouldn't understand, Westie, you're too young, but passion is what we're made for. Without it . . ." She shrugged, cast her eyes at the ceiling, searching for the right words. "Without it, we're just animals."

This about a man who's gut-punched her. A man who split my lip when I tried to protect her because he was smacking her around, calling her names, slapping her silly while she cried and begged him not to, not to hurt her so bad, "Please, honey, don't."

The love of her life.

And I look just exactly fucking like him.

The hostess, Jessica, sticks her head through the door. "Sixteen's ready for the check, eight's stacked the menus up by the edge of the table, and I took a dessert order for you on twelve. If you don't get back out there, I'm telling Sheila to fire you."

"Coming."

I open the outside door, drop the half-finished cigarette on the concrete step, and grind it out under my shoe.

Jessica waits until she actually sees me moving before she heads for the front.

I take the check to table sixteen, get table eight's order, deliver dessert to twelve. Then I check on my other tables. The whole time, my mother's words are drilling a hole between my eyebrows.

The love of my life.

I've dedicated almost ten years to trying to be the man my father should have been but isn't. A man who will put the family first, no matter what. Keep them safe, keep them fed, keep them happy.

I never wanted to be her love. Her kind of love—it makes you weak. It drags you under.

But tonight, more than any of the past twenty-two nights I've spent without Caroline, I can't help thinking there's more than one way to drown.

Another waiter passes me and says, "Jessica just gave you six."

"Thanks."

When I take the water pitcher over, I find my econ teacher at the table. A plump woman, she once brought along four kids and a bag of powdered-sugar doughnuts to a study session and let them go to town. She's with her husband tonight, dressed up nice. She shows me off a little. "One of my best students last semester," she calls me, and she says she hopes to have me in her seminar next year.

I take their order and wish them a happy Valentine's Day.

I like her, so I make an effort to uncurl my lip when I say it.

Back in the kitchen, I put the order in and pick up appetizers for another table, a four-top. I push through the kitchen door with a plate in each hand, two more balanced on my forearms, thinking about another dinner with another woman old enough to be my mother.

Two years ago on Valentine's Day was the first time I ever set foot in the Tomlinson house. Mrs. Tomlinson had a candlelight dinner prepared at the resort kitchen, and she said she'd pay me two hundred bucks if I played waiter for a couple of hours.

I served the food and stood in the corner where she'd told me to stand, watching them eat—this man who'd taken me under his wing and the woman he married. His love.

This man I wanted so badly to be like, because he had everything I wanted. Respect, money, security, skill.

Mrs. T wore a black dress cut low in the front, her tits half hanging out, diamonds dripping from her ears, down into her cleavage, sparkling on her fingers. She cooed at her husband, talking about their wedding day.

"The happiest day of my life," she said.

The next week, I fucked her in his bed. She wanted me to take her from behind. I climbed on top of her, did her until she scratched at the sheets, arched her back, came with a yowl like a cat.

I remember holding her hips, pushing into her. A mindless pistoning piece of meat.

No better than an animal.

My mother's love is a disaster, but I wasn't doing any better for myself until I met Caroline.

I came to Putnam thinking love was a weakness and sex was a tool. Maybe I was right. I think, with the life I've had, I'd have to be some kind of dumb-fuck not to be at least a little afraid of the way I feel about Caroline.

I've been worried that *deeper* is an undertow that will take away my control and leave me as helpless and deluded as my mom. I've thought if I let that happen—if I let myself get distracted by Caroline, broke the rules, said *fuck it* to my common sense—then I couldn't respect myself, because I'd be no better than my father. No smarter than my mom.

But here I am, hustling steaks and salads and quinoa cakes to one couple after another, smiling and being charming even though I fucking hate this, I hate all of it, I hate everything when I'm not with Caroline, and I'm thinking the whole time, *What's it going to take, a mallet to the head? A neon fucking sign?*

I love Caroline. I want her. I want everything she'll give me, and it's not going to stop. It's never going to stop.

And I'm not my father.

I look just like him, but I'm not him. I've known that for a long time.

What I need to get through my head, maybe, is that I'm not my mother, either.

I'm not in love with a woman who doesn't deserve me. I'm not throwing myself at passion like it's a drug and I need a hit, begging it to take me in, shoot me up, wreck me if it has to.

I waited more than a year to even kiss Caroline, and I had plenty of time before then to learn what she's all about.

She's good. She's smart. She's fucking fierce.

Honestly, I'm glad she told me off. I was being a dick, and she called me on it. The woman I'm in love with is strong enough to insist I treat her the way she deserves.

I haven't. I haven't told her anything about me, my life, my family, my people, because I've been afraid she'd use it against me. Pick me apart. Break me open.

But why would she do that? She's not my father. Not my enemy.

She's Caroline.

Three weeks without her has taught me the same thing I should have figured out in the eighteen months since I met her: That she's amazing. That I'm in love with her. That passion feels fantastic.

Loving Caroline hasn't thrown me off a cliff.

I'm still me. Not my father. Not my mother.

If I get called home, I'm going, because I have to. It's not negotiable.

I don't know what's going to happen before then—not with Caroline and me or with anything, really. I could have to leave tomorrow. I could bite it in a convenience store holdup. We could all die from fucking bird flu.

But tonight, it's Valentine's Day.

If the world ends in the morning, I'm going to do

everything I can to make sure it ends with Caroline in my bed, her hair on my pillow, my hands on her ass.

And I mean that in the most romantic possible way.

I'm at her door, a dozen cheap gas-station roses clutched in my hand. I smell like sweat and dishwasher steam, and she's in her pajamas, her eyes slitted against the brightness of the hallway.

I woke her up.

I woke Bridget up.

If I stand here long enough, I'll probably wake up half the hall, and I don't give a fuck.

"What do you want to know?"

"What?" Her voice is thick with sleep.

"Tell me what you want to know. Ask me a question, I'll answer it. I'm an open book."

Her hair's all snarled at the crown of her head. I want to smooth it down, kiss her, take her in my arms.

Too soon. Too soon, even if this works out. And if it doesn't . . . I can't think about that.

"You're an open book," she repeats. She must be waking up, because she injects some skepticism into the words.

"Anything you want to know."

"Let's start with why you're here at—what time is it?"

"Eleven thirty-five."

"At eleven thirty-five at night on Valentine's Day"—and here she kind of eye-rolls at the bouquet in my hand—"when you haven't called me or texted me or given the least sign you remember I'm alive in almost a month."

"Twenty-two days."

"You're counting?"

"I can tell you how many hours if you want."

"Because . . ."

"Because when it comes to you, I'm a fucking moron. More than you know. Probably in a bunch of ways you don't have a clue about."

That almost makes her smile. I can see her lips twitch. She decides not to allow it, but lip twitching is a good sign, so I barrel on. "Look, I didn't mean to wake you up. I would've come sooner, but I was on at the restaurant, and there was this couple who came in right before ten and stayed for fucking ever, so this was the soonest I could get here. I guess I should have come tomorrow, but . . ."

. . . but I couldn't stand it anymore.

. . . but I needed to see you.

. . . but once I made up my mind, I didn't want to wait even four seconds longer than I had to.

"I brought you roses." I hold them out, the only gift I've ever given her, blood red and, I hope, so cheesy she has to like them.

"I see that."

I wait for her to say something more, give me a clue how I'm doing here. She scrubs her hands over her face—something I've seen her do a hundred times at the bakery to wake herself up.

"Okay," she says. "Okay, Mr. All-of-a-Sudden-I'm-an-Open-Book. Where are you from?"

"Oregon."

"What town, idiot."

"Silt."

"You're from a place called *Silt*?"

"Yes."

"What's it like there?"

"It's close to Coos Bay, which is on the ocean. Coos is

pretty—they get tourists. Silt is farther inland. It's kind of . . ." *A shithole.* "There's not much to it."

"So do you have parents, or are you, like, the product of spontaneous generation?"

She's teasing, but not really. My family's a sore spot between us, and she's pushing right into it. "Everyone has parents, Caro."

Bridget says from somewhere in the darkness, "Don't forget, you can slam the door on his foot."

I think about pulling my foot back, but I'll risk it. "I've got a mom. My dad's . . . not around. Most of the time. Which is much better for everybody involved. He's . . . bad news."

She meets my eyes, a slight pucker between her eyebrows. Fully awake now—this is how she looks in class. Listening hard enough to hear everything I'm not saying in between the things I am. "What's her name?"

"My mom? Michelle."

"Is she married to your dad?"

"No."

"So is she the Leavitt, or . . . ?"

"It's my dad's name."

"Any more brothers and sisters?"

"Just Frankie. I told you about her."

"No, you didn't."

Fair enough. "I will."

She tilts her head, thinking. "What's your favorite color?"

"Green."

"Best place you've ever been on vacation."

"We never went anywhere. California, I guess."

"Best present you ever got."

"That book you gave me."

Her eyes widen a fraction. "It's just a book. About bread."

"I liked it."

"What kind of presents do you usually get?"

"Clothes. Stuff I need. Shit my mom thought was funny but isn't particularly. Bo gave me a fifth of whiskey at Christmas."

"Who's Bo?"

"My mom's boyfriend. She and Frankie live with him."

"Why did you dump me after break?"

I'm not expecting the question. My eyes flick to the darkness past her shoulder. "Do you think . . . if I promise to tell you anything you want, will you come back to my place?"

She doesn't answer right away. Instead, she plucks the flowers out of my hand, peels back the clear plastic and tissue paper around the top, and studies them. "If this is just a cheap attempt to get laid on Valentine's Day, it's not going to work."

"It's not that."

After a long moment, she looks up.

I've seen her face a hundred ways. Cautious and hopeful, brave and fierce, happy and crying. I've seen her soft and open, her mouth thoroughly kissed. I haven't seen her look like this but once: that first night when I walked out to her car and invited her into the bakery.

Scared. She's scared of what's going to happen.

But she wants it anyway.

"What is this, then?" she asks.

I wish I could think of something perfect to say. I wish I had words that took in her and me, eighteen months of watching and waiting, nights I've lain awake, midnights we've passed together mixing dough and making each other laugh. Every dream I've had about her. Every time I heard her voice or got a text that made me smile or shake my head. Every night I held the phone to my ear and said whatever I could think of to make her squeak and moan and fall apart.

With all the ways I *know* her, I still don't know how to

make her understand how I can be standing here, completely unsure what it is I'm doing, where we're headed, what this is—and how I can still be so positive this is where I belong.

She's what I want. More than my plans, more than I want to be smart, more than I want to follow the rules—I want to be with her.

I need to. I have to. I want to.

I can't waste any more time trying to figure out which of those it is. Not when I doubt we have all that much time left to waste.

"I want to be your boyfriend," I blurt out.

Immediately I wish I'd thought of another way to put it. *I want to be your boyfriend*—worse than lame. Childish. The words drop into my gut, leaden.

I've never said them before.

Caroline is looking right at me, those big brown eyes full of interest and . . . sympathy, maybe.

Fuck it all, she feels sorry for me.

Too late. You waited too long.

But her mouth is soft, and so is her voice when she says, "Hang on a second."

I wait in the doorway, a hook tied to a line held in Caroline's hand. Just waiting to see where she'll drag me.

Keys jingle. She comes back with her coat and the lanyard she uses as a key chain dangling from her fingers. Her boots are by the door. She shoves her feet into them, yanking them over her pajama pants. "Don't wait up, Bridge," she says, and moves through the door, closing it behind her, jiggling the handle to make sure it's locked.

She's coming with me.

She turns around, her face close to mine, her body close, the flowers pressing into my coat, rustling and crinkling.

"Am I driving?"

I just stare at her. I haven't got a clue what I said to get this lucky.

Maybe she's a gift. The universe paying me back for my dad being such a hopeless shithead.

I'll take it.

"West?"

"Is . . . is that a yes?"

Her shoulders lift and fall with another plastic crinkle. "Do I ever tell you no?"

"You did once."

She smiles—her smile like the pink and orange at the horizon when I walk out of the bakery into the alley and get surprised by the morning.

I've been in the dark. I've been solitary, single-minded in pursuit of a life that felt like it might be enough—until she walked into it and it wasn't.

Deeper or nothing. My new motto.

"I didn't tell you no," she says. "I told you to make up your fucking mind. And look!" She waves the flowers in my face. "It worked. Now I'm being wooed."

"That's what you wanted, huh?" I smile. "Some good old-fashioned wooing?"

"Maybe it's some of what I wanted."

I lean in, on solid ground at last. "I'll woo you until you can't walk, sweetheart."

"Promises, promises."

She closes her eyes when I kiss her, but I keep mine open.

I want to watch the sun rise.

I think it's supposed to be awkward—walking to her car, the night cold enough to freeze my balls off. Driving to my apartment with the heat blasting and quiet all around us.

We go up the fire escape, leave our shoes by the door, pass through the common area into my bedroom. I hang my coat over my desk chair and sit down on the bed, legs stretched out, back against the wall.

She considers for a moment, then does the same thing.

We're side by side on my bed, and I keep waiting for it to go wrong, to feel wrong, but all I can feel is relief, if relief feels like walking with nothing dragging behind you after you've been towing a trailer of misery around for most of your life.

I turn a little so I can look at her.

Her hair's still all screwed up. She's got crud at the inside corner of one eye, and her bottom lip has a raised elliptical pad on it like you get when your lips are too dry because of the weather or because you've been biting them.

Which she does, while I watch. She catches her lip between her teeth, sucks it into her mouth, releases it with grooved white lines that pink up as I watch.

I want to devour her.

I'm pretty sure it's not time yet.

"You have to tell me what you need me to do now," I say. "I mean, you want to talk, but I'm not sure . . . I'm complete shit at this."

It's another kind of relief, it turns out. To be shit at it, and to just be able to say so.

"This being, what? Girls?" She's smiling.

"Yeah, you'd love for me to admit that."

"It would make me pretty happy to hear you say you're shit with girls, yeah."

"You didn't used to have any complaints about my skills."

"But that was, like, a practice environment. Make-out homework."

"You're saying I might be the kind of person who can't hack it in a real-world application."

She turns toward me, resting her shoulder against the wall. "I'm saying I have a feeling you've never had a girlfriend before."

"That's true," I tell her. "I've been with girls but I've never—"

I think about how to put it, and I start to tie myself up in knots before I remember that it's just Caroline and me. I get more than one shot at putting it right if it comes out wrong the first time.

"You're the first girl I ever cared about this way."

I thought admitting that to Caroline would be like taking a piece of myself and handing it to her.

It is.

And it isn't.

It's more like . . . like there's all this stuff I've packed into myself, a defense against what I'm afraid of. Rocks and dirt, bits of rebar and junk that I've found by the roadside. And what I'm giving her isn't *me,* it's a clawed-off piece of this barrier that I've gotten used to thinking of as me.

I don't need it. Not to keep me safe from her.

She's smiling, looking down at her hands where they're laid out on the bed. Just an inch or so from my hands. She nudges her fingers over until they overlap the tips of mine. "You know what the magic word was, at my room?"

"No, what?"

"Boyfriend." She glances at my face, then back down. "That's why I came with you. Because you said that."

"I should've said it a long time ago."

I mean it, too. I wish I'd been able to. I wish I hadn't wasted every night I might have been able to spend with her. "Friend. Boyfriend. You deserved both."

She reaches up to touch my face. Her fingers stroke over my forehead, past my temple, over my cheekbone, curling into a loose fist so she can skate her knuckles over my mouth. "You'll really tell me anything?"

"Yeah." The word is a whisper, the movement of my lips against her skin.

"If I asked you why you got so upset when I gave you that money at Christmas . . ."

God damn. Way to pick a woman who goes for the throat.

"Yes. If you asked me."

She sits, watching me for a moment.

"If I asked you why you came out to my car that night at the bakery?"

I nod and turn her hand over. Kiss her palm. It's corny, I guess, but I'm just so fucking happy she's here.

"How many . . . partners you've had."

I kiss her wrist. "Yes."

"How you feel about me."

"Yes."

But I think maybe she knows that already. I think it's there when I look at her, when she looks at me. If it wasn't already there, we wouldn't have lasted so long. We wouldn't have put each other through so much when it would've been easier to just not.

I like her, and I love her, and I want her.

If she asks, I'll tell her.

For now, though, because I want to and she's staring at my lips, I kiss her neck. I find her pulse and pause there, lick it, imagining the rush of blood and heat at her throat. Flattering myself that her heart's beating faster because of me.

I keep thinking she's going to stop me, but she doesn't, so I kiss all along beneath her jaw, behind her ear. I kiss her eyelids and her nose, her cheekbones, her chin.

I get my hand at the base of her spine, press up so she'll lift her hips, ease her down onto the bed.

I kiss her mouth.

She tastes like everything I've been starving for.

I keep on kissing her, and she keeps letting me. Her arms sneak around my back and rake down my spine. I'm over her, hips centered above hers, hard against soft. I didn't plan this, but her lips shape the welcome I've been waiting for my whole life, her arms are the anchor I need, her body is my home.

We're right together, Caroline and me. Even if I'm doing this wrong, completely fucking wrong, it doesn't matter.

We're right.

"Tell me what you need me to say."

There has to be something. I can't just get to kiss her. Nothing in my life is this simple.

She pushes me away and sits up. I follow her, think she's going to start making demands now. Insist on the answers to all the questions from a minute ago, which, okay, some of them aren't pretty. The answer to that first question, in particular, might mean she never wants to kiss me again, and doesn't that mean I *have* to tell her?

Does it? I'm not sure.

Caroline reaches down for the hem of her shirt, pulls it over her head, and throws it on the floor.

She's not wearing a bra.

Fuck, this isn't fair. I'm already having trouble with the ethics of the situation. I can't think about right and wrong while Caroline's tits are exposed, her nipples puckering in the cool air, her arms an open invitation.

"I should . . . We should. You know. Talk. If you want to?"

"I'm good. But you've got too many clothes on."

She unbuttons my dress shirt, working from the bottom while I hold on to her waist and gawp at her like I've never seen a naked woman before. There's just something different about Caroline. There always has been.

She takes her fingers off my buttons to snap them right in front of my eyes. "Up here."

I blink and shake my head, breaking the spell. "Sorry."

"And here I thought you missed *me*."

I kiss her forehead. "I did."

She yanks the last button free and says, "Off."

"You sure?"

She goes up onto her knees, so she's taller than me. Puts her hands on my shoulders, stares me right in the eye. "All I needed to hear was that you'd tell me. That you trust me."

"I always trusted you."

"No. You can't keep everything to yourself and still call it trust. Take off your shirt."

I shrug out of my button-up but hesitate on the T-shirt. I worked a long shift, and I had to hustle. "I stink."

She casts her eyes at the ceiling and grabs my hem, so I lift my arms above my head and let her pull the shirt off me. When I open my eyes, her breasts are in my face, and I don't see that I have any choice in the matter. I have to touch them.

God, she's so fucking *soft*. I hold them, testing the weight in my hands. I haven't forgotten the taste of her, the pressure of her nipple against the roof of my mouth. When she moans, I knock her over and fall on top of her, going after her with no art or plan or restraint. Sucking and licking, molding and squeezing, rubbing myself against her thigh, between her legs, over her hip bone, like a stupid kid.

Which is what I feel like. Young and dumb and lucky.

She's just as bad, grabbing at me in fistfuls—hands in my hair, on my ass, gripping my hip, raking up my back. And still I make one more half-assed attempt to talk to her. "Listen, about the questions—"

She rubs the heel of her hand up and down my cock, and my jaw goes slack. My brain goes slack. All the tension in my body is busy flooding to where her hand is working me over.

"Later," she says.

Later works for me.

She urges me onto my back and straddles me, centering herself over my hard-on, rubbing back and forth and swaying her tits in my face. I'm the luckiest guy alive.

I suck her and she rides me. Her skin's so pale, one nipple swelling and softening, darkening as I twist the other between my fingers. Her eyes are closed, her throat mottled pink, her body rising and falling in a slow, even rhythm I can hardly bear. It's been too long since I came. The first few days after she walked out of my room, I was seething with misplaced resentment. I whacked off like I was planning to make a profession of it. But after a while I lost interest, lost heart.

I'm out of practice.

Which is another way of saying I have the stamina of a fourteen-year-old.

I grab her hips and hold her still. She whimpers and rocks.

"Don't. Baby. Seriously."

"It feels good."

"I know. A little too good. You keep that up, I'm gonna . . ."

She pulls at my wrists until I let go, puts them on her tits. "Go ahead."

"You want me to come in my pants?"

Her eyes drift closed. When I thumb her nipples, she sucks in a breath like I'm hurting her, and it's really, really good. Then she bears down on me even harder.

"Caro, I mean it."

"I mean it too," she says.

"It'll be messy."

"You have to wash those pants, anyway."

"Yeah, but still."

"I'll clean you up. With my tongue."

That's the end of the conversation. My whole upper body breaks out in goose bumps—a sure sign I've only got seconds left. I get my hand behind her back, draw her down, stick my tongue in her mouth, and I'm kissing her when my toes curl and I have to throw my head back, close my eyes, the head of my cock unbearably sensitive, tingling fluttering clamping tightness moving up, out of me, hot against my skin, slick and slippery as she slows, kissing my neck, mouthing over my collarbones.

Jesus. *Jesus.*

I put my hand on the back of her head, and she giggles, tucked into the hollow between my shoulder and my neck. "That was an interesting noise."

"Shut up."

"Like you were dying."

"Swear to God."

"It didn't sound pleasant."

"It was pleasant. Never doubt it."

She's shaking against my chest, my arms wrapped tight around her.

"We'll do you in a minute." I sound like I'm underwater. "Then we'll see who's laughing."

That sets her off again, and I watch her, smiling, because we're ridiculous.

Ridiculous and happy.

Me and Caroline.

After I catch my breath, it starts to sink in that I'm a dick-head.

Like, literally. I just let the head of my dick call the shots. Genius.

I rub my hand up and down Caroline's back. She's tense, her muscles twitching and tight.

"How close were you?"

She breathes a little laugh. "Um, close?"

If I was her, I'd be annoyed. First she gives me an ultimatum and I ignore her for three weeks, then I wake her up, coax her back to my apartment, and don't even get her off?

"I suck."

She props herself up on my chest and smiles. "I don't know, I was kind of enjoying how completely useless you got there at the end."

"I bet."

"No, seriously. You're always so in charge. You've made me come, like, a million times, and I've only . . ." She gets bashful, looks away.

"I like making you come."

Caroline shifts to the side and gives my chest a shy smile. She strokes her hand over my chest, down my stomach. "I like making you come, too. A lot."

"You sound surprised."

"I didn't always like it. Before."

I'd guessed as much.

"It wasn't—it wasn't bad, really. It just wasn't . . ."

"Like this."

"Yeah."

Her fingers find the button on my jeans. "So I said a minute ago that I'd, uh, clean you up."

"You don't have to."

"But if I want to."

"If you want to, knock yourself out." I catch her chin, tip up her face so I can see her eyes. "But if you *don't* want to—

tonight, or if you're still coming around next week or in a month, and you don't want to then, either—that's fine. I mean, I know you love lists and schedules and all that shit, but there's not, like, a list of stuff we have to do or some timetable we have to do it on. Where we are now . . . it's good."

I laugh at myself. *Good.* "Okay, it's fucking awesome."

She pushes her nose into my neck and kisses me there. Not the kind of thing I ever would've thought I wanted a girl to do, but Caroline can do it all night long if she wants. It's nice. Like when Frankie used to wake up in the middle of the night and crawl into my bed, all warm and soft. Comfortable.

"Thanks," she says.

"Don't thank me. We already established that I'm a dick."

Her arm tightens around me. "You're not. You're great. I mean, you're kind of *also* a dick. But mostly great."

She's quiet for a minute, and I'm thinking about how right I feel with her and how I've never had this with anyone else. Never let any girl this close.

I'm glad it's the same for her. I know that makes me a jerk, because it means everything that happened to her with Nate had to be kind of shitty in order for her to come to me and think what we've got is anything different—anything special at all.

But I'm glad anyway.

I want everything with Caroline to be special.

After a while, her hand starts meandering down my stomach, and she unbuttons my slacks and lowers the zipper. I lift my hips to help her peel them off. She slips the pad of one finger underneath the waistband of my briefs and follows it across my stomach, which makes me suck in a breath.

I could go again. Soon.

"Take these off," I say, grabbing a fistful of her pajama pants.

She does, while I take off my briefs. She's a little shy about it, and she leaves her panties on. They're purple, with dark purple lace at the top.

"Nice," I tell her.

That makes her smile. She shoots a nervous look at my crotch and starts to maneuver her way down there, but I grab hold of her armpit and haul her back up so I can kiss her. She's pressed against me, skin to skin, nothing but a tiny scrap of panties separating us. I kiss her slow and lazy, knowing how lucky I am and wanting to soak it in for a good long time.

When she finally pulls her mouth away, I'm hard again, and she's squirmy, pressing herself into me.

She starts to kiss her way down my chest.

"Let me get you off," I say.

"I promised."

I can only see the top of her head, and I can't tell if she means that funny or serious.

"You don't have to," I remind her.

"Shh." She takes her time getting down there, and the way she does it . . . *Jesus.* All those shy glances, somehow I got thinking she didn't know what she was doing, but by the time she puts her tongue on my cock, one quick swirl around the head, I'm already half dead.

"Tease," I choke out.

She grins. Sticks out that pointed pink tongue of hers. Licks me clean.

I keep my hands fisted in the blankets so I won't put them in her hair. Caroline and me have messed around a lot, but tonight's different, and I don't want to fuck it up. Traumatize her or whatever. She can do whatever she wants to me, but I'm not going to push her.

It's fucking hard, though. To keep still. To keep from showing her exactly what I want her to do to me. She wraps her fingers around the base of my cock, and there's this spot where she could put pressure and doesn't. She licks and sucks the underside where I'm so sensitive, but she flicks right over the place beneath the head that makes me insane.

I give up on the blankets and rub my hands over her shoulders, up her neck, into her hair. Not clutching at her, though it takes a monumental effort not to. Just touching her.

She cups my balls, but her fingers are so gentle, her mouth so . . . polite. It's nice.

It's good.

She lifts up her head. Crawls up until she's a couple of inches from my face. "Hey."

"What?"

"You don't come with a guidebook. Tell me what you want."

"You're doing great."

I jerk off the bed before I understand why. She pinched my nipple, twisted it. Not in a cute way.

"The fuck? That hurt!"

"Tell me what you want."

Her eyes are intent, her mouth set in this no-nonsense line. She looks like classroom Caroline, sure of herself, ticked at me for keeping her from completing this lesson to her satisfaction.

I love her like this.

"Suck me," I say. "Hard."

She smiles this little smile. Totally satisfied with herself. "*Thank* you." Her head drops down again. "Now, keep talking to me, or I'm going to drive home and you'll be all alone with your right hand. Or is it your left, since you're left-handed?"

I don't think I'm supposed to answer the question. Not when she's crawling down my body, ass in the air. I want my hands on that ass. Get her turned around, pussy in my face, dripping all over me while she sucks me off.

I've said shit like that to her on the phone, when I was too far gone to stop myself, safe because I was a couple thousand miles from her. But it's different to think about saying it to her face. Does she like that, or does she just put up with it? Where do girls like Caroline draw the line?

When she wraps her hand around me, I reach down, show her where to pull the skin tight. "Here."

She takes over. Then she's licking me again, flicking her tongue over the head, sucking me into her mouth. Sucking *hard*.

"Jesus fucking *Christ*."

She pops me out of her mouth long enough to say, "That's more like it."

There are no girls like Caroline. Just Caroline.

She's more than enough.

She sucks me, licks me, tongues me in the spot I show her until I'm lifting off the bed, my legs stiff, my dick so hard I can't possibly last. When she goes for my balls this time, I show her where to stroke behind them, where to press—oh, *fuck*, she's a quick study.

"Turn around," I say, but I'm not sure she understands me. Not sure I can make words that actually come out sounding like English.

"Caroline. I—can you—*gnuh*."

"Eh?" she teases.

I sit up, grab under her arms, haul her up my body. Her

lips are shining, wet, and I kiss her, get my tongue inside her, get my hand in her panties and my fingers into her slickness. She's slippery, soaking. God damn.

She moans into my mouth. "West."

"Turn around," I tell her.

"What?"

"Turn around. Get your hips up here"—I tug her toward my face—"and your mouth back down there."

"That's . . . Can't we just have sex now?"

For a second I'm dumbfounded. When I manage to gather a few brain cells together, I say, "Honey, we *are* having sex."

Her cheeks are already pink, but now they turn red. Which is hilarious. I mean, I've got my fingers inside her, she's riding my hand, still moving in this soft up-and-down even as we're talking, hair all loose around her shoulders, fucking beautiful—and *now* she's going to get shy on me?

"What did you think this was?" I ask.

"I know. I mean, yes, I've heard Quinn's sex-doesn't-have-to-include-a-dick lecture, too. But I meant, you know, were we going to have *sex* sex. Penis-in-vagina sex. *Sex*."

I raise an eyebrow. "Penis-in-vagina sex?"

"Shut up."

"No, I mean, that's romantic. That's probably the most romantic proposition I've ever heard."

She's laughing. "Shut *up*."

I move my fingers and push her onto her back. Look deep into her eyes. Say, real serious, "Caro, I would *love* to have penis-in-vagina sex with you."

She smacks my arm, and then I kiss her, and then . . . *damn*. It's like we've been playing around and now we're not. At all. The kiss gets intense, fast, her hands are everywhere, grabbing at me, positioning my hips where she wants me, where I'm grinding against her. Her panties are in my way, and I've had enough of that. I yank them down, pull them off her ankles, push her knees apart and lick between her legs until she's making these quiet, helpless sounds that I fucking love.

"West," she says.

Yeah. I know. She wants me inside her, and if I don't get there in the next thirty seconds, the world might as well end.

"Hold on. Don't move. Not one inch."

I get up, grab a condom from the desk, rip it open, and roll it on with my eyes on Caroline on my bed, legs spread open, wet and ready, her body, her mouth, her smile, her eyes.

"I'm getting cold."

"Yeah, yeah."

Then I'm back over her, my dick sliding over her warm, soft pussy, our mouths meeting, her arms around me. "You sure?"

"I'm sure."

I reach down. Find the right spot, the right angle.

I ease into her. Inch by inch. Slow, because I don't want to hurt her, because it's been awhile for both of us, because I don't want to embarrass myself and come before we're even hardly started.

Slow, because I want to watch her face, and, fuck, it *is* romantic. It *is* special.

It's Caroline.

When I'm all the way in, her knees spread wide, her eyes right with me, I kiss her. I just stay there, not moving, because I've wanted to be here, with her, for so long, but I didn't think I ever would.

It's torture. The worst best torture of my life.

This is what deeper feels like.

This is what sex feels like, if you're doing it right.

If you're in love.

It's incredible.

I frame her face between my palms, smooth her hair off her forehead. "You okay?"

I thought this couldn't get better, but it does when she smiles. And when she moves, rocking her hips experimentally into me, then back away—Christ Jesus. I suck in a breath and close my eyes.

"I'm great."

"Good."

I'm not ready to move yet. I've been told I have amazing stamina, but it's obvious now that this is only true when I don't give a shit. With Caroline, I'm going to have to work hard just to not be the king of the premature ejaculators.

"West?"

She rocks again.

"Hunh?"

"Are you going to fuck me or what?"

"I ever tell you I don't like bossy women?"

She slithers away beneath me, then thrusts up. Her mouth falls open in a soft O. Then she smiles and looks at me, like, *I'm such a genius.*

She does it again. "You—*oh*—like me, though—*oh my God.*"

Whatever tiny piece of control I was holding on to, I lose it. I start to move, and she's right with me. I suck her tits, kiss her neck, behind her ear, everyplace she likes. I drive into her, savoring every stroke, the tight clasp of her cunt, the way she moans, the slide of our bodies, the sex stink better than any perfume, the taste of sweat at her throat.

"Can you come like this?" I ask.

"I don't . . . know."

I get a hand under her ass, angle her up. She squeaks.

"Better?"

"Oh, wow." After a few seconds, she says, "Harder."

Music to my ears.

I speed up, stop banking my thrusts, let her have more of my need, more of my greed, and she takes it. She *wants* it. She gets her legs around me, digs her heels into me on every stroke, lifts up into me, and says, "West, yeah, oh, God." I didn't think she'd be like this, this open, this loud, but she is and I love it.

"This gonna work?"

I don't have to ask, though. She's tossing her head, heels back on the bed, digging in, getting restless and desperate. "Please," she says. "Please."

She always begs me when she's about to come. I love that, too. I love making her so crazy that she loses her pride and just begs.

"So fucking sexy."

Then we're moving fast and frantic, and I don't have any way to describe it that's worth anything. I push into her until there's nowhere to get to, until I've already got there, and there's no her or me, just us, our bodies, our heat, this gathering pleasure white-hot and dangerous, too dangerous, but I don't care. I can't think.

I can only move with Caroline, deep, deeper, all the way toward the center of something bigger than either of us.

She tightens. I groan. She grips me. I kiss her.

She moans and her voice breaks, a beautiful cracked-open sound. My balls tighten, the joy searing through me, her eyes closing, her arms clenching, my heart open as I watch her light up with pleasure.

Caroline

We got five weeks.

I'd teased West for counting the days of our separation, even though I spent them dragging around, doubting myself, wrecked with missing him. But when we were together—the last two weeks of February, the first three weeks of March—it was so good that every day felt like an anniversary. Every day felt special, worth pressing into a scrapbook, sealing in amber, tucking away.

Nights at the bakery. Showers at the apartment, a snack in the quiet kitchen, trying not to wake Krishna, laughing behind my hand. Mornings in West's bed, hands and mouths and the slow, beautiful rhythm of his body rocking into mine.

The way he moves has always made me crazy, but there is nothing like the way he moves inside me. Nothing.

I didn't know it could be like that. So dirty and so good. So gorgeous and perfect.

For five weeks, we were always together. I went back to my

vampire schedule, napping in the afternoons, waking up in the middle of the night and meeting him at the bakery for his shifts. I studied at the library when he was working there, set myself up in a carrel on the fourth floor and waited in the quiet for him to find a cart of journals that needed shelving. I pushed my fingers into his hair when he dropped to his knees beneath my chair, bit my thumb to keep from crying out, came against his fingers and his tongue, scandalous and forbidden and happy.

He kissed me in the dining hall. I took his hand when we walked across the quad. We raced each other down the train tracks, one on each rail, balancing with our arms out, pushing at each other's hands to see who could stay on the longest, who would fall off, who would win.

Those were the best weeks. In the dead of February, the frozen cold, I had West, and we were beautiful and bright, friends and lovers, laughing all the time. Laughing until my cheeks ached and my stomach hurt and I had to ask him to stop, because it was so good, it hurt.

I loved him.

I didn't tell him, but it was obvious. Obvious to me, obvious to West.

Obvious to anyone who was paying attention.

West is sitting on the edge of the mattress, bent over his phone. He's got an eight o'clock. I don't have to be up for another hour, but I'm up anyway. West had ideas.

Or, okay, West's penis had ideas. I woke up to his mouth on my neck, his hand heavy and hot against my stomach, his erection pressing against my ass.

"Good morning?" I said. Because I wasn't all that sure. That it was good, or that it was even morning.

"Mmm."

That was pretty much all it took to convince me. He has this way of humming under his breath, this low, delicious sound that vibrates right up against my clit. It's so sexy. It's so *West*. One *mmm*, and I'm in.

I mean, what's there to complain about when you're with a guy who's gorgeous and nice and who wakes you up with the slow, inexorable press of his fingers into your panties, parting your folds, sliding over your clit and inside you?

Nothing.

He got me breathing heavy, flipped me over, eased a pillow under my stomach, and moved into me from behind, his hand at my clit, kissing my neck, my shoulders, until I came so hard I saw stars.

After he was done collapsing on top of me like a giant slug-man, he took a shower, so now he smells like soap, wet hair, West. I'm still all snuggly and sex-relaxed, and he's whistling, rubbing my bare leg, scrolling through his texts.

"Who wrote to you?"

"Franks."

"What's she up to?"

"She got on Mom's phone and sent me a whole bunch of selfies."

"Let me see."

I crawl half onto his lap, and he shows me. "She's so cute."

She looks a lot like him—West with round cheeks and a sharp chin, eye makeup, and a sparkly shirt. She's in love with taking selfies, too. I've seen probably thirty of them in the past three weeks, because West has been as open as he promised to be. He told me all about Frankie, about his mom and Bo, about his dad.

There are some things he's holding back, I think. Something about sex, about that money I dropped in his lap. But I know enough. I don't need to know absolutely everything to understand what makes West tick.

Sometimes I think about what life gave me compared to what it's given him, how hard he works, and I get so angry. He doesn't like to talk about fairness and unfairness, though, or to dwell on the gap between how we grew up.

"It is what it is," he said last time I brought it up. "You hungry?"

He says now, "She's got all that crap on her eyes."

"It's called eye makeup." I peer at the phone. "Actually, that's a good nighttime eye. I can never get my eyeliner to look that awesome."

"You don't wear that stuff."

"Not for everyday, but sometimes if there's a party or whatever."

He frowns at the pictures. "She's too young."

"She's just trying it out. I was the same at her age. In a big hurry for bras and lipstick, all that stuff."

"Yeah, but I doubt you had anybody sniffing after you in Ankeny. It's different with Franks. She's got to be smart, or some useless jag-off will get her knocked up before she's even old enough to know what she wants yet."

I watch him type out a text. Wash that shit off your eyes. You're pretty enough without it.

"Heartwarming."

"I'm her brother, not her boyfriend."

He's more like her father, though, I think. The closest thing she has to one.

Standing up, West stretches and drops his phone on the desk. "Can you hand me mine?" I ask. "I need to see if Bridge is going to breakfast before class."

He does, then pulls on a pair of jeans and a T-shirt. I

watch his bare chest and stomach disappear from view, sad as always to see them go.

West is smiling when I glance at his face. "What?"

"You. You look like you're ready to go another round."

I swipe my finger over the screen of the phone. "I was barely awake for round one."

"Oh, I don't know. You woke up pretty good by the end. I thought I was gonna have to shove a pillow over your head, keep you from waking up Krish."

"You'd probably accidentally suffocate me, you were so busy back there doing your business."

"Doing my business?" He sounds offended. I love offending him.

"You know." I stare at my phone, flapping a hand at him. "That man-business. Thrust thrust, pant pant. I swear, sometimes I'm not sure why I put up with it."

I barely see him coming before he's grabbing my ankle and yanking me down the bed. I'm all tangled up in the covers, thrashing and laughing, when he crawls on top of me and braces his arms on either side of my head. "Thrust thrust, pant pant? I should spank your ass for that."

"I'd like to see you try."

His eyes are blazing. "So would I. But I'm gonna be late for class." He dips his head and kisses me. "You coming to the library later?"

"Yeah, but I have a group-project thing after lunch, so I'll be downstairs."

"Come up after."

He means the fourth floor. Our floor.

I swear, we're going to get caught, and then he'll get fired.

He says it'll be worth it.

"Sure."

One more kiss, with tongue, a bump against my hip that's a hint and a promise, and then he's moving away. He shoulders his bag as I navigate from texts to missed calls.

I've got a bunch. I had the ringer off last night, my phone deep in my bag, and I didn't realize.

They're all from my dad.

"See you later, babe."

One at nine o'clock last night. One at nine-thirty. One at ten. Ten-fifteen. Eleven-thirty. Six o'clock this morning.

My stomach sinks like a rock.

"What's a guy have to do to get his woman to say goodbye around here?"

I look up. West is leaning in the doorway, hand braced against the jamb.

"My dad called six times last night."

"That's—that sounds excessive."

"Yeah."

Bad news, cunt, the Internet Asshats whisper.

I'd almost forgotten about them. I'd let myself forget. Let myself pretend.

Not ready to listen to Dad's voice mail, I switch to email. Fifty new messages. I scroll through the list, seeing strange email addresses and threatening subject lines.

Seeing my dad's name. *Call Me. Urgent Matter.*

An email from my sister Janelle. *I NEED TO TALK TO YOU.*

I don't click on any of them.

I open the web browser and type in my name.

Caroline Piasecki. Advanced search. Limit to last twenty-four hours.

So many hits. All the worst sites. All the same pictures, all over again.

This isn't supposed to be happening, but it is.

West is behind me, hands on my shoulders. The phone's hidden from view by the fall of my hair, and I wish I had something better to hide behind. Some place, some world where I could take him, where everything wasn't already being ruined.

"It's bad," he says.

It's not a question. He can feel it. He knows.

"Yeah. It's bad."

But after that, it only gets worse.

I walk into my dad's office armed to the teeth.

West stays in the car, parked all the way down at the end of the driveway. I feel shitty about that, but he said I can only fight one battle at a time, and he's got a point. Probably the day to reintroduce West to my dad and fess up to his being my boyfriend is *not* Sex-Picture Day.

Still. Just knowing West is out there, waiting. Knowing he's on my side. It helps.

We both skipped class this morning. He called in sick to the library. I don't think he's skipped class all year, and he's definitely never missed work, so I appreciate the gesture. Plus, I need him. He's not much good with computers, but he's good with *me*. He sat next to me for hours while I pulled up my spreadsheets, Google-searched until my eyes itched, ranted and raved as I uncovered layer after layer of Nate's assault.

It's worse this time. Way worse than before.

The pictures are everywhere, of course, freshly posted at all the meat-market sites along with my name, my school—yeah, yeah. I've long since lost the ability to find them shocking.

What's shocking is all the other stuff.

Hateful posts on my Facebook wall. Personal notes to my school email from strangers who want to rape me, fuck me, punch me in the cunt. My Twitter account is sending out spam messages with links to my vulva. And somehow, God, my professors all must have been contacted, because I've gotten concerned-sounding email from three of them and a phone message from the Student Affairs office requesting that I set up an interview as soon as possible.

In six hours, I've cycled through hurt and anger, disgust and fear, resignation and fury. I'm a hundred-pound bag of flailing feelings. I'm sad. I'm mad. I'm a wreck.

But West is with me.

More than West: After her eight o'clock, Bridget showed up with Quinn. They called Krishna, who pulled his laptop, mine, and Quinn's into a temporary network on the living-room coffee table. Within an hour, he was directing a search-and-record-keeping operation with Quinn and Bridget. They're doing screenshots of everything, calling in favors with a MathLab geek friend of Krishna's who has crazy computer skills, combing through the student handbook to figure out what kind of rules Nate's breaking and what can be done about it.

I'm a wreck, but they're all on my side, and that helps. So much.

Krishna's friend is the one who figured out what started it all. Tucked away on one of those unmoderated sites where bros like to hang out and be dickheads together, there's a thread about me. A link to the pictures, a standard complaint about what a frigid, evil whore I am, and then a call to arms: *What can we do to teach this bitch a lesson?*

Dozens of them took up their weapons. While I was at the bakery with West, sleeping in his arms, having sex with him—all that time, I was being attacked. By strangers. For no reason at all.

If this had happened to me seven months ago, I think I would have crumpled under the weight. Knowing my professors have been sent those links, that my sister and my aunts and maybe even my grandparents have been Facebook-spammed with naked pictures of me—it sucks. It hurts. It makes me want to cry if I dwell on it, if I think too hard about what it means for my future, what it says about the shape of the rest of my life.

But it also makes me so, so mad.

I'm ready to fight. I have a stack of printouts in my arms, a bag with my laptop in it weighing down my shoulder. I have West at the end of the driveway.

In front of me, my father sits in the maroon leather recliner by the window, his own laptop open on his thigh, his glasses pushed up into his thick gray hair, ruffling his otherwise dignified appearance. I study his familiar face—thick eyebrows, that dumpling nose Janelle inherited but I didn't, his jawline jowlier than I remembered. He's putting on weight. Too many drive-through cheeseburgers.

He called me home, and I came.

My palms are sweaty when I sit down in the other chair in his corner. It's deep and tall, and my feet just barely reach the floor. All of my memories of being punished as a girl begin here, with the helpless weight of my swinging feet. I know the number of brass studs anchoring the upholstery onto the end of his chair's arms. Nine around the arch. Twelve more down each side. I've studied each pucker in the leather and memorized the geometrical arches and whorls in his abstract office carpet in order to avoid having to look him in the eye.

Today, I sit with my spine straight, damp palms clasped in my lap. I pulled up my hair into a ponytail and wore jeans and the sweater he paid for at Christmas, pale-blue-green cashmere the color of West's eyes. My armor.

I sit quietly and wait, because Janelle is the one who sucks up to him, and Alison is the one who cries. I am the daughter who comes to him armed with counterarguments, clever defenses, tricky maneuvers.

I am the daughter who fights.

For months now, I've been too scared to fight. I've been trying to live in a bubble that Nate popped way back in August. I didn't want to believe it. I told myself I could fix it. Throw some patches on there, paint over the cracks, avert my eyes, and pretend everything was fine.

Everything's not fine.

The bubble is well and truly fucked.

But outside the bubble, I've found rugby parties and new friends who don't care about my stupid sex pictures. Outside the bubble, there are nights at the bakery, phone sex, and long naps in the middle of the afternoon with my arms wrapped around a boy who smells like fresh bread and soap, and who makes me feel like I *matter,* no matter what I look like, what I've done, what's been done to me.

The world hasn't changed. It's full of men who hate women. It's stuffed to the gills with assholes who will mount an attack on a stranger just because she's female and they're small-minded monkey-boys with an inferiority complex.

The world hasn't changed, but *I* have.

Outside the bubble is life. West.

I like it out here. I'm staying.

Dad clicks on something, closes the lid of his laptop, and looks at me. "Caroline," he says.

Just my name, for a moment.

Just my name, because you begin by identifying the accused.

"I received a call last night from your aunt Margaret. She'd seen something distressing on your Facebook page, and she wanted to know if I was aware of it."

His eyes are my eyes, dark brown and full of sympathy. His manner is reasonable. His diction is clear and measured. He doesn't yell in the office. He *judges*. We come to him like criminals, and he passes sentence on us, calmly and rationally.

"When I told her I didn't know what she was referring to, she sent me the link, and I checked it out for myself. The link took me to a website where . . ."

He clears his throat—the first sign that any of this is disturbing to him.

". . . where I found several pictures of you unclothed. Some of them compromising. Sexually compromising. Although it wasn't possible to positively identify each of the pictures as you, there were certain . . ."

He looks away from me for a second.

This is not your fault, I tell myself. *You didn't do this. Nate did.*

Dad clears his throat again. "There's no question that at least one, if not more, of the sexually explicit photographs is of you. I followed a second link to much the same thing, and I can only assume that the additional links were also to these photos."

There's a long pause, and I wonder if I'm supposed to say something. But what can I say?

Yes, that's me.

That's me, giving Nate a blow job.

That's my vagina, my hand between my legs, stroking my clit.

Yes, that's me riding Nate's cock. My face with his semen on it.

Yes.

That's your baby girl. Your pride and joy.

I sit silent. I knew this would be hard, but it's harder than I expected. I'd thought about his judgment, feared his disgust, but I'd never thought about his *grief.*

The grief is in his face, in his eyes.

These pictures make him sad, sad because of me, sad *for* me, and it's unbearable.

"So." He folds his hands on his stomach, over the top of the ratty beige cardigan that he wears on top of his oxford shirts at home. "Tell me how this happened."

I take a deep breath and imagine a string tied to the crown of my head, pulling me up straight and tall. An exercise that our high school choir director gave us, but one that comes in handy anytime I need to be perfectly poised, perfectly careful.

"Nate took the pictures. When we were still going out. And he—they showed up online right after we broke up."

The lines around his mouth deepen, twin parentheses framing his impatience. "Am I correct in remembering that you broke up with Nate soon before returning to school in August?"

"Yes. It was August when he first posted them."

"You know that he posted them."

"No. I assume it was him, but I can't prove it. They were submitted anonymously to the sites. He denied it."

"Caroline." My father looks right at me, leaning in a bit. "It's March."

"Yes."

"Tell me what happened between August and March."

"I made a systematic effort to remove the photos from the Internet. I set up automatic searches, sent out cease-and-desist email—"

My dad makes an impatient sound. He doesn't approve of homegrown lawyering.

"—and whatever else I could think of to get them off-line. And then, when that wasn't working, I hired a service to help me scrub my reputation. On the Internet, I mean. They do the searching for you, get photos wiped, try to push the legit results up on the search pages . . ."

And I haven't heard from them in weeks. The reports they did send me were late, sketchy, and incomplete. It's possible they're frauds or just crap at what they do.

It's possible I threw away fifteen hundred dollars of West's money on a pipe dream.

How many hours of his effort, his sweat, did I waste so I could cower in my dorm room, wishing life were fair?

On the list of my regrets, that loan is way up near the top.

"But this latest attack was launched from an online bulletin board," I continue. "Presumably by Nate. A number of others participated in it with him. I don't know their identities. What I do know is that the pictures have spread so far and wide, it's probably a wasted effort trying to get them removed. I'd like to focus my energy at this point on—"

"A wasted effort? Do you have any idea what's going to happen to you if you *don't* remove the pictures?"

"I have a good idea, yes."

"You'll have trouble getting into law school. Recommendations will be difficult, but even assuming you can present a good application—admissions committees search the Internet. Internship applications, scholarships, job applications. There's no chance at the Rhodes Scholarship, the

Marshall. Getting the pictures off-line will have to be your top priority. You should have brought me in from the beginning, Caroline. So much damage has already been done."

So much damage.

But to what? To whom?

"I'm not damaged."

"That's not what I meant."

"It is, though. You're talking about this—about my future—as though it's this white, pure thing that I've gotten dirty. Like you sent me out to play in a white dress, and why wasn't I more careful with it?"

He frowns.

"I'm not a white dress, Dad. And I didn't take those pictures. I didn't share them. I didn't say all that stuff about me. *Nate did.*"

"You don't know that for sure."

"Fine. Someone did. The important thing is, that someone wasn't me."

He grunts and looks out the window at our yard. Our house is in the nicest part of Ankeny, with a big shaded lot and an acre of lawn that I had to mow in high school if I expected to be allowed to go out on the weekends. Today it's overcast, patchy snow still on the ground, spring weeks away.

It's not my yard anymore.

This isn't my house.

I'm not a child.

"Did you report this incident to the college?" he asks. "Or to the police?"

"No. But I intend to."

"You say you suppose Nate posted these photos in the first place because he was upset. Does he have any reason to continue to be upset with you? Something that prompted this second attack?"

It's West, of course. West and me, together. Out in public, around campus, so obviously a couple, so obviously into each other.

What did Nate tell me that night at the party, when he blocked me from leaving the room? That he was worried about me. That we were friends, we'd *always* be friends.

What did he want that night when he came to West's apartment with Josh and offered to buy weed? To stake some kind of claim over me? To prove he was better than the guy I ended up with?

"I think he might still have feelings for me."

"I see."

Then my dad is silent, and I have to endure the ticking of the grandfather clock and await his judgment.

"I'm going to have to speak with Dick," he says. "He might have some insight into the best course of action on matters like this."

Dick Shaffer is my dad's friend, a prosecutor.

"I've looked into that," I say. "And I have a meeting with the Student Affairs office this afternoon, where I'm going to ask about possible approaches. It's not illegal to share sex pictures online, provided they're pictures of an adult and they're the possession of the person who shares them— that they're not stolen and they weren't coerced. Which means, I think, there isn't much of anything the police can do. But if we go after Nate for violating the technology policy—"

My dad's gaze sharpens. "Go after him?"

"Yes, because the post he made last night, if he was using the campus network, that was a violation of the campus tech policy, and I think if it goes to a hearing—"

My dad stands up abruptly and carries his laptop over to his desk, where he leaves it, silver and shining. He tucks his hands behind his back and begins to pace, deep in his own thoughts.

I've lost the thread of my argument. I don't think he was listening, anyway.

I don't know what to say to get him to listen.

"Do you remember," he asks, "what I told you when you turned fifteen and I allowed you to have your own Facebook account?"

"Yes."

He twirls a finger at me. *Repeat it.*

"You told me to be careful, because the Internet is a public forum and nothing I do or say online will ever go away."

"And I told you it was especially important for *you* to be careful, didn't I? More than your sisters. Because you want to be a lawyer. You want to be a *leader of men.*"

I did.

I do.

"Is this the behavior of a leader of men, Caroline?"

That question—it makes me dizzy for a second. It sends a wash of fire through me, a hot rush of some feeling that I can't immediately identify.

Before my sophomore year at Putnam, I'd never understood that your whole world can pivot on a few words.

A text message that says OMG.

One question from my father: *Is this the behavior of a leader of men?*

The answer comes up from deep inside me. From that place beneath my lungs, that ripped-open wound that's been cut and kicked and battered. The part of me that has refused, *still* refuses, to give up.

Yes is what it tells me. *Yes, it fucking* is.

If there's anything I learned from a childhood spent poring over the biographies of world leaders, it's that people who make a difference in the world succeed not *despite* what's happened to them but *because of it*. Being a leader— it's not about only doing things your father will approve of. It's not about being good and smart and pretty and lucky. You can't lead from inside a bubble.

You have to *live* to lead, and the past few months I've been alive. I've been falling in love with a boy my father forbade me to talk to. Hell, not a boy, a *man*. A smart man who works hard and never skips class except when he has to because I'm in the middle of a crisis.

A drug dealer. A brawler. West is both of those things.

But he's also a son, an older brother, a generous lover, and a kind, amazing guy.

This year I've been figuring out who I am. I've been learning what I want, and it's the same as what I've always wanted, only *I'm* different.

Leaders live and grow and learn. They run into dragons, get burned by them, temper their swords in the fire, and take them on.

That's what I want to do. That's who I want to be. Not this girl cowering in her father's office.

I want to be *fierce*.

So I stand up, too. I plant myself in the middle of his rug, cross my arms to match his. I let my eyebrows draw in, the corners of my mouth fall, and I ask him, "What do you mean by *this*?"

"Sorry?"

"You said, 'Is *this* the behavior of a leader of men?' What do you mean? Are you asking me if leaders have consensual sex with their long-term monogamous partners? Yes. They do. Are you asking, are leaders ever betrayed? Yes. All the time. The question is—"

"The question is one of *judgment*," he interrupts. "There's

a reason you've never seen a sex-photograph scandal involv-
ing the president of the United States, Caroline, and it's
because—"

"It's because Monica Lewinsky didn't have an iPhone,
Dad. Are you kidding me with this? Do you know how many
senators have been caught sending pictures of their penises
to staffers?"

"Enough that you should have known better."

That catches me up short. Catches my breath in my lungs.

I should have known better.

Of course I should have. Things with Nate were never
quite right, and I should have known that I liked him for the
wrong reasons, that I had to work too hard for his regard,
that he didn't *care* about me the right way. I think that was
always part of his mystique—the sense that I might never be
quite enough for him, that he'd picked me out but I was a
little too brainy, a little too naïve, and I needed to prove myself in order to make his deigning to go out with me worth-
while.

I figured it all out eventually. I broke up with him because
it wasn't working, because at Putnam I had more confidence
that I might find someone better. Someone like West.

I just didn't figure it out soon enough.

Be careful what you put on the Internet. I've heard it a
hundred times. *Be careful what you do in this digital age.
Don't let yourself be made a victim, because if you do, it's
your fault. Your mistake.*

I knew the pictures were a bad idea. I had my mouth on
Nate's dick when he lifted the phone in the air and took the
first one, and it didn't feel sexy. It didn't feel risky or clever, a
secret shared between us. It felt *wrong*.

I decided to give him what he wanted so he would be nice

to me. So he would approve of me, act like he loved me, like he was proud of me.

He took that picture. He came in my mouth.

Afterward, he wanted to do body shots. *One, two, three, four.* My cleavage sticky, my senses dulled, my jaw sore, I did what he asked me to.

I was eighteen years old, and I thought I loved him. I should have known, but I didn't.

And I don't deserve to be abused for it. Judged for it. Called names.

I don't deserve to have my life ruined.

"I *trusted* him."

"You shouldn't have. Do you think Professor Donaldson will be able to write you a recommendation letter for law school now, with these photographs on his mind? Do you think he'll be able to attest to your intelligence, your drive, when he's seen this?"

"Probably not."

"Do you think you'll be able to get an internship this summer, next year? That you'll be able to apply for scholarships with this on your record?"

"I know it's an embarrassment, Dad, but—"

"It's not an embarrassment. Embarrassment fades. This is a black mark. You might as well have committed a felony, Caroline, and all because you didn't use your head."

"Nate is the one who posted the pictures."

"And you're the one who let him take them."

"I trusted him."

He makes a disgusted sound. Looks away from me. Wipes his hand over his mouth.

"You shouldn't have," he says, for the second time. And he looks at me, more sad than angry. "I thought you had better judgment than this. I'm disappointed in you. I'm . . . I'm disgusted with those pictures, and I'm disappointed."

It breaks something inside me to hear him say that.

It hurts.

But I think the thing it breaks—it's not my heart. It's some last delicate fragment of the bubble. It's the part of me that was still my daddy's girl, living in hope that if I were perfect, he would love me best. Love me most. Love me always. And his love would make me powerful.

It hurts to hear that I've disgusted him. It hurts to know that from here on out, he'll never love me in quite the same way, if he finds a way to love me at all.

But I don't need his love to be powerful.

I'm already powerful.

And there's enough work for me in the world, just trying to fix this one thing, that I could spend the rest of my life doing it.

"I'm sorry you're disappointed," I tell him. "But I'm human. I'm nineteen. I make mistakes sometimes. And I think . . . you know, maybe I should have told you right away. Maybe that makes this harder for you, because I've had seven months to think about what these pictures mean and you've had, like, seven hours."

I step closer to him and put my hand on his arm.

If he flinches slightly—if my heart contracts—I ignore it.

I'm not disgusting. I'm his daughter.

"But, Daddy? Here's what they mean to *me*. They're an act of hate. They're vengeance against me, from someone I never treated badly. They're *undeserved*. And even if they were deserved, what does that mean, exactly? That if someone takes naked pictures of me, I'm a bad person, so they get the right to call me a slut on the Internet? Are you trying to tell me that just because I didn't stop Nate from aiming his camera, I deserve whatever happens to me, forever? I deserve this attack because I *asked for it*? Do you hear how ugly that is?"

"I never said you asked for it." He sounds different, his voice choked and unsettled.

"Yeah. You did."

My father has always told me that the first step toward getting what I want in life is to *know* what I want. You figure it out, and then you go after it.

So I make him look at me. I make him hear me.

"You did."

This is my power now, and he doesn't have to like it.

I'm going to use it whether he likes it or not.

I'm going to keep using it until people start listening.

West stands up as soon as he spots me.

He's been waiting in the Student Affairs reception area, sprawled opposite the office assistant in a high-backed pink chair that is too small and entirely too fussy for him.

I was in the meeting for over an hour, but he's in exactly the same place where I left him. The only thing different is that his hair has arranged itself into grooves—plowed-through furrows that I stare at blankly for a moment until I figure out they're from his fingers.

How many times did he have to run his hand through his hair to leave it looking like a springtime field?

"How'd that go?"

He touches my elbow when I get close, slides his hand to my waist. With light pressure, he steers me through the door and into the hallway.

Student Affairs takes up part of the basement level of the student center, along with a gallery and some other offices.

It's a bright white labyrinth down here, and I'm always getting lost in it, but I'm pretty sure we came in on the other end from where West is leading me.

"Okay, I think. I told them a bunch of stuff, and they asked some questions. Then I gave them all my log printouts. They're supposed to talk to Nate next, and then we'll see."

West's expression darkens. "That's it? 'We'll see'?"

He's been like this since we left my dad's. Keyed up, bitter, a little sarcastic. I think he must have been under the illusion that just because I'm right, everyone will take my side. As if that's the way the world works.

For my part, I've moved beyond thinking anything is going to be handed to me without a fight.

"Well, yeah. What did you think, they'd tie him to the back of a horse and drag him around campus?"

He doesn't find the joke funny. I reach up and feel the deep worry line between his eyebrows. "Hey. What's this for?"

"Nothing. You hungry? You should eat something. Get some rest. I want you to sleep while I'm on at the bakery tonight."

I stop walking. "West."

"What?"

"What's the matter?"

Because there's something more going on with him than can be explained by disappointment with how my interview went. There's this energy coming off him, a gathering storm cloud, dark and dangerous. I can feel it when I stand close, and it reminds me of that day when I found him at the library after he'd punched Nate—a physical violence, vibrating atoms, primitive chemicals.

"Nothing. I'm fine."

I take his upper arms in a firm grip, pull him closer, go up on my tiptoes to kiss him. He just stands there like a block of wood, and when I come down he tries on a smile that's so pathetically *not* a smile, I want to wipe it off his face.

"Yeah, you totally feel fine," I say. "That was such a great kiss, I'm about to rip off my panties and do you in the hall-way."

No smile. No humor in him at all. He tugs at my hand. "Let's get out of here."

"Not until you talk to me."

"Not here."

"Why not? There's no one around."

His eyes dart past my shoulder to the other end of the hall.

"*Fuck,*" he mutters.

I figure out why he's swearing—the only likely reason for him to be so tense—as I'm turning around. The sight of Nate standing where there was no one a few seconds ago is more confirmation than surprise.

"You knew he was coming?"

West doesn't answer. Maybe he overheard something, maybe the secretary told him, but somehow he knew.

"It's fine, West. I mean, it's sweet that you're so worried, but I was going to have to see him sooner or later, I just—"

One glance tells me he isn't listening to me.

One look at his eyes informs me that West's attempt to railroad me out of the building wasn't for my protection. At least, not in the way I assumed.

He's flushed. Focused.

Homicidal.

"Don't you dare," I tell him. "Don't even think about it."

"You should go," he says.

Nate has spotted us. He's about thirty feet away—close enough that I see him go still.

I think if I were closer, I'd see fear in his eyes.

"You'll get expelled."

My hand is over West's galloping heart. I'm not sure he can even hear me, and I've already had enough of not being heard today. My dad, the dean of students, the residence-life supervisor who sat in on the meeting—none of them really listened. And now West.

"Get out of here, Caroline."

He's pushing past me, moving steadily down the hall toward his prey, and I'm certain—certain that West isn't going to hit Nate. No, he's going to beat him until someone pulls him off. He's going to put Nate in the hospital. Maybe even kill him.

I guess I should be worried for West, or for Nate even, but I'm not. Figuring out what's about to happen doesn't scare me. It ticks me off.

West has peed on this particular tree already. Twice.

I grab a fistful of the back of his T-shirt and yank on it. Fabric rips. West whirls around.

"This is my fight," I tell him. "*Mine*. Not yours."

"Get out of here if you don't want to see this."

"Do you hear yourself? This isn't an action movie. Knock it off."

"Let go of my shirt."

"It won't help anything, West. You'll just get in trouble, maybe go to jail, and then I won't have you and I'll still have to deal with this. It won't *help*."

He tries to get my hand off his shirt, but I've got a good grip. So he just takes his shirt off. Right there in the basement of the student center, he whips off his shirt and stalks down the hallway toward Nate.

I drop my bag and run.

I never got very good at rugby, but I learned a few things about tackling before the season ended. None of them has anything to do with this graceless tumble into West. I collide with the backs of his thighs, get my hands around his knees, slide down to his ankles.

I'm tenacious, though. I don't let go. If he wants to fight Nate, he'll have to drag me along behind him. I'll cling to his back like a baby monkey. It won't be dignified, but I don't care.

"Caroline, for Christ's sake."

"I'm not letting go."

Hands on his hips, he glares at Nate, who's smirking now. He really does *deserve* to get punched in the nose.

But that's neither here nor there. I made my feelings about violence clear when I puked in West's toilet. I don't like it. I don't want it. I didn't ask for it.

"Get off me," West says. "This is between me and him."

"No, it's *not*."

"He called the cops on me."

"And that was one move in a longer war, and the war is about *me,* and I say no. No fighting. I hate it. It doesn't fix anything. It just gives you an excuse to let off steam, which isn't fair, anyway. I mean, I've got steam, too, and I don't get to punch people." I look up at West, arms around his ankles, pleading with him. "I get that you're frustrated, okay? I get it. You're mad. You want to fix this for me. But *you can't fix this for me*. All you can do is make it worse."

I can see the moment when it sinks in. Maybe not what I'm saying so much as the fact that I'm practically laid out on the floor, tangled up in his legs. He's not going to accomplish anything this way.

Nate sees it, too. He walks into Student Affairs without another glance.

The breath explodes out of West in a loud, frustrated sigh.

After a few seconds, when I've started to feel silly—I mean, how is it, exactly, that I ended up wrapped around the legs of a shirtless man in such a short span of time?—he gives me his hand. "Come here."

His palm is hot and damp, his grip strong. When I'm on my feet, he frames my face between his hands. "You're mine. He hurt you. I want to hurt him."

"I know."

"It's the only thing I can do for you."

"It's not, though. It's not what I need from you. You have to trust that *I* can do this. It's my fight."

"Feels like my fight, too."

I turn my face into his palm. Kiss him there, where I can feel his pulse in his hand. "That's because we're a team." I smile against his skin. "But I'm the leader."

He snorts. "You're not the leader."

"I am, too. You should've seen me in that meeting. I kicked ass."

"I bet you did."

"West?" I look up at him. There's more ease in his expression now, softness in his eyes that I put there. "I need you to believe in me. Even if there are times nobody else does, I need you to be the one person in my life who trusts that I can kick all the ass that needs to be kicked."

"Of course you can. But it's not—"

"And then," I interrupt, because this is important. "And *then,* even though I know it's harder and it's not what you *want,* I need you to let me do it."

He gazes past me at the doorway where Nate isn't anymore.

"West, look at me."

He does.

"There's going to be some other chance like this. Sometime when I'm not around and you get a shot at Nate. I'm asking you to promise me you're not going to take it."

"Caro."

"Please." I touch his cheekbone. Pet his neck. He feels so dangerous, right on the edge, and I need to pull him back, because I know that this decision—right now—is one of those pivot points. A make-or-break moment.

I can't be with him if he won't let me fight my own battles.

He covers my hand with his and holds it against the bend between neck and shoulder.

I love his eyes. I love the way he looks at me, what he sees in me, who we are together.

"I hate not being able to do anything for you," he says.

"You're doing everything for me. Just by being you." I kiss him. "Promise me."

His breath against my mouth is a sigh and a capitulation. "I promise."

"Thank you." I stroke his neck and kiss him again. He's so warm, wired, animal.

Also, shirtless.

When his tongue parts my lips, I go weak against him. The kiss gets serious, fast. My back bumps into the wall, his hand catches behind my thigh.

"Let's go home," I say.

We don't even make it to the parking lot before he's pushing me up against a tree, the bark rough at the back of my head until his hand is there, protecting me.

Then, scorching heat and roving hands. I'm wet, was already wet in the hall, wetter still as I pushed through the door and he gave it a shove from behind me, groped my ass with his free hand in the deepest, dirtiest way.

"Home," I say on a gasp.

"Yeah."

"You drive."

"Keys."

I fish them out of my purse, although I'm not sure how. West is no help. His hands are all over me. "Here."

I have to dangle them in front of his face to get his attention.

Back at the apartment, Krishna and Bridget are waiting.

"How'd it go?"

"Did you nail his ass?"

West doesn't even let me talk. He pushes me in front of him, says, "Give us a minute," and slams the door to his bedroom in their surprised faces.

"That was rude."

He's too busy unbuttoning my pants to answer.

A few quick jerks, a shove onto the bed, a condom retrieved from the desk, and he's on me, pushing my knees open, testing me with his fingers. When he feels how wet I am, he makes that *mmm* sound that drives me crazy. "Hurry," I tell him.

It doesn't last long, but oh, God, it's amazing. One confident thrust and he's filling me, our tongues dancing, his belt buckle jingling as he moves into me hard and deep. We don't talk. I'm not sure we breathe. He needs to claim me, and I need to claim him, too, his flaws and his anger and his stupid macho protective bullshit, his promise and his body and the way he is, frustrating and imperfect, gorgeous and hot, violent and intelligent and real.

He sucks my nipple into his mouth, laps it with his tongue the way he knows drives me crazy, gets his hand up under me and tilts to put friction where I need it. It doesn't take much. I'm close. So close already, and he feels bigger and harder and deeper than ever, driving fast, breathing ragged against my neck. "Come on, baby," he says, and I make this sound like a sob, but I've never felt this good.

Tighter and harder, I dig into his shoulders when I start to come, needing to hold on to him, to keep him here, right here, this close. He groans, pushes his forehead into mine, kisses my temple when I turn my head, comes inside me holding my hands, our fingers interlaced, his grip so tight that the ache in my joints is the first thing I feel when I'm capable of feeling anything but bliss.

I wiggle my fingers, and he lets go.

"Holy crap."

He grins.

"That was—holy crap."

He kisses my nose, still smiling, and shakes his head.

"Seriously. That's all I've got. I'm sure there are other words, but . . ."

West starts laughing, his belly moving against mine. "Never let it be said the caveman thing doesn't turn you on."

"It doesn't!"

He keeps laughing, so I pinch him. "Last time you hit Nate, I *puked*!"

"You just came in, like, fifteen seconds. And that time at the library—"

"Don't *even* bring that up."

"After I decked him. You were hot for me."

"I was not!"

"You would've let me do anything to you that day."

"No, I wouldn't."

"You so would have. I should've kissed you. Skipped all those months we spent kidding ourselves. Don't tell me you weren't thinking about it."

"I wasn't."

"Right, because you're such a good girl."

I get my hands around his head, pull him close, kiss him. "Okay, maybe I was thinking about it. But only because you so clearly needed an outlet for all that rampant testosterone."

"You would've volunteered to be my outlet?"

"Your receptacle. Because I'm a giver."

"I just gave you an orgasm that made your eyes cross."

"Well, sure. Giving has its benefits."

He starts laughing again, and I hug him tight, loving the way his body feels against mine.

Loving him.

When we come out, we bump through the bedroom doorway, West's hand at my hip, a shit-eating grin on his face that I can't see but can feel with my whole body.

Happy.

It's amazing, I think, that we can find so much happiness at a time like this. I mean, yes, sex. But it's not really the sex. It's what's underneath the sex. It's how he makes me feel, how I make him feel, how we are together. This golden ribbon of something beautiful we've always had between us, there even when I was peering into his car and trying not to look too hard at the bare slice of flat stomach reflected in the car window. Even when we were arguing at the library, not-touching at the bakery, kissing on the train tracks.

Even when I told him to make up his mind and walked out on him, that ribbon was there—a shining possibility underneath.

I do feel a little awkward, though, about Krishna and Bridget. Who are sitting on the couch, watching TV kind of . . . tensely.

I think the tension must be in their bodies. Bridget sits ramrod straight, the back of her neck pink. Krishna's got his arm braced along the top of the cushions, his whole body turned toward her, one knee up on the couch, even, and I get this impression of haste, like maybe he just moved away from her, even though I would have seen it if he had.

If he'd been two feet closer to Bridget, his arm right behind her, leaning over her, leaning *into* her, and then hastily moved away to where he is now when I pulled open the bedroom door—I never could have missed it.

Except I think maybe I did, because when Krishna turns around, this kind of hard, glistening *something* in his eyes reminds me of a horse about to buck.

I've never even seen a horse about to buck, but that's what I think of. A terrible impulse, barely contained.

"What are you *watching*?" West asks.

It's a fair question. Because they're watching *My Little Pony*. With the volume weirdly low. Like, barely audible low.

Bridget is picking at her track bottoms, pinching little tents at the spot where her knee bends and the material wrinkles up.

Krishna is looking everywhere, at nothing.

I don't think I've ever seen the two of them in the same room together but not talking. They are both Olympic-medal talkers. Talking is practically their religion.

I've definitely never seen them look so awkward.

Nor have I known Bridget to fail to answer a direct question.

That's the point at which I would like to crawl into a cave for a while so I can sit with my humiliation, because of course this is our fault, West and me with our door-slamming and our probably loud loud *loud* sex noises through the thin walls, and Bridget and Krishna out here listening for God knows how long.

How awful are we?

Totally awful. I'm not a good friend. They're here to support me after my meeting with the administration, and I let them be sexiled to the living room to marinate in the discomfort of West's and my grunting horrible coitus sounds.

If that's even what they were doing. Marinating in discomfort.

I don't know. I'm just thinking about the best way to sweep the whole thing under the rug—apologize? But how can you apologize for sex noises? I would die—when West takes the conversation in completely the other direction.

"Is this one of those things where you mute the TV and replace it with another sound track? Like watching *The Wizard of Oz* while listening to *Dark Side of the Moon,* except with *My Little Pony* and Caroline and me fucking?"

I punch him in the arm. "West!"

Krishna starts to laugh.

Bridget covers her face with her hands and buries her head in the couch cushion. I think she says something about Twilight Sparkle, but it's hard to hear her with her mouth against the leather.

"Dude," Krishna says. "That was epic."

"Right?" West is smiling in this way only a guy could— 70 percent ego, 30 percent swinging dick. "I should get a medal."

"Do you guys want a ruler?" I ask. "You know, for measuring your penises?"

Krishna makes a dismissive noise. "He'd win."

From the depths of the couch cushions, Bridget makes this noise that's like a scream crossed with a squeak.

"Do you want some ice cream?" I ask. Because that's all I've got to offer. I don't have one of those laser-gun things that can erase memories with one bright white pulse of light.

"Yes," she says. "But only if you have the kind with the pretzels with peanut butter in the middle and chocolate on the outside, in the vanilla ice cream with peanut butter stripes."

"Chubby Hubby."

"Yes. Or I guess I'd take mint chocolate chip. But not that terrible stuff you had before with the fruit in it, because you know how I feel about fruit in my ice cream."

"Why don't you come with me and see?"

She gets up. I expect her to climb over Krishna, whose leg is partially blocking the path between the coffee table and the kitchen, but instead she goes the long way around and doesn't look at him.

"Twilight Sparkle, huh?" West says to Krishna. "Is that what's got you two all hot and bothered?"

"No, it's that picture your mom sent me of her in her panties."

"Oh, yeah? Was it as good as the video I got from your grandma last week?"

"Dude. Leave off my grandma."

"That's what your sister said when she wanted her turn."

"Oh my God," Bridget says. "Make it stop."

My head's already in the freezer. I take it out to call, "Settle down, boys! You're both pretty."

I try to sound scornful, but it's hard to pull off when you're smiling so hard that your cheeks hurt.

The week after Sex-Picture Day is crazy.

Spring break is coming up. West and I both have midsemester papers and projects due. I endure another meeting with Student Affairs because my dad has decided he wants to be part of everything, except once he's in the meeting he doesn't say a word. It's this weird repeat of the first meeting but with more people in the room.

The Internet-Asshat emails keep flooding into my in-box. I guess they've found my phone number, because now I'm getting all these hang-up mouth-breather voice mails and ranting, insane threats. I have to screen all my calls, delete three-quarters of my texts. I decide to suspend my Facebook account and shut down my Twitter altogether.

All of it has to be documented, too. Everything needs to be tracked. I'm already tired of it. I wish I could just switch off the phone, turn off the computer, and ignore the whole river of garbage that my life has become.

And, as if that's not bad enough, West can't get his mom on the phone. Frankie hasn't sent him any texts for a few days. He's worrying.

There's nothing I can do.

I'm overwhelmed, weary of being hated, worn out from so much hard work.

There's nothing *he* can do.

We stick together like we've been glued to each other.

We're at the bakery when his phone finally rings. I'm mixing up the dill, and he's slitting open a bag of flour to dump into the bin. Since I'm closer to his phone, I look at the screen. "It's Bo."

He drops the blade on the floor. I meet him halfway with the phone. I know he's been hoping Bo, his mom, *someone*, will call him back.

"Hey. What's up?"

I turn my back to adjust the volume on the music, and the

ten seconds the job requires is all the time it takes for the color to drain from West's face.

"How long ago?"

He paces the length of the table as he listens.

"Did you try to talk her out of it? Or . . . No, I know. . . . No. All right. And what about Frankie, is she—"

His shoulders sag.

His fingers are white where they curl around the phone.

"All right. Thanks. It was decent of you to call. I'll . . . I'll take it from here."

When he hangs up, he just stands there.

He stands there for so long, I'm afraid to touch him.

"West?"

"She took him back," he says.

"Your dad?"

"She fucking took him back."

This is the possibility he's been afraid to name for the past few days.

The worst thing.

"How did it happen?"

"I don't know. Bo didn't even—he didn't kick her out. He came home and all her stuff was gone, with a note saying she was sorry but she had to follow her heart." He pounds his fist on the table. "Her *heart*."

"Did they leave town, or . . . ?"

"They're at the trailer park. Her and Frankie. They moved in with my dad."

"Oh."

I'm not sure what to say. There aren't any words that will fix the defeat in his posture. The heavy dead sound of his voice, like someone has ripped all the fight out of him.

I know it's bad because, when I stand in front of him and

try to put my arms around him, he slumps against me hard enough that I have to lock my knees to hold him up.

Not for long. He gives himself ten seconds—surely no longer than that—and then pulls away.

He doesn't look at me when he says, "I'm going to have to go home."

"Sure." He'll have to make sure they're safe. Talk to his mom. Check on his sister. "Tell me what I can do to help."

"I have to fly. Pack up my stuff. Right after this shift's over."

"Will you stay for your exam?" He has a midterm at ten tomorrow morning.

"No, there's no point. Listen, can you look up flights for me? See what's the earliest I can get out of Des Moines."

"I will, but maybe you should take the exam, at least. So when you come back—"

It's how he glances away that stops me.

It's the pain I see before he turns his face so I can't see it at all.

"West?"

He grips the tabletop with both hands. I'm looking at him in profile, his braced arms, lowered head, the straight line of his spine.

I know before he tells me.

He's not coming back.

"It was never going to work out, anyway," he says quietly. "I never had any business thinking it would."

"What wasn't?"

"It's not something I should have let myself think I could do."

"I don't know what you're talking about."

He shakes his head. "It doesn't matter."

"It matters a *lot*. West?"

When he looks up at me, he's so far away. He's in a state

I've never been to, a place I've seen pictures of but can't imagine, can't smell. A town by an ocean I've never seen.

Oregon. I can't even pronounce it right. He had to teach me how to say it like a native.

"Come on. Talk to me."

"I'm sorry," he says. "But she's my sister, and I have to watch out for her. Nobody else is going to do it, nobody ever has. It's my fault for thinking . . . It's my fault."

The way he looks at me, it feels like goodbye, but it can't be. We're mixing up the bread. We're going to be here for hours—firing the ovens, slicing into the loaves, venting the steam. After we get through tomorrow, it's spring break, and I probably won't see him much for the week, but then we have the rest of the semester. Junior year. Senior year.

We have all this time still.

This can't possibly be happening.

"You can't just *leave*. You have to at least go talk to your adviser, take a leave of absence, or—"

I'm just getting warmed up when there's a sharp rap from the other side of the room. The alley door is open, like always, because the kitchen gets so hot. Standing there, framed in it, are two uniformed policemen.

"Mr. Leavitt," the one in front says. He's blond, middle-aged, nice-looking. "Officer Jason Morrow. We met in December."

"I remember," West says. "What do you want?"

"We have reason to believe you've been engaged in the illegal sale of marijuana from these premises. We'd like to have a look around."

I move closer to West. He puts his arm around me and kisses the top of my head. Mumbles, "Keep quiet."

To the policeman, he says, "This isn't my property. I can't consent to a search."

"Is this young woman an employee?"

"No. She's with me."

"So you're the only employee here, is that right?"

West steps away from me, toward the door, and blocks my view of the officers.

I've been here before, so many times, staring at his back as he puts himself between me and trouble. But this time the trouble's come for him.

"Yes."

"As the person in charge of the premises, you can consent."

"You're going to have to call Bob. He's the owner. It's up to him."

"Mr. Leavitt, we have a team at your apartment right now with a trained dog. It's in your best interest at this point to cooperate with our investigation."

West takes the door in his hand and uses his boot to nudge away the wedge of wood Bob uses as a doorstop. "Until you come back with Bob or a warrant, I'm not opening this door."

And then he shuts it and flips the lock.

"Call Bridget," he says. "I'm calling Krish."

"West, do you think—"

But he's not even listening. He's crouched down, rooting around in my bag. He finds my phone, puts it in my hand. "We have a god-awful mess and not much time to sort it out. If they're in the apartment, I need to know what's going on. Call her."

My fingers do the work.

I feel as though I'm watching all of this happen from a few feet outside my body, like I can't do anything but the task in front of me, and I don't *understand* enough. It's all swirling around in my head. *West is leaving. The police are outside.*

He closed the door on them. They're searching the apartment. He's got to take care of Frankie. West is leaving. He could be arrested. So could I. I'm an accessory. I can't do this.

It's all so thoroughly, confusingly screwed.

The phone rings and rings, but no one picks up. West's got his own phone by his ear, and he's staring into the middle distance. "No answer?" he asks.

"No."

Then my phone chimes with an incoming text. What's going on???!!!

"It's from Bridget."

"Ask her where she is."

I do, and she replies, At W & K's. On fire escape. Police r here w/ drug dog!!!

West is right behind me, reading over my shoulder. "Shit. I was hoping they were lying about that. Find out where Krish is."

The minute we have to wait feels like a lifetime.

In West's room w/ cops & dog.

"Did you have anything there for them to find?" I ask West in a whisper.

"No. I haven't sold all semester, you know that."

"So there's nothing to worry about."

The look he gives me is almost pitying. "I wish that was how it worked. Ask if she can call you. We shouldn't be texting this shit."

Bridget says, There's a cop watching me. Didn't want me 2 answer phone.

A pause.

She tried 2 take it, but I asked if I was arrested, she said no, so I kept it. But text is better.

"Surprised she thought of that," West says.

"She watches a lot of crime TV."

After a few seconds, another text. They're in Krish's room.

West has his hand at my waist. He's right behind me, right with me.

I don't think I could stand it if he left.

They found something.

"Fucking hell," he says. "That little wanker. I told him. I *told* him."

"Told him what?"

"Not to keep weed in the apartment. Ever. Under any circumstances. But he's a lazy little fuck, and he doesn't think. God *damn* it."

He takes the phone from my hand and starts typing with his thumbs.

"What are you saying?"

"Shh. I'm going to call her. I'm just telling her to listen to what I say when she picks up. She doesn't have to talk."

He must get Bridget's okay, because after a second he taps a few times, puts my phone to his ear, and waits.

"Bridge, listen, I need you to do something for me. I need you to just *do* it, if you want to help Krish, and I know you do. In a few minutes it's going to be too late, so this is the deal. I need you to barge in that bedroom and get right up in the middle of everything and tell the police the weed belongs to me. Act like you're Krish's girlfriend, like he's being noble trying to take the blame and you hate me, you want me to go down for trying to pin it on him. Say whatever you have to. You might have to go to the station for questioning, but just keep acting like you don't know shit—which you don't—and keep saying that weed belongs to me. You'll be fine, and so will Krish. They don't want him. They want me. And if he gives you a hard time about it, you find a way to tell him, 'West says to do this. He *insists*.' You hear me?"

West glances at me, then looks up at the ceiling. "And after it's all done and you get released, I want you to find Caroline and take care of her for me. Take good care of her. I know you can't talk right now, but you promise me just the same. She's gonna need you."

A booming knock at the bakery door makes me jump. "Mr. Leavitt!"

They're pronouncing his name wrong. *Leave-it* rather than *lev-it*.

For no reason at all, that's the thing that makes me cry.

"Thanks, Bridge," West says, and disconnects the call.

He taps open the address book on my phone.

Bang bang bang. "Mr. Leavitt!"

Bo, he types. And then a phone number with a 541 area code.

He hands me the phone. "I'm going to open that door," he says. "I'm going to let them in here, because there's nothing to find, and they'll get a warrant and be back tomorrow bothering Bob, anyway. So they're going to search, and we're going to make bread, okay? It might take them ten minutes, it might take them three hours, but at some point they're going to decide to take me to the station. You stay here and finish the shift. I don't want Bob to get screwed over any worse than he has to. Then just lay low, Caro. They couldn't have found more than half an ounce in Krishna's room. Maybe a quarter. It's a misdemeanor. It's nothing."

"Why are you doing this?"

"In the morning, you call Bo and tell him what happened. He'll take care of whatever needs taken care of. Tell him I said if he's got one more favor in him, I need him to keep an eye on Frankie until I get this all sorted out."

"West—"

Bang bang bang. "Mr. Leavitt!"

They have his name wrong.

I can't stand it. I can't.

"I need you to do what I said," West says. "I *need* it. Okay?"

"Okay."

When he kisses me, his mouth is warm and alive, his arms tight around me, but something is over, something is dead already, I want to scream. I ball up his shirt in my fists.

"I love you," I tell him, without planning to. It's not the right time. It's not the right thing. It's only what happens when I open my mouth, when I try to say what has to be said, now, before it's too late.

His eyes are so full of caring and regret. Such a beautiful color, such a beautiful face. I tell him again. "I love you."

He kisses me one more time, but all he says is "I'm sorry."

Then he opens the door.

I have to throw out the French. The yeast proofed before West finished the mixing, and the dough looks strange. But the rest of the bread is okay, and I carry on with the work, checking the clipboard, manning the mixers alone in the shrieking silence.

West is gone.

West got arrested.

West is lost, and I'm here, surrounded by a hundred jobs, objects, scents, tastes, that remind me of him.

I cry. A lot.

I stay, and I do the work.

At five-thirty, Bob comes in. He's bewildered to meet me.

"West told me about you," he says after he works out who I am. "Is he sick?"

"He got arrested."

I don't know—maybe I wasn't supposed to tell him. But he's going to find out, and I figure West would rather he find out from me.

The conversation takes thirty minutes. It's unpleasant. I wish, after it's over, that I'd handled it better. By the time we're done, Bob looks sad and defeated, and I feel as though I've done a bad job of defending West.

Maybe when I go to law school, I'll learn the right way to defend the man you love when he's turned himself in for possession of drugs that weren't his but may as well have been.

I think, though, it's possible there is no right way.

When I leave the bakery, I call Bo, who is monosyllabic and a little bit scary. I think I woke him up. It's not important.

Then I'm not sure where to go. I could walk to the police station, but what would I do there? West said to stay away. I want to do what I said I would, but I can't stand this. I don't know what it looks like where he is. I've seen a lot of cop shows, just like Bridget. I've read detective stories. All I can imagine is West in an impersonal room being interrogated by the blond cop. West being urged to name names.

West with that smart-ass mouth of his, saying the wrong thing. Getting himself in deeper trouble.

But then I think of Frankie, and I know I've got it wrong. There's only so far he would go for Krishna, only so much he'll give up.

He'll be on a plane. This afternoon, tomorrow, the day after—nothing will stop him from going.

I wish I didn't know that about him. I wish I weren't so sure of him, so unshakable in my conviction that he'll do exactly what he thinks is right, always.

I wish the right thing could be the thing that I want, but it's not, and that leaves me here. Worried about West. Stuck with myself, alone, on the verge of tears because he's going to go and I'm going to stay and I love him.

It's not fair.

It's just not.

I walk a few blocks to the police station and sit on the steps outside. No one's around this early. Only the occasional car putters through the cold morning. It's spring break as of tomorrow, but Iowa is stuck in winter, freezing and thawing only to freeze again.

I hate this place today. I hate Oregon, too—the ocean, the buttes I've never seen. I hate trailer parks. I hate West's mom for being such a failure, for loving a man who doesn't deserve to be loved and taking the man I love away from me.

So much hatred. But my hate doesn't feel poisonous or toxic. It feels true, inevitable. I have to hate these things, because here they are, parked in the middle of my life. A giant metal box of Impossible, seams sealed, and when I kick it, it echoes. When I knock, no one answers.

Hating it is the only option I have.

I'm still sitting there on the steps an hour later when Nate's friend Josh walks out of the station and pauses to light a cigarette.

"Caroline," he says when he sees me. He's inhaled, and he chokes on the smoke and takes awhile to recover his voice. "Jeez."

He doesn't ask, *What are you doing here?*

He knows why I'm here.

Long-haired, loose-limbed, floppy Josh. I thought he was my friend. I thought he liked me.

He ratted out West.

"Is Nate in there?" I ask.

"What? No."

"So it was just you snitching on him."

He looks like I've smacked him in the forehead with a mallet. Totally unprepared for this conversation.

I stand up for the sole purpose of taking advantage of his surprise. Thinking of my dad in his office—the way he rises to pace when he wants to take a position of power over me—I even put myself a step above Josh. Why shouldn't I use whatever advantages I have?

Why shouldn't I *prosecute*? Haven't I earned the right by now?

"What did he ever do to you?" I ask. "What did I ever do, for that matter, to make you hate me so much? I don't get it. I need you to explain it."

"Nothing. I mean, I don't hate you."

"You turned him in."

"No, I didn't, I swear. I—"

"What happened? Did you call in a tip, or did they pick you up?"

I watch his face with narrowed eyes, waiting for a sign. But I don't need to be sharp to see it—it's obvious. "They picked you up. What did you do?"

"I was smoking a blunt in my car."

"Where, on campus?"

"In the Hy-Vee parking lot."

"You're kidding me."

He shakes his head.

"You got picked up for smoking dope in your *car* at a *grocery store*? How stupid are you?"

Now he won't look at me.

"So they asked you who sold you the pot, and you gave them West's name. Even though it was a lie."

"I didn't have a choice."

"You had a choice. You just chose what was easy. Why not pin it on West? Nate hates him, anyway. It's not like West is your friend. He's just a dealer. He's expendable. He's nobody. It's not like anybody loves him or anyone will care when he's kicked out of school, right? He's not as important as *you*. No one is as important as you."

And the longer I'm talking, the angrier I'm getting. Not even at Josh. At Nate.

I was never really human to him. Never fully a person. If I had been, he wouldn't have treated me the way he did—not while we were going out, not in August, not *now*.

He's behind this. I don't care if it's Josh who turned West in—it's Nate who made it possible. Nate who convinced all our friends, Josh among them, that I was a psycho bitch. Nate who treated me like shit, hurt me, and assaulted me, and Nate who got away with it.

I've spent so many months not being angry with him.

Why the fuck have I not been *angry*?

"Where's Nate?"

"I don't know. Sleeping?"

"Is he home?"

"Huh?"

"Did he go home to Ankeny for break yet? Or is he still here?"

"He went home."

"Thank you."

I jog down the steps, leaving Josh there for . . . whatever. For the crows to pick at. For April's rains to wash away.

I don't give a shit. I've finally got force and velocity, a direction to point in, and as soon as I hit the sidewalk, I start to fly.

By the time I get to Ankeny, it's nearly eight, and the highway is clogged with people on their way to work. The traffic in

Nate's neighborhood is all headed in the opposite direction from me, so I already feel like I'm breaking rules when I park in his driveway. Even more so when his mom comes to the door.

His mom is so nice. She was always great to me. She seems not to know what to do with the fact that I'm standing on her doorstep, which I can understand. I used to be allowed to come in without knocking. I practically lived here senior year.

Now I'm dangerous—to her son, to her peace. She knows it. I can tell.

"Is Nate here?"

"He's not up yet."

"I'd like you to wake him up."

"You shouldn't be here."

"I am here."

"You ought to let the college handle this, Caroline."

I'm tired of the word *this*. I've heard it a lot since I first heard it from my dad—a word employed as a refuge, a little piece of slippery language that can be pulled over the head and hidden behind. *This situation. This trouble. This disagreement.*

I'm a prosecutor. I won't allow her to hide behind words.

"Did you see the pictures?"

She can't look at me. "Caroline, I don't want to talk about this."

"Did you see them or not?"

"Yes."

"Did you recognize Nate's comforter in the background?"

She crosses her arms. Stares at a spot on the ground by her foot.

"It's me in those pictures," I say. "But it's your son, too, whether he likes it or not, whether he wants to admit that he's the one in them with me. And I didn't tell a single person they existed, so the fact that the whole world knows now? That's on him. Nate has things to answer for. I'd like you to wake him up."

For half a minute we stand there. I think she must hope that I'll go, change my mind, but that's not happening.

Eventually she turns and ascends the carpeted staircase. She leaves the door open. I stand on the threshold in the gray light of morning. An unwanted gift on the doorstep.

I can hear the radio on in the kitchen. From upstairs, a murmur of voices, a verbal dance between Nate and his mother too muffled to make out the specifics of.

A complaint. A sharp reply. Then the conversation gets louder—a door has opened.

"Why are you taking her side?"

"I'm not. But if I find out you did this, don't expect me to support you just because you're my son. It's despicable, what happened to her."

"What she did is despicable."

"What she did, she did with you. Now get dressed and get down there."

Footfalls. Water running in the upstairs bathroom.

Nate comes down barefoot in a red T-shirt and jeans, smelling like toothpaste.

He rubs his hand over the back of his neck. "I'm not supposed to talk to you."

"Who says, the dean of students? Please."

"I could get expelled."

"Maybe you should have thought of that before you tried to ruin my life."

His eyes narrow. "Melodramatic much?"

"You think I'm *exaggerating*?"

"Nobody tried to ruin your life, Caroline. Your life is fine. It'll always be *fine*."

"What's that even supposed to mean?"

His lips tighten. He doesn't answer.

"You have no idea."

It's just dawned on me that he doesn't. I mean, he really *doesn't.*

When he said we'd always be friends, in some twisted way, he meant it.

"You think it's . . . like a prank. Like the time you and the guys soaped all the windows at the high school or rolled the football coach's car to the park and left it on top of the teeter-totter. What did you do, stay up late with a six-pack of beer, jerking off to porn, and then think, *I should put Caroline up here?*"

"Someone stole my phone," he mumbles.

"Oh, bullshit. That is such a giant, steaming pile of shit, I'm not even going to—God. You did, didn't you? You thought you could do this and it would just be *funny* or *awesome* or *what I deserved.* You didn't think it was going to mess up my chance of getting into law school. Ruin my relationship with my *only living parent.* You didn't know it would make it so I couldn't sleep for months, couldn't look at a guy without flinching, couldn't pull on a shirt in the morning without thinking, *Does this make me look like a slut?* I thought about changing my name, Nate. I get phone calls from strangers telling me they want to stick a *razor blade* in my *cunt.* That's what you unleashed. That, and a million other awful things. I want to know why."

"I didn't do it."

His voice is small, compressed. This is a lie, a bald and ridiculous lie too feeble even to back up with volume, body language, anything.

"You did it."

He shrugs.

"You're pathetic," I say. Because he is. He's so pathetic. Hiding behind his hate, looking down on me, looking down on West. "I feel sorry for you."

"Yeah, well, you're a bitch."

"Why? *Why am I a bitch?* Is it because I broke up with you? Because I'm standing here? Because I wouldn't let you put your penis in my butthole? I was *good* to you, Nate! I loved you! For three fucking years, I did every nice thing I could think of for you, and then you paid me back with this. I want to hear, from you, what you think I did to deserve it."

"I'm not telling you shit."

His expression is so mulish—I wish his mom could see him right now. I honestly do. He looks like a four-year-old.

He's a boy, too stubborn to tell me the truth, too childish to comprehend the consequences of his actions.

He hates me because he can.

Because he's been allowed to.

Because he's male, he's well off, he's privileged, and the world lets him get away with it.

Not anymore. The life those pictures ruin? It's not going to be mine.

"Enjoy your break," I tell him. "Enjoy the rest of your semester. It'll be your last one."

And I can see it in his eyes—the fear.

For the first time. Nate is afraid of me.

I like it.

When I get into my car, the slamming door seals me into silence.

I'm in the metal box now, but it's fine. I can come and go as I please. I can find a way to get comfortable with all the impossibilities in my life.

I don't know what I'm going to do about Nate, whether the administration will back me up in a fight against him, if there's any way I can go after him legally—a criminal trial, a civil trial. I've poked around a little bit online, but until this month I didn't want to think about fighting, so I haven't really considered what this fight is going to look like. How long it might take. What I even want from Nate, now that I'm allowing myself to want things again.

Today's not the day I'm going to worry about it. Today there are other impossibilities to think about.

West is leaving, and I love him.

I can't change that. I can only find a way to cope.

I have work here. I have things I need to do, power to exercise, wrongs to right.

I back out of the driveway, headed to my father's house.

There's a favor I need to ask, and he's the only one who can grant it.

"I need you to get my boyfriend out of jail."

It's a sentence I never expected to have to say to anyone, much less to my dad, but it comes right out, fluid and easy.

All the fluster, the confusion, is on his side.

"You need me to—your what? Out of *jail*?"

Maybe I should have worked my way up to it.

I wish I could have picked another time, some morning when I walked into the kitchen and he actually looked happy to see me. As opposed to this morning, when I found him reading the paper with his coffee, the circles under his eyes too dark, his mouth too sad when he caught sight of me at the French doors.

There's no other time, though. Only this time, this pain twisting in my guts as I think about how my future with my dad could be like this forever—this disappointment perpetual, our old relationship impossible to recover.

"His name is West Leavitt, and he's being held in Putnam by the police. At least, I think he is. It would be good if you could find that out for me, actually. He was planning to confess to misdemeanor possession of marijuana."

"You have a boyfriend. Who smokes marijuana."

"Sort of. I mean, yes, he's my boyfriend. And he occasionally smokes it. But mostly he just . . ." *Sells it.*

Gah. I need to pay more attention to what I'm saying, because my dad is sharp. He's been talking to accused people for a long time. I guess he's pretty good at hearing what they don't say.

When it dawns on him, I can see it in his eyes. The lines deepen in his face, and his jowls look saggier.

I always used to think he was the handsomest dad. I've never seen him as old before, or weak, and it hurts so much to be what's weakening him.

"This is that kid," he says. "That kid from across the hall. Last year."

"Yeah."

"You promised me you'd stay away from him."

"I did stay away. For a long time."

Then there's silence and snow tapping at the windows, because the weather has turned foul.

He takes a sip of his coffee.

I grip the back of a kitchen chair and wonder about my mother. If she would have taken my side, if she hadn't died.

I think of my sister Alison in the Peace Corps. She's got email where she is, and the Internet. I wonder if she knows yet.

I wonder about my sister Janelle, too, who does know. She wrote me this email—this long, long email that I had to close and not look at, because the first paragraph contained the words *I forgive you,* and I don't want anyone's forgiveness.

I'm not the one who has to be forgiven.

"Tell me what happened," my dad says.

"With the drugs?"

"The whole thing."

So I try.

I try in a way that I didn't try the other day because I was too angry.

I try even though I feel like there's no time for this and I wish I were with West right now, and I'm not sure how much of what I tell my dad can even reach him through the filter of his pain and disappointment.

I try because I know him, and I know that he's fair, and I know that he loves me.

I start at the beginning. I work through to this moment, this kitchen. I tell him everything I think he really needs to know. What Nate did to me. What West has given me. Everything that's happened, everything that's pertinent, and more.

I use the word *love*. I tell him I love West. Because that, too, is pertinent.

And because, now that I've said it to West, I could say it to anyone.

I love West. I love him, I love him, I love him.

When I'm done, my father walks out of the room, but I don't go after him. I take his coffee cup to the sink and rinse it out. I take the beans from the freezer and grind them and make another pot, and I collect some dishes from the countertop and the table to load the dishwasher.

I give him some time.

I think, if I were him, I would need time.

I'm his youngest daughter, his girl who lost her mother earliest, when I was still too little to remember her. He was the one who rocked me to sleep against his chest when I had bad dreams. He was the one who came to every awards ceremony, every debate tournament, every graduation.

He has a picture of me in his chambers with a gap-toothed smile, my hair in pigtails.

I think maybe when your last baby, your motherless daughter with her hair in pigtails, grows up and leaves, you console yourself with the knowledge that she's smart, and she'll be safe, and she knows how to make good choices.

It must be so difficult for him now, to deal with the fallout of the choices I've made.

I'm not a white dress. My future is not a thing I can dirty, tear holes in, or ruin. Not in any way that's real. But for him, I guess that dress . . . it's a dress that he laundered, a hope that he cherished, and he's got to find a way to adjust to what I've done to it.

His daughter is naked on the Internet.

His baby girl is in love with a drug dealer.

I give him time.

It only takes him ten minutes to come back to the kitchen.

He accepts the cup of coffee I offer him. He stares down into the black brew. He meets my eyes and says, "I'll make a few calls."

"Thank you."

He sighs.

He puts the coffee mug down.

"Don't thank me yet. There's probably not a lot I can do. And I have to tell you, Caroline, I'm not certain I'd do even this much if this boy—"

"West."

"If this . . . West didn't have one foot out the door."

"Okay. Thank you." It's a big concession on his part. If

he's going to make some calls, it means he's putting his own reputation on the line for West—and that means he does trust me. At least a little.

I put my arms around him. His neck smells like after-shave. Like my dad.

"I love you," I tell him. Because I do. I always have. He's the world I was born into, and he gave me so much. Safety and strength, intelligence and courage, the knowledge I arm myself with.

He's a great dad, and I love him.

When I squeeze, his arms come up, and he squeezes back.

"After this, can we be done for a while with the bomb-shells?" he asks. "You're going to give me a heart attack."

"I hope so. Although maybe now is when I should tell you I'm not going to be around for break. Once you get West out, I'm staying with him until he flies home."

Another sigh.

A long minute, with the snow hitting the glass, and my dad not letting go, and me not letting go, either. His shirt collar is stiff, his body warm, the size of him surprisingly wrong since I've spent so much time snuggled up to West.

My dad isn't very tall. I've always thought of him as taller than me, but he's not, after all.

He's just ordinary.

We're both doing the best we can.

"I talked to Dick," he says. "We have some strategies to consider."

"Okay. Why don't you set up a meeting for the three of us, and I'll take anything he has to share under consideration."

My dad backs up a step and looks down at me with his eyebrows steepled. "You'll take it under consideration?"

"Right." I touch his arm. "This is my fight, Dad. I'll take

your help, if it's help I think I need. But don't get confused about who's in charge."

And it's funny—he laughs. Not a big laugh. Kind of a snort with half a smile attached to it, and a slight shake of his head. "You always were a ballbuster," he says.

But he says it like he's proud.

SPRING BREAK

West

I wish I had a picture of what she looked like that day.

I'd told her not to come, not to get involved, but I didn't really expect her to listen. It's like she said to me—we're a team, and she's the leader.

There are guys who'd have a problem with that, her asshole ex among them. And, sure, even I threw out a token protest when she said it, but that was mostly to make her smile.

Caroline's being the leader—it doesn't mean I'm her flunky. It doesn't diminish me. It's just who she is.

I always liked that about her. How she could walk into a classroom with her books, her binder, her pens, and you could see by the way she raised her hand, the questions she asked, the straight column of her spine: She's the leader.

It's what makes her so awesome.

So I wish I had a picture of Caroline on the steps of the police station, and it's not because I've forgotten.

Her perfect posture. The way her hair bumped over the collar of her jacket, shiny and smooth.

The look on her face, serious one second and radiant the next.

The light that came into those big brown eyes of hers when she saw me walk through the station door.

I won't forget. I could never forget what Caroline looked like the first time I saw her after she told me she loved me.

She's the only person who ever said that to me, other than my mom or Frankie. The only girl to give me her heart, and I hate that she handed it to me right when I was leaving. When I fucked up everything—school, my home situation, the weed, my job. I got fired from the bakery. I missed my midterm, nearly got her arrested, and that's when she decided it was time to say the words.

I didn't know what to say back to her. I still don't.

I love you, too.

She knows it, I think. If she doesn't, I was doing something wrong all those weeks we had together.

She knows it, but it wouldn't do either of us any good to have it out in the open. If I'd said it, it would've been just another loss for us to carry around.

I thought about saying, *You shouldn't,* but I couldn't bring myself to say that, either.

She shouldn't. She does. I'm glad.

More than glad, I'm greedy over it. I can't find any piece of me—a finger bone, a molecule, a single atom—that wants her to feel different.

She's in love with me.

Thank fucking Christ.

So I wanted that picture. Caroline, standing in the sun with our friends gathered around her. Bridget and Quinn on the steps, listening as she told them something. I'd asked Bridge to take care of her, but seeing Caroline there, I realized she doesn't need to be taken care of anymore, if she ever did. She had those two arrayed around her and her dad in a car by the curb, awaiting her commands.

She was the leader.

Her dad pulled a few strings, got me out on probation with permission to leave the state as long as I complete some kind of drug program back home. There's still hoops to jump through, but the public defender said the misdemeanor's going to drop off my record once I've hopped on through them. The PD said I was getting a sweet deal—maybe sweeter than I deserved.

Her dad said he'd be glad to see the back of me.

I get where they're both coming from. If I were them, I'd feel the same.

Sweeter than I deserved—that was Caroline. Head to toe, beginning to end, every day I had her.

I ought to be sorry I slept with her, sorry we got to be friends, sorry I ever walked out to where she was sitting by the curb in the dark and pulled her into my life.

There's things I am sorry for. That I left Frankie. That I thought I might have a place in the world somewhere other than home, thought I could put down the responsibility I picked up ten years ago and trust somebody else to carry it.

I'm sorry I ever came here, because if I'd stayed in Oregon, maybe I could have kept this from happening. Kept Mom away from my dad. Kept her together with Bo, and kept Frankie tucked away safe with stuffed animals in her bed and glitter on her fingernails. I should have been there, telling her bedtime stories. Telling her she can be anyone, anything she wants to be.

That's what's in my power—to give Frankie that. Not to take it for myself.

I'm sorry I tried.

But I'm not sorry about Caroline. Not even a little.

I wish I had that picture, though.

Her smile.

Her eyes in the first instant when she looked up and saw me walking out, a free man.

I wish I had it, just to have something of Caroline to keep.

Caroline

I had him for one more week while they got some legal stuff sorted out.

Seven days.

He tried to pull away from me, but no way was I letting that happen. I slept in his bed. I kissed him and licked him, bit him and scratched him, put my tongue on every single spot on his body it wanted to be.

He was mine. *Mine*, and I knew I had to give him back, but I didn't have to do it yet. I refused to cry over losing him when he wasn't gone.

I helped him pack. I helped him sell his car to Quinn.

I took him to bed.

I walked him to Student Affairs and forced him to formally withdraw. Not because I thought he might come back, but because that was the right way to leave. With deliberation. With care.

I deliberately, carefully, slowly drew his cock into my mouth and sucked it until he stopped saying my name and started bucking off the mattress, his heels catching the fitted sheet so it rucked up underneath him and he came with his hands tangled in my hair, his fingertips gentle behind my ears.

I held him.

I touched him.

That last night, I stroked his back and his shoulders, his hips and his ass, his arms, his neck, his face.

For as long as he was still mine to love, I loved him.

Then I let him go.

At the airport, I don't know what to say.

We hold hands on the walk from the parking lot to the check-in counter.

We hold hands on the walk from the check-in counter to the security line.

We hold hands until the moment is finally here when he has to go and I have to stay and we can't hold hands anymore.

He drops his backpack on the ground and pulls me into his arms.

I can't think of words to tell him that mean anything. It's easy, with my body, to press up against him. To rub my damp eyelashes against his shirt, feel his lips on the crown of my head, his arms so tight around me.

I won't tell him I wish he didn't have to go. There's a little girl on the other side of the country who needs him. There's a place he fits into, a life that's not this life, and I can't question the claim it has on him. I don't have the right.

I can wish things were different. I've wished it a thousand times. But as long as they're not different, this is the way it is, and I won't tell him I wish he would stay.

"Hey," he says.

I look up at his face. I push my hands up his neck, cover his ears where they stick out because he's wearing his black baseball cap. He'll get on a plane next to some lady who thinks he's an anonymous college student, nobody important. She won't know that he's everything.

"I'll miss your ears," I tell him.

"I'll miss that gap in your teeth."

"I never did show you how I could spit through it."

"That's all right. We found some other stuff to do with our time."

That makes me smile, which makes him smile, and we just look at each other. I study how his eyes crinkle at the corners, how deep the lines sink in around his lips, how nice his teeth are. His slightly crooked nose. The smile fades away, leaves his mouth so serious, as serious as his eyes.

I pet his ears. Pinch his earlobes.

"I don't know how to do this," I tell him.

"There isn't a way. We just do it."

I reach for the brim of his cap, pivot it all the way around on his head, and go up on my tiptoes to kiss him.

Goodbye. I'm kissing West goodbye.

His hand clamps down on the back of my neck. His tongue moves into my mouth and the kiss goes deep, deeper, until we reach the place where there's no boundary between us. The place where I've given him a piece of my heart, my soul, a prayer flag with soft, fraying edges that flaps in the wind, claims him as my own, forever.

I tell him, with this kiss, that I want him to be well. That I want him to thrive. I want him to use his mind and his hands, his curious restless energy, his creativity—to put them in service of something that feeds his soul.

I tell him I want him to remember to eat, to make good

bread, to pay attention to what he does with his days, what he puts into his body, what *feeds* him.

I tell him I love him, and my love means I want him to be happy, I want him to be whole.

My love means I have to let him go.

When he moves his lips away, pushes the tip of his nose along my cheek, I'm crying, messy and wet, and he says, "Caroline. God, Caroline. Don't."

"It's okay," I say. "It's just the way it is."

His hands. His hands are on my shoulders, my neck, his thumbs smoothing over my mouth, and I'm stroking his forearms, the muscles firm and tight, following the grooves, ruffling his arm hair, wishing we had more time.

I don't think it's fair that we don't have more time.

There isn't anyone to complain to.

My fingers catch on the leather bracelet at his wrist, the letters of his name. I find the snap and work my thumb beneath it, flicking it off. The cuff falls to the floor, and when I reach to pick it up, our heads knock together, because he bent down to get it for me. Just one more thing he would do for me if he could. One more way he wants to help me with the work of being alive.

"I need to keep it."

He smiles and says, "Okay."

He puts it on my wrist, and then he kisses my arm, right by the snap, right over my pulse.

There are flags inside me, too, with his prayers on them. I'll carry him everywhere, for the rest of my days.

"Take care of yourself," he says. "Don't let anybody get away with any bullshit."

"I won't."

"Bridget and Quinn will look out for you. And try to keep Krish from self-destructing, if you can."

Krishna.

Krishna is a mess.

He let West take the fall for him, walked out of jail and straight into a bar. He hasn't come back to the apartment, and he won't answer West's calls.

Only Bridget seems to know what he's up to. She's talked to him a few times. She's worried about him, but none of us knows what to do.

I can't really concentrate on Krishna right now.

"I'll do my best."

My voice is full of tears. My heart is so full of cuts, nicks—every second this goes on makes the blood flow more freely. Cleans me out. Empties me.

He rests his head against my neck, kisses me at the nook where neck becomes shoulder. "Don't cry because of me. You're going to be fine. Great. Better than great. You'll get a whole lot more sleep, too, which is good. You'll live longer."

Come back to me.

The words are shouting inside me, bouncing around like manic ghosts, but I clamp my mouth shut and rest my hands on his body, just to feel his warmth and the way his back rises and falls with every breath. The ridges of his spine.

I don't know if I'll ever see him again.

"Promise me," I say, even though I wasn't going to. Even though I swore to myself I wouldn't make a single demand. "Promise me you'll be my friend. Promise me you'll call me, text me, tell me what's going on with you. Promise if you're awake in the middle of the night, if you're alone, if you need somebody—"

He lifts his head and wipes my tears away again, this time with his thumbs. "I promise."

"You're going to need a friend."

"Yeah."

"I want to be your friend, West."

He kisses the tip of my nose. "You're already my friend, Caroline Piasecki."

I just close my eyes. I close my eyes and open my hands and let go of the tail of his shirt. "You should get in line."

"Yeah."

"Text me when you land."

"I will."

"Tell your sister I said hi."

"She'll like that."

This time, when he kisses me, I don't let myself touch him. Not anywhere but at the mouth.

His lips are so soft.

They tell me all the things I told him and more.

Live. Breathe. Fight.

Be who you are. Be better.

Be fierce.

"Don't wait for me," he whispers, and he kisses me again. "I don't want you to wait."

When he picks up his backpack and walks away, I think of the day we met.

How he drove his car almost right into my feet. How he teased me, made me smile, made me faint.

How he looked with that dumb rubber chicken dangling from his fingers, grinning, asking me, *Want to play?*

I think maybe I've always been waiting for him.

Always.

I don't know how I'm ever going to be able to stop.

The thing about being a good girl is, you spend your whole life developing a finely honed radar for detecting anything that could potentially cause people to love you less.

Girls like the one I was last August—we eat approval. We live for it.

So when we're attacked viciously by a guy who goes out of his way to make us feel dirty and disgusting, our first reaction is always to take all the blame on ourselves.

My fault, we say. *My fault, my fault, my fault.*

It takes a special kind of person to pull our hands off our eyes and show us what it is we're really looking at. Whose fault it is. What a useless exercise blame can be.

West taught me to make bread. He hoisted me up on a roof and kissed me until I saw stars.

He taught me that deeper is worth going after.

Because one text message can crack the solid ground of

your life wide open. One bad decision, one flash of the camera, and the sunny, perfect part of your youth is over.

Then you get to decide. You look around, sift through the rubble, make your choices.

You arm yourself with love, friends, knowledge.

You figure out who you are. What you want.

You figure it out, and you go after it with everything you've got.

And that means sometimes you have to let yourself be scared. You have to turn left and take risks and make mistakes, because, otherwise, how do you find friends who will teach you how to tackle, to drink butterscotch schnapps for no reason at all, to strip down to your bra and dance?

When you've got a shot at deeper, you have to fist your hands in its T-shirt and pull it closer. Tug until fabric rips. Yank at it, reel it in until it's naked up against your belly and you're starving and full, desperate and satiated, dizzy and grounded.

You *have* to, because ugliness is everywhere.

Because life's not fair.

Because the world is a seriously fucked-up place.

You have to, because beauty is out there, and it's worth every sacrifice we make to seize it.

It's worth it even if we don't get to keep it.

Note from the Author

Dear readers,

What happened to Caroline is called "revenge porn" or "nonconsensual pornography," and it sucks. It's also perfectly legal everywhere in the United States with the exception of New Jersey and California.

Revenge porn is a form of abuse that uses sexual imagery *without the consent of the women (or men) pictured* as a way of shaming, hurting, and denigrating its victims. It happens all the time, right out in the open, with the consent of our legal system.

It needs to stop.

If you'd like to learn more about revenge porn or lend your voice to support its criminalization, I'd urge you to visit End Revenge Porn (www.endrevengeporn.org), a campaign that is working to raise the public profile of this issue, support victims, and lobby legislators to change the law.

All best wishes,

Robin York

Acknowledgments

I'd like to extend a personal thank-you to all of the women who have chosen to speak out about their experiences as the targets of nonconsensual pornography. Their stories shaped this one, and I can only hope that *Deeper* will play a small part in raising awareness of revenge porn and changing public attitudes for the better. There's plenty of room for improvement.

In writing *Deeper,* I benefited enormously from the support of the team at Random House. A huge thank-you to my editor, Shauna Summers, who was invaluable in helping me shape the story, and to associate publisher Gina Wachtel, whose enthusiasm for West and Caroline made the writing a pleasure (mostly).

In this, as in all my writing endeavors, I would have been lost without the help of my friends-slash-critique-partners. Mary Ann Rivers has always understood West better than I have, and thank goodness for that. When I wasn't sure what was supposed to happen next, she told me. She also wrote Caroline-and-West fanfic for me when I was feeling weepy about the ending of this book, which I had no choice but to gild and put it in a special folder because it was so awesome. (There was spanking involved.)

My agent, Emily Sylvan Kim, and my most excellent friend Serena Bell both read successive drafts with flattering avidity and offered a million excellent suggestions for improvement. *Deeper* is a better book for their feedback.

I'm also indebted to a number of people for sharing their thoughts and experience at the research phase of this book, including Maisey Yates, Phoebe Dantoin, Morgan Tuff, Laura Bickle, and Curt Johnson. My brother Austin reminisced with me about his nights as a baker, and I supplemented his memories by watching the adorable Vincent Talleu's YouTube bakery videos six or eight times. Or ten. Who's counting?

My thanks, too, to the Not by Bread Alone bakery in Green Bay, Wisconsin, where baker Angela allowed me to shadow her in the wee hours one weekday morning.

Few characters have given me as much pleasure and satisfaction to write as West and Caroline. I hope I've done them justice. Any and all mistakes that remain are my own.

Caroline and West's story isn't over yet,
but everything is about to get . . .

HARDER

Read on for an exclusive sneak peek at the next
novel in Robin York's New Adult series.
Coming soon from Bantam Books

THE END

West

When I had to say goodbye at the airport, I thought, *This is the last time.*

The last time you get to kiss her. The last time you get to touch her.

This is the last time you're ever going to see her face.

And then, after I turned and left, *That was it. It's over.*

I guess I went to the gate. I must have boarded a plane. Someone sat next to me, but I don't remember any of it. What I do remember is thinking everything would have to get easier from that point forward, because nothing could be harder than walking away from Caroline.

It almost makes me laugh now, if you can call it laughter when it comes with the salt-copper taste of blood at the top of your throat. If it's still a smile when you have to swallow and swallow around it, unable to get rid of the bitter flavor of your mistakes.

I went home to Silt thinking I was heading into some kind

of Wild West showdown. I'd call my dad out onto the public street at high noon and we'd draw our pistols. I'd fire straight and true and take him down, and then . . . well, that was the part I had to avoid thinking about. That was the part where the screen starts to go dark, the edges drawing in around a black-bordered circle that shrinks down until it's the size of a quarter, a nickel, a pinhole, nothing.

Nothing. That was where I would live after I drove my dad out of my life once and for all. Inside that blackness where the pinhole used to be, where the light had disappeared from, I'd pitch a tent, pull a blanket around me, and endure.

I was the sheriff, right? And he was the bad guy. But after I took him down, my reward would be an eternity of nothing I wanted. Maybe a gold star to pin on my shirt.

I was so sure I was the fucking sheriff, it almost makes me laugh, because what happened when I got home was that everything sucked in a completely different way from how I thought it would.

I did the impossible and walked away from Caroline.

After that, everything in my life that was hard got harder.

Caroline

When West's ringtone starts playing in my darkened bedroom, it slips into my subconscious and I have one of those last-second-before-you-wake-up dreams that's pure sensation— his skin warm against me everywhere, his weight and smell, the muscles in his thighs against the backs of mine, his hand sliding down my stomach. All of that, slow and melting and *West*, until the song finally manages to pierce through the haze of my sleep and pinch me awake.

I fight my way from under the sheet, turned on and pissed off because I know how this goes. The rock in my stomach, the day ahead during which I'll try and fail to shake that flood of sense-memory.

I'm going to have to live through it, and then I'm going to have to lose it, every good memory I have of West, *again*, when what I want is to drop back into that dream and live there instead.

It sucks. It *sucks*, and I'm so distracted by the suckage that I'm picking up the phone and swiping at the screen with my thumb before I completely clock what's going on.

West's ringtone. West is calling me.

West is calling me at one a.m. when I haven't heard from him in two and a half months.

If he's drunk-dialing me, I'm going to fly to Oregon and kick him in the nuts.

That's what I'm thinking when I put the phone to my ear—but it's not how I feel. I wish it was. I wish I could say "Hello?" and hear West say "Hey," and not feel . . . I don't even know. Plugged in. Lit up. *Juiced.*

I stand in my dark bedroom, breathing into the phone, aware in every centimeter of my skin that he's breathing on the other end, somewhere on the far side of the country. I have too many memories that start this way. Too many conversations where I told myself I wouldn't and then I did anyway.

This enormous burden of shame and guilt, longing and pain, so heavy I can hear it in my voice when I snap, "What do you want?"

"My dad's dead."

My head clears in an instant, my attention sharpening to a point.

"He got shot," West says, "and it's . . . it's a fucking mess,

Caro. I know this is—I shouldn't ask you. I can't ask you, but I just need to tell you because I can't fucking—" A crackling kind of whooshing noise interrupts him, loud as though he's in an open boat in a gale-force wind. It's the kind of interference that fills your whole head with white sound, and I just stand there, waiting for his voice to come back.

I'm pushing the phone so hard into my ear, my breath coming shallow and fast, aware with the kind of clarity I've only ever found in moments of crisis that it doesn't even matter. Whatever he says next. It doesn't matter.

The thing I never understood before West was that there are some people who, when it comes to them, reason and logic are never going to be in charge.

He left me. He betrayed me. He broke my heart.

But I stand there in the dark, holding the phone, and I know that in a few hours I'll be on a plane.

SILT

I emerge from baggage claim to the sight of West leaning against a dirty black truck. The first thing I think is, *He cut his hair.*

The second thing I think is, *He looks scary.*

Stubble covers his scalp, a dark shadow that throws the shapes of his face into relief: jawline, cheek bones, eye sockets, protruding brow, jutting chin, scowling mouth.

The muscles in his crossed arms belong to a brawler.

The West who left me in Des Moines more than four months ago was a guy, sometimes a boy, but this person who's waiting for me is a big, hard, mean-looking man, and when he glances in my direction, I freeze. Mid-step. I'm wearing a white cardigan over a new green top that cost too much. Designer jeans. Impractical flats. I wanted to look nice, but I got it wrong.

I got everything wrong, and yet I think nothing I've done is as wrong as whatever is wrong with him.

He straightens and steps forward. I start moving again. I have to.

"Hey," I say when we meet a few feet from his truck. I try on a smile. "You made it."

He doesn't smile back. "So did you."

"Sorry you had to pick me up."

He doesn't reply. I texted to tell him I was coming right before I boarded the first flight. I didn't want to give him a chance to say no, so I just said my flight number and when I'd get in.

When my first flight landed in Minneapolis, I had three texts and a phone message from him, all of them variations on the theme of *Turn your ass around and go home.*

I waited until I was boarding for Portland to text him again. *I'll get a rental car.* I walked off the flight to find his reply: *I'll pick you up.*

Since that was the outcome I'd been angling for, I said, *Okay.*

It doesn't feel okay, though. Not even close.

West wears cargo shorts and a red polo with a landscaping company's logo. He's tan—a deep, even, golden brown—and he smells strongly of something I don't recognize, fresh and resinous as the inside of our cedar closet after my dad sanded it down. "Did you come from work?" I ask.

"Yeah. I had to take off early."

"Sorry. You should've let me rent a car."

West reaches out his hand. For an instant I think he's going to pull me into his body, and something like a car accident happens inside my torso—half of me slamming on the brakes, the other half flying forward to collide with my restraint.

His fingers knock mine off the handle of my suitcase, and the next thing I know he's heading for the truck with it.

I stand frozen, gawping at him.

Get your act together, Caroline. You can't freak out every time he moves in your direction.

He opens the passenger-side door to stow my bag in back of the cab. The truck is huge, the front right side violently crumpled. I hope he wasn't driving when that happened.

By the time he emerges, I'm comparing the musculature of his back to what his shoulders felt like under my hands the last time I saw him. The shape of his calves is the same. He's West, and he's not-West.

He steps aside to let me in. I have to climb up to the seat. The cab smells of stale tobacco, and it's sweltering. I leave my sweater on. Even though I'm sweating, I feel weird about any form of disrobing.

I turn to grab the door handle and discover him still there, blocking me with his body.

That's when I figure it out. It's not his hair or his tan or his muscles that make him different: it's his eyes. His expression is civil, but his eyes look like he wants to rip the world open and tear out its entrails.

"You need to eat?" he asks.

I don't think the simmering cynical hatred I hear in his voice is directed at me. I'm pretty sure it's directed at *everything.* But it scares me, because I've never heard West sound like that before.

"No, I'm good. I had dinner in Portland."

"It's almost three hours back to Silt."

"I'm good."

He's staring at me. I bite my lip to keep from apologizing. *Sorry I came when you called me. Sorry I needed a ride from the airport. Sorry I'm here, sorry you don't like me anymore, sorry your abusive asshole dad is dead.*

My own father didn't want me to come. At all. I had to

quit my job a few weeks early and hand over almost everything I'd earned as a dental receptionist this summer to pay for the plane ticket—a move Dad called *boneheaded*. We argued at breakfast and then again when he dropped me off in Des Moines.

Sometimes my dad is right.

"You don't have to fuss over me," I say. "I'm just here to help."

Without another word, West slams my door and gets behind the wheel, and we're on our way.

I thought Eugene was a city, but after we leave the airport we're instantly in the middle of nowhere, and that's where we stay. Oregon isn't as green as I expected. The only mountains I see are faint bumps in the distance, smudges against the horizon line. The road is flat and straight for a while, the sky wide open and pale blue. It's nearly seven, which I guess means we'll get to Silt late. I don't know where I'm staying tonight or how long it is until sunset.

A few hours from now, I could be sitting in this truck with West in the dark.

I take off my sweater. West fiddles with the air conditioner, reaches across me to redirect a vent, and suddenly it's blasting in my face. My sweat-clammy skin goes cold, goose bumps and instantaneous hard nipples. I shudder.

He turns the fan down.

"You're doing landscaping?" I ask.

"Yeah."

"Do you like it?"

The look he gives me reminds me of my sister Janelle's cat. Janelle used to squirt it between the eyes with a water gun to keep it from jumping on her countertops, and it would glare back at her with exactly that expression of incredulous disdain.

"Sorry," I say. Then I try to count up how many times I've apologized since I walked out of the airport.

Too many. I'm letting him get to me when I promised myself on the plane I wouldn't let *anything* get to me. This is a crazy situation. Someone's dead, guns are involved, West was torn up enough to call me—my job is to be unflappable. I'm not going to get mad at him or act heartbroken. I'm not going to moon around or cry or throw myself on him in a fit of lust. I'll just be here, on his side.

I'll do that because I promised him I would when he left Iowa. I made him swear to call me, and I told him he could count on me to be his friend.

He called. Here I am.

After a while, I start to get used to being in the truck. I find myself scanning West all over again, looking for similarities instead of differences. His ears are still too small. The scar hasn't vanished from his eyebrow, and the other one tilts up same as always. His mouth is the same.

Always, for me, it was his mouth.

The scent coming off him is like a hot day in the deep woods—like a fresh-cut Christmas tree—but it's not quite either of those. On the seat between us, there's a pair of work gloves he must have tossed there. I want to pick them up, put them on, wiggle my fingers around. Instead, I look at his thigh. His faded shorts, speckled with minuscule pieces of clinging bark. His knee cap.

I look at his arm from the curve of his shoulder to the banded edge of his sleeve where the polo shirt cuts across his biceps. He doesn't have a tan line. He must work with his shirt off, and the thought is more than I know what to do with.

The last time I saw him we were kissing at the airport, holding each other, saying goodbye. Even though I know everything's different now, it doesn't entirely *feel* different, and that's cruel. It's cruel that it's even possible for him to have done what he did and for me to still be sitting here, soaking him up.

It's cruel that I'm not over him. I've tried to reason myself into it, but I'm learning reason doesn't have anything to do with love, and West has always made me softer than I wanted to be, more vulnerable than was good for me.

But there's another side to it, and I can't seem to forget it. Before we crashed and burned, I liked the person I was with him. He made me vulnerable, but he helped me be stronger, too. I'm not going to sit here cringing away from him because his biceps are bigger than they used to be and his eyes scare the crap out of me. I'm going to do what I came here for. If he doesn't like it, he can deal.

"You want to fill me in on what's going on?" I ask.

A muscle ticks in his jaw. "I've been at work. I don't know what's going on."

"What was happening when you went to work?"

"My dad was dead."

I roll this around in my mind for a while. It's such a West thing for him to have done, I hadn't thought twice about it. Of course he'd go to work on the morning after he found out his dad had been killed. He's West. Work is his religion.

"Where's your sister?"

"She's out at Grandma's. I have to pick her up."

"Does she seem okay?"

He shakes his head. A terrible thought occurs to me. "She wasn't there, was she? When he got . . ." I don't want to say it.

"Mom says she was at a sleepover."

His knuckles are white on the steering wheel. I watch the color drain from his skin all the way to the base of each finger as he squeezes tighter.

"You don't believe her?"

"I'm not sure."

Then we're quiet for a minute. He's got a cut on his right hand in the space between his thumb and his index finger. The skin is half scabbed over, pink and puffy around the edges with curls of dry skin. I can see two places where it's cracked.

A burn, maybe, or else a bad scrape.

Back in Putnam, I'd have known where he got a cut like that. I'd have nagged him to put a Band-Aid on it or at least spread some lotion around so it would heal better. I probably would have made a disgusted face and told him to cover it up.

I wouldn't have wanted to touch it the way I do right now.

I want to reach out and touch that newborn pink skin with my fingertip. I'm dying to know how he would react. If he'd jump or draw away. If he'd pull over and turn off the truck and talk to me. Touch me back.

He called me. That's the thing.

"What do you smell like?" I ask.

He lifts his shirt to his nose and sniffs it. I glimpse his belt buckle, which is all it takes to slice clean through the twine I'd used to tie up a tightly packed bundle of conditioned sexual response. My cheeks warm, and pretty much everything below my waist ignites. *Jesus.*

"Juniper," he says.

"Is that a tree or a bush?"

"Both, kind of."

He taps the steering wheel with flattened fingers. His left knee jumps, jiggling up and down, and then he says, "It's a tree, but most of them are short like a bush. Eastern Oregon's got too many of them. They're a pest now, crowding other stuff out. The landscaper I work for uses the lumber for decking and edging, but I've seen it in cabinets and stuff too. They make—" He stops short. When he glances at me, I catch sight of a strained sort of helplessness in his eyes right before it disappears. As though he's dismayed by how difficult it is to keep himself from talking about juniper trees.

West clears his throat. "I was chipping up scrap wood for mulch. That's why I stink."

I wait, because I know there's more. His knee is still jittering. *Come on,* I think. *Talk to me.*

"They make gin from juniper berries," he says finally. "Not the Western juniper we have here. The common juniper over in Europe."

"Is that sloe gin?"

"No." Another pause. "Sloe gin is made with blackthorn berries and sugar. You start with gin and pour it over the other stuff and let it sit forever."

For the first time since I landed, I almost feel like smiling. Whatever's wrong with him, however twisted and broken he is, this guy beside me is still West. When it comes to trivia like gin berries and juniper bushes, he's a crow, zooming down to pluck shiny gum wrappers off the ground and carrying them back to his nest. He can't help it. I wonder how much else he knows about juniper and if he has anybody to tell all these useless facts to. The girl who took my place—does she listen when he does this? Does it make her like him more?

If there even is a girl. Whoever she is, she's not the one he called last night.

"I like the smell," I tell him.

"When I'm here I don't smell it. But when I fly from Putnam to Portland, it's the first thing I notice when I get off the plane." This time when he glances at me, he's got himself under control. His eyes aren't giving anything away. "It was, I mean. When I used to do that."

"I bet when I get back to Iowa, I'll smell manure."

"Only if you time it right."

The silence is more comfortable this time, for me at least. West remains edgy, tapping his fingers against the steering wheel.

"Is this your truck?" I ask.

"It's Bo's."

"Is Bo still in jail?"

"No. They questioned him and let him go."

"Was he . . ." I take a deep breath. "Did he really kill your dad?"

"Nobody will say. He was there, shots were fired. The gun was my dad's. For all I know it could've been suicide." The anger is back, flattening out his voice so he sounds almost bored.

"Not likely, though, if they took Bo in for questioning," I say.

"What the fuck do you know about what's likely?"

"Nothing. Sorry."

That's where the line is, then. Junipers are an acceptable topic of conversation. His dead father is pushing it. Speculation about what's going to happen next? Out of bounds.

West leans forward and flips on the stereo. The music is loud and unsettling.

I reach out, calm and slow, to turn it off. "When's the funeral?"

"Whenever they get the body back from the coroner."

"Oh."

"I'm not going."

"Okay."

More silence. The scenery changes from dry brown land to dark green forest crowding both sides of the road. I'm surprised by the abruptness of it. In Iowa, changes in the landscape tend to be visible from a long way off.

"How long are you staying?" West asks.

"As long as you need me to."

He stares at me. I start to get nervous we're going to drive off the road. "What?"

"When's school start?"

"The twenty-eighth."

"Two weeks."

"Two and a half."

"You're not gonna be here that long."

"Whatever you want."

West looks out the driver's-side window, frowning. "You shouldn't have come."

I've already thought the same thing, but it hurts to hear him say it. "It's nice to see you, too, baby," I drawl.

"I didn't invite you."

"How sweet of you to notice, darling, I *have* lost a little weight."

His eyes narrow. "You look scrawny."

I drop the act, too stung to play games. "I'll be sure to put on a few pounds for your visual enjoyment."

"If you want to say *Fuck you, West,* go ahead and say it."

"Fuck you, West."

His jawline tightens. When he reaches for the volume knob, I bat his hand away. He puts it back on the wheel. "I don't know what I'm supposed to do with you," he tells me.

"You're supposed to let me help."

"I don't want you anywhere near this shit."

"That's sweet, but too bad."

He glares at me. "I'm not being sweet. You don't belong in Silt."

"I guess I'll see for myself in a few hours."

"I guess you will."

He reaches for the stereo again, and this time I let him turn it on.

I think about how we're driving toward the Pacific Ocean, which I've never seen.

I think about West and what I want from him. Why I'm here.

I don't have any answers. I'm not kidding myself, though. Inside a makeup pouch at the bottom of my suitcase, there's a leather bracelet with his name on it.

I shouldn't be here, but I am.

I'm not leaving until I know there's no chance I'll ever wear that bracelet again.

PHOTO: © STUN PHOTOGRAPHY

ROBIN YORK grew up at a college, went to college, signed on for some more college, then married a university professor. She still isn't sure why it didn't occur to her to write New Adult sooner. She moonlights as a mother, makes killer salted caramels, and sorts out thorny plot problems while running, hiking, or riding her bike.

www.robinyork.com